Praise for *Hope Farm*

'Peggy Frew is an amazing w   . The complex story of Silver and   ip is beautifully written, acutely obs   rbing. I could almost feel the crisp Gippsland mornings, hear the birds warbling, and smell the stale dope smoke. *Hope Farm* is elegant, tender, and very wise.' — Chris Womersley, award-winning author of *Bereft* and *Cairo*

'Frew's deceptively slow-burn tale of a teenage girl — adrift, bewildered, seeking solidity — moves inexorably to its climax, laying bare a certain darkness at the heart of the alternative lifestyle. But it's the tale of a survivor, too.' — Luke Davies, award-winning author of *Candy*

'An original tale, drawing into the body of Australian literary fiction, a world between the cracks. Frew's voice is contemporary, her observations sharp and sensitive. *Hope Farm* describes the cycle of loss and damage when there are no boundaries to protect us.' — Sofie Laguna, author of *The Eye of the Sheep*, winner of the 2015 Miles Franklin Literary Award

'[E]legiac, storied … aligns itself with other novels in which children — out of rashness, anger or even ignorance — act out to terrible consequences. As with Briony in Ian McEwan's *Atonement* or Leo in L.P. Hartley's *The Go-Between*, these decisions are usually compounded by circumstance … Frew does not want to pass judgment though. She understands that the sadness of childhood is to grow up in circumstances over which you have little or no control.' — Jessica Au, *Sydney Morning Herald*

'Frew is a gifted writer, evidenced here by finely balanced observations and atmospheric description … Silver is poised at the beginning of adult understanding and Frew handles the challenge with deftness. Silver's insight and compassion are juxtaposed with naivety and the idealistic force of her first crushes.' — Ed Wright, *Weekend Australian*

HOPE FARM

Peggy Frew's debut novel, *House of Sticks*, won the 2010 Victorian Premier's Literary Award for an unpublished manuscript. Her story 'Home Visit' won *The Age* short story competition. She has been published in *New Australian Stories 2*, *Kill Your Darlings*, *The Big Issue*, and *Meanjin*. Peggy is also a member of the critically acclaimed and award-winning Melbourne band Art of Fighting. *Hope Farm* has been shortlisted for Australia's 2016 Stella Prize.

HOPE
FARM

—

PEGGY
FREW

SCRIBE
Melbourne • London

Scribe Publications
18–20 Edward St, Brunswick, Victoria 3056, Australia
2 John St, Clerkenwell, London, WC1N 2ES, United Kingdom

First published by Scribe 2015
This edition published 2016

Part of this book was written during a residential fellowship at Varuna,
the National Writers House.

Typeset in Adobe Garamond 11.5/16.75 pt

Printed and bound in the UK by CPI Group (UK) Ltd, Croydon CR0 4YY

Scribe Publications is committed to the sustainable use of natural resources and
the use of paper products made responsibly from those resources.

9781925228533 (UK edition)
9781925106572 (Australian edition)
9781925113778 (e-book)

CiP records for this title are available from the British Library and the National
Library of Australia

This project has been assisted by the
Australian government through the Australia
Council for the Arts, its arts funding and
advisory body

scribepublications.com.au
scribepublications.co.uk

'You don't look back along time but down through it, like water. Sometimes this comes to the surface, sometimes that, sometimes nothing. Nothing goes away.'

Margaret Atwood, *Cat's Eye*

I try to imagine going back. I picture it as it was, that stretch of road — the land on one side still not cleared, the trees leaning outwards, reaching as if ready to wrench free their roots and spring over the raw-edged strip of asphalt to the waiting paddocks. I see again how closed-up that bush looked from the outside, how protective of its secrets.

In my mind, I find the turn-off, the dark mouth open and fringed with branches — and I take it, and I begin to drive down the dirt road. But that's as far as I ever get. Long before I reach Ishtar's hut and long before I reach the gate to Hope itself, just short of where the bridge flattens its back and the sunken runnel of the creek sends up its cool vapours, my vision slips, slurring like the tyres of my city hatchback on the loose surface. I'm skidding, I'm sliding, I'm going too fast, into a spin; I'm slamming into a tree. Or I'm slowing down, losing power — I drift to a standstill. Or the car simply disintegrates. The steering wheel comes off in my hands, the doors unfasten and fly away, the roof lifts and vanishes, then the windscreen, the dashboard, the seat below me, and I am hanging in space. Whichever way, after that it's always the same: the gravel darkens and the trees close in, and the whole thing shuts down.

I don't believe in ghosts, but still, perhaps that is what keeps me away, even in fantasy — the fear of conjuring them somehow, of unblocking some channel, providing at last an audience for the enduring, impotent rage of a dead man. And there would be other ghosts too, and not only of the dead. There would be the ghost of my long-ago self, that girl. There would be the ghost of Ishtar as she was then: a young woman, a young mother. As I stepped into the ruined hut and imagined a trace of incense and wood smoke in the chill, there would be the spectre of our union — the possibility of us sorting things out, of getting it right, of doing justice to the bond that, however frayed, did exist.

And then, if I was to walk down to the creek and along to what, if anything, remained of Hope, there would be the echoes of that place, of those who had lived there when I knew it, with their foolhardy but ultimately gentle intentions. Freedom, tolerance — these banners, propped at exhausted angles, limp in the soupy air of a confused and bitter inertia, doubtless played a part in what happened. But I don't blame the hippies. It wasn't their fault; it wasn't anyone's fault, in the end.

Maybe what I'm most afraid would happen is this: that I invoke all of those ghosts, in my imagination or otherwise, and they rise, dragging at the air, pressing in on me. And then, somewhere on the path leading from one to the other, the hut and Hope Farm, they fall back, thin out, dematerialise — and I am left alone with the ceaseless rustle and tick of the bush, the whisper of insects, the relentless busyness of birds, the ruthless constancy of nature.

Before

It's hard to remember much from before Hope. We lived in so many places — and in my memory they've merged to form a kind of hazy, overlapping backdrop. Certain details leap briefly to catch the light: a kitchen where I climbed into a cupboard and watched a woman's feet shuffle back and forth as she cooked, the hem of her orange robe lapping; the chain-link fence of a school yard, cool under hooked fingers and tasting, when I put my tongue to it, of tears; a dog with new puppies under a verandah, lifting her head to growl when we came squirming in on our elbows, me and a girl whose name is now lost but whose pierced ears I recall perfectly — the wonder of those gold circlets entering the downy, padded lobes. None of these details are anchored though — there is no sequence, no scaffold on which to hang them.

What I do remember, as a constant, is our belongings. Our shapeless, worn duffel bags, and Ishtar's old case. There were clothes, but not many of them, and a couple of bathroom things — toothbrushes, soap. Then there were the papers Ishtar kept in a bundle in the case, and the Indian bedspread she always put on the bed, wherever we were. That was all. But I can remember every aspect, every angle and facet of those things, even down to the scratches on the suitcase — one of them in the shape of a knobbly, malformed horse's head, ears back, mouth agape.

It was always the same. We had to leave because the energy had changed — something had faded, failed, gone wrong. There was probably a specific reason, probably to do with a man, but I never needed to look that far. I just saw it coming in Ishtar, in the flattening of her voice and movements, the dulling of her colours.

She went quiet, she stopped smiling, she didn't touch me or, often, even respond if I spoke directly to her. She still went to work and upheld her domestic obligations; she never faltered in these things. In fact, as the shutting-down phase went on, she almost seemed to vanish into the endless rhythms of chores, of labour — they took on a new quality, a busy screen beyond which she was even less reachable. Slicing onions in the drab kitchen of a group house. Sweeping the hallway of an ashram. Buttoning one of the various uniforms she wore — for mopping the floors of a hospital, or changing sheets and scrubbing bathrooms in a motel — slipping my lunch box into my school bag and handing it to me without a glance as she strode to the door.

Then one day she'd come back to whichever room we had, in whichever house, and the switch would have flicked; she was alive once more — the veil lifted, her skin lit — and I'd know even before she spoke that we were packing and leaving. We were going somewhere else, to start again. And the old criss-cross of feelings would tug at me: the relief and the mistrust, the hope and the anger. And each time it happened, the mistrust and anger were stronger, the relief and hope weaker.

During these transitions something would change in the way I saw the world. Everything — an unlined curtain leaking light, a dash of spilled turmeric on a bench top, the chalky line of scalp that showed at the parting in the hair of a girl at school — seemed to become at once very clear and slightly removed, as if I was peering through a viewfinder. It was a glassy, sliding feeling, and it continued until the ending had been completed, and we were on our way to the new place, when suddenly all the details would be lost, and the girl's hair and the turmeric and the curtain blurred and swam into the uncertainty of the past.

Men were usually involved, in both the endings and the beginnings. Boyfriends, lovers, partners — whatever they were to her in the varied and loose lexicon of the circles in which we moved. I can glimpse them still, a collage of faces, mostly bearded, mostly framed with quantities of hair. I can dredge up the sounds of their voices, some of them, or a small physical detail — a bracelet of plaited flat strands of copper on a sun-damaged, ginger-haired wrist; a combination of a long nose and bushy eyebrows that called to mind the letter 'T'. But I have no memory of any actual break-ups, of men begging or raging at having been left. I recall no messy scenes. Ishtar was so good at it, I suppose, so practised. She simply withdrew and allowed things to collapse.

This time it would be different. And I imagine now — when that pocket opens in the haze and Miller first appears, first spreads and cups his hands, first unfolds the smooth carpet of his voice — that I could tell from the beginning.

Before Miller, before Hope, she had decided we would go overseas. At night she sat cross-legged beside me as I lay on the mattress we shared, and talked about countries. She brought an atlas up from the communal bookshelf in the yoga room and turned the pages, running her hand over maps, sounding out place names. *Istanbul. Prague. Varanasi.*

For a while I held back, like I always did. It was so hard to resist though, the heat in her, the energy that hummed and leapt. When she read aloud she sounded like another person, uncertain, effortful, with her pointer finger creeping across the page. She seemed nearer to me, nearer even than all the times we'd slept in the same bed, back to back.

She got stuck on a word, frowned, peered, muttered. Then she threw me a grin. Her face was pink. 'Gibraltar,' she said, straightening her spine. 'Gibraltar.'

I pulled the covers up to my nose, my own mouth splitting in an unstoppable, answering smile.

We went to get passport photos at the chemist's. Mine had to be taken twice because I blinked the first time, and Ishtar laughed. 'Be cool,' she said, and then I watched as she faced the camera, still and strong and lovely, and my throat filled with helpless, fluttering pride.

Afterwards she bought me jellybeans to eat while we walked back to the ashram. Their chemical sweetness made me feel like a little kid again. It was a Brisbane winter, clear and bright, and somewhere somebody was burning leaves.

'I love that smell.' Ishtar's arm went round me. 'Remember the picture, in the atlas, of the chestnut seller in Italy?'

I remembered him, olive-skinned and stern, standing with his stall and his fire in a metal burner, the street behind him shining and slick and cold-looking.

'We'll go there,' said Ishtar. 'We'll eat chestnuts. And spaghetti.' Then she let go and started walking faster and I had to run to catch up.

She kept the passports in her suitcase, inside a yellowy-orange envelope that closed by winding a string around a little paper button.

Then Miller came and the plans were changed. We weren't going overseas any more — we were going to the country instead, down south, to live.

'It's a farm,' said Ishtar. 'There'll be goats. And potatoes.'

The atlas was gone. I stood in its spot on the threadbare rug.

She folded a jumper. 'Goats are good for milking. And wool, some of them. Angoras.' The word had a soft, fleecy sound, and in the way she said it, drawing it out, I heard another voice, and knew it must be his — Miller's. 'Cold down there.' She pushed the jumper into her bag. 'We'll need to rug up.'

On the maps I'd copied at school, Victoria had always looked cold, squashed down the bottom in a jagged wedge, shaded green or blue.

'Oh, it's far,' said Ishtar, although I hadn't asked. She folded and stuffed, knelt and stood, her movements fluid, unhesitating. 'It's a long way. Further than we've ever been.' She paused, touched her hot palm to my cheek, leaned closer and kissed me, three quick kisses that pushed me almost off balance. 'It's going to be a whole new life.' Reaching past, she began to fold her Indian quilt, with the pink and orange pattern. Her hair brushed near my lips and I breathed her smell, sweet and smoky.

I got up and went to the window, which showed part of a brick wall and a yard with a Hills hoist sprouting from concrete. I put my face close to the glass and looked up into the sky. Flat, angry phrases slid rhythmically through my head. *Of course, of course. You should have known.*

'Angora goats,' came Ishtar's new, Miller-tinged voice. 'And potatoes, all kinds. Sebago. Coliban.'

Of course. I stared up at the sky and opened myself to disappointment, pinching, cold, lonely. How could I have been so stupid, to have believed in the overseas trip, in us — just the two of us — getting on a plane and taking off into some whole new life? I was as bad as she was.

'Well, that's about it.'

I turned from the window. The mattress lay stripped, showing its stains and hollows. Our two duffel bags and her old brown case stood by the door.

'I'm off to work now, to give this back.' She was holding her uniform, folded into a small pink slab. 'To let them know I'm finished. I've scrubbed my last toilet.' She gave a little pretend stamp with one foot, put her free hand on her hip, and shook back her hair.

I was supposed to join in, to say something or return her smile. And, unbelievably, the urge was still there — to concede, to go to her and feel those arms round me. But I stared down at the rug, at the webbing of its exposed fibres.

She didn't notice anyway — the door swung and she was gone.

Another ending, another new start. But with a difference, and not just because of Miller. When he steps out of the murk of memory, solid and bold, his gestures sweeping with the promise of change, another figure materialises, sharp edged, beside him. It is me, as I was then: thirteen, scrawny and suddenly tall, angry and sad and full of shame and reluctance — but changing, coming into something, waking up to a power of my own.

I heard his voice first, coming from the front room downstairs, where they did the yoga classes and the satsangs. I couldn't make out the words — there was just the sound of it, rich and rolling. I went down to the hallway and looked in at them.

There was a slant of sunlight from the window, and he stood square in it, taking it all up, the honeycomb halo of his hair ablaze. Ishtar was a still shape before him, slender and dark. I could hear the words clearly now, and see the way he gestured, how every phrase had a movement to go with it.

'Ishtar,' he said, raising his arms and widening his fingers. 'Fierce, proud goddess.'

Embarrassment tickled in my chest, and I glanced up the empty hallway and then back at Ishtar's motionless figure. Why was he speaking like that?

'My heart is yours. My heart and my new shovel. And a few other things besides.' A burbling, deep chuckle — and an answering nod of Ishtar's head.

So it was a joke. He was acting, putting on a show. In a moment, he would stop and return to his normal self, whatever that was.

But when he dropped his arms and stepped closer to her, his voice grew breathy, almost girlish. 'Oh, I am so excited,' he said. Now his hands were clasped at the level of his chest, the fingers lacing and unlacing. 'I am so happy to be on this journey with you, this path. One year, it'll take, to get set up. And after that, independence. Self-sufficiency.' Back went the great head, the tawny beard jutting. A shrill whoop flew towards the ceiling and he began to circle her, passing in and out of the wedge of light. 'Our new life! Thank you, beautiful lady, for your love, for your gifts, for your trust.'

I lowered my eyes.

'Oh, Ishtar, Ishtar,' came Miller's moan, and my mouth twitched in an awful, involuntary smile. Again, I glanced around for someone to share this with. Sonia the house mother, with her glasses and the black hairs sprouting under her loose chin like insect feelers, who might pad up beside me to peek in, then turn and grin and make a face, confirming that this was funny, ridiculous, not to be taken seriously. But the hallway was still empty, and when I took a last look into the room he had his arms right around her and his huge woolly head turned away from me, his face pressed against her throat. Ishtar's eyes were closed and her lips were moving. Her voice was very quiet.

'I'm with you,' she said.

Back upstairs I sat on my duffle bag and made a shape with my hand, touching my thumb and ring finger together. I don't know when I'd learned it, or who had shown it to me. It was meant to ward off bad vibes — I didn't really believe in it, but I did it anyway. The feeling of wanting to laugh had gone away completely.

Ishtar made me go with them to the used car yard.

'Come on.' She took my wrist, pulled me to my feet. 'It'll be fun.'

Out the front she stood behind me, her hands on my shoulders. 'Miller,' she said, 'this is Silver.'

'The pleasure is all mine.' His voice boomed, making me jump, but his eyes were on her. 'Shall we?' He held out his arm and she took it, keeping hold of me with the other hand.

On the bus they sat together, and I sat behind on my own. Miller talked and talked, his voice dipping in and out of the rumble of the engine.

'... has lapsed somewhat, as these places can. But that's as it should be — these things function cyclically, like the seasons ... Not a difficult climate, down there. Good, rich, soil ...'

I felt very far away and low down. The back of his halo of hair looked solid, densely packed. When he lifted a hand to gesture, I saw how the muscles of his arms pressed outwards against the fabric. When he turned towards Ishtar to nod, pinching his fingers in emphasis, his face came partly into view. The fleecy bronze hair ran down in front of his ears to join with his beard, and then there were his eyebrows in between, so the bits where actual skin showed — his forehead, his nose, the places under his eyes — had a sudden, beaming quality. This skin was pinkish and smooth, not like a man's at all.

The car yard had strings of triangular flags looped along the top of its high, metal fence. They flapped lazily, and the rows of clean, empty cars below had a forlorn look. A man wearing a suit and carrying a clipboard came out of the office and shook Miller's hand, and the two of them moved off between the cars. Ishtar stayed by the entrance with me. She reached to pull me close, but when I looked up, her gaze was on Miller. Her face was as composed as always, but I saw the softness at the corners of her mouth, the wet, wide eyes.

Miller strode among the cars. His voice came floating over in waves. He kicked tyres, opened doors, flung up bonnets. The salesman followed with quick, light steps — I could see the small nods he gave as he spoke, and the neat movements of his hands as he pointed at things with his pen. Eventually they stopped by a station wagon, brown and with dents in the doors. Miller threw out his arms and said something, and the two of them laughed, too loudly, as if acting. They spoke some more, the salesman writing things on his clipboard. Miller got in the car, sat in the driver's seat, and got out again. Then they shook hands and began to walk towards the office. Halfway there, Miller called to Ishtar and beckoned her over.

I trailed along and hung around outside the door of the little room. All I could hear was Miller's voice, running on endlessly, billowing into laughter. It wasn't the same voice he had used with Ishtar; this voice was faster, with a brisk, jokey edge to it.

'Looks like we've got a deal, mate.' He said *mate* like it was a foreign word.

When I looked in the open doorway, I saw how it was Miller who leant to sign the papers on the desk. It was Miller who shook the salesman's hand again, and clapped him on the shoulder. But it was Ishtar who took an envelope of cash from her bag and counted out a pile of notes.

What did she see in him? I wasn't old enough to ask that question, to consider her motives. She was my mother, all I had ever known; maker of decisions, ruler of my life. What she chose — for herself, for me — was as inexplicable, as far outside the realm of my control as the weather. What I did notice though — because I was always watching, because wariness was second nature to me — was what changed in her when she was with him.

When the salesman ripped the rectangle of paper off the outside of the windscreen and handed Miller the keys, Miller opened the passenger door and turned and grabbed Ishtar, scooped her up like a child, and put her in the seat. A sound broke from her, an unlikely, breathless squeak. He settled her into position and, as if the salesman and I were not standing right there, reached in with both hands, took her face, and kissed her on the mouth. When his woolly head moved away I saw Ishtar's flushed skin, her parted lips, the glow in her eyes.

There was a lot of talk about love in the ashrams. Love was supposed to be deep inside us and in everything we did and thought — and everywhere else, too: in plants, animals, the earth, the air. Like carbon molecules, which I'd read in a book were the building blocks of our planet. We sang about love at satsang, chanted mantras over and over — *love is everything, love is all*. I didn't think of it as a personal thing, an intimate thing, between two people. Early on at school, when I first heard loving someone being used as a taunt, an accusation — 'Oooh, you *love* him' — I was confused. I couldn't grasp it used this way — sharpened, pointed.

But being *in* love, that was different. That had power. When a girl was charged with this at school, I understood her agony, the heat of her denial — *I am not!* To be in love was to be in a state, to be possessed, taken over. There was something crude in it, something base.

This was what I saw for the first time in Ishtar. When she packed the bags, when she talked about the angora goats, when Miller put her in the car and kissed her and she gazed up at him. And when we returned to the ashram and they went upstairs, and again I saw him lift her, carry her into the room. From the bottom of the stairs, I saw her head fall back against his arm. I saw the smile she gave him, her face transformed, a stranger's face. Miller pushed the door open with his shoulder and carried her in, and the door slammed shut.

We didn't travel with him in the station wagon, down to the farm. He had some stops to make on the way, which included collecting some tools and things that would take up all the space in the car.

'We'll meet him there,' Ishtar said, as we carried the bags down the stairs. 'We're going to catch the train. It'll be fun. Exciting. Come on, he's waiting to drive us to the station.'

As we were loading the car, Sonia came out onto the path with the straw broom in her hand.

'Oh,' she said, 'you are off so soon? On your big adventure? Is this your ride to the airport?' She peered at Miller in the driver's seat. 'A very hairy taxi service?' The sagging flesh below her chin wobbled with her laugh.

Ishtar didn't answer, just put another bag into the boot. Sonia came up to me where I stood on the footpath. She bent so her watery eyes behind their glasses were close to mine. I could smell her, the dried-flower smell of the tea she always drank. 'Give my love to Europe,' she said. 'My homeland. If you go to the Alps, breathe some extra of that clean air for me.'

I looked at Ishtar, who had finished with the bags.

'Where is your first port of call?' said Sonia.

From nowhere, tears were forming. I bit my lip. Even though I had never touched her, not even the waxy-looking skin of one of her hands, now all I wanted was to bury my face in Sonia's

16

orange robes. I stared hard, blurrily, at her feet, her thick beige socks and navy slippers.

'Ishtar?' Sonia's voice was louder this time. 'Where is your first port of call?'

Ishtar's boots trod towards us and came into view alongside Sonia's slippers. Her voice was cool, dismissive. 'We've changed our plans. We're going somewhere else.'

'Oh. Well, that is a surprise.'

The boots stepped away again, and Ishtar's legs disappeared into the passenger's side of the car.

I went to the door behind and opened it.

'Well, I wish you all the best,' said Sonia. 'All the best for your new adventure.'

The inside of the car smelled of lemon cleaning stuff. I bent my head and blinked so the tears fell quickly into my lap. We began to drive and I didn't look to see if Sonia was waving or had already gone back into the house.

It felt right that Miller did not travel with us. I couldn't imagine him sitting up for two days and nights in a train carriage, confined and not in charge. As the trip wore on and my tiredness increased, my impressions of him warped — in the muzzy chamber of my recent memory he expanded, bear-like, his voice unravelling into growls and grunts, his hands becoming paws as they reached for Ishtar. It was hard to picture this creature driving a car. Nodding in and out of sleep, my temple against the chill window glass, I began to imagine I could see him out there on the spool of shadowy dawn paddocks, carless and huge, jogging without fatigue, rising proudly to clear a fence — a giant travelling under his own power.

We changed trains twice, both times in the grey light of either evening or early morning; the second time, I felt the cold cut at me as I traipsed along behind Ishtar. I slept and woke and slept again. Beside me, she seemed always awake, upright and still. When it was dark outside, her reflection hung behind mine in the window, smudged and unknowable.

I saw him watching. Every Sunday he worked on his car out in his drive way and I rode my bike past and back letting my skirt slide up my legs. One time he was waiting he left the car with its bonnet up left his tools out on the concrete he stepped in to the footpath and blocked my way. Down behind the old fruit trees on the empty block I saw myself through his eyes. Sinking in to the long grass I put back my head and showed my throat like an animal but I could feel his want and Id never felt so strong so full of power, staring in to the wide open sky. It did hurt like girls at school said but that was only the first few times then it started to feel good. We didnt ever realy talk, I always had to hurry any way before my father finished the mowing or my mother got back from afternoon tea with the church ladys or Linda came out from studying in her room and noticed I was gone. Some times Id see him when Linda and me were on our way to school, getting in his car to go to work and hed give me a smile. He was a mechanic I think, any way he wore those overalls and his nails were always black but he smelled clean.

Hope Farm

WINTER

It was still not completely day when we arrived, and the cold was ferocious. Nobody was there to meet us at the station, although Ishtar did not appear to have expected anyone. We hitched a lift with a farmer and I fell straight into sleep again, wedged in the middle of the ute's bench seat, the wool of Ishtar's coat rough against my cheek. I woke when we scrunched to a halt.

'There's Kooralang,' said the farmer. 'Down that way.'

I sat up. The morning was opening into light. Through the spotted windscreen the sky sat high and cool; the road ran in a dark tongue between paddocks. Far away, right at the bottom, a white fence turned a corner, and edges of buildings showed like stragglers on the outskirts of a crowd.

'Not much to it.' The farmer hung one hand at the crest of the steering wheel. 'Not since the mine closed.' He leaned forward, squinting doubtfully, as if the town might have actually disappeared. 'And that was twenty-odd years ago, now.' The ute shuddered like a restless animal. 'But you want to be going this way.' He gave a shove at the gears and we bounced forward, swung round into a side road. It grew darker as the trees closed in. 'Friends of yours, are they?' said the farmer to Ishtar. 'These people?'

'Yeah.'

'Don't know much about the place meself.' He shifted on the seat, his voice rising like someone arguing a point. 'I mean, I don't care what they do. Long as they're not hurting anybody.'

I closed my eyes, tried to let my head flop against Ishtar's arm, but it didn't work — I couldn't get back to sleep. I gave up, straightened myself again, and watched the trees flicker past.

'Here it is.' The ute slowed.

The gate was open, the sign beside it crooked on its post. *Hope Farm*. The rainbow letters were faded, the timber grey.

The farmer looked over at Ishtar again. 'I'll take you down. Save you lugging all that gear.'

'Thanks.'

'Get up early did you? For the train?' He eased the ute through the gateway.

'We've come from Brisbane.'

'Crikey. That must've taken a while.' Then he added, quietly, as if to himself, 'That kid's exhausted.'

The trees thinned, trickled into cleared paddocks that sloped down then up to a clump of buildings, the hill banking behind them. The farmer held back for a moment, bending to peer across. Then off the ute went, rattling downwards. I turned and saw the short train of dust that tumbled roundly at our back, shepherding us in.

We stood on the porch, our baggage in a heap at the bottom of the steps. Down at one end, the boards were rotted through and straps of long grass stuck up out of the hole. From inside the house there came the sound of a baby crying. I stepped across to one of the windows. The little squares of glass were furred with dust, two of them cracked. I put my face close, but there was a curtain drawn on the other side.

'Hello?' Ishtar tapped on the door.

A small girl came around the end of the porch. 'Just open it,' she said. 'No one'll hear you.' She had snot in a slug on her upper lip; without taking her eyes from me, she wiped it onto the sleeve of her jumper.

Ishtar knocked again.

'My name's Jindi,' said the girl. 'What's your name?'

I turned back to the window and ran my finger along its sill, making little pellets of grime. From inside, the crying continued.

'That's Willow's baby,' said Jindi in an important voice. 'He cries all the time. He's gunna drive Willow crazy.'

Then the door swung open. A woman stood there. She was tall and seemed to lean over us — even Ishtar in her boots with the heels — and her hair looked pressed onto her head, running flat from its centre part down either side of her long face. She had small, fast-blinking eyes.

'Hello.' Ishtar did one of her quick smiles, pulled her coat tight, and folded her arms. 'I'm Ishtar. I'm a friend of Miller's.'

The woman's head twitched. She crossed her arms as well, and under her jumper the shapes of her breasts drooped onto them. From behind her the crying went on, loud and rhythmic.

'He's on his way,' said Ishtar. 'He'll be a week or so.'

The woman craned further forward, blinked past us at the pile of bags. 'Oh, well,' she said after a while, and stepped back. 'You'd better come in then.'

We followed her into a dim corridor, then through a doorway immediately to our right, which was hung with a thick curtain. The room was dark and warm and smelled like incense and dirty clothes. There was a fireplace with a fire burning, and a low wooden table with cups and bowls and candles on it. A wrinkled rag rug. Two heavy armchairs with rips in the fabric. The baby was on a mattress against one wall, half tangled in a crochet blanket. It lay on its back and bellowed, lifting its feet into the air every now and again.

'I'm Ishtar,' said Ishtar. 'And this is Silver.'

'Willow,' said the woman distractedly. She went over to the fire and stood looking into it as if we weren't even there. Then she gave an extra big twitch, said, 'Oh all right,' and turned to the baby. She snatched it up, flopped into one of the armchairs, and lifted her jumper.

The crying stopped. No one spoke. There was just the gulping of the baby feeding, and its noisy, wet breaths. I went to the window and pushed the curtain aside a bit. Out on the porch, Jindi marched up and down, bending her knees and bobbing her head. She was singing quietly, a thin song that came and went. After a while she stopped, stuck a forefinger in each nostril and rotated them briskly. I let the curtain fall back again.

Eventually, the baby's swallows slowed, broken by long periods of heavy breathing and the occasional snort. Then they petered out completely and there was just the breathing. Willow rose, the baby limp and horizontal in her arms. She went to the mattress and slowly lowered the little body, pulled across the blanket, and moved away.

'Well,' she said, in a low voice. 'Come and see the place then.' She turned and without looking at either of us went to the curtained doorway and ducked through.

The narrow hall was dark as well, but cold. There were doors either side, open, and I looked in as we passed. More mattresses,

26

an old dresser with a dim, flecked mirror; a tie-dyed length of fabric hung at a window, turning the air orange. Signs of freshly departed inhabitants: clothes piled on a chair; overflowing ashtrays; a glass of water on a windowsill.

'It's a big old house,' said Willow. 'Plenty of space.'

The last room was a kitchen, with lino worn through in places. There was a table and a mess of chairs, and rows of shelves with plates and bowls, and jars of lentils and beans. Dishes were piled on the bench beside the sink. A squat fridge groaned in a corner; beside it a doorless opening led to a smaller room where a bucket overflowed with nappies. I tried to breathe shallowly, through my mouth.

Willow crossed to the far door. She opened it and leaned part-way out, twitching towards a low building nearby. Chickens stepped and pecked along the dun-coloured walls. 'Mud-brick,' said Willow. 'Built it from scratch. Well Sunny did, and Ken. Mostly them.' She pushed the door closed again. 'They started the place up. Good workers, they were. Got things done.'

I leaned over the back of a chair, hollow with tiredness.

She thrust her face at me, blinked. 'Hungry?'

We sat down and she scooped out some dahl and rice from pots on the stove. I was so hungry I shovelled it down, trying to ignore the smell of the nappy bucket, and Jindi, who had come to stand beside me with her chin resting on the tabletop, her snot-clogged breathing loud and close.

'There's more.' Willow twitched at the pots.

'Thanks,' said Ishtar.

'Do you go to school?' said Jindi, edging nearer.

I kept eating.

'Sam and Jarrah went to school,' said Jindi, her breath on the back of my hand. 'They used to live here, but they've gone now.'

'So what happened?' said Ishtar. 'To Sunny and Ken?'

Willow gave a hoot of a laugh. 'Oh, there was some bust-up.' She gave her hair a shake, put her hands on her hips. 'You know —' Her lips spread in a smile, her tongue showed pale. 'Divisions.'

'I don't go to school,' said Jindi with satisfaction. 'I was going to, but then I got sick, so now Val says I can just wait till next year.'

I angled myself away from her, scraped up the last of the food.

She pressed on. 'I'm five. How old are you?'

'Thirteen.'

I thought this might put her off, but she only widened her eyes in a reverent way, and repeated, breathily: 'Thirt-een. Thirt-een.'

'Well —' began Ishtar, but Willow spoke over her.

'So,' she said. 'You'll be staying on then.'

I put down the spoon and stared at the yellowy grains of rice stuck to it. Under the table, I made the magic shape with my fingers.

'Yeah,' said Ishtar, and I changed my hidden fingers into a fist.

There was the slam of a door at the other end of the house, and a moment later the baby started to cry again. Willow's hands fell away from her hips. She swayed, as if preparing for movement, but then just stood, stooped and blinking.

Jindi took her chin from the table and skipped out into the hallway. I squeezed my fist harder. A woman's voice called from one of the front rooms, and Willow came unstuck at last and followed Jindi.

Ishtar's hands came down on my shoulders. 'Don't worry,' she said, 'it won't take long to fix the place up.'

I tried not to feel how warm her hands were, but I couldn't help it. I was overwhelmed by a quick, hopeless wish to be a little kid — as small as Jindi — able to be lifted and carried somewhere, to a bed, to be wrapped in blankets and laid to sleep. I let my head droop, but then the hands were gone, the cold air sudden on my shoulders, and Ishtar was moving away, stacking the plates and going to the sink.

I didnt tell any one. I knew though. I never kept track of my months so I couldnt tell that way even if Id known about that which I didnt. It was the 1970s but you wouldnt know it in our house my mother told me nothing about sex and it was the same at school. But I felt sick all the time and my breasts went all hot and sore and I couldnt stand any thing touching them not even the towel when I dried myself. I climbed up on the edge of the bath to see in the mirror. The swelling the shock of them. I knew what it meant that it was to do with him with the things we had done. I knew that much. Even though I didnt believe in religion it was hard not to feel it as a punishment. Now when he touched them and kissed them it hurt and I had to try hard not to push him away. I still went to meet him but there was a sad feeling to it because even though I didnt know exactly what it would be I knew some thing was going to have to change. There was a girl called Evie Dyer in Lindas class, she disappeared for a long time, months. Got in to trouble whispered the church ladys sipping there tea. You could see how brave Evies mother had to be pretending not to hear but her lips shook just a little bit. Evie came back but she didnt finish school she went to work at the chemist instead all lumpy in her uniform folding over the paper bags and sliding them across the counter with her eyes down like shed done some thing wrong. But she wasnt there long either. She vanished again. Got married someone said. I thought I saw her pushing a pram up the hill near the football club one time, her drooping head her steps slow. On Sundays in the long grass with him I narrowed my eyes against Evie Dyer against what was to come. I opened myself to his touch to his hunger, I let it fill me up. I never told him.

Until Miller arrived, Ishtar slept with me on a mattress on the floor of one of the bedrooms in the main house. I recall this time as a kind of lull, imbued with a sense of waiting. I also recall being knocked sideways by the penetrating, constant cold, which no chilly Brisbane winter morning could have prepared me for. I only ever felt remotely warm in that front room. In bed, even wearing a jumper, tracksuit pants, and socks, and with Ishtar's back against mine, I slept curled like a slater — stretching out an inch in any direction meant touching mattress so cold it felt wet. It was this sensation that woke me in the mornings, the icy chill crawling across Ishtar's emptied side to surround me completely.

The cold inside the house was seeping and heavy. Outside, there was also the wind, which blasted and stung relentlessly. My ears hurt, my eyes watered, and my fingers and toes went numb. None of my clothes were adequate; I soon learned to wear almost all of them at once.

Before Hope, we must have stayed in communes that were more or less self-sufficient, living off their own produce and bartering with the leftovers — there were dim memories of helping pack up cartons of eggs for a market, and boxes of tomatoes — but these places would have been in the minority. This set-up, where values and reasons slumped, deflated, in the background while everyone plodded round under the weight of the type of resentment that comes with unacknowledged compromise — this was more familiar to me.

Reminders of what had been were everywhere. In the kitchen a series of hand-made posters, sagging, faded, and blackened with cooking grease were pinned to the wall: instructions on the care of goats and chickens; a guide to composting; a planting schedule with delicate illustrations of vegetables and herbs. There were chickens, of course, but the coop was in bad repair and, until Ishtar did it, had not been raked out for a long time. Of goats there was no sign at all, and the veggie patch was full of weeds, its fence partly collapsed. A scarecrow drooped, waterlogged, grass sprouting from its shoulders. There was a compost heap — it was huge, overfilled, spilling from its chicken-wire frame. *No cooked foods*, said the discoloured poster, but the tower of compost held small pools of curry and slops of milky porridge. It smelled rancid, and Jindi proudly informed me that she'd seen rats there.

The residents were as you'd expect: long-haired, worn-looking, with bad teeth. There were around eight or ten adults, most of them women, and — most disappointing of all Hope's disappointments — no children other than Willow's screaming baby and disgusting, snotty, close-breathing Jindi.

'When we get our own crops going again,' the women would say, seated at the kitchen table, passing a joint, 'we won't have to worry about all that.' *All that* being either bosses or the dole office — because those of them that weren't on some kind of benefits worked picking fruit or vegetables for local farmers, or in the nearby powdered-milk factory. They would nod vaguely towards the window, the darkening paddocks outside. 'Feed ourselves then, like we used to.' The hollow, automatic quality to their voices reminded me of doing the chants in the ashrams, sitting cross-legged on the floor. Nobody made any mention of Miller and his new regime.

So the crops had failed, the goats were gone, the compost was rotten, but still they stayed, these people. I suppose they had nowhere better to go. It was the eighties — they were a dying breed. And they were tired; their ideals had seized up and grown heavy somehow, and they didn't know how to put them down. That's the only explanation I can come up with now. At the time, of course, I gave it no thought. They were just there, they did what they did — or didn't — and we were there as well, and I would simply, like always, have to put up with it.

I was used to this, to arriving, to having Ishtar seamlessly meld with the household — working, working, weaving herself into new patterns — to being left to manage my own slow and reluctant settling. I doubt I was a typical thirteen-year-old. I imagine I was very naive in some ways, and unusually worldly in others. What I cared about first, always, was if there were other children my age, who I might make friends with. Then, where would I go to school, and might I make a friend there? Were there sweets in the house? Licorice? Halva? Dates? Honey? What kinds of books were there to read? There was never a television. Hope, it was clear from the beginning, lacked on every count.

I spent that first week or so — before Miller came and school started — just hanging around. I was alone a lot of the time, which suited me. The farm workers and those with factory shifts went off early, piled into the assortment of rattle-trap vehicles that returned later to skirt the front porch like dilapidated beasts at a waterhole. Those who were left behind — Willow and the baby, Jindi, plus a few random extras — beetled around the place in what appeared to be established routines, not interacting with one another much. The daylight hours seemed to stretch on forever.

There was a small shelf of books in the front room and I worked my way through them, taking one and finding a place to hide with it; I was always avoiding Ishtar because she might give me a job to do, and Jindi for obvious reasons. There were only a few kids' books and they were horribly childish — still, I churned through them and then moved on to the adult ones, which were all about Tarot and healing, or rainforests or permaculture, and that kind of thing. There was also a guide to the care of goats, which I found surprisingly enjoyable; I spent a lot of time mooning over the photos of different goats, mentally naming them and attributing personalities. It was depressing to close the cover on those clean, well-fed animals in their tidy, lush pastures and return to the reality of broken-fenced paddocks containing only thistles.

I watched Ishtar sometimes, from a place up on the hill behind the buildings where there was a huge fallen tree I could lean against, hunched, shivering in my jacket. Even though I had resolved never again to be drawn in by her fervour, the brightness to her movements as she came and went — raking, chopping, sweeping, pegging out loads of washing — every now and then I was struck by a kind of unwilling wonder. From her figure there below, a current seemed to rise through the chill air, to fan out warmly, indiscriminately, stirring the leaves of the clotted ivy that covered the outdoor toilet, the straw of the chicken coop, the ruined vegetable garden, skating up the sodden grass of the hill and, in passing, filling me with shivers.

One evening I sat watching as she went along the back wall of the house, stooping to pull the lanky weeds that lapped at its base. Beyond, the rust-pocked, wheezing cars were slipping one by one down the track with their loads of potato-pickers and factory hands. The heavy sky was darkening, but just as Ishtar threw the last weed onto the pile, there was a shift low on the horizon and a swathe of watery, greenish blue appeared, and the unexpected edge of a platinum sunset sent everything shining. The kitchen window blazed, and below it the wall met the ground unhampered, seeming to shout its illuminated glory — the simple beauty of a clean line. Ishtar caught the weed pile with a garden fork and tossed it in one swift, elegant movement into a wheelbarrow just as a returned worker came past on his way to the mud-brick building. The worker said something and Ishtar put back her head in a laugh that seemed to puncture the clouds overhead, the light catching her long throat, and I throbbed with reluctant pride. She was amazing. She could gild the edges of even miserable, freezing, grey Hope.

I had always known there was something special about her, registered it in the way other adults reacted to her. I had never given this any thought; it was just the way things were. And besides, I understood. I'd always wanted her, too — or more of her, anyway. Perhaps every young child wants more of their mother, finds her the most beautiful woman in the world — perhaps this is normal. I wouldn't know.

It was at Hope Farm though, it seems to me now, that I began for the first time to pay attention to this, to the machinations of her charm. As with all memory, it's difficult to know how much I have since manufactured with my retrospective preoccupations, but when I think back to eating dinner in the crowded fug of that front room, seated on the floor with a plate of curry in my lap, I get a strong sense of tuning in properly for the first time to the disturbance, the little maelstrom of interactions that

Ishtar, her presence and her looks, always prompted. Perhaps it was the dawning of an adolescent awareness of social nuances. Perhaps it was simply because Hope was far and away the most uncomfortable, ugliest, and most depressing place we'd ever lived, with the most flaccid, uninspiring residents, and therefore the ideal setting for the showcasing of her charisma. Or perhaps, and most likely, it was because of what I'd seen back at the ashram: Ishtar with Miller, Ishtar *in love*; a glimpse of a new territory, a relationship in which she might not hold all the power.

I understood that it was because she was beautiful — I'd always known that. The way her skin caught the light, creamy and golden, the darkness of her brows and lashes, the fullness of her lips. The rich brown hair falling heavy and smooth, lightening to caramel at the ends. There was something else though, that shook things up in them, that prompted such a range of responses — the open, soft-faced stare; the covert glance; the bodily adjustments, use of a louder voice, bigger gestures — and it was to do with the way she wore her beauty, her ownership of it. It was there in the way she walked, the straightness of her spine, the reserved grace of her movements, in her speech, her laughter — and in the way she bestowed these things on others, measured them out. She was in charge. She made people want her. I sat in the firelight with my plate cooling against my thighs and saw the gazes that were drawn, helpless, towards her, pulsing with greed, envy, admiration, rivalry — but all of them with desire, either for her or for something she had.

'Why'd you leave?' said a woman on one of those first nights, when the emptied plates had been stacked and another joint lit.

Ishtar gave a brief, noncommittal smile. 'It was time to move on.'

'Did you stop believing?' said the woman. 'In the guru? The meditation and all that?'

Ishtar shrugged.

The woman frowned. 'Well, did you ever believe?'

Ishtar shrugged again.

'But aren't you s'posed to?' The woman dragged on the joint and then held it to the lips of the man seated beside her, whose plinking on an acoustic guitar went out of time as he inhaled.

Ishtar didn't answer.

'Isn't that the whole point?'

Ishtar sat with her back straight, hands on her knees, her face hard and beautiful. 'I respected them,' she said after a while. 'I pulled my weight.'

There was a pause, and then the guitar man said, 'Sometimes it's just time to move on.' His eyelids lifted, and he gave Ishtar a blurry, slow-smiling look.

The woman saw and did a kind of head-tossing wiggle, then leaned into him and placed a hand on his leg, right up near his crotch. Someone handed her the joint again and she sucked viciously on it. 'So how long were you there for?'

'About a year.'

The woman's mouth hung open. 'But you can't do that.' She turned to the man but he didn't seem to be listening any more. She looked back at Ishtar, grimacing. 'You have to believe. It's, it's … *lying* if you don't.'

Nobody responded. Ishtar sat quietly.

The woman went on. 'That's just bullshit. You have to believe, or you're bringing everyone else down. Like this place. We're all here 'cause we believe in the same things.' Her fingers tensed on the man's thigh. 'Freedom … and …' Her eyes were almost closed, but her brow had an angry crease in it. 'Freedom,' she said again. 'A better way, a better future ...'

There was quiet for a while. More and more spaces fell between the guitar man's notes. His head drooped. Ishtar stood, smoothly, and walked to the curtain. I followed, but not before catching the dulled, resentful dagger of a look the woman sent after her.

There it was, contained in those two actions, in Ishtar's unhurried, poised departure and the impotent fury of the woman's stare: the essence of what made people hate and want her. I'm sure I didn't fully comprehend it at the time, and the irony would not be revealed until much, much later, but now I think, to them, she must have appeared free — or at least closer to what they thought freedom was than they were.

My mother guessed in the end. She kept asking if I had any thing for the incinerator and when I said no she stared at me. Then she said Where have you been putting them? You know you cant leave them lying around some where even wrapped up, theyll start to smell. And I said I havent got any. Then she went to the bathroom and checked the cabinet and said You havent used any, did you buy them for yourself? I didnt answer because of course I couldnt buy them for myself what would I buy them with? She came back in to my room then and knelt down in front of me where I was sitting on the bed. She stared at me at my face and then at my breasts sticking out all swollen under my dress. She got that voice. What have you been doing? she said.

Miller arrived, and Ishtar helped him unload the car. They carried clinking bundles of tools to one of the falling-down sheds at the back — spades and long-handled gardening forks, and then some boxes that gave off a shimmying rustle.

'Look, girls,' said Miller, sliding a pile of boxes to the ground and squatting. He opened the top one and took out a small paper packet. Jindi rushed forward. Miller ripped off the end of the packet and shook something into his hand. 'Look,' he said again. 'Seeds. The stuff of life.'

'Wow,' breathed Jindi.

'Can you believe that from these tiny things will burst whole plants? Bearing fruit?'

The girl bent closer, her face almost in his palm. 'What kind of fruit?'

Miller didn't answer. Swivelling, he raised his hand to his own face and blew, sending the seeds rushing out in a disintegrating cloud.

Jindi gasped, grabbing at the drifting particles. 'But what kind of fruit will they make?'

Miller, seeming not to hear, was gathering up the boxes again, slinging them haphazardly into the shed. Then he strode away towards the mud-brick building, where Ishtar had taken another load of cartons and bags.

After making a few more grabs at the air Jindi ran to me, fists clenched. 'Silver!' she panted. 'There's going to be fruit!' She opened her fingers but the minuscule seeds had vanished into the grime of her palms. She held her hands nearer to her eyes, then shook them before staring up at me in confusion. 'There were seeds,' she said. 'I had them.'

I could see some of them, a constellation of dark flecks

trapped in the yellowy green globule of snot that was descending from one of her nostrils.

Miller and Ishtar didn't come back out of the mud-brick building. I had a pretty good idea what they were doing in there. While Jindi was busy pawing through the dirt, I took off.

The other side of the hill ran down to a belt of scrub and past that was a creek, which swung in a wide curve around the back of Hope's cleared paddocks. Directly behind Hope and off to the right, the scrub, while only a narrow strip, was choked with blackberry and almost impenetrable, but in the other direction it widened and was much easier going, with a faint path that ran a few metres up from the water, parallel. Quite soon this came out at the dirt road, just a bit further along from Hope's gateway and weathered, pathetic sign, where a small timber bridge straddled the water. The almost-path continued on the other side of the road, where there were no more paddocks or houses, only bush, and I was able to walk along there for probably fifteen or twenty minutes without coming across any other sign of human life. It was a delicious feeling, to leave Hope behind.

It was loose bush, easy to move through — a combination of tall gums, ti-tree with their ragged, papery branches, and the occasional explosion of bright-baubled wattle. There were places where the creek's bank opened out into miniature meadows of patchy pale grass that steamed under the winter sun.

That creek! The lightness of the flow of water; the warm, brown look of it — even though, when I put my hand in, it was so cold my fingers turned white and numb — the wet fissures in the big rocks that sat half submerged; the refractions of amber light deep down, and the mossy-looking spotted fish that lazed there. Birds seemed to burst with pleasure out of the canopy of bush, hurtling their calls around, landing with an extra flourish to dip their heads and then lift and shake them, brash drops flying from their beaks.

I went there often. I took a book and read, hunkered at the base of a tree, folded in on myself against the cold. My feet would go to sleep and I'd have to ease my legs out slowly in order to stand up, the electric tingle of pins and needles jagging in pure, enlivening streaks.

It was down by the creek I met Ian.

I'd had the feeling that there was someone else around. Once, huddled in the lee of my enormous, silvered hillside log, something had made me turn and stare up at where the wind-raked grass met the sky, and I thought I saw a flicker of movement. In the bush there were always noises — stirrings, rustlings — but sometimes I thought I heard the swish of a branch, as if someone had pushed through it, or the weight of footfalls. I put it down to wallabies, which I saw occasionally, if I stayed out late enough, nosing down to the water, stopping to pull at grass clumps or put their heads up to twitch their ears. Sometimes one would stop very close and fix me with a trembling gaze, and I would stare right back, and the moment seemed to go on forever.

Then one time I was down there in the afternoon. All day it had been raining, but the sky had cleared and there were splashes of sun on the wet ground and little ribbons of light moving in the brownish water. I was squatting, keeping as still as I could, watching out for one of the fish that moved almost invisibly in and out of the shadowy depths. The creek was rushing faster than I'd seen it, with bits of bark and twigs and leaves being carried along, and swirls of water frothing at the places where the bank made a curve, or where rocks stuck up above the surface. I had seen a fish, and was watching it dart in and out as if excited by the creek's new energy, when something appeared at the edge of my vision, and came floating along near to my side of the bank.

At first I thought it was a big, funny-coloured bubble. But then it got closer, and didn't burst but swung with the current in a quick, clean arc, coming neatly to rest like a docking boat in the shelter of a big tuft of reedy grass that hung out from the bank right next to me.

It was a ball of some sort, greyish white. I was about to reach for it when another one appeared, the same size and colour, and whisked itself in to halt beside the first. Side by side they jiggled there, surrounded by floating leaves and yellow wattle blooms.

I stood up. I took hold of one of the branches of a nearby ti-tree — a low, strong one — and leaned out to see upstream.

Down they came, twirling and bobbing, one by one. Two more small, greyish balls — and then a tennis one, waterlogged green. A short break and then another grey and another tennis ball, and at last, like the main attraction in a parade, lower in the water and right out in the middle, a cricket ball, bright cherry red, turning slowly in the current.

The grey balls came shooting in to bob with the others in a little cluster, hemmed by the mat of floating leaves, and the two tennis balls stopped slightly further out. The cricket ball, though, was too far away and too heavy to be sucked in close like the others. It was on a different course, and unless I did something it would just keep going past. I reached for a long stick, gripped the ti-tree branch harder, and leaned further out. The ball was almost level with me now, and I swung with the stick, missed, then swung again and just connected — and in it cruised, still turning its lazy shining somersaults, to join the bobbling jostle of grey and green.

No more balls came, and after a while I pulled myself close to the ti-tree and let go of its branch, and dropped the stick. It made a dull *thunk* on the grass. At the same time, I heard another noise and turned, and there he was, pushing his way through low wattle branches.

He was gangly and pale, with colourless eyelashes and brows, which gave his eyes an unprotected, dazzled look. There were bright blobs of wattle on his shoulders and in his hair, which was almost more green than blond, like the tennis balls. He was wearing a blue jumper and brown pants, and desert boots that made his feet appear big and clumping below the skinny legs — and he had a stick, too, held upright like a staff. He was breathing fast, as if he'd been hurrying, and he stepped forward and peered past me.

'Did they stop here?' he said, his voice breathy and impatient.

I moved aside to show the balls floating in their little pocket of calm.

He went over and knelt, letting his stick drop. 'Even the cricket ball?' He reached down and grabbed it.

'Well …' I indicated my own stick. Shyness made my voice come out strangely. 'I sort of … tapped it in.'

'Yeah, you have to. It's heavier — it doesn't go with the current as much.'

There was a long pause. He sat back on his haunches, the ball clasped between his knees. He tilted his head, half shut one eye, and aimed the other at me. 'So …' he said. 'New digs?'

I didn't answer. I didn't understand what he meant; it was not a term I'd come across before, even with all my reading. He waited a moment and then, with the air of someone accustomed to having to rephrase his sentences, said, 'You've moved house, have you?'

'Yeah.' I wasn't going to offer any more information.

'Oh, I know where you're from.' He gestured downstream. 'Hope Farm. With all the hippies.'

Before I could help it, my voice leapt out, quick and defensive: 'Well, we don't live there. We're just … staying for a while.'

'Ah.' The boy opened both eyes properly. I became acutely aware of my ill-fitting, unlaundered clothes, the tangle of my hair. 'But you *are* a hippie, aren't you?'

The blood rose to my face. 'I'm …'

'I don't actually *care*.' He waved a hand. 'I really don't. I am not,' he got to his feet, 'in a position to *judge*.'

I smiled — I couldn't help it. There was an old-man quality to him I found comical: the frail body, the stalk-like legs, the desert boots planted in the grass. My suspicion ebbed. There was just something so — harmless — about him. I looked at the dripping ball in his hand. 'Doesn't the water ruin it?'

'What do you mean?'

'The cricket ball. Doesn't the water get inside it?'

He held it up as if he'd forgotten he had it. He gave it a little toss but then failed to catch it, and it fell and rolled towards the creek. He threw himself after it, grabbed it, and sat up. 'I don't know,' he said. Then he put it down carefully on the grass and began to take the others from the water, one by one.

'But if it gets wet it's probably no good.'

'No good for what?' He had his back to me.

'Well, for cricket.'

He turned and stared. 'Why should I care,' he said, 'if it's any good for *cricket*?' He spat the word out like it was poison. Then after a few moments he grinned. 'Oh, I see,' he said. 'You think these balls are *mine*.'

I waited, confused.

'Yes, yes, of course you would,' he said, as if to himself, clambering to his feet. 'But I am afraid you are *labouring* under a *false assumption*.' He bent and picked up the cricket ball again, and passed it to me. 'See that?'

I turned the glistening red surface to follow the trail of black letters. The writing was tall and reached almost all the way around. *DEAN PRICE*, it read, in aggressive capitals, *HANDS OFF!* I raised my eyes to meet the boy's. He lifted an eyebrow.

'Dean Price?' I said, hesitantly.

'Is not me.'

There was a pause while I waited for whatever it was that he was so clearly looking forward to revealing.

'My name.' He spread his wet hands. 'Is Ian Munro. And I stole that ball from Dean Price. All these balls.' He indicated the pile at his feet. 'And that is because Dean Price is my *nemesis*.'

It wasnt our usual doctor it was a different one in a different part of town. He didnt look at me he pointed at the high bed and said Take off your underwear and hop up there. I took them off and then I didnt know what to do with them. I looked at my mother but she had her head down like she was praying so I just bunched them up and kept them in my hand. He put a sheet over me and said Knees up, then he went round to the end of the bed. I looked at the ceiling. Knees apart he said and put his hand in under the sheet and his fingers were cold. He felt the out side too, pressed around my belly. Yes he said to my mother. About four months. In the car my mother said Who was it? What do you mean I said. I mean who is responsible she said. I only knew his last name so I said it. She stared at me. Who lives at number fourteen? she said. Yes. She hit me on the ear. That man is married she said. I didnt answer, I put my hand over my ear. I had seen a woman of course, going in and out of the house but she never seemed to have any thing to do with him. My mother was quiet for a long time then she said Theres a place youll have to go in Brisbane, theyll look after you until its over and then you can come home, it will be like it never happened. It was hot and she took out a hanky and wiped under her nose. She put her hands on the big white steering wheel. Nobody needs to know she said but I couldnt tell if she was talking to me or to herself. I thought about Evie Dyers mother and her sorry smile her teacup shaking in her hands. Back at home my mother made dinner and I set the table. Linda was there in her room studying like always, she didnt have to do as many jobs round the house as me. When my father came home we had dinner like there was nothing different but afterwards when I was in my room I heard him shouting. Who did it? Who did it? Whats his name? he shouted. Wait wait my mother said, She doesnt know his name and

any way hes gone now, hes left town. Its all right she said, It can all
be dealt with nobody needs to know. He stopped shouting then.
Quietly he said Of course theyll know, everyone always knows,
her life is ruined now dont think it will be the same again because
it wont. Shh said my mother, She will hear you.

Ian lived on the next farm over, on the far side of the stretch of bush. Despite being so skinny and brittle-looking he was in fact a year older than me and in Year Eight at Tarrina High, where I would soon also be going. Tarrina was a much bigger town than Kooralang; it had the train station where Ishtar and I had arrived that first morning. It was there at Tarrina High that Dean Price made Ian's life a misery. Or *misery*, as Ian said; he seemed to enjoy straining at certain words with his rusty voice, wringing out extra meaning.

'It's *brutal*,' he said, as we sat on the damp grass, the pile of balls between us. 'Just *brutal*. But it always *has* been. I'm pretty tough, you know. I might not look strong, but I've got resilience.' He took an apple from his pocket, bit into it, and spoke wetly. 'They're just *brutes*, Dean Price and his … *cronies*. When they can't understand something, they just stomp on it. I've been getting stomped on for eight years now, but they'll never truly crush me. Because I —' he made a sudden, rattling noise and began to cough.

Timidly, I reached out and banged with the heel of my hand between his shoulder blades. The knobs of his spine were sharp through his jumper. He nodded, still coughing, and I banged harder.

'Okay, okay. Enough.' He held up a hand. 'Thank you.' He cleared his throat and wiped his eyes. 'Where was I?'

'They'll never truly crush you.'

'Oh, yes. They'll never truly *crush* me because I —' he looked intently at me with his still-watery eyes. 'You're going to need to know all this,' he said.

'I know.'

'I have *strategies*.' He leaned back on one elbow and gestured with the other hand. 'Three main ones. The first is *avoidance*.

49

Simple. Keep out of their way. Know the safe places. Know their movements and plan yours accordingly.'

'Where are the safe places?'

He held up a finger. 'I'll get to those. But first, the other strategies. The next is *resilience*. You can't always hide. There will be situations in which you are unable to.' He paused for a moment and his face darkened. 'Phys Ed,' he said, in a terse voice. 'Changing rooms. Toilets.'

'I know what you mean.'

He heaved a sigh. 'It's unavoidable. And when they find you, you just have to endure. Don't provoke them. Don't fight back. Just put your head down and wait for them to tire of you.'

I swallowed. This school sounded rough.

Ian was looking at me earnestly. 'You think that's cowardly? You think I'm *weak*, not fighting back?'

'Oh no. I —'

He spoke over me. 'I'm a realist,' he said. 'I plan to survive, and move on. I have no desire to enter their primitive battles, to *engage* with them on their level.'

'I didn't —'

He went on, finger upheld. 'And now for the third tactic. This one is equally as important as the first two, in fact it's *crucial*, because it preserves morale.'

I waited.

'Revenge.' He smiled. 'Revenge is very important. Without revenge, you go under.'

We both looked at the heap of balls.

'Yes,' said Ian. 'That's what the balls are for. I have taken something from Dean Price, and I can *revel* in the knowledge that I have caused him some suffering.'

I smiled.

'But,' he went on. 'You must be as vigilant in carrying out your revenge as you are in practising your avoidance. You must plan, and use *stealth*. You must never take risks. It is absolutely not worth it.' He reached out and picked up the soggy cricket ball. 'Dean Price will never know why his precious balls keep disappearing. And that's important for two reasons: one, my relative safety is assured, because if he was ever to find out it was me that was taking them he would quite possibly actually *kill* me; and two, the thought of his ongoing anguish makes my revenge so much more *delicious*.' For the second time he tried to toss the ball and catch it again, and for the second time he missed. It rolled to nestle with the others. 'I like to picture his face,' he said, 'as he tries to figure it out. The cogs in his head slowly crunching round.'

I tried to smile politely. But I had a vision of Dean Price, bullish and mean-eyed, with angry pimples — and stealing something from a person like that, for any reason, just sounded way too dangerous.

Ian went to the edge of the water. 'Shall we toss this lot in again and see what happens?' he called. 'They can go quite a way, almost to the bridge. There's a bend just before there that always stops them.'

I joined him, and one by one we threw the balls into the rushing stream. We started with the small grey-white ones, which barely made a sound as they hit the water. Then we did a tennis ball each — they plopped in satisfyingly before surging off. We watched them go, and then Ian raised the cricket ball. He stood for a moment with his skinny arm tensed, but then lowered it again.

'What's your name?' he said, and for a moment all the

old-man oddness dropped out of his voice, and he just sounded like a kid.

'Silver.'

'Here, Silver.' He held the ball out. 'You do the honours.'

'Oh, no.'

'Oh, yes. Go on.'

'Okay.' I took the ball. It was heavy. I lifted my arm and threw, and up it went in a long streak, then over and down and in, right at the middle. A little clear frill of splash rose and marked its entry and sank away again, and then the ball broke the surface gently and seemed to settle for a moment before commencing its slow, grand twirling, and its journey downstream.

My mother drove me all the way to Brisbane for a special mass. She didnt take Linda just me. It was there in the church pew that I felt some thing move right down low, the lightest tap. I sat still but it didnt happen again. When my mother prayed she laced her fingers and her knuckles went white. Afterwards we went to a park near the Valley. She took me to a bench. I have to go to the shops wait here she said and walked away. I watched her leave, her spiky steps. In one week I was to go to the place, the Home she called it. I didnt think about what it might be like, I kept my mind shut against any thinking but some times like now out in the light open park I couldnt help seeing what would come after, that I would be like Evie Dyer. I felt panic and the tap came in side again like a message and I wanted to get up and walk away in the opposite direction from my mother. I stood up and then I saw them. They were getting ready for a picnic putting out patterned cloths on the grass and unpacking metal pots of food from big baskets. Some had dark skin and wore robes that glowed orange in the sun but the clothes of the others were beautiful too. Most had long hair centre parted and worn loose. A man sat cross legged with a guitar and played and some women sang they all had smiling calm faces. I could smell the food and it was like nothing Id smelled before. I felt so hungry all of a sudden. I knew what hippies were Id seen pictures in the paper and some times the real thing in the city, once some had been busking when Id gone to a film with friends from school. My friends pointed and laughed and pulled me away but Id wanted to stay to see more. At home I often looked at the pages on India in my Geography book, the photos. Foreheads stained with red dye and wreaths of yellow flowers, the jewel saris of women working in a field, there beautiful slim brown arms. Patterns even in a sack of dried beans. Every tiniest thing decorated everything beautiful so far away from the plain white house of my parents its square lawn and concrete paths and the empty ugly streets I rode my bike down. I had moved from the bench to get closer and then I saw a woman, she had long brown hair down her back and tied onto her with a length of fabric a curled shape close against her chest like it was part of her. She stood near the guitar man, her eyes closed moving gently from side to side. Then I saw what it was bound to her chest because a little arm came up, a tiny hand touched her chin and she opened her eyes and smiled and held the hand and kissed it not stopping her dance. Over the grass two women came to me. One maybe in her twenties wearing robes, dark skinned her smile clear and white the other older almost my mothers age with hair in plaits over her shoulders the breeze puffing her silk blouse and long skirt making ripples in the tiny diamond shapes that covered them. They didnt speak. The younger one gave me a pamphlet but when I tried to look at it my eyes were full of tears. The panic happened again, the tears ran down. Can you help me? I said. I covered my face my ears burned. Then I felt hands touch me arms close round me. I smelled incense and perfumed skin the spices from there cooking, I dropped my hands and sobbed against them. Little girl, whispered the dark woman. Little girl. Even though I was taller than her. She wiped my cheeks with her fingers. Then she let go and over my shoulder my mother was calling my name. I turned and there she was half running in her low heels her stiff skirt waggling her hat crooked. She was shooing with her arms her shopping bags flapped. I felt the older woman take my hand. We can help you she said, If you ever need. Her warm dry hand squeezed mine and then let go and then my mother was there grabbing me pulling me away.

The whole drive home my mother didnt speak to me, two and a half hours. At home she unpacked one of the shopping bags onto my bed.

Two dresses like tents one brown one navy. Two wide cotton nighties plain white. A bra with huge cups that sat up by themselves. Now I knew why she didnt bring Linda on the shopping trip or take me in to the shop with her, in case any one saw and guessed. Thats how worried she was because what are the chances of bumping in to any one from our town all that way away and in a big city like Brisbane. You wont need much my mother said Its only for while youre there, once youre back home you can wear your old clothes again. When she had gone out I opened my wardrobe and looked at everything so plain and ordinary. I thought of the silks of the woman with plaits the diamonds scattered like stars. I thought of that baby curved against its mothers chest there two bodies like one, the mothers smile no pram no Evie Dyer plodding sad and lumpy. I closed the wardrobe door again, pushed the new clothes to the end of the bed and sat down. I looked at the pamphlet and traced the image of two hands joined and pointing upwards, not like my mothers all white against the church pew these fingers were elegant the shape of freedom. Join Us On The Path it said. I touched my belly low down, the place where it was growing.

Ian and I met again the next day. He brought a pad of paper and a pen, and drew a map of the school for me, marking out the areas to avoid whenever possible, and also the safe places. There were only four days left until the end of term break, when he would have to return and I would have to begin. The library, he explained, was open before and after school hours and at lunchtime and morning recess, and you could stay in there as long as you wanted, providing you were quiet. There was always a teacher around, and anyway, people like Dean Price didn't even know it existed. 'And — bonus — it's heated,' he said. 'And — *double* bonus — it has its own toilets.'

We were by the creek again, near the bridge, sitting on a steep bit of bank, Ian with the notepad propped on his knees. He drew two small rectangles near the big shaded section he'd marked *Oval*. 'So save your toilet trips for the library,' he said, and put big crosses through the two rectangles. 'These other toilets are not at all safe.'

'Okay.'

'Now. The bus. There are a few oafs that catch it, but the driver's all right, he's got control, so sit near the front. Nobody else gets on or off at our stop, so you don't have to worry about that. And, most blessed of all blessings, Dean Price himself does not catch it. His *den* of *idiocy* is, I believe, in the other direction from school.'

'Where's our stop?'

'Just up on the main road. About halfway between the turn-off for your place and the one for mine.' Ian put the cap on the pen and clipped it to the notepad. He dropped them to the ground, drew his arms round his knees, and turned to me with a pinched sort of smile. 'Now, this is a difficult thing to say, but I'm sure you'll understand.'

I waited. Again I felt like laughing at him, at his seriousness, his old-man speech, and funny, clumsy stork-like body. But there was pride there, too — it glowed in his thin face.

'As far as school goes,' said Ian, 'we don't know each other.' He gave the small, apologetic smile again. 'We don't *speak* to each other, we don't *look* at each other — we do not *communicate* in any way. All right?'

I opened my mouth, but he spoke again, quickly.

'It's just too dangerous. They're like sharks — you can't make any kind of splash or it *attracts* them. And when I say "as far as school goes", I am in fact referring to any *public* interaction.' He waved in the direction of the main road. 'On the bus. At the bus stop. In Kooralang or Tarrina, or any other town. Basically, anywhere other than *here*.' He stubbed a finger at the ground between his legs. 'Understand?'

'Yeah.' I did understand. I wouldn't want to be seen in public with him, either. It seemed sad that it had to be a secret, conducted under such rigid conditions, but still — and my heart lifted — it was a friendship.

'But you know,' said Ian briskly. 'I'll be with you, in *spirit*.'

There was a sound from the dirt road, an engine, far off but getting closer.

He jumped up. 'Quick!' Down the steep bank and along towards the bridge he went, feet first, hands grabbing at stones and clumps of grass. He looked like a giant, spindle-legged crab. 'Come on!'

I followed, sliding down in the same position.

The car was coming not from the main road but from the other direction, the other side of the creek. It was close now. I could hear the gravel spitting from its wheels.

'Quick!' Ian scuttled into the space under the bridge.

I went after him.

Side by side we clung to the bank, in the cold half-light, our heads inches from the timber sleepers. The car was closer, the engine roaring, its vibration already running through the bridge. And then it was on us and we were inside the dense, thundering ripple of sound, and I thought of aeroplanes, of waterfalls, of massive machines going full tilt, and I clapped my hands to my ears, almost slipping down, and then it was over. I realised I was screaming, and Ian was screaming beside me, and the two screams went on for a while, reedy and small in the deaf silence, and then stopped — and there was just the hammering of my heart and the panting of my breath, and the soft sifting of the dust coming down between the timbers above.

He turned to me. His face was white with dust and his tongue came out and licked his lips and they showed suddenly red. 'I'll be with you in spirit,' he said.

I woke alone in the cold room at Hope, which was bare of furniture apart from the mattress I slept on and a poster of Joni Mitchell stuck to one wall — and bare of Ishtar's things, too, now that she slept out with Miller in the mud-brick building. I lay, listening to the moan and clatter of the morning around me — voices from the kitchen, the strained jigger of someone starting one of the cars out the front, Jindi's footfalls thudding up and down, the steadfast howling of Willow's baby — for a moment not remembering, and then it filtered in, set up a buzzing under my ribs and in my fingertips. I had a friend.

On the day before my mother took me to the Home I rang the number on the pamphlet. It was a Sunday my fathers mower roaring in the garden Linda studying, my mother at the church hall. I didnt think about the fruit trees on the other side of the fence about him waiting there with his black rimmed fingernails what he might wonder now that I wouldnt come again. He didnt fit in to any possible future. There was only the tunnel of my mothers plan leading to an Evie Dyer life or the thing that made my heart beat fast. The phone was answered by someone with an accent. I met a woman I said, In the city. She told me I could call if I needed help. Wait please they said and then someone else came on. Hello? Hello I said and began to cry because I recognised her voice. Ah she said, The girl from the park. How are you? Im going to have a baby I whispered, Theyre sending me to a Home. I dont know what to do. We are here she said, You can call any time day or night.

In the back of the station wagon I dozed to the tireless stream of Miller's voice.

'It was the Andeans who first cultivated the potato. More than two hundred species are still to be found, up there on the *altiplano*.'

He seemed to go out of his way to use foreign words, reaching with his tongue right into their difficult corners. Even the names of the different kinds of potatoes he spoke as if the words themselves were tasty foods in his mouth, sweet or spicy. *Sebago. Pontiac. Sequoia.*

Sometimes he recited bits of poems. For this he gathered his voice up and urged it into faster rhythms.

Season of mists and mellow fruitfulness
Close bosom-friend of the maturing sun
Conspiring with him how to load and bless
With fruit the vines that round the thatch-eves run

He snipped off the end of the word *fruit*, rounded out *bosom* with a purr.

The poetry voice seemed to have a trace of an accent, crisp and proper, like the voice that read the ABC news on the radio. It wasn't the same as the one he'd used with the salesman at the car place, breezy and light, when he'd said, 'Looks like we've got a deal.'

We parked outside the Kooralang pub. There were lights on in the bar, and faces turned to look.

'Meet you at the book shop,' said Miller. Before he walked away he reached for Ishtar, kissed her, and I saw his hand on her bottom, squeezing.

Once he had gone, it seemed very quiet. The road was wide

and the buildings seemed to lean away from it as if resenting any activity that might occur between them. Ishtar glanced up and down and then started to cross the broad black expanse, boots ringing. I followed, feeling the eyes from the pub.

Inside the op-shop, Ishtar went through the racks of clothes, occasionally bringing something over and holding it up against me; the purpose of this visit was to put together a uniform for me to wear to school.

I stood at the window looking out. A few people passed — farmer-looking men, in hats and boots. A tall, shambling woman pushing a pram with two dogs in it.

After a while, Ishtar went through to the back room and the two women behind the counter began to talk about her. One had a slow voice that went on and on like a ribbon unwinding, and the other kept sticking in sharp little sounds, like pins.

'She'll be from that place then.'

'Mm. Yes.'

'You know, up the hill, near the Munros'.'

'Mm. Mm.'

'You know, those people.'

'Yes. Yes.'

'The hippies.'

'Yes.'

A pause. The rustling of newspaper as they unwrapped things from a box.

The ribbon voice lowered. 'Thought there was only one or two kiddies, but here's another.'

'Mm. Yes.'

'Running wild, no doubt.'

'Mm. Mm.'

I was standing between the two window mannequins. One of them had its hand out and the fingers were chipped, half-moons of chalky plaster scarring the flesh-coloured paint.

'Used to be a couple of them at the school,' continued the ribbon voice. 'One was in Mitchell's class, Gail's little boy.'

'Mm?' pricked the pin voice.

'Filthy dirty, Gail said.'

'Mm. Oh.'

'Crawling with parasites, probably.'

'Mm. Yes.'

'*Worms.*' The ribbon voice dropped to a whisper, and I turned to see that Ishtar had come back in.

'*Lice.*' The woman took another newspaper-wrapped shape from the box.

'Just these, thanks,' said Ishtar.

The farming supply building was shaped like a shed and built from the same metal, which sighed and shuddered in the wind. It was enormous; inside, it felt like standing in a big-city train station — not a real building at all, but a strange, covered part of the outside, porous and booming. Standing in the entranceway, between the slid-open doors that could have fitted two side-by-side buses, I couldn't see the far wall. Tractors hulked in the shadows and smaller machines stood with their attachments — scoops out front, or cutters — gleaming faintly like the jaws of insects. There were corridors made of open, towering shelves, with piles of shovels and axes and hoes and clippers, hoses and sacks of grain, or boots and hats and raincoats — each shelf so wide and deep and high I imagined making one of them a room for myself, with a bed and even a chair.

Miller stood out among the farmers and the salesmen; it was as if he was too clearly in focus. Where their clothes had a soft look, the colours muted, their jeans grease-stained and white at the knees, his held a freshness, the colours too bright, too evenly distributed. It was the same with the hands. The farmers' hands were battered, the fingers blunt and clumsy-looking, often black at the knuckles and nails. Miller's hands in comparison glared their unmarked cleanliness, their softness — he mostly kept them in his pockets.

'G'day, mate. Got any Sebago?'

Here was another of his voices — lazy, the words oozing from somewhere between his nose and throat. Still, it rang out too loudly, and I saw the way the men looked at him and then cut their eyes at each other.

When they brought the sacks of planting potatoes, they stood back and watched as he heaved the first few into the back of the car, bending awkwardly to hug them round their knobbly middles, his face reddening.

'Give you a hand there, mate?' They stepped in, their movements casual, took the sacks by the top corners and used their knees to buck them up and into the boot as if they weighed nothing at all.

Miller stood by, panting, eyes elsewhere. His pink lower lip shone.

Later, in the car, his clipped, newsreader's voice took on a bitter, nasal edge. 'Lot of inbreeding in these places,' he said, slowing to overtake a tractor that was trundling half on and half off the road. 'Pity. The gene pool becomes muddy. Results in all kinds of inadequacies.'

Ishtar didn't answer, but nodded.

We passed, and I glimpsed the man on the tractor — hat, flannel shirt, work-scarred hands on the big steering wheel — and then Miller swung his own wheel so we cut very close in front, crossing partly onto the verge, and I felt us accelerate, heard the engine rev and the hard flick and ping of flying gravel — and, receding, the shouts of the farmer.

After dinner he would sometimes go on a rant, pacing in front of the fire, scooping air with his hands.

'What have we lost, in our comfort, our ease, with our televisions, our houses chewing up electricity, driving around in our cars, sitting on our arses?' This voice was a mixture — it swung between the proper, neat-edged one and the squashed *bewdy mate* one.

A murmured response might rise from an armchair, or from one of the shadowy figures seated cross-legged on the floor, but Miller's questions weren't meant to be answered — he made no pause, left no space for other voices.

'What have we given away? What power?' The firelight burnished his hair. 'Understanding.' He clapped the back of one hand into the palm of the other. 'Consciousness. Awareness. We have tried to push the earth away, cut ourselves off from it. And from each other! We don't know how to live closely any more, how to cooperate. We're each in his own little box, driving off to our offices every day, working, working — doing what? Making money. What for? To spend. What on? Our little boxes, keeping comfortable, warming our soft white arses, staring at our tellies, driving our cars.'

Somewhere in the gloom, Willow's baby began to cry, and there was a shuffling. A woman got up and began to collect empty plates, but Miller talked on as if giving a speech to a vast crowd. He jabbed a finger in the direction of the road to town.

'They're all stuck in it, in their isolation, this endless, meaningless scrambling for money. They think there's no way out, no other option. But we know.' He tapped his broad chest with a thumb. 'We know how easy it is! How simple. To return to the earth, to commune with nature, with each other. To simply step outside of the circuit.' He tilted back his head and gave it a slow, disbelieving shake. 'It's all so simple,' he said, and the flash of a smile broke open his beard. 'All we need is a patch of land and some seeds.'

Ripples of approval and agreement did stir among those listening when Miller gave these performances, but to me there always seemed to be a feeling of detachment, of separation. And it didn't only come from him, from the one-way nature of his speechifying, the fact that he treated them like a faceless crowd. There was almost an air of indulgence in the way they watched and listened, and in the way — despite the supportive nods and murmurs by the fireside — they went on with their lives, heading off to work the next morning as usual while he strode alone out to the weed-filled veggie patch with a hoe.

Later I would realise that of course people like him had already come and gone, making little difference. The established residents accepted him as they accepted most things, with the particular combination of indifference and tolerance that seemed to be their specialty. I've heard that those who last the distance in communal living situations tend to be the ones without any strong motivations or ideas of their own. The leaders — the movers and shakers, the Utopian dreamers — care too much about their visions and are too uncompromising in them to be able, in the long term, to get along with others. And now, when I dredge up the faces of some of those Hope Farm stayers — Willow; Jindi's mum, Val, who did most of the cooking; the joint-smoking woman and her guitar-playing boyfriend — I imagine I see, in the settled lines at their mouths and the corners of their eyes, and in the way those eyes gaze out, a sort of enduring and strangely contented apathy.

They were certainly more than happy to accept the drugs Miller always had a lot of. I'd been around plenty of pot smoking — not in the ashrams, but in the group houses, and Ishtar often had a little stash of leaf in her bag, along with her tobacco pouch and packet of papers — and the smell of it and the sight of equipment such as bongs was something I was so used to I barely paid attention. But even I noticed how full the pot bowl on the low table in that front room always was once Miller had come to Hope, and how much stronger and riper the smell of the smoke that filled the room. And regularly, over the next couple of months, he would produce acid, which got everyone going much more than any speech.

Although an unpleasant, thick-headed feeling always came over me when there was pot smoke in the air, I had never actually taken any drugs myself, nor tried alcohol. It would have been easy enough — nobody watched what children were doing; I had seen kids not much older than I was drinking and smoking joints at parties. But I had never been interested. I didn't like what I saw happen to people when they drank booze, smoked dope, dropped acid. The bleariness, the slurring. The loss of control, I suppose that was it. And I didn't like being around people who were in that state, in those rooms with that building tension, that feeling of unpredictability, danger.

One night in those early few weeks at Hope, when one of these acid parties was just getting started and I was making my way out of the front room, ducking between the dancing bodies, the smells of armpits and greasy hair, someone moved out of the way and I had a sudden clear view of Miller and Ishtar. She appeared, as she often did, to be a solitary calm point in the midst of the action. Miller stood before her, and I watched as he licked his forefinger and dabbed it in his palm where a tab of LSD must have lain. He held out the finger, and like a shy horse — or someone acting the part of a shy horse — she dipped her head, and then tilted up her chin, opened her lips, and took the finger into her mouth.

I had seen Ishtar in many situations that were adult, mysterious, threatening. Naked flesh moving in the half-dark, under candle flames or firelight, or the cool glow of the moon and stars. Low voices, giggling, soft kissing sounds. Parts of bodies that my gaze skittered away from. More than two people — three, or four, or five. That heavy smell that hung in rooms the morning after a party, of bodies and booze, pot and Indian perfume. Tiptoeing out, the only person awake in the house. The whispery loop of a record left spinning on the turntable. Sleeping figures on floors, long hair and beards and tangles of bare limbs. Ishtar there somewhere, an arm slung over her, the soft peak of her exposed breast.

This moment though, watching her take Miller's finger into her mouth, seemed to bring down in a sick, spinning tumble all those other times I'd glimpsed her there in some dark, adult scene, giving her body, herself, over to things I didn't understand, things I feared — things I knew, even at the time, that someone should have been protecting me from. And standing there, my hand gripping the coarse fabric of the doorway curtain, I felt all that accumulated fear and disgust — and sense of betrayal — rise and harden, forming into a sharp point of hatred.

But then she began to dance. She stepped away from Miller and put out her arms. She shook back her hair and I saw her cheekbones, her open lips, the curves of her closed eyes, and all I could see was how strong she was, how beautiful; all I could feel was how much I wanted her, longed for her to put her arms around me, to swallow me up with her warmth, her softness, to look right into my eyes, my face, to put me to bed and sit with me until I fell asleep. And the twisted needle of hatred — vibrating with a power that couldn't be dissolved, that had to go somewhere — propped and skidded sideways.

And there was Miller, moving in his own lumbering dance. He tilted back his great, furred head and his wet tongue showed. Out went one fist, trapping a sweep of Ishtar's hair, and then he had her, her back to him, his paws all over her, that mouth at her ear. I saw his teeth part and then nip at her earlobe, I heard his laughter, low like a growl, and my hatred found a target and took off.

I pushed through the curtain and gulped at the cold air of the unlit hallway as if it was some kind of antidote.

He was easy to hate, to despise, as he prowled in his circle of light, talking endlessly. The unfixed gaze directed out somewhere over the heads of his audience, the chop and swirl of his hand gestures, the heedless, blustering assault. The different voices, and the way he slipped in and out of them as if nobody noticed or understood what he was doing.

When he said, 'Thank you kindly, madam,' to the gaunt woman who ran the coffee shop in Kooralang and I saw the flush bloom over her craggy face and at the collar of her blouse, I had to drop my eyes. *He calls you Typhoid Mary behind your back*, I wanted to shout. *He says you're inbred.*

When he wielded the mattock, I noted the laboured arc of his great arm through the air, the muscles in his back heaving as he dragged it through the earth, the patches of sweat on his shirt, the way he had to stop often, panting. For all his heft, he was bad with tools, inefficient. Even I could tell he didn't know what he was doing.

His smell. Dense, bulky, threatening. Pot and sweat and something else, something that made me think of bulls and billygoats.

The way he grabbed hold of Ishtar and took her from where she sat on the floor by the fire, like a toddler snatching up a toy. The way he kissed her in front of everyone, kneaded her flesh with his hands — her breasts, her buttocks — then turned and walked with his arm round her neck, pulling her in close beside him, locked to him, steering her through the house and out to the mud-brick building.

And the way she loved it! The gentleness that came over her, the softening. I narrowed my eyes, clenched my teeth in disdain. *Pathetic*, she was. *Sucked in.*

It was before dinner, early evening, and I had been sent out to empty the compost bucket. Jindi was followed me, her prattling a rude trail at my back in the cold darkness, when suddenly she broke off with a squeak. I turned and saw the bush of Miller's hair, gold in the light from the kitchen window. He had her in his arms, and was holding her above his head.

'Look, look, my little pup,' he rumbled. 'The stars are out for us tonight. Can you touch them? Can you? Reach up your arms, my girl. I'll help you.' He lifted her higher. 'Go on, reach.'

Against the studded sky, Jindi's figure wriggled. I could hear her eager breathing.

'Did you touch one? Yes? Ah — look!' He swung her to the ground again. 'See?' He stepped back and spread his arms. 'You did!' The girl tottered like someone who had just gotten off a ride. 'You know how I can tell?' Miller went down on one knee and lowered his voice. 'I can see it shimmering all through you, the starlight. You've got sparkles in your hair.'

Jindi's hands went to her head, and she crooked her neck and twisted and turned, trying to look down at herself. 'I —'

Miller's croon, warm and full, slid over her timid whisper. 'Oh you can't see it. Nobody can but me.'

'But why —'

'Because, my little puppy dog, I see things other people don't.'

Then he rose and turned and went into the house, leaving Jindi gasping and voiceless, clutching her hair. I waited for her to rush across to where I stood by the compost heap, to appeal to me to check her over for shimmers and sparkles, but she didn't.

I squinted at her. Against the yellow glow of the window she was a solid, definite, black. Not one shimmer. But once I'd dumped out the kitchen scraps and walked back with the plastic bucket bumping against my thigh, I saw, up close in the light, how wide and moist her eyes were, the fevered brightness of her cheeks, her parted lips.

From inside the kitchen came a round of Miller's laughter. I took the steps slowly. I didn't want him near me, I didn't want those big, strange, soft hands to touch me, couldn't stand the thought of his face close to mine, his breath entering my lungs. But still, I felt myself stiffen with the heavy, lonely pride of the excluded.

I don't know why he didn't ever scoop me up in his arms, purr into my ear, try to summon in me the thrill that set Jindi sparkling, brought the tiny but significant smile to Ishtar's lips. I wasn't as young as Jindi. I had no puppy-dog charm — I'd long since passed the age where any adult might want to sweep me up, to hold me in their arms. I was scrawny, my limbs were too long; my face, when I caught sight of it in the small, dark mirror that hung from a nail on the bathroom wall, appeared to have been outgrown by its features; my hair had neither Ishtar's chocolate-and-caramel sheen nor Jindi's babyish silkiness, but snaked heavily in all the wrong directions. That could have been the reason: my adolescent awkwardness, and the untouchability that went with it — although it's hard to believe Miller would notice any such thing. Perhaps he did pick up something of my reaction to him, my hatred, strong as it was. Perhaps that was it.

If he'd seen me as at all significant, as any kind of threat, then he might have put some effort into winning me over — but he didn't. He ignored me. And that might have been his biggest mistake.

In the Home there was only work and prayer time and sleep. High brick walls and a circle of lawns like a moat. I fell in to the busyness, lost myself in it levering sheets out of the giant boiling vats in the laundry chopping piles of carrots in the kitchen scrubbing floors kneeling with the others while a nun said prayers. I forgot everything and became a dumb beast that worked and worked and never thought. My back ached the skin on my hands cracked my mind sank in to a murk. There were some girls pregnant like me and some just in for punishment, those ones were pretty tough. I kept to myself. I was scared, I didnt even talk to the other pregnant ones not even at night when we went in to our tiny bedrooms with there partitions so thin they were like curtains. Some times I heard other girls crying and some times my belly jerked with the kicks like calls for help but I was always so tired I just fell in to black sleep. A girl who was getting big would just vanish and nobody said any thing a new girl arriving to take her place. I didnt know how long Id been there the days stretched endless in both directions. It got harder to reach over the laundry and kitchen benches and to get up and down off my knees with the scrubbing brush or at prayer time but I barely noticed when we were told to have a wash I didnt look down or touch my belly. I didnt think about the people from the park or Evie Dyer or my mother or any thing, the past and the future didnt exist in this place. Some of the girls got visitors some times and phone calls or letters but not me. Then a girl came who was different. Pat she was called or any way that was the name she used some girls kept there real names a secret. She was pregnant she went around behind the laundry to smoke cigarettes and when the nuns caught her she just took a last drag and threw the butt away smiling and went back to work like she could just as easily choose not to.

They cant do any thing she said to me We are fallen already we cant be punished any more. She had been there before, this was her second time, she was all the way from Adelaide. There were girls from everywhere, most people sent the pregnant ones as far away as possible just in case any one saw them and found out although how any one could see you in side this prison I didnt know. This is my last chance Pat said and laughed but it was not a happy laugh. Once I followed her out when she went to smoke. Whats it like? I said. It hurts she said Like hell and the nurses are all mean old bitches. And then they take it off you straight away before you even see it and then they make you sign the papers. What papers? I said. She grinned and blew smoke. The papers that say youre giving the baby up for adoption. So it can have a good life. I tried not to look around when she said the word baby, it made me nervous and I kept expecting a nun to come. She ran her hand down her front, smoothed her dress so I could see the shape, kept her hand there. I will tell you some thing she said, You dont have to sign. They tell you you do but you dont. When she drew on the cigarette she looked much older like a grown up woman. The thing is she said, They say its for the best that you can forget about it and get on with your life. But you dont. I said What will you do this time? She dropped her hand then. She had peroxided her hair and there was a stripe of dark at the parting. Oh I will sign. Course I will. What choice have I got realy? Where would I be otherwise on my own with a kid? Id be on the street just ask my mum and dad.

I told one of the nuns I needed to ring my parents. She took me in to the office downstairs and I dialled the number on the heavy black telephone. My mother answered. Is everything all right? she said. Yes I said. Well what is it then? said my mother. The nun was standing behind me near the door and I had to speak quietly. What if I want to keep it? I said. You cant. Why not? Couldnt you — You cant she said, Dont ask me again. My father said some thing in the background. Nothing, she said to him, Shes just being silly. To me she said This is a respectable family, if you cant be respectable then you are not welcome in this house.

School started.

Across the shining, wet road I clomped in my op-shop shoes, my frozen hands pulled into the sleeves of my jumper and my breath sharp in the early air, over to where Ian waited at the bus stop. He was always there first, tall and skinny in his green and grey uniform. Side by side we stood, steadfastly ignoring each other, taking it in turns to peer up the road.

Cockatoos rasped and shrieked high in the facing wall of bush, and sometimes a beaten-up car would chug out from the Hope turn-off, windows misted, the blurred figures waving as they passed, the dry-throated bleat of a horn sounding. I never waved back.

The bus, with its tough, craggy driver — smelling of instant coffee and cigarettes, and ever-ready with his yell of, 'Pipe down or yer can get off and walk' — took us, sliding on our vinyl seats, past soggy-looking paddocks that erupted every now and then into sudden, bald hills. Ian and I sat separately, of course. At intervals we stopped to let more kids on — all the same kinds of kids that were at every school. There were the bully-boys, loud and dangerous, spreading themselves across the back rows and being shouted at by the driver. Then there were the prissy girls, grouped in twos or threes, with neat hair, who all wore their uniforms, I knew, in mysterious, significant ways, like another language. Then there were the freaks. All sitting near the front. An enormously fat boy. Two girls almost as big — sisters — both with orange curly hair. A boy with glasses, who breathed heavily through his mouth. And me, of course, and Ian. Finally, there were the others, the in-between kids. Ordinary kids with freckles or buck teeth or sticking-out ears, sitting in pairs and talking. I snatched secret looks at them. These were the ones I envied, and always had.

The hills and paddocks were eventually interrupted by increasing numbers of houses and then, all at once, rows of shops and low-rise office blocks; and finally, the tall, ugly orange-brick school buildings, flanked by an oval on one side and a vast car park on the other.

'She's from that place, I bet.'

I sat at a desk by the window, pretending to be interested in the view of the oval below.

'What place?'

'You know, that *hippie* place. Near Kooralang. Hope Farm, or whatever they call it. I saw her get on the bus.'

Other voices joined in.

'Awww! That place!'

'What farm? Where?'

'You mean *Dope* Farm.'

'You know, near the Munros'. It's a commune.'

'What's that?'

'It's where a whole lot of lazy bastards sit round taking drugs in the nude, that's what my dad says.'

'Euw.'

I gripped the metal bars under my desk, bowed my head, waited.

'Yeah, and none of them are married and they all just *do it* with each other all the time.'

'Euw! Stop!'

The teacher came in then, and the talk broke off.

Later, as I searched for the library, trying to look like I knew where I was going, I expected something more. A mob of boys passed and called out, 'Hippie shit!' and a pair of prissy girls sliced me with their eyes, but nothing else happened. I found the library and gratefully entered its stuffy, overheated calm.

'Hippie Shit' became my nickname. I spent morning tea and lunch in the library, was picked last in Phys Ed, and when we had to make pairs in Science, I was always with one of the freaks. But this was all bearable. I was used to it. I was cloaked in layers of difference, thirteen years deep; I didn't expect this not to go unnoticed. And it could have been much worse — I could have suffered what Ian did with Dean Price: committed, focussed bullying from someone who has decided to really hate you.

Also, my teacher for all subjects apart from Science and Phys Ed was Mr Dickerson. Mr Dickerson had once thrown a kid from a second-storey window, Ian said — and whether or not this was true didn't matter, the important thing was that everyone was terrified of him. He was an egg-shaped man with only a few wisps of white-grey hair, and he always wore the same formless beige trousers and a red jumper with a small flag of untucked shirt showing at the bottom. He rarely spoke, and all of his classes were the same. First he wrote a list of instructions on the blackboard. Then he turned to face the class, casting his yellowish gaze out over our heads and banging with his fist on the board as he recited what he had just written in an almost melodic, mournful tone and chalk dust ran off the end of the shelf in a shivery stream. Then he sat motionless in his chair as we all rustled and scribbled away, until it was time for him to read out the answers from a book. We corrected our own work, and I doubt anyone bothered cheating; there would be no point since every now and again, without warning, we were given a test, which we had to hand up to Mr Dickerson himself and which would be returned next lesson stippled with red ticks or crosses and a simple grade — no comments, ever.

I liked schoolwork. I was good at it and always had been, but in the past I'd feared drawing attention to myself. Now, in the safety of Mr Dickerson's reliable silence, I was free to do well, and to take secret pride in my test results — the rows of tidy ticks, the circled grade at the bottom, lovely in its unadorned completeness.

So I was lucky, really. But Ian was not.

I saw Dean Price on the first day, after school. At the edge of the oval a huge boy stood with a much smaller boy tucked under one of his arms. I could tell it was Ian just by the legs. They stuck out, skinny and unmoving. The bigger boy swung round and I saw Ian's face. His arms pointed to the ground and his head hung down, too, eyes half closed; his whole body seemed both passive and wary. The bigger boy — who had to be Dean Price — didn't have the pimples I'd imagined, and at first his eyes looked quite normal, but then they narrowed and his face twisted, and I saw the cruelty in it. His mouth opened and his tongue showed, red and fat. Bellowing something unintelligible, he lifted Ian higher and began to shake him.

I got on the bus and stared out the window in the opposite direction. My heart thumped and my hands shook, and I thought of what Ian had said: *As far as school goes, we don't know each other.*

As kids got on and went up the aisle, I flicked my eyes to check — and eventually saw Ian, dishevelled and pale. He passed without meeting my gaze, and later when we met at the creek he said nothing about it.

Every day after school we met — and on the weekends, too, if he didn't have too many chores to do at home. He brought sandwiches his mother made: white bread with a rubbery slice of something he called *straz*, which I suspected was a kind of meat, greyish-pink and salty. Sometimes it was sweets: caramel slice or yellowy cake that squeaked against my teeth, the cream in the middle oily on my tongue.

One day he brought a camera on a strap around his neck, its clunky body impressively big and black against his bony chest, the scuffed case undone and swinging below. It was from school — Year Eights did photography and were allowed to borrow cameras over the weekends, although there was a waiting list. 'Too many dumb girls,' said Ian, 'taking photos of their *horses*.'

The camera did have a worn, institutional look to it, and there was a number engraved on the bottom, but he handled it with such practised, proud skill that I soon forgot it wasn't his.

'This is my ticket out of here,' he said, lying on his back under a tree, the viewfinder to his eye, his fingers delicately rotating the focus back and forth. 'Get a portfolio together, send it off to *National Geographic*, wait for the call: "Is that Ian Munro, oh gosh, we just *love* your work," then off I go, international man of *mystery*, out on *assignment*.' He peered out at me. 'Jet-setting around the place, helicopter into the Amazon, undercover job in Beirut.' With the camera still to his face, he got up on one knee, pointing, adjusting the focus, and clicking so quickly I didn't get a chance to change my expression.

'Hey.' I raised a hand.

He lowered the contraption. 'You don't believe me.'

'What? Yeah, of course I do.'

He grinned his narrow grin and said nothing, but the next time we met he brought the print and I saw for myself the doubt in my own face, the assessing eyes, the mouth ready to curl in disbelief. I also saw the skill in the shot, the angle of it, the way the light seemed to radiate from my skin, the perfect clarity of the lines, my eyebrows and lashes, the faint dabs of freckles across the bridge of my nose. I stared, entranced. This was *me*; this was how I looked from the outside: a clever, tough girl.

Ian leaned in. 'Pretty good, wouldn't you say? It's just a *bit* overexposed, but I like that. Gives it a kind of magic glow.'

I was still gazing down at my own face. With a further jolt of surprise I realised that I found it beautiful — not just the shot but the face itself, the double peak of the upper lip; the wide, clear eyes; the neat, pointed chin; the wild hair snaking against the tender-looking earlobes and neck. A skirl of something — pleasure and embarrassment — went through me, and I passed the print back to Ian and began swiping leaves into the creek with the end of a long stick.

'See?' said Ian. 'I know what I'm doing.'

'Yeah, okay. You do.'

I sent the leaves into the water, keeping my head down, holding in a smile. I had a feeling of incredulous pleasure, like the time years before when a kid at school was giving away a pet rabbit and it was my name that the teacher picked out of a hat, the room seeming to stretch, the faces of the other kids tiny and far away as they turned to look. It was like a dream, but it wasn't one — the next day the kid brought the rabbit in a box and gave it to me. The feeling lasted for ages — a thrumming, disbelieving joy — and it was not just because of this wonderful thing that had happened to me, but also because it was still happening, had not ended. It lasted until we had to move out of the place we were living and into one of the ashrams where, Ishtar said, pets weren't allowed, and we had to leave the rabbit behind.

Now I glanced at Ian standing with the photo held out in front of him, and then back at the water rushing like cold black tea at my feet. I felt the sun on my back. I bent and picked a blade of reedy grass and pulled it, squeaking, between my fingernails, put it to my tongue. I had a friend. I had this place. Impossible to believe, but things had turned out kind of okay.

Ian's voice was musing. 'I'm very happy with it actually.' He tilted his head. 'The hippie child. The gypsy girl.'

'I'm not ...' I began, but then stopped. I was what I was, the photo showed that. I stole another look at the picture and the thrumming feeling went on, undeterred.

Ian squatted to slip the photo carefully back into its envelope, and then the envelope into his bag. He glanced up at me. 'Shall we *repair* to the bridge, my gypsy friend?'

'Okay.'

Following his back — lean, purposeful, oblivious — through the wattle, I let the smile out at last, and my cheeks hurt with it. The watery sun turned the round blooms into golden explosions that smelled of honey.

One night I waited till it was realy late then I got up and went along three doors to Pats room. I knocked quietly. Yeah? she said and I opened the door. I could just see her lying in the bed. Can I ask you some thing? I said. Yeah. We were both whispering. If you did have some where to go, if you did have someone to look after you, would you do it? What, keep it? Yes keep it, if someone could help you take care of it. Yeah she said, I reckon. Especially after giving up the first one. He was a boy. I never saw him but they told me he was a boy. So you going to keep yours then? I think so I said. Have you got some where to go? After? Yeah I said, I think I do. Well she said, When my boy was born I suddenly thought Oh no I cant give him up I have to keep him, but I had nowhere to go you see. I did put up a bit of a fight but it was pretty weak, I knew I couldnt keep him realy. You might be all right if youve got some where. Youll have to be strong though, they have that many tricks you wouldnt believe it. They want those babies. Someones making money in all this you know and its not us. Someones making money? I said. Course they are she said. There are these agencies where people go who cant have kids and they pay good money to get a nice little baby. Yoursll be beautiful I bet if its any thing like you. Whos the father? I didnt answer. I felt my face go red, I was glad it was dark. She laughed. You dont have to say she said, But I bet he was good looking. Yeah I said, He was. Well listen she said, Youll need to be that strong theyll stop at nothing to get there mitts on your baby. But just remember if you dont sign the papers they cant take it, doesnt matter what they say. Theyll tell you if you wont sign theyll take the baby any way and make it a ward of the state but if youve got some where to go where youll be safe and looked after Im sure they cant do that so dont believe them.

82

I sent a letter to The Path, I had the brochure with the address hidden in the lining of my suitcase. I didnt know who to put so I just wrote To the lady I met in the park, then I wrote that I needed there help please I didnt have anywhere else to go. I wrote down what Pat had said about the agencies and someone making money, that although it sounded crazy in some cases they were making girls give up babies who didnt want to. It was embarassing because I knew I probably made a lot of spelling mistakes and my writing always looked like a stupid persons but I had to swallow my pride, this was important I had to contact them they were my only hope.

Ishtar got a job, at the milk factory. On the powder line, whatever that meant. Most weekday mornings she went off in one of the cars, and came back after I'd returned from school, fine grains of yellowy stuff sometimes caught in the hairs at her temples.

'Decided to join the rat race, have yer?' said Val, banging the wooden spoon on the edge of the porridge pot.

Ishtar didn't answer, just took her bowl and began to eat, standing up. The chairs around the table were all full. The morning meals were quieter than the evening ones, and more people ate in the kitchen. Miller was rarely there. I hardly ever saw him on school mornings, and on weekends he usually didn't emerge from the mud-brick building until breakfast was long over.

'Pity.' Val leaned against the fridge and took out a tobacco pouch and some papers. 'It was nice seeing the two of you out there, slaving away, side by side.' She dug in the pouch. 'Cute.'

The word sliced above the spoon-scraping and chomping. A couple of heads lifted, and I also watched for Ishtar's reaction. It was always hard to tell whether Val was teasing or not. She was a large woman with coarse hair dyed a brassy henna-red, growing out grey at the roots. Her gravelly voice could be heard ordering Jindi out of the kitchen from the other end of the house.

Ishtar kept eating, taking her time.

Val rolled her cigarette, lit it, and began to smoke, one arm folded across her wide middle. There was a half-smile on her lips, but she didn't say anything more.

Ishtar finished her bowl and put it in the sink just as one of the men — Gav, they called him — weedy, glasses, bald on top and with a thin ponytail behind, rose from his chair with a gust of patchouli and stretched his arms above his head.

84

'Better get going,' he said. Two women also got up and they all left the room, Ishtar in tow. There were the sounds of banging doors from the front of the house, and then a car starting and driving away. The three or four adults who remained went on eating.

From another room came Jindi's voice: 'Va-al! Val!'

'Just a minute, love,' called Val. She went to the window above the sink and let out a blurt of smoke. Through the glass, the mess of Miller's handiwork was visible: the vegetable patch dark and bare, stripped of weeds but also of its fence. Miller had obliterated it in an afternoon, but rebuilding had apparently stalled. A couple of posts stuck up out of the ground, snarls of wire at their ankles, but nothing more had been done, and I realised now that things had been like this for some time — perhaps even weeks. At one end of the patch sprawled an out-of-season pumpkin plant, which had seeded itself.

'See?' Miller had said, 'we don't even need to lift a finger. Nature is eager to provide,' and as if in response the vine had spread quickly, its hollow creepers licking across the raggedy grass towards the shed. Jindi had waded into it, searching for fruit, but found nothing — it seemed to be putting all of its energy into growing more leaves.

Val tapped ash into the sink and sniffed. 'Good thing he's got her,' she said, casting a look at the shuttered entrance to the mud-brick building.

I got a letter back from the woman although it didnt say The Path on it anywhere and it was in a plain envelope. I could tell she had written it very clearly so she must have known from my letter to her how bad I was at writing and reading, that made me feel ashamed like always but still at least I could read it. Thank you for your letter it said, Yes of course you would be welcome to stay with us for as long as you need to. You are doing a brave thing and it wont be easy but we will help. Let us know when the time comes. With love from Mira.

It was night when it started. I stayed lying in the bed. I knew I was probably supposed to tell the nuns but I lay there for ages. With the pain I came even more alive like at last I had realy woken up from my daze. Its a baby I whispered out loud, youre having a baby. I thought about the hippie woman with her baby tied on, her smile her kiss the freedom of her body. I tried to imagine my mother holding me when I was little but all I could see was the gloves she wore when we started going to church. When it began getting realy bad I got up and put my things in my case and checked in the lining for the pamphlet. I went down to Pats room and tapped on her door and opened it. Your time is it? she said. Yeah. A pain came and I had to hold onto the door. When it was finished I said Which hospital? What? she said. Which hospital do they take you to? She told me and then she said, Well good luck then, stick to your guns and dont sign any thing. I went downstairs. It was nearly morning, the windows showed light grey. I thought the door to the office would be locked but it wasnt, maybe they forgot to lock it. I went in. I took the pamphlet from my case and rang the number. Mira answered. I didnt cry this time, I could hear someone coming and I had to be quick. Im having the baby I said and told her the hospital. Please help me I said and hung up.

'What's he doing?'

Ian and I were up at the fallen tree, leaning across it to look down on Miller, who moved slowly along the fresh brown rectangle of the old veggie patch. The remains of the fence still lay in a rusty tangle at one end; shaggy circlets of weeds had drawn themselves up round the lower reaches of the abandoned new posts, obscuring the coils of wire. Miller had a spade and a sack. He would dig, then take something from the sack and squat with it a moment, then step forward and dig again.

I shrugged. 'Planting potatoes, I think.'

'That's what I thought. Bit early, isn't it?'

'What do you mean? It's almost dinnertime.'

'I mean in the year.' Ian slid his camera in front of his face, pointed it down at Miller and fiddled with the focus. 'We don't do ours till spring.'

I watched Miller probe with the spade.

'And there's no fence. The chooks'll scratch everything up.' Ian clicked the shutter. 'Not sure he knows what he's doing, your dad.'

'He's not my *dad*.' The words shot out, louder than I'd meant. I felt the blood rush to my face and there was a gaping, shocked feeling in my belly at the idea of somebody seeing us as a unit — me, Ishtar, and Miller, with equal connections between the three — that it was not obvious that the only thing that brought me and Miller anywhere near each other was Ishtar, in the middle.

Ian was looking down at the camera. His ears had turned red, and I felt the silence between us throb with all the things we'd never talked about, never even ventured near. School, Mr Dickerson, Dean Price, photography — all these had been gone through, taken apart, talked over from every angle. But us, ourselves, our families — what it was that made us different, that had us sitting up the front of the bus with all the other freaks — that, through some unspoken rule, had been off limits.

I swallowed. 'He's just my mum's boyfriend,' I said. Then, seized by a sudden recklessness, shoving the words out quickly: 'I don't know anything about my dad.' My heart pounded. I had never told anyone this before. At school whenever we'd had to do projects about our families, I'd always made mine up. My fictitious father — and grandparents, aunts, uncles, and even, sometimes, siblings — looked just as feasible as anyone else's when drawn and labelled in coloured pencil.

'Really?' Ian was still fiddling with the camera, and his voice was soft, respectful.

'Ishtar says she didn't know him. They weren't … together.'

Below us, Miller put down the spade, squared his legs, and began moving his arms in a series of ponderous circles.

'Miller is her new boyfriend,' I said. 'I don't know anything about him either.'

I did know some things. I looked in his room one time, when they had gone off somewhere in the car.

The room was like a burrow, right down the end of the low, dim hallway of the mud-brick building. There was one window and it was small and high, allowing just a trickle of light. The air felt thicker in there, and was full of his musk. Only a small patch of floor was clear for walking on; everywhere else stood piles of boxes, bags, and suitcases, some opened and with the contents spilling out. There was no furniture other than the mattress, the chair, and two bookshelves, side by side, both crammed full.

Books formed wonky towers in every possible space between and on top of the boxes. I picked up a couple. One was on Ancient Egypt, with big colour photos of tombs and mummies, and illustrations of gods with heads of animals; another had a murky cover showing a woman with very long hair and billowy white clothes sitting by a pond, and was full of poetry.

Nearby, a briefcase, deep reddish brown like an office worker's, overflowed with pieces of paper. From these I learned his full name: Walter Ronald Miller. A few of the papers had swirly writing at the top saying either *University of Melbourne* or *University of Sydney*. Some of the others were from Telecom or the SEC with bold red letters saying things like *FINAL NOTICE* and *PAY IMMEDIATELY.* Some of these had Miller's name, some had other names — names of women.

Next to the briefcase was a tall carton full of clothes, still in their packaging, from a shop called Henry Buck's. Five or six neatly folded shirts with pieces of white card showing at the undersides of the collars. Three soft jumpers in sleeves of tissue paper that had snagged and torn where the sticky tape was, but which still held a clean, new-wool smell. A jacket and pants of dark grey, heavy fabric — these had been badly folded and stuffed in and so were very creased, but they were brand new, too, and *Miller* was handwritten on a bit of paper pinned to the sleeve of the jacket.

Another box held a diary, bound in leather, with *1978* embossed on the front. Listening for the sound of Miller's car, I riffled through it: it was mostly blank, the pages opening with reluctance, as if for the first time, but the early couple of months had entries, a few words on each page, marked in a close, sloping script. I struggled to make one out. *J. Banner,* it said, *2.15 Prelim hearing*. Underneath the diary were some spiral-bound notebooks, filled with writing in that same hand. None of it made sense to me — it was all about affidavits and pleas, and prosecutors, and had lots of names I'd never heard of, some marked *vs*. with another name I'd never heard of. There was a big fat hardcover book, too: *The Law of Torts in Australia*.

I glanced at Ishtar's one suitcase and duffel bag sitting in the corner. They looked their usual compact, neat selves, but even they were being encroached on by the huge, looming tide that was Miller's mess — and her bedspread, crumpled down at the foot of the mattress, appeared more worn than I remembered, and smaller. I turned slowly in the small central clearing. So much stuff. As if he conjured it with his hands, brought it bouncing and skittering into his orbit, to then fly along in his wake like iron filings following a magnet. Into my mind came the twin images of Miller lifting Ishtar and putting her into the car, and then lifting and carrying her into the room at the ashram — her yielding body, her transformed face. Then I saw him raising Jindi towards the night sky. The power in those arms, and the speed with which they snatched something up — a body, a whole person — and then just as quickly let it go again.

The feeling of dread that had lapped at me since I entered the room was becoming unbearable. I made for the door, but then stopped. Above the bed, someone had stuck a picture, hand-drawn with coloured pencil on a large piece of yellowing butcher's paper. It was better than I could do, but amateurish nonetheless — perhaps Year-Nine or -Ten level. The detail and choice of colours were impressive, but the scale was out, giving a sense of vertigo, and the figures had clumsy, too-big heads, and hands without enough fingers. I moved closer to examine it properly.

At the bottom there were layers of green and brown, with tiny things dotted here and there: networks of tunnels with rabbits and rats in them, bones both animal and human, snakes and lizards, minuscule worms and bugs that I had to get right up close to see; veins of gold with borders of dashes to show sparkling, faceted jewels with their own dashes in ruby red and emerald green; and then, massed into clots, rubbish — scrumples of paper or rag, apple cores, cans and bottles, even a toilet bowl with a crack pencilled across it and, down low in one corner, the carcass of a half-flattened car. All through this section, reaching among these objects, snaked the root system of a tree. This took up the lower third of the paper.

Then there was a middle section with a background of light blue and the trunk of the tree rising up in the centre, reaching its wide limbs to both sides, bristling with leaves all shades of green. Below this canopy, taking up every inch of space, were plants, animals, people, buildings, even a pool of water with a boat on it, all jumbled in every which way, sideways and upside down, as if packed as closely as possible. I stood for some time taking in all the different elements, because there was a lot happening: a nest of eggs; two people seated at a table, a roast chicken on a plate between them; an aeroplane crashing into a mountain in a grey, red, and yellow explosion; a silver horse twisting her neck to lick her suckling foal; a group of grinning skeletons holding the body and separated head of a naked baby aloft, blood spurting. It was all mixed in together, the lovely and the awful, all shoved in every which way in the cramped blue. My chest felt tight. I glanced at the doorway.

The last, highest, part of the paper had no background colour, so what was drawn there appeared to float in jaundiced space above the busy scene below. In the middle was a swollen sun, flecked with red and sending out a semicircle of rays. At the end of each ray were the same two figures drawn over and over again in different positions. In every one, the figures were locked together by the man's penis, which was enormous, almost as big as one of his legs — the man was meant to be Miller, clearly, with his bronze halo. Each snaking penis was sticking into some part of the woman — Ishtar, with her draped hair, her calm eyes. The places where the penis stuck into Ishtar's body had been drawn as if transparent, so the whole penis could be seen going into one of the two passages drawn like wormholes between her legs — or in some of the pictures her mouth, and throat. In every picture, a spray of droplets burst from the end of the penis, from a dark point marked there precisely in black; the liquid, all colours of the rainbow, shooting into the shaded pink of Ishtar's body.

I couldn't get those enjoined figures out of my mind. In they came, as I lay sleepless on my mattress in the Joni Mitchell room: the brutal, stabbing, oversized penis; the explosions of sperm; the awful angles of Ishtar's bent-back limbs. The strange peace in the two pencilled faces, as if disconnected from the actions of their bodies.

I tried to bring a blackness down over them, or to replace them with shimmering blobs of silvery blue by rubbing my eyes hard, but they always came back. I tried to stop the cartoon heads and clumsy hands from turning into the real Miller and Ishtar, with skin and wet tongues and other parts, but I couldn't.

I'd glimpsed those dark, adult places before, at those parties —
Ishtar there in some sprawl of candlelit flesh — but this was
different. And somehow worse. I didn't know why, but it seemed
to have something to do with the towers of junk in Miller's room,
evidence of a vast, messy past that he trailed so blithely, as if it
was weightless.

Pat was right the nurses were mean. They left me alone mostly, on a high bed in a hard white room glaring with lights. Every now and then they came in and looked under the sheet told me to open my knees like the doctor had all that time ago and it hurt when they touched me. It went on and on, it got worse than I could have ever imagined. I made noise I couldnt help it and they came and told me Shh now pull yourself together. Right at the end a doctor came, he was nicer than the nurses. Come on he said, Be a good girl youre nearly there. Then she was born and I heard her cry. The nurses tried to stop me seeing, they took my arms and tried to make me lie back again but I pushed them away and sat up and for a moment I saw her at the end of the bed under the doctors big hand with its white glove. I saw her dark hair all wet and her little pink ear and her skinny arms out wide. I saw she was a girl. And then she turned her head and I saw her face and it was funny because I heard one of the church ladys say once that all newborns look like there fathers but she didnt, I looked at her and all I saw was myself. The doctor cut the cord and then a nurse wrapped her in a cloth and took her away.

Something went wrong with the plumbing in the bathroom. The bath wouldn't drain, and had to be bucketed out every time someone had a shower. The room became wetter and mouldier, with puddles collecting on the slippery lino, and the floorboards swelled with damp in the places where the lino had already worn away. Then one day an elongated hole appeared near the base of the bath, from which freezing air blasted upwards, smelling of dirt and rodents.

There was a meeting of sorts, in the kitchen. It was a weekend morning, Miller not yet up.

'Three letters, I've written,' said Gav, in a tone that managed to be all at once incredulous, aggrieved, and triumphant.

'They promised to send a plumber,' said someone else. 'Straight away. That was last week.'

'And Val's rung them on the phone, and even gone in to the office.'

Val's rattling laugh. 'The woman said, "Oh, so yer use the bath, then, do yer?"'

No one joined in the laughter — instead there was a round of tongue-clicks.

'Fascists.'

'Arseholes.'

Heavy sighs.

'Ah, well …'

Arms folded, away they slouched.

People began washing in a small tin tub in the laundry. It was only knee deep, and not wide enough to sit down in. I didn't use it — there was no door. At any time, a figure might be glimpsed from the kitchen, bending and sloshing, luminously naked in the gloom.

'We're not paying the rent,' said Val grimly, setting the envelope of cash on the kitchen windowsill, 'till something's done. That's the only language they understand, the bastards — the language of money. They'll get off their arses soon enough.'

I came back from the creek late one afternoon to find Miller out at the wood-splitting stump with a chainsaw, in a storm of noise and spraying woodchips. On the back steps, Jindi jumped up and down, her mouth moving, her voice a tiny peep under the frenzied revving of the machine. Two men also stood by: Jez, who was the guitar-playing man from that earlier night; and Gav, with the glasses and ratty ponytail. Gav also sometimes wore a sarong that showed his hairy white legs above socks and sandals.

Miller held the chainsaw with braced arms, angled it this way and that, applying it to a chunk of wood. A shape emerged — a wide, shallow, scooped-out grin. The wood inside was a lighter colour, rough from the teeth of the saw.

At last the noise stopped, and he laid the machine down. 'Right,' he said, and Gav and Jez moved forward.

There were two sections of a large tree trunk turned sideways, the bottom edges trimmed to form a flat base, the tops cut away into half-moons. Gav and Jez took one between them, Miller the other. Away they moved, bodies bent with the strain, past the chicken coop and the compost heap to a level bit of relatively clear ground that lay at the bottom of the hill. There they arranged the logs either side of a small, freshly dug pit.

The bath they laid on top was the old cast-iron one I'd seen down the side of the farmhouse, rust-streaked and belly-up in the weeds. It had already been flipped and washed out — and with help from Val and Ishtar, Miller and the others got it off the ground to waist height and shuffled with it to the waiting log cradles. With yells and much grunting, it was settled into place.

Jez, Gav, and Val wandered off. Miller, sweating, retired to the kitchen steps with a glass of beer, and Ishtar took over. Before the sun — indistinct behind an even sheet of cloud — crept away completely, she had the bath filled from the hose and a fire built beneath, banked and settling into coals. A black mark merged with the rust where the flames touched the underside of the bath, but when I looked down through the water the inside was unblemished. When steam began to rise, Ishtar took a shovel and put out the fire. There was the smell of wood smoke and a faint metal tang. Darkness had gathered in the bush and along the fence lines; the light was on in the kitchen, casting a warped, yellow rectangle onto the ground. Someone brought a candle.

Most people were back from work now and a small crowd applauded as Jindi, her bare skin starkly white in the near-dark, rings of dirt at her neck and wrists, was lifted, shrieking with glee, into the water. The bath was so deep she had to hold onto the edge; grubby trails dripped from her fingers down the newly cleaned rim.

'How is it, Jindi?'

Jindi wallowed and grinned, her double chin bulging. 'Nice!' she declared. 'Very nice!'

The kitchen door banged open and out came Val, naked and whooping, arms flung upward, the loose flesh of her belly and thighs quivering. To renewed cheering from the crowd and the engine-like chug of her own laugh, she skipped across the grass, breasts bobbling. The orange-red of her hennaed hair flared in the candlelight as she hooked one leg over the edge and clambered in with a splash.

'Who's next?' yelled someone.

Gav began to unbutton his shirt. 'Shove up, girls,' he called. 'There's room for one more.'

I went inside, which meant passing Miller where he still sat on the step, now with Ishtar on his lap. I approached with my head lowered, and at the edge of my vision they appeared to be one merged being with two heads and a sprawling, many-limbed body. Miller's drawing rose, unbidden, into my mind and I took the steps quickly, gut shrinking with distaste. I imagined the two of them were waiting, with a kind of benevolent tolerance, for everyone else to finish with the bath — Val and Willow and Gav; lesser beings, who belonged in the overcrowded middle plane of Miller's picture — so that they, who were special and belonged up high in clear space, contorting themselves joyously at the end of each pointing ray of sun, could have it all to themselves.

'Where're you off to?' Ishtar's voice was a half-hearted murmur, and I felt her hand pat briefly at the leg of my jeans as I passed — an absent, dismissive pat.

In the kitchen I made myself a slice of bread with honey. By the sink lay some potatoes, half of them peeled. A frying pan was on the stove and starting to send up black smoke. I turned off the hotplate and went into my room.

Lying in bed I could hear them, singing, yelling. Eventually there were the sounds of someone moving around inside the house, followed by the smell of pot and then, after a bit longer, the smell of cooking. My stomach twitched with hunger but I didn't get up. I thought about Jindi descending naked into the water, the uncomplicated joy in her face, the way she kicked and wriggled, free in her child's body. I curled on my side under the blanket, pushed with my forearms at the hateful tender places where my breasts were starting to grow.

The outside bath was popular for a while, until a man came and fixed the bathroom, and everyone started using that again.

'It is glorious, out in the clean air,' said Val. 'Just glorious. But it's also fucken freezing!'

They put me in a different room. Go to sleep they said, You need to rest. I want to see my baby I said. You cant keep her from me. Not now they said, The babys sleeping now. You need to rest. They went round the bed straightening things. They took my temperature and looked under the sheet again, they were always looking without asking first or saying what they were doing. Please I said. Its best if you dont they said. A new woman came in, a woman in plain clothes. Hello she said and smiled. She had a singsong, false kind of voice. She said Im an almoner thats a funny word isnt it? I almost laughed it was such a joke her talking to me like I was a child, me who had just had a baby. My job is to help girls like you she said. I saw the papers in her hand, I knew what she was doing. Now you just need to sign these she said. No I said. She smiled. Youre tired she said, I will come back later. A nurse gave me an injection. I was so sore and worn out I couldnt help it I fell asleep. When I woke up I didnt know how long Id slept, the lights were off the blind was down and I couldnt tell if it was day or night. A nurse came and I asked again about the baby and she said Later. They brought me food and I was so hungry I ate it all and then I fell asleep again. Next time I woke up the blind was open and it was day. Can I see my baby please I said and the nurse said Not now. Then I thought of some thing. Dont I have to feed her? I said. No no she said, Dont worry about that, shes being taken care of. I dont know how much time passed, I slept again and when I woke up the almoner was back sitting beside the bed in a chair. Well youre looking much better now she said in her put on voice and set the papers down over my knee and held out a pen. I didnt take it, I didnt look at the papers. Please can I see my baby I said, I dont want to give her up. She tried to hold my hand but I pulled away so she put her hand on my arm. We already have a couple she said, Waiting. Theyre a lovely couple and they cant have any children themselves. Now dont be selfish. What kind of a life do you think you can offer her? She deserves a good life in a comfortable home and a good education. You cant give her any of that now can you? Mm? I tried to think, my mind wasnt clear. The papers nearly fell off my knee and she put them back again. She slipped the pen between my fingers. I just want to see her I said. Well she said, How about you sign these and then maybe ... I felt so foggy and tired I nearly did it, it would have been so easy and maybe she was right maybe I was being selfish. But under the fog I felt hate, I hated her I hated all of them the nurses the nuns my mother, I didnt want to be a good girl I didnt want to do what they said to enter the tunnel like Evie to shut my life down. Id seen that babys face and it was like a reflection of myself. I let the pen go and it fell on the floor. She bent to pick it up and I tipped my knees and the papers slid off and just missed her head. She straightened up all flushed and her voice wasnt singsong any more. Youre a silly girl she said, Why wont you cooperate? Think about your baby, dont be so selfish. Then I saw some thing in the doorway and it was her, Mira, except she didnt have the plaits she had her hair pinned up and she wasnt wearing her silk clothes, she had on a skirt and a blouse very old fashioned. The almoner got to her feet. Who are you? she said, There are no visitors allowed in here. Help me I called. I pulled back the covers and sat up. What are you doing? said the almoner, Lie down now please. She went over to Mira. No visitors in here she said, Youll have to leave. Help me I called, They wont let me see my baby theyre going to make me give her up. The almoner pushed Mira out the door then went out herself.

I thought it was all over then, I thought theyd won. It was lucky the almoner didnt come back because I probably wouldve signed the papers. Nobody came in for hours. I got up but the door wouldnt open it must have been locked from the out side. Then at last it opened and I thought it would just be another nurse come to poke around and jab me with needles but I couldnt believe it, it was Mira again in her strange clothes. There was a man too in a suit with a briefcase and there was the almoner all huffing and puffing and red in the face. Only Mira sat down, she held my hand then she nodded at the almoner. The almoner wouldnt look at me. There has been a misunderstanding she said, We were not aware you had a safe place to go and someone to support you. Then the man said to me Now just to make sure we all understand whats happening could you please let the social worker here know what you want to do with your baby. He meant the almoner. I want to keep her I said. I dont want to give her up. The almoner looked like steam might come out her ears. Is that clear enough? said the man. Yes said the almoner and went out.

From time to time Ian would cop it especially hard at school. I'd see him at the morning break with Dean Price's sausage fingers hooked into his armpits, his toes barely touching the ground, his head slack, eyes lowered while something unintelligible and foul was bellowed into his face. With this came a corresponding increase in attention from Dean Price's cronies who caught our bus; they were kept pretty well under control by the driver but still managed to deliver menacing looks and comments as they sloped, pack-like, up or down the aisle.

When these things happened there were changes in Ian's own behaviour. He went missing — sometimes arriving at the creek bank late, and sometimes not showing up at all — and he never said where he'd been. His face looked extra thin and pinched, and he would hardly keep still, talking a hundred miles an hour, maniacally adjusting settings on the camera, sending the collection of balls hurtling into the creek, his whole body almost flying down after it.

His actual speech also changed, became even more affected. 'Ah, manna from the *gods*,' he would intone, when I brought some honey sandwiches. 'Come *sup* with me, fair maid, and let us forget our *woes*.'

He began branching out, too, with his acts of revenge. One afternoon he boarded the bus with a swollen lip and a graze on his chin, composed but slightly unsteady as he approached his seat. The next day at the creek, he produced with trembling hands an exercise book that had *D. Price: Maths* printed on the front cover. I stood by while Ian tore the pages out one by one and dropped them into the brown flow, the paper turning translucent so little clusters of numbers appeared to float directly on the water.

Another time, I saw him up against a wall near the boys'

changing rooms with the flat of Dean Price's hand against his ear, his cheek pressed against the bricks. A couple of days later it was a single, knobbled football boot that entered the creek, laces trailing, its opening like a mouth gulping as the water went in.

These attacks and retributions were not acknowledged by Ian beyond his sharing, wordlessly, the celebration and disposal of his spoils. Afterwards — once the pages had all floated away, or the boot, glugging its last breath, had sunk below the surface — he turned as if waking from a trance, blinking his invisible lashes, and I saw that it took effort for him to rejoin me, to bring himself back.

'Well,' he might say, dusting off his hands with exaggerated briskness. 'What shall we do now, gypsy girl? How about a *scene*?' His latest passion was Shakespeare, and we spent a lot of time reading scenes from the matching tattered copies of *King Lear* that he'd got from a box of discards from the school library. Ian was an excellent reader, rarely stumbling over even the most obscure language.

When he read aloud, all of the usual drama — his flamboyant emphasis on certain words — left his voice, and it grew clear and steady. His face, too, became calm, the skin softening, losing its pallor. But this only lasted while he was reading, and too soon the book was closed and his jumpiness returned, and a sad, protective feeling swelled in me as I watched the white spots reappear over his cheekbones, like the skin was stretched too far.

Not long after the almoner left, a nurse brought me the baby. She was so tiny and she did look just like me, even Mira said so. I had my first try at feeding her which didnt go very well but Mira said that was all right if I just kept trying my milk would come. It was strange because normally I would be so embarassed showing my breasts and especially with the man there but I didnt mind at all. The only thing that mattered was that my baby was crying and it seemed right to feed her. It must have looked so silly but when she had finished drinking I hardly even thought to cover myself up again. I just sat there staring at her and saying Isnt she beautiful isnt she beautiful? Yes Mira said, Shes lovely. Then the nurse came to take her away again, I got upset but Mira held my hands and said Dont worry theyll bring her back when shes due her next feed. What if they dont? I said. I will make sure they do she said, I will visit every day. Still, I couldnt believe her. They were all so mean I said, And what if that almoner comes back? Mira kissed me and stood up. You just stay strong she said, Dont sign any thing. If they bother you tell them you have a place to go and Welfare have been informed you are keeping the baby. I will be back tomorrow and Im going to visit every day until they discharge you.

They took me out of that room and put me in a ward with other women who were all new mothers but married. I saw some of them look at my finger that had no ring on it, none of them spoke to me but I didnt care as long as my baby was brought to me like all the others for feeds that was all I cared about. Some of the older nurses were rude to me and nobody helped at all with the feeding which was hard. All I wanted was to hold her and feed her and kiss her she was so beautiful. Mira came every day like she said. She was always dressed in the skirt and blouse and with her hair up, she looked so different but she had that calm way about her and she sat very straight and just her being there made me feel better. The man in the suit didnt come again. But a funny thing happened on about the third or fourth day. One of the married women walked over to my bed and said was it true I had a lawyer in and caused a big scene with a social worker? I didnt know what to say. I thought about the man with his briefcase and how hed made me say that about keeping the baby to the almoner in front of him and Mira. Is it true? said the woman. Because thats what we heard and she nodded at all the other married mothers who were just about falling out of there beds trying to listen. I didnt cause a scene I said. Well not you said the woman, Your friend you know Mary Poppins. One of the other women laughed. Shes not your mum is she? said the first woman. Its none of your business I said, Please leave me alone. She said some thing snippy going back to her bed but I didnt care, the nurse was coming with my baby and I was looking forward to feeding her. My milk had just started properly. I still hadnt got the hang of feeding and it hurt a lot but I was just so glad that at last she was actually getting some thing in her little stomach. The almoner never came back and nobody brought any more papers for me to sign but I still worried. Then one day a nurse came and said Your aunt is coming to take you home this morning. I guessed she meant Mira. This nurse was new, she was actually nice and she was the only one whod tried to help me with breastfeeding. She brought me my case so I could get dressed, all I had was one of my horrible tent dresses and it was ridiculous it was so big. The nurse was very polite though, she didnt say any thing. But she did ask where were the babys clothes and I didnt know what to say. Dont you have any? She spoke quietly because all the married mothers had there ears flapping. Yes I said, but my aunty must have forgotten to bring them. Never mind she said, Lets just keep this nightie on her shall we and the little blanket. Thank you I whispered. I was so grateful. She whispered right in my ear You are very lucky, I used to be on the ward for unmarried mothers and there are so many girls like you whod keep there babies if they had the opportunity and the way they are treated its just plain wrong. I didnt know what to say back so I just said thank you again. I thought about Pat and all the other girls at the Home and Evie Dyer and how I never couldve understood before what it felt like to have your baby taken away and how I still couldnt imagine never having gotten her back. I would want to die. Then Mira came and it was time to go.

One Saturday, Ian and I were by the creek sharing the lunch his mum had made him, me sitting on the ground, Ian pacing around, waving his arms and talking. He had been out of sorts for a few days. The lunch was white-bread sandwiches with Vegemite and rubbery cheese. He had gone quiet for a minute or two, which was unusual, and was standing still. Then he gave a stern nod, as if confirming something to himself, and turned to me.

'I want to show you something.' He scrunched up the wax-paper wrapping from the sandwiches and stuffed it into his pocket. 'Come on.'

Through the scrub we went, back towards Hope. We reached the bridge and climbed up and crossed it, the ringing of our shoes bouncing off the water below. Ian turned back into the bush, staying on the same side of the road, and before we climbed too deeply into the trees I was able to look across and see all our landmarks — the steep part of the bank where we sat near the bridge, and an especially big wattle tree, and the clump of grass where the balls had collected that day — from this new angle. Everything looked strange, small and lonely somehow.

We moved up, diagonally climbing the slope, and after a while Ian stopped. 'There used to be a track here — can you see?'

I looked around. 'Not really.'

'See how there aren't any really *enormously* big trees in this bit?'

I looked, ahead and behind, and saw the line of lesser growth: smaller trees with thinner trunks, more bracken and low shrubs. The greens seemed brighter too. 'Oh yeah.'

'It's how they got in.' He started walking again. Some colour had come into his face.

'In?'

'The miners.'

'Miners?'

But he wasn't going to give any more away. On he marched, his steps springy with importance, and I followed. After a bit longer he turned and went between two big trees that had pinkish-white trunks, wrinkled at the joints, like skin. There was a line of rusted wire, very low to the ground, and some fallen timber posts — the remains of a fence. We stepped over them and Ian halted. 'Stop!' He spread his arms dramatically. 'Careful!'

I stopped, and looked ahead. My eyes were still adjusting to the shadows under the bigger trees, and at first I thought there was something there, lying on the ground a couple of metres away: a square, black thing, about the size of a car door. I blinked and squinted, struggling to make it out, because there was something funny about it. As my vision cleared I realised that it wasn't a thing that I was looking at, a car door or sheet of black plastic — it was nothing, it was space. It was a biggish hole in the ground.

'It's a mineshaft.' Ian flung himself down beside it. 'Well, actually, it's not. They go in sideways, usually, and then slope down gently. This is a kind of testing hole. They made these to assess the coal seam, so they knew where to actually mine. My grandad told me. He worked in the big mine, the real one, before it closed. But these little ones, up in the hills, they're really old — from the *olden* days.'

Slowly, I moved closer and got down on my knees. The opening of the shaft was lined with planks of decayed-looking wood, broken away in parts. I lay on my front next to Ian, and looked right in. It went straight down into complete darkness, the higher reaches of wall showing earth and more ruined and missing boards. The air that rose from it had the cold, dead smell of a place where no light penetrates.

'It's really deep,' said Ian, his voice sinking echoless into the void. 'More than a hundred feet, according to my grandad. Probably more than a hundred and fifty. That's fifty-odd metres.' He dropped a handful of twigs in and there was a long pause before the faint splashy patter of them landing. 'Hear that? There's water at the bottom.'

I wriggled back and away, sat up. 'So there are more?'

'Of course. They're everywhere round here.'

All the times I'd run, unthinking, through the scrub, feet crashing down, landing anywhere. My skin tightened.

Ian looked at me properly, without staring through me the way he'd been doing for the past week. 'Don't worry,' he said. 'They're only up here, on this side of the creek. Our side's fine.'

'You sure?'

'Of *course.*' He made a dismissive gesture. 'That's why all the houses are down on that side. Up here it's just mines. Old, old, forgotten mines, full of skeletons and ghosts.' He leaned on his elbow and spat the words down into the hole, which swallowed them up.

'Careful.' I scooted further back. 'I can't believe it's just open like this,' I said. 'I mean, anyone could just …'

'Ah.' Ian also sat back. 'Well, there was the fence.' He tipped his head in the direction of the lines of rusty wire that we'd stepped over, and that I now saw ran in a square around the shaft.

'Yeah, but it's fallen down.'

'Well.' He threw me a grin, and despite the feeling that I was about to find out something I didn't really want to know, I felt a little twirl of happiness — it was so good to see him smile again.

'It wasn't quite so fallen down. I helped it a little bit. And there's the sign, didn't you see it?'

I scanned the entrance to the clearing and eventually made out a rectangular shape lying in the undergrowth, off to one side.

Ian took up a long stick and began breaking bits off and tossing them into the hole. 'I didn't knock *that* down,' he said. 'It was already like that.'

The sign was too well covered to read. 'What does it say?'

'Oh, you know. *Danger. Keep out.*' He waved a hand. 'Most of the mines are marked. My grandad says the government did it, years ago, when they shut everything down. And there would've been a cover.' He indicated some splintery remnants of timber at the edge of the hole.

'Did you …'

Again he grinned.

I moved further away. The uncomfortable feeling was growing, a lump in the pit of my stomach.

Ian had started on another stick. 'I hardly had to do anything,' he said. 'It was only a couple of *tiny* bits left, and they were really rotten. I mean the whole thing was pretty badly secured. A lot of them are like that — nobody bothers to check. Nobody comes up here.' He glanced at me. 'It's *cool*, isn't it?'

I didn't answer. It was good to see him looking less miserable — but this thing was scary, and dangerous. We weren't supposed to be here; even if they had all fallen down, the sign, the fence and the cover had been put there for a reason. I pictured the one-hundred-metre sprint track that was marked out on the oval at school, cut in half and then made vertical. Fifty metres was a long way down. 'I don't like it,' I said.

'Pardon?' He had gone back to lying with his head out over

the lip of the shaft, and was dangling one arm in.

'I don't like it.' I knew I sounded prissy, uptight, worrying about the rules. I felt myself flush. 'I mean,' I added, 'I've just got a bit of a thing about heights.'

Ian sat up again. 'Fair enough.' His tone was determinedly light and casual.

There was a long, uncomfortable silence, with no eye contact. At last I cleared my throat. 'I might go then.'

'Rightio. I'll come back down soon. Meet you at the bridge?'

'Okay. Be careful.'

'Always.' He gave me a comical wave, wiggling his fingers.

There was, of course, more to my dread of that shaft than a simple fear of heights, or depths, rather — of falling. It was to do with what the discovery of it meant to Ian, the way the white spots over his cheekbones coloured when he showed it to me, the animation in him, the excitement. That this jubilant engagement with something so risky was how he picked himself back up, recovered from what Dean Price had been doing to him. I didn't reflect on it in this way then, or articulate it to myself — it was just another thing that made me feel bad, and that I therefore tried my best to take no notice of. And it was such a relief to have Ian back to more or less his normal self. Neither of us mentioned the shaft after that, and we returned to meeting by the creek most afternoons.

If he didn't show up I didn't think about where he might be — a kind of blankness came over me, and I'd take on some repetitive task, like carefully removing petals from the tiny purple flowers that grew on the bank, until it began to get dark and was time to get up on my frozen legs and jog back along the path and over the hill to Hope.

Then one day, somebody was doing a clear-out, and had put a pile of books on the kitchen table for everyone to help themselves from. In the pile was a beautiful leather-bound copy of *The Tempest*. I snatched it and ran to the creek, calling for Ian — but couldn't find him. Thoughtlessly, and in the heat of my excitement, I crossed the bridge and ran up towards the two big pink gumtrees.

I kept calling as I got closer, but he mustn't have heard. He didn't notice me even when I got near enough to see him, just before I reached the fallen fence. He was standing in the clearing, turned away from me, and he had a lump of wood — a small log really — in his arms. I had drawn in breath to call again, but I faltered, thinking either I was going mad or there was something wrong with my eyes. The hole appeared to have vanished. Ian stood on a perfectly uniform carpet of clear ground, evenly sprinkled with leaves and twigs. As I watched, groggy with confusion and forgetting all about the book, he took one step back, bent his knees and bucked his hips forward, letting go of the log. The hunk of wood went out in a slight curve away from him, fast and heavy — but instead of landing, it plunged through the ground, dragging a portion of grass and dirt and leaf litter with it in one quick, fluid movement, like the last surge of water draining through a plughole. And there it was — the sudden, gaping square of black space.

'Ah *ha*!' yelled Ian, hopping on the spot. 'Down you go!'

A horrible, tipping sensation came over me, worse than the bewilderment it replaced. I turned and ran, back between the twin trees and down the hill, over the bridge and along the other side of the creek. There was a place where the bush grew thickly, and I pushed my way in, far enough that I was well hidden from the path. The growth was so tight I couldn't even squat down, and I stood with the book held to my chest, my heart thundering. It was a trap. By covering the hole with something — paper or a sheet of fabric — and then arranging dirt and bits of grass and twigs over it so it was indistinguishable from the surrounding ground, he had made a trap. I tried to lick my lips; my mouth was dry. Ian's voice hammered in my ears: *Down you go!*

After that it wasn't possible to completely ignore the presence of the shaft. When we were together, embroiled in some activity — then I could forget. But whenever he didn't show up at the creek bank, I couldn't help but know where he most likely was instead, and wonder what he might be doing. Why would you make a trap like that, so real and deadly? Who was it he imagined breaking through that carefully constructed seal, and dropping — *Down you go!* — into the dark? And when we saw each other again after these absences, there was a strangeness there, and I found myself watching his face carefully.

Sometimes we would meet on the path and it would be obvious he was on his way back from the shaft, and something in the determined, breezy nod and greeting he gave made my chest feel squeezed. It was the same sad, adult feeling I got whenever I felt the growing lumps behind my nipples, or thought about getting my period — of something having been lost. Of unwilling acceptance. Of compromise.

Mira had a taxi waiting. The house was in a suburb I didnt know, Id only ever been in the city. By the time we got there the baby was hungry and crying. Some women were waiting, they took me to a room and put me in a bed on the floor and I lay back against pillows, it had been a week since the birth but still I was sore. An older woman with dark skin and acne scars knelt beside me. Shes a midwife said Mira, She knows all about babies. Feed, feed said the midwife. I pulled at my stupid tent dress and tried to balance the baby against my knees. The midwife helped me take the dress off and put a long shawl thing round my shoulders. Everything smelled smoky and foreign. The baby snorted her head against me. The midwife put her palm to the back of the tiny head and with the other hand pinched me quickly in to the right shape, I got such a surprise I yelped and then I felt that feeling that little hungry strong mouth and for once it hardly hurt. See? said the midwife and grinned.

The next morning Mira came to see me. She was back in her own clothes and had her hair in plaits again. I tried to say thank you to her for all her help but she put her hand up to stop me. We do what is right she said. Now your parents will be worried, I think you should ring them and let them know youre safe. She helped me out to the phone in the hallway. Who did you say? said my mother. Who are these people? I told her again, I said the name slowly and clearly, I had nothing to hide. I heard her tell my father Its them the ones I told you about from the park. Then she said to me You go straight back to the hospital now, its not too late. No I said, Im not going to do that Ive made my decision. My mother was quiet I could hear her breathing then she hung up the phone.

'Is she going to have a baby soon?'

It was morning, and Jindi had waylaid me as I came out of the toilet.

'Who?'

'Her.' She pointed a dirty finger at Ishtar's outline in the kitchen window.

'Ishtar?'

'Yeah.'

'What makes you think she's going to have a baby?'

'Miller told me.'

'What?' I bent to see her face, which seemed engorged with importance. 'What did you say?'

'I was helping him with the digging and she brought out a drink for him. I didn't get any, but I didn't mind, I think it was coffee or something yuck.' She paused, luxuriating in a long moment of thoughtfulness. 'Or maybe it was a cup of beer. Beer is really horrible. I like the foam, but the underneath is —'

'Jindi!'

'Mm?'

'Come on. What did he say about Ishtar?'

'Oh.' She pursed her lips and gazed off somewhere over my shoulder. 'I can't remember now.'

I straightened and began to push past her. 'Never mind,' I said, 'I'll find out some other —'

'No, no — wait!' She grabbed my wrist. 'I can remember — I just remembered.'

I stopped. 'Okay then — quick.'

She kept hold of me. 'I was helping him and Ishtar brought the drink and then she went back inside and Miller said, "She is my woman and just like I plant these seeds to grow food for us

116

to eat I will plant my own seed in her.'" She grinned. 'And you know what that means, don't you?'

I observed Ishtar for signs of swelling, but her stomach stayed flat. She was different though. Still busy — always busy — but something had changed, and as I watched her move through her endless cycle of chores I realised that the brightness was missing from her. She had settled; her movements were now more efficient than eager.

'What we are doing here,' boomed Miller, pacing in front of the fire, 'just by being alive and present in our bodies, close to the earth, letting the elements in — the wind, the rain — welcoming them, allowing them to touch us, this is *profoundly subversive.*'

'Yeah,' came a feeble cry from the gloom. 'Right on.'

I looked for Ishtar, for the almost-undetectable signs of pleasure at the corners of her mouth, but when I found her face in the flickering light, it had the emptiness of someone waiting for something to be over.

Then I heard them arguing one night, outside, on the stretch of ground between the back of the toilet and the hill, where the bath stood. Their voices slipped through the gaps in the tin over my head as I shivered on the wooden toilet seat, trying not to breathe the smell.

'What do we have,' Miller said, 'if not trust?'

'Well, how long then?'

'A week. Maybe even less. I have to help. It's an obligation. I know you understand.'

Ishtar clicked her tongue. 'I didn't mean how long will you be gone. I meant how long till I can have my money back.'

Miller made a long sound, part laugh, part exhalation, low and weary. 'Money? Really? Ishtar. My love. You disappoint me.'

There was a long silence, and then when she spoke again Ishtar's voice had completely changed. It wavered, weak as a child's. 'Well, it was my money — and you said …'

Miller spoke in a teasing purr. 'If you care so much, my sweet lady, I will bring it when I return. I will repay you, and with interest. All will be settled and square.' His voice lowered and grew slightly muffled. 'And then you'll stop taking those dreadful pills, won't you.'

This was followed by loud breathing and kissing sounds. I wanted to sneak off but was afraid they'd notice me if I moved. They sounded very close, just on the other side of the bricks.

He went away. The next morning, early for him, throwing a canvas bag — roughly packed, clothes showing at the unzipped opening — into the back of the brown station wagon. He kissed Ishtar, as I watched furtively from a corner of the front porch. He kissed her for a long time, his bushy beard seeming to eat up her face, then he stood with one large hand at the back of her head, his forehead pressed to hers, whispering. Ishtar didn't answer. But she dipped her chin, once, twice, in nods that to me looked reluctantly obedient.

When the car had reached the top of the slope and turned out onto the dirt road, she stood for a long time staring after it. She had her arms folded but she didn't look strong or tough like Val, whose crossed arms as she rested a hip on the edge of the sink made me think of words like *buttress* and *fortress*; nor were they like Willow's when she locked them under her heavy breasts, which had a comfortable appearance, like the closed wings of a roosting chicken. Ishtar's hands gripped the upper sleeves of her own jumper as if underneath was a structure that had not been fitted together properly, an unsteady frame that might collapse at any moment.

The midwife helped me, she brought me nappies and showed me how to change them and wash them. I didnt have any clothes but they gave me some light silk things like they all wore. The baby didnt have any thing apart from the little hospital nightie but the midwife showed me how to wrap her up in cotton cloths. It was summer any way so she didnt need clothes realy. I had that room to myself with the bed on the floor and apart from going to the toilet I stayed there for what felt like a long time two weeks maybe. The midwife visited every day for a while and then she stopped coming so often. Other people brought me food and sat with me and held the baby. Nobody spoke realy, they were all very quiet and still but they smiled. They brought me books to read but I just looked at the pictures mostly I wasnt supposed to learn from them they were just to keep me entertained. In some of them the drawings were very dramatic, people with animal parts a donkeys head the tail of a snake a man bursting out of a wolfs body with blood splashing. The pages were thin and grainy feeling. Through the open window I could smell frangipani. My old life seemed so far away already, when I got up and felt my full breasts under the floating silk dress and looked down at the baby sleeping on the bed I felt like a different person. I moved slowly the way the others in the house did I spoke in a gentle quiet voice like they did. In the small bathroom mirror I smoothed my hair with my hands parting it in the middle feeling it hang around my face. Mira was the house mother she did all the shopping and cooking and she was always around. There were others who lived there, about twelve people, men and women but they went out most days. Then in the evenings there was this thing called satsang in the living room. They asked me to join in after the first week, they said of course I could bring the baby. There were no couches or chairs and only one bookshelf and a table with candles and flowers and fruit on it and a photo in a frame of a smiling dark skinned man with glasses. Everyone was there and usually extra people too, teachers in robes to give talks and lead us in meditation and yoga. We all sat cross legged on the floor. It was very quiet. I didnt know the words of the chants but after the first time Mira gave me a booklet with them in it and the meanings in English and also stuff about the man in the photo, what he taught and the things he had done. The typing was small and reading was so hard for me any way I skipped most of it but from what I could tell he was a nice person, he believed in love and peace. I did try to learn the mantras so I could join in, it was slow with my reading, I mostly learned from just listening at satsang. At first I felt embarassed and kept my voice quiet but after a while it was just automatic and my voice seemed to blend with the others without me even thinking about it. I liked satsang, everyone sitting so close it was like the calm collected in a pool around us and you could feel how deep it was. The baby lay across my lap and slept.

'What,' said Val, spilling out the contents of the kitty tin onto the table, 'none at all?' With brisk fingers she clicked coins on the scarred tabletop, swept a pile into her hand. 'With all those shifts you've been doing?'

'I'll have to owe you. Till next week, when I get my pay.' Ishtar's voice was low and cool, but she had turned her back, was hiding herself in the busyness of wiping the pots stacked on the draining board, bending to put them in the cupboard.

Val, a wedge of folded hessian shopping bags under one arm, tipped the coins into a pouch. 'You won't get anything back from a bloke like him,' she said, in a voice much gentler than her usual one. Then she sniffed and turned to the door. 'But I expect you know that.'

Jindi was waiting when I came out of the toilet.

'When is Miller coming home?'

'I don't know.'

'Maybe he's not coming back. Does that mean you and your mum will go, too?'

'I don't know.'

She butted against me. 'Can't you stay?' Her cold fingers tried to worm themselves into my pocket, where my own hand was.

Miller's runaway pumpkin plant sighed and rustled its fibrous stems against the wall of the shed. In all its vast, undulating carpet of green not one orange bloom was visible.

I dug my hands deeper into my pockets, angling myself away from Jindi. A lash of wind brought hot, unexpected tears into my eyes.

'Can't you stay, Silver?'

Ishtar passed us, walking from the house to the mud-brick building. Her stride was even; her upright back, as she entered the dark doorway, inscrutable as ever.

'Silver?'

A jet of anger rushed up in me and I pushed past, knocking her. 'I don't know!' I made for the house, not looking round. 'I don't know everything that's going to happen!'

After school I raced into the bush and down to the creek, through showers of wattle blooms, to submit to Ian and his bossiness.

'Now you run to the bridge, and grab them,' he ordered, getting ready to toss an armload of balls into the water. 'Go. And make sure you remember the *sequence* they come through in. Here, write it down.' Passing me a chewed pencil and a scrap of paper. 'Okay. Be *gone*, gypsy girl. I'll count to ten and then I'll chuck them.'

Back and forth I ran, welcoming the scratches of twigs and leaves, keeping my heart racing, my breaths full and busy in my chest. I gave myself over to it: to the chill rising from the ground, the mossy, wet smells, the secret black soil where the smallest plants sent hair-like roots too fragile to touch. To the endless onward hurtle of the creek, the rip of birdcalls, the sting of the air, the creak and whisper of the canopy above and the patient, sturdy trunks below.

Willingly I yielded to the demands of Ian's repetitious games and lengthy readings, animated lectures on apertures and lenses, f-stops and film speeds. Gratefully I sank into my role as audience, sidekick, player of bit parts, photographer's assistant. The photography sessions were better than the play

123

readings, because I didn't have to speak. Unable to see what he saw through the viewfinder — a perfect composition of clouds, or bracken fronds, or swirl of water around domed peaks of rocks — I nonetheless stood, dutiful and happily vacant of thought, casting my shadow just where he needed it, or holding a piece of white paper below or to one side of the camera's lens.

A car came along the road and we raced to get under the bridge. Breathing the metallic, sunless air, stones jabbing my shoulder blades, I pressed down on the wild fear churning low in my belly as the approaching growl widened and the timbers overhead began to tremble. On it came, the ruthless descent of tyres, the terrifying roar of sound; the vortex that took everything else away, that shook me empty and left me licking the chalky dust from my lips, grinning with a vast, brainless joy.

She was so beautiful I could look at her for hours and kiss her and smell her skin. When the others said how beautiful she was I felt so proud and strong I couldnt believe she was mine, I was her mother all she had in the world and I had fought to keep her. I didnt show how I felt though that wasnt what these people did, you couldnt talk about yourself or be proud or vain. Once or twice I imagined showing her to my father and Linda and even my mother too, I thought if they saw her surely they would love her and understand. I did try to ring again one more time but as soon as she heard my voice my mother hung up. So I didnt think about my parents after that, it wasnt hard because the baby filled everything and she belonged to this new life she was what made me who I was now. I thought about names. Everybody in the house had strange names, some were lovely. Mira, Kali, Rani, Skye. There was a woman called Rainbow. Some of the men had more normal names, Ronnie and David but there were also Kabir and Jasper and Jaskaran. Lying on my bed I turned the thin pages of the books, I looked at the captions and whispered the names to myself. One time the phone rang and I was right there in the hallway and nobody else was around so I answered it. Someone asked for Kate. I hadnt met any one with that name. Then Mira came out of the kitchen. Who do they want? she said. Oh they mean Kali, shes not here ask if you can take a message. Later I watched Kali during satsang sitting tall with her auburn hair and face all peaceful, it was hard to believe she could ever have been a Kate. Mira brought me some papers in a long clean envelope, they were for the registration of birth. I looked at them and my reading was even worse than usual, all I saw was lines of type and spaces. My hands shook. Please will you help me? I said. Mira was folding laundry, she stopped and set everything carefully aside she did all tasks like that never rushing. She took me to the kitchen and sat down, I sat beside her with the baby in my arms. Mira gave me a pen. Just put our address she said and told it to me. She had to say it four times for me to get it right. Then she tapped her finger where it asked for the fathers name and said You can put Unknown if you think thats best. I did it, full of shame but Miras face was the same as always, still and not judging. What about the babys name? she said. Have you thought of one? I felt embarassed, I wrote it down without saying it out loud, I did it so carefully making the letters neat and checked it over and it looked so bold there written for the first time. Mira leaned across to see. Her voice changed then, Oh now that is just perfect she said and I smiled and felt my face get hot. She took the paper and folded it, put it in an envelope that already had a stamp and the address on it. Would you like to post it yourself? she said, The post box is just at the corner of the street. Yes I said. Wait a moment then. She went out and came back with a long orange cloth. Hold her there she said, Close to your chest, and she used the cloth to bind the baby to me. I thought about the woman in the park that day with her baby tied on. You can let go, you can have your arms free said Mira and I took them away, I wasnt sure at first but then I felt how firmly the cloth was tied and I relaxed. Out side, the sun glared. I looked down but the baby had her head tucked in her little fists up by her face, sleeping and peaceful. I walked along with the letter in my hand feeling the swish of my long skirt. An old lady came the other way and I saw her run her eyes over me my clothes and the baby tied on, the leather sandals Mira had given me. She was about to look away but I caught her eye and smiled. Hello I said. Oh hello dear she said. She looked confused. I swished by, still smiling. She had never seen any one like me before. Later when Id come back Mira said And have you thought of a name for yourself? I realised then that none of them had ever asked my name and not even Mira who knew what it was had called me by it. At first I wasnt sure what she meant but then I remembered Kali who used to be Kate and then a picture from one of the books came in to my mind of a goddess with a sword and a bow and arrows standing with one foot on the back of a lion. Ishtar I said. Mira took my hands. Ishtar. Welcome. She kissed my cheek.

SPRING

It's difficult to tell how much I took in when it was all actually happening and how much I have since pieced together, or made up. There are times I recall that year of my life in bright snatches of mindless physicality, and I wonder if that's mostly how I did experience it. Stretching out my legs under the rough blanket as the early light coated the empty walls and Joni's face greeted me, grave and faded. The ache of frost at the bus stop. The bus smells of exhaust and vinyl and sandwiches. Air zapping fresh as I ran to the creek, my toes blocks of cold in my shoes. The comfortable flow of Ian's voice. The bush flexing its great, porous hide as we moved, tiny and blissfully unimportant, between its bristles. Maybe that's all that registered and it was all the other stuff that ran on underneath, managing every now and then to surface into consciousness but mostly embedding itself for later. And then there are times it seems to me that they were inescapable, the tensions of the adult world — the fraught and febrile aura that surrounded Ishtar and those in her orbit, that whined and creaked like a wire pulled too tight.

In and out she dips, in my memory, wheeling like a star, cutting the chill, dank air of the farmhouse. Bleary with sleep, I pull back the rough fabric of the front curtain to glimpse her getting into one of the cars, the white puff of her breath in the grainy morning light, the sweep of her hair, the belt of her coat trailing. I am always just missing her. In passing she might touch me, run a quick hand across my shoulder blades, kiss the top of my head, pull me to her so I feel the brief softness of a breast or the point of a hipbone. And then I am released, as on she goes, and on, to the next thing.

'How was school?' she might murmur, taking up the peeler and a handful of carrots — but her back is to me, and if I don't answer she never turns around, just goes on whisking the blade down and down, the slivers of peel flopping one by one, waving their weak arms as they fall.

Or is this only how I remember her? Perhaps she did turn, did set down the peeler and come to sit by me at the table, to put her arm round me, to lean in close so her warmth filled my breaths, asking me a question and then waiting for the answer. I often wonder if I have done her a disservice in the way I recall her, in what I have managed to haul from the murk and lay out under the harsh beams of examination and analysis. But I am at the mercy of memory. All I can do is hang on, attend to what I'm supplied with, squint and puzzle over it.

Miller, also, has most likely suffered from some stereotyping, some streamlining of character. Did he really only appear when in the grip of inspiration, ablaze with ideas, rattling them off in volleys, resonating with their urgency? It might have been just one or two impassioned speeches, a couple of LSD-fuelled rave sessions. Maybe, at times, he acted like the rest of us — came to the breakfast table, spoke in an ordinary voice, made regular conversation, went off to work.

I don't know. I can't remember, not clearly. But this is my story, I suppose. To me they were not ordinary, either of them;

they were strung up in some straining net of intrigue, suspended, pulsing with impending drama, with the approach of a veiled but certain ending — an explosion, or a collapse.

This is how it all seems to me now, the way it has lodged in my mind, and so this is the only way I can tell it.

After a while they started me working. Everyone must contribute Mira said, And Silver is not a newborn any more, your time of rest is over. Before I just stayed in the house, I slept a lot during the day when Silver did I was so tired from feeding her and changing her nappies at night. I didnt know that about babies the tiredness the not sleeping. But before it hadnt mattered I just slept when she did, day or night. I didnt have any thing else to do. Some times I helped in the kitchen or cleaning the house. I didnt mind those jobs, I wanted to help to show how grateful I was. But now there were real jobs that took up the whole daytime, there was no time for sleeping or just lying on the bed with Silver watching her face making her smile. There were three different jobs delivering storeroom and housekeeping. Delivering was walking around the streets putting pamphlets in peoples letterboxes. I went with three or four others straight after breakfast, we left with our bags of pamphlets and me with Silver tied on too. Usually we caught a bus to a different neighbourhood, some times in to the city where we offered the pamphlets to people on the street. Delivering was the best job even though I got so tired with all the walking and carrying Silver, but she liked it the walking kept her happy she always wanted to be rocked and bounced, it helped her sleep. Storeroom was taking things out of big crates and sorting and packing them in to smaller boxes, clothes and bags and little jewellery cases and things they came from India and were sold at markets to raise money. It was across town and we caught the bus there too I didnt like doing storeroom much because it was hard to keep Silver happy while I had to stand at the sorting table I had to sort of sway from side to side while I worked. Housekeeping was just helping Mira but it meant doing all the shopping, there was a lot of it and even though we had a trolley each we always filled them right up and had to carry bags too weighing down our shoulders. It was hard getting on and off the bus with all that and a baby as well. Then we had to cook and I worried about Silver I wanted her near me but there was never anywhere safe to put her down so I just kept her tied on with the cloth but then she was so close to the big boiling pots of food and hot oil and it got so hot she always cried. All the jobs were tiring and Silver was growing getting heavier to carry. I went to bed exhausted every night some times I fell asleep at satsang sitting up. I knew I needed to contribute like Mira said but it was so hard with Silver I didnt know it was going to be like that I suppose I never thought about what it was going to be like realy. I tried to be like Mira not hurrying not making mistakes doing everything in order and neatly but I was so tired and Silver cried so much I felt clumsy and slow always behind I got things wrong. Sorry, I was always saying, my voice and Silvers cries too loud in the quiet house. Sorry, sorry. Mira never said any thing she just kept on with her work. One time in the kitchen it was such a hot day the air choking with frying smells and steam and Silver crying and crying, and Mira just took her just untied the cloth and took her from me. She put her in my room and shut the door and then shut the kitchen door when she came back. But I knew she would still be crying in there even if I couldnt hear it. As soon as Id finished work I went in and there she was still screaming in the middle of the mattress all red in the face and she had vomited. I felt like I couldnt breathe and the milk hurt in my breasts. I grabbed her up and kissed her and kissed her. Im so sorry, I whispered. But I had to do it after that, shut her up in the room if she was crying too much, Mira never said any thing but I knew it was what was expected. It broke my heart, my love for Silver was still so easy then all I wanted was to be with her every moment.

It was while Miller was away that Dan came to Hope — quietly slipped in. His entrance didn't boom and clang with importance the way Miller's comings and goings did; in fact, from the very beginning, he seemed to exist as a kind of demonstration of how to be the exact opposite of Miller.

Dan was younger than all the other adults — even I, to whom most grown-ups appeared either old or really old, could tell — the whiskers on his cheeks sparse and soft-looking, and with big wet-dark eyes like those of the wallabies that hid down by the creek. He was always in the background, in the shadows, and I wouldn't have paid any extra attention to him if it wasn't for something that happened on one of the first nights he was there.

I'd gone to bed early with a stomach-ache, heavy and low in my gut, and woke some time later to a different kind of pain, stronger, dragging. I sat up and there was a sudden warm seeping feeling in my underpants. I snapped properly awake, clenching my muscles — had I just wet my pants? But it happened again, another ooze, and the strange dull tug of pain again. A numbness came over me. *It's your period*, I thought distantly. *This is what it feels like.*

My body was still, my breathing even, but underneath the stillness something squirmed and twisted, fought blindly. I held the muscles between my legs tight, but the leaking kept on, persistent, frightening.

For some reason an image leapt up: a woman, a house mother in orange robes, from a long time ago. Kara or something, Khana — the name swam just beyond my reach. Her smell, like cooking; the pink of her palms as she worked dough thin for samosas; her fingers nipping my cheek; the crooked shine of her teeth in a smile. How big this woman loomed — I must have been very small — and how importantly. Some of the house mothers had been mean; sometimes they'd shouted, or hit, or shut me in a room. But this one had been different — this one had been kind. I turned on my side, hoping to prevent the leakage from running between my legs to the mattress. More memories barged through, marched out in a bright string — the woman clapping her hands in a back yard, under a lemon tree, the chant of her song; following the orange swish of her robe back into the kitchen where the first samosa would be set aside; waiting, watching it steam; the taste of its crumbling, sweetish shell and fresh, soft inner. A desperate feeling rose and swelled, a lost, sad, grown-up feeling. I couldn't even remember the woman's name.

I got up, cast around in the half-dark, put my boots on. I reached into my duffel bag, right down to the bottom, for the packet of pads that Ishtar had given me at some point, perhaps a year earlier, along with a factual but typically removed explanation of fertility and sex, things I already knew about anyway. I pulled a pad out, and some spare underpants and a pair of old corduroys that were getting too small, bundled them all to my chest and went into the hallway.

There were voices from the front room, and the strum of an acoustic guitar. Most of the bedroom doors were closed and dark.

Through the kitchen I crept and out, trying not to rattle the loose doorknob, shivering in the fresh cold. There was light coming from a window in the mud-brick building, and by it I could just see the shape of the outdoor toilet, leaning wonkily by the woodpile. I stepped down into the grass and tried to walk quickly, hugging the bundle, stumbling on the uneven ground.

I'd never had to use the toilet so late at night before.

The timber door scraped and the stink slid in the chill air. I couldn't see anything inside. I fumbled against one wall for the shelf I knew was there, the matches and candle, but caught a fistful of cobwebs. The pain rippled in my belly. Something scuttled in the dark. The toilet smell choked me and my stomach heaved.

I let go of the door and stepped back, sucking in clean air, wiping the cobwebs on my jacket, then my nose with the back of my hand. The bundle came undone and there was a fluttery sound as something landed on the grass. I sank to my knees and felt around.

'Everything all right?'

There was a figure between me and the lit window — a man, slight, with longish dark hair. The red dot of a lit cigarette flared and I caught more of his face, a curve of mouth and cheekbone, dark eyes. It was him — Dan.

'Got a torch here, if you need one.'

'Oh, no, it's all right, it's —'

But there was a *click*, and a circle of light broke over the grass, showing the underpants with leg-holes gaping, the awful, incriminating oblong of the pad. I sprang and seized them, then stayed crouching, face burning, staring at the edge of the light's sphere where his legs showed: blue jeans, worn brown work boots.

'Thank you,' I said, after a moment, the word hardly coming out, a scratchy whisper.

'No worries. Here you go.' He bent and the light neared, then its dazzle turned away from my face, its beam playing out towards the black slope of the hill.

'Thank you,' came the whisper again, and I reached with

my free hand and took the heavy metal cylinder. I could smell the smoke from his cigarette. I still couldn't look up. The blood drummed in my face.

'You can just leave it on the doorstep there.'

'Thanks.' I didn't raise my eyes or get to my feet until I was sure he'd gone.

Dan never said anything about that night. I fully expected him to. There were a lot of good things about how open most people were in the places we lived — about sex and other matters of the body — but there were also some behaviours I would now consider inappropriate. I'm talking about a certain attitude in which the aversion to prudery or preciousness is so strong that a kind of brutal honesty is affected, and there is a focus on drawing attention wherever possible to sex and bodies, often in the form of teasing or jokes. Someone less prudish than I suppose I already was would perhaps not have minded this at all, but I experienced it as unnecessarily heavy-handed, and at times actually quite cruel. So I expected from Dan some kind of public humiliation — a lewd joke at the breakfast table, an announcement. Incredibly, he said nothing. We passed one another in the hallway the next morning and he only gave me one of his gentle smiles, which I, blazing with shame, almost missed and certainly didn't respond to. It took a few days and two or three repetitions of this — the friendly smile, the lack of comment — for me to accept the fact that he was not going to mention what had happened.

Perhaps out of gratitude for this unexpected kindness, or perhaps because, like Ishtar — and Miller I suppose, although he would always be in a category of his own — Dan stood out from the rest of the Hope residents in having some special vitality, I developed a kind of crush on him.

Unlike Ishtar, he appeared to be completely unaware of his own charm. He was so understated, so undemanding, there in the place he'd chosen for himself — off to one side, removed yet assured — that I thought myself alone in appreciating what he had to offer. Which was plenty.

Dan got things done. He had plans that would be realised. Not that they were on parade — I only found out what they were because I questioned him. He was absolutely not going to stay on at Hope Farm. He was only there because it was cheap and he wanted to save up quickly the last of what money he needed for a plane ticket to America, where he was going to play in bands. I don't know what made me believe his story any more than anyone else's, or trust in his ability to follow through, but I did.

Maybe it was this that I was drawn to, this sense of purpose, of connection with the outside world; this logical, sensible sequence of actions through which — calmly, without any need to involve or inform others — he was making his way. Where Miller was all bluff and bluster, a human hurricane churning in ineffective circles; where Ishtar continued to erode my faith in her with inexplicable, fraught decisions and extreme, untenable commitments; Dan, I had decided, was in complete possession of personal integrity. Dan made sense.

I sought him out, waiting on the front porch for his arrival back from work, or lying on my mattress with a book, listening for him to emerge from his room across the hallway so I could follow him into the kitchen and be there while he made a cup of tea. I never entered his room to snoop, but was thrilled just to inhale the air near its doorway, to catch sight of its interior — a guitar propped against the wall, a jumper across the back of a chair. He took over the splitting of the firewood from Ishtar, and as he worked I stood in attendance. I became his Jindi — his follower, waiting around corners, overflowing with questions. I knew this and sometimes, with a spasm of guilt and embarrassment, admitted it to myself; but mostly I managed to ignore it, curtain it off with the rosy cloud of my adoration.

He tolerated me. Maybe I wasn't really as annoying as I think I was, or maybe he was just a patient, generous person. Maybe he felt sorry for me. Whatever the reason, he never asked me to leave him alone, or seemed irritated by the way I gazed, rapt, as he rolled and lit a cigarette, as if his long brown fingers were the only fingers ever to do such a thing; ever to deftly fill and massage the flimsy scrap of paper, to put it to the pink tip of his tongue for the fast, sealing lick; to give it one last reshape before raising it to his lips, before the strike of the match.

'Where will you live again? In New York?'

A slow exhale of smoke, a thoughtful nod. Setting one foot on the wood-splitting stump and laying his forearm across his knee. 'Well. There are a few different places. I've heard in the Lower East Side you can get a cheap room, and it's near where all the clubs are. You know, where the bands play. Then there's Chelsea.' Another drag. A fringe of fine wood splinters hanging from the underside of his sleeve. 'But I'm not sure what the rent's like there.'

The Lower East Side. Chelsea. I shaped the names silently in my own mouth, storing them up for later.

A couple of times he let me go with him into Kooralang. I almost burst with pride, riding up there in the high cab of his truck, the privileged sole passenger, listening for the surprisingly low, rich notes of his voice as he sang along to the songs on the radio.

'Now. I need to visit the hardware,' he might say, as he pulled on the handbrake. 'Would that be all right with you?'

The thrill of being consulted! Giddy with importance, I would clamber down and swing shut the heavy door, wait for him to come around to the footpath.

The town had a dingy collection of shops and businesses: a butcher's, a chemist's, the hardware place, a post office, a coffee shop with empty booths and buzzing flies. An old theatre, long closed and with boarded-up windows; a small building painted a faded mushroom colour with a sign that said *Kooralang Coal Mine Historical Museum*, the door of which was secured with a rusted chain and padlock. There was a church and a hall, whose abandoned appearances made their noticeboards advising of upcoming events difficult to believe in. Down the other end of the main street was a supermarket, and past it, on the far side of some paddocks, sprawled the powdered-milk factory where Ishtar worked, its black-streaked chimneys leaking smoke.

Walking down the street with Dan, stretching out my stride to match his, I felt for the first time in my life immune to the way people looked at me. And people did look. The town existed in a kind of parallel time-warp to the one at Hope; it was 1985 but it could have been twenty years earlier.

I had been jeered at for my clothes countless times in the past. I had been sent home from school with notes of concern or outrage from teachers — regarding my lack of proper footwear, the state of my fingernails, my hair. But in the main street of this small town with its meaty, red-faced farmers, its scrawny, wind-whipped farmers' wives, and bands of flannel-shirted youths, the tide of antagonistic attention was the strongest I'd yet experienced. Here our difference glared as if we were spot-lit, and the judgement was absolute.

When I was with Ishtar, or Miller and Ishtar, I slunk along, feeling the stares, hearing the whispers, wishing I was invisible. But with Dan it was different. Dan didn't care what people thought, and neither did I, because I was with him.

At the post office, he picked up shipments of records and copies of American *Rolling Stone*. I watched him, the flop of his hair as he bent his head, his long brown fingers on the square, shallow cardboard packages. Records. Mail order. America. All the vast potential of the world was in him. He brimmed with it. He was the exact opposite of everyone else at Hope, carping about nobody giving them a fair go, sighing and staring out at their imaginary crops and goats and freedom.

A little vision glowed in my mind: Dan climbing the stairs into a jumbo jet. It was his body mounting the steps but somehow I was inside it, looking out through his eyes. Sitting down beside one of those little oval windows, feeling the engines roar. Taking off into the sky.

One time there were some people visiting from India. They were staying with us for a while and giving talks at satsang and being taken round to all the other houses. There was a picnic in the park to celebrate there visit, it was funny because it was the same park where my mother had left me on the bench when Id first met Mira that day. Everybody sat round eating in the warm sun, someone played a guitar. It was just like it had been back then except now I was one of the group wearing my own silk clothes that fluttered in the breeze sitting on the bright patterned cloths eating the food that had smelled so strange and different. I wasnt looking in from the out side any more imagining what it might be like, I was there and suddenly I got a strange kind of sadness it was like homesickness but it wasnt about my old home or my parents or that life I had before. It was like I was homesick for a feeling, for the feeling Id got when I first saw Mira and the others the woman with the baby how theyd looked like freedom to me then. I hadnt realised I didnt feel that way any more. I smelled the top of Silvers head and kissed it because at least I had her. Back at the house in the kitchen Mira and I did the dishes. People didnt speak much, most things were done in silence but I wanted to know. Do you remember I said, That day in the park when I first — Yes, yes she said. She seemed annoyed. Well I said, There was a woman with a baby. Mira didnt answer she kept her head down scrubbing a pot. Do you remember her? Yes said Mira running the tap. From my room down the hallway I could hear Silver starting to cry. I waited but Mira didnt say any thing more. Well I said, What happened to her? Nothing said Mira, She was just one of a group of people who came along to our open meditations for a while. So she wasnt an actual member? Mira poured water from a pot and held it out to me. No she said. Lets get this done now before satsang. I took the pot and began to wipe it. Silver was still crying and I started to cry myself, I didnt know why. I dont think Mira noticed she didnt say any thing any way. In satsang I could hear my own voice in the chants but it didnt blend with the others like usual. During the meditation I watched the others secretly, the peace in there faces. We were supposed to forget our surroundings everything we could see hear feel, forget we even had bodies but how could I when I had to know what Silver was doing all the time be ready for if she woke up and cried and disturbed everyone else? All I could feel was my body my sore neck and shoulders how tired I was, the weight of the baby in my lap. I closed my eyes, the stiffness in my back felt like anger. None of them had babies they didnt have to worry about another person and get woken in the night they didnt have to feed another person from there own bodies. The teacher began the chant for the end of the meditation and I couldnt join in it was like my voice was gone. I wondered if the others could sense all my poisoned energy, I thought they probably could but there wasnt any thing I could do about it. Not long after that a new woman arrived and Mira put her in with me to share my room. But what if Silver cries in the night? I said, my voice too loud. Mira didnt answer just smoothed the cover on the bed. They werent actual beds they were mattresses on the floor. Mira smoothed the cover neatly and got up and went out. She didnt speak but I knew her answer, that I was thinking of myself too much and that wasnt what we were supposed to do.

Miller was probably only gone two weeks, but it felt longer. The days passed with no real difference, apart from the fact that I spent more of my spare time hanging round Hope — and Dan — rather than down at the creek. There was a feeling of lightness, of respite, and I'm fairly sure it wasn't just in me; the whole place seemed to breathe and shake out its limbs, and even the weather came good, sun steaming in the paddocks each morning, and the relentless wind dropping from time to time.

People stayed longer in the front room after dinner, smoking and chatting, playing cards and listening to records, presumably enjoying their freedom from the tyranny of Miller's grandstanding. Here, though, was where Dan and Ishtar came into one another's company, and this made me uncomfortable. I knew Dan liked her. I saw him watching her in the firelight; I caught the way the smile leapt to his lips if she spoke to him, the readiness of his response. This was unbearable — this dog-like devotion, and the indifferent way in which she fed it, allowing her light to fall on him so casually, so randomly. It was the only time I didn't like him. I wanted to stub out that eagerness, to crush it into nonexistence. It made me feel tired and old. *Forget about her*, I wanted to say. *You won't get what you want.*

There were a couple of big parties while Miller was away, lasting late into the night. I got up one Sunday morning to find the house sunk in sleep and Jindi alone outside, splashing nude in the outdoor bath, which had a mound of fresh ash under it.

'Silver!' she called through chattering teeth. 'The bath's on!' Her lips were blue, her skin blotched and goose-bumped.

I put my hand in; the water was only tepid. 'You'd better get out,' I said. 'You'll freeze.'

'But it's on — the fire's on.' She climbed out though,

shivering violently, and squirmed on the grass in a threadbare towel, yelping. After a while she quietened, and the plump soles of her feet showed pink with warm blood. At the sight of them and the beads of water drying on her legs, an unexpected fondness entered me and I lay down beside her. I closed my eyes to the morning sun and let her prattle away at me. There were tiny flowers in the grass, purple and white, their scent thin and elusive, but sweet.

For a long time it was the only brightness my love for her, it was the thing I held warm to myself against everything else the tiredness the loneliness the sick feeling in my stomach that came whenever I had a moment to think and wonder if what Id done was right. It was hard to even remember that feeling from that long ago first day at the park when it all started. It was hope I told myself, it was freedom but the words were as empty as the way I felt now at satsang. I had Silver though. Every chance I got I kissed her I squeezed her I looked in to her eyes and made her smile. When we went to bed she wriggled and laughed against me put her hand under my cheek and her face right up close so I could smell her sweet breath and I let her even though it kept us both awake. I let her because it was like it charged me it filled me up and all the lonely sadness of the day would be gone for a while. But then that changed too, it was like some thing soaked in and I couldnt protect either of us from it like it wore me down and got through to her. More and more when she needed some thing I was just so slow and tired it was like the air went thick and I could hardly move. I felt myself just staring with my empty face not answering or looking at her. She could walk now and some times she would come to me and hold onto my leg and Id just move on not trying to push her or any thing but the movement of my leg would knock her and she would fall and I wouldnt stop or go back because I couldnt, it was hard enough just wading through the fog to the next chore. And then one night came when I was so tired and everything had gone wrong during the day, Id tried to give a man a pamphlet in the city and he called me a stupid fucking hippie and told me to get out of the way then there was a problem with the buses and we were late back to prepare dinner and then I dropped a full bowl of cooked rice all over the kitchen floor. Silver was sick, I hadnt known that was why she was so strange all day wanting to climb on me and sit in my lap which she never normally did, moaning when I tied her on my back to get the bus. Then after dinner she vomited on the hallway rug. I put her in bed and went back to clean the rug then I had to wash out her clothes and the rags Id used and everything because they all smelled of vomit. Finally when I went in to bed she was still awake she must have been feeling better because she laughed and reached out her arms but all I wanted was sleep. I looked in to her face and no warm feeling came. I lay down with my back to her. She cuddled up to me and touched my hair but I lay like a block of concrete, there was this heavy sadness and some where deep under everything I wanted to break the spell to turn over and face her, it felt like an important thing to do but I just couldnt. I didnt move or make a sound and after a while she left me alone. And after that it was like some thing had broken and I couldnt fix it, I seemed to feel more and more tired like the love had been buried under the tiredness and every night I turned my back on her I lay there but I could never fall asleep because of the sad feeling I just lay listening to her breathing until she fell asleep. Turn around I told myself, kiss her love her but it was like I was paralised. Then once she had fallen asleep the guilt came and it got stronger and stronger and at last I would roll over and look at her sleeping face and I would cry and whisper Sorry, but I couldnt touch her not even then, even though all I wanted was to pull her little body close and kiss her hair.

I hit her once when she was about three. Three and a half, because it was winter it was after I moved to the second ashram right out on the edge of town. It was early morning and I was so tired, there had been a special teaching and dinner in a rented hall the night

146

before, raising money for a school or some thing. By the time we got back and cleaned everything up it was very late and when she woke me it felt like Id only been asleep for a moment. She stood up on the mattress and the covers fell off and I felt the wetness in the cold air, she had wet the bed and it had gone on me too on my clothes that Id fallen asleep in. I had nothing to wear my other clothes were at the bottom of a pile of dirty stuff in the laundry. She was crying quietly, she never made much noise once she grew out of being a baby. Under her nose was all raw and snotty she had a cold and she was just standing there with her arms held out her pyjamas soaked the pants dragging down. Crying with a tiny high sound like a dog whining. I got up on my knees and grabbed her arm and tried to pull her pants off tugging hard with my teeth clenched so much my jaw hurt. The pants got tangled round her legs and she fell onto her side right in the middle of the wet patch and she just lay without moving her pants around her ankles her legs bent, and some thing in the way she didnt even try to help herself brought the anger whipping out of me and I hit her on the thigh as hard as I could over and over the slaps loud my hand stinging. Across the room one of the other women stirred and I stopped. Silver crawled away a bit and curled up with her arms over her head and I sat with my hand empty across my lap, my own blood roaring in my ears. I never hit her again I made myself that promise and I kept it. Some thing opened up that one time a black hole that had no bottom and I knew I had to never do it again. Later when Id cleaned everything up and got her dressed and found my own dirty clothes in the laundry and put them on we went in to the kitchen and I started the breakfast even though it was early and no one else was up yet. She sat at the table waiting, she was so small she had to kneel on a chair and she had never looked so beautiful, the shape of her face her eyes so clear everything about her so pure and lovely I had to look away. I had made her and I had kept her and now I was ruining her. I put some yoghurt in a bowl and mixed in two big spoonfuls of honey more than we were supposed to use then I gave it to her and told her to be quick before the house mother came. She took the bowl and started eating but her eyes were wary.

Dan came back from work with a bike in the tray of his truck.

'Found it on the side of the road,' he said, lifting it down and propping it against the front porch.

It was tall and old, with a wide seat of cracked leather that still had a little tool pouch hanging behind, attached with miniature metal buckles fuzzy with grime and corrosion. Its frame under the rust was a deep green. There was something old-fashioned and dignified in its shape that made me think of the retired racehorses that lived on the far side of the Munros', which, despite their dull coats and jutting hipbones, occasionally broke from the shelter of a row of cypresses to go racketing in a stiff-legged mob across the swampy grass, pride in their still-beautiful high tails and arched necks.

Dan crouched beside the bike, head bent, hair licking at the back of his neck. His brown hands moved over the metal, brushing away dust and leaves, testing the moving parts.

'It's pretty rusted up.' He jiggled one of the pedals, which ground a couple of centimetres in each direction. 'Chain needs cleaning. And oil. But the tyres haven't perished. It's a nice old bike.' He looked up at me. 'What do you reckon?'

Late afternoons on the front porch, the bike upside down, the white walls of its tyres revealed through scrubbing — my job, wielding the bucket of hot soapy water, wringing out the rag with red fingers, a film of steam on my face — its smaller parts laid out on a grease-stained sheet, or soaking in a dish of soupy, browny-orange liquid. Dan kneeling, sleeves pushed back, cigarette between his lips, selecting a spanner from the flat container where they slotted tidily in order of size.

The smells, of fresh smoke and oil and the moist air that came sliding up from the creek. Crows rasping in the bush beyond the paddocks, black already below the streaky sky. Voices from inside and lights coming on, but out on the porch a circle of hush as Dan used a stick to lift the chain, glossy, dripping, from the oil bath and lower it into the rag I held out with both hands.

I don't recall being disrupted during those afternoons, although I'm sure we were — by Willow or Val, pausing on the steps to see how we were going; or, more likely, by Jindi, standing too close and talking too much. But those interruptions have not stayed in my memory. Only the unhurried calm in which Dan worked and I stood by, hoping for the gift of a task.

When it was finished, he put the seat — bearing its cracks, but clean now and softened with neatsfoot oil — down as far as it could go, and I tried to climb on. It was a big bike; my feet dangled above the pedals and I had to lean right over to reach the handlebars. I wobbled and tipped onto the grit of the car-parking area.

'Never mind.' Dan took it and readjusted the seat. He got on and bumped part-way up the drive and back. 'Not bad.' He threw me a grin then hefted the bike up into the tray of his truck. 'Come on,' he said. 'Let's see how it goes on the open road.'

We drove in the same direction the school bus went, past the Munros', and Dan stopped where the road went up in a long gradual slope before dropping into a steep hill. It was about six o'clock, the sun going down. The road shone. A battered ute popped over the peak of the hill and came drumming down past us, but then there was nothing, just the wind in the long grass.

Dan straddled the bike with his feet still on the ground. 'Come on.' He tapped the crossbar.

It took a couple of goes but then I was on, balancing, twisting to grip the middle of the handlebars. Dan shifted his position and I felt the power of our combined weight, the potential for it to swing too far, and my heart began to race.

'Hang on.' His voice was close. He pushed off and his body came forward, his arms either side of me. His chin scraped my temple. 'And keep your feet clear.'

I tightened my legs and felt the bike sway then settle into the regular beat of his pedalling. Up the slope we went, in steady strokes, the sounds of the chain and the tyres on the road smooth and reliable. Then we were at the top, and there was no longer that feeling of effort, of drag; Dan's weight shifted back, so I could lift my head a bit, and there were a few seconds of easy rolling before we slid into speed and the paddocks flattened into blurred lines of yellow-green, the fence posts blipping by faster and faster. My eyes slitted and I heard my shrieking and Dan's yells whipping away behind us. Down we swooped, and down — my fingers white on the metal, my legs stiff, my whole body braced. When we got to the bottom and the hum of the tyres eased back from their supercharged whirr, I realised I was laughing in loud, ragged gasps and there was a cold, wet trail from the corner of each eye back to my hairline.

We did it three times, walking back up after each one. Only a couple of cars passed us; they seemed to whizz by apologetically, as if aware that this hill, this close sky, the paddocks spread each side, this silvery-black stretch of road belonged, this evening, only to us.

When it got too dark we trudged for the last time up and back to the truck. My face felt raw; my grinning lips caught on my dry teeth.

The market stall was once a month. It was the only job I liked, out in the sun and people everywhere, different people not just the kind you saw in the city. Sitting there behind the bench all heaped with beautiful things and the racks of clothes like bright curtains either side some thing magical happened, I could forget what my life was realy like and almost feel the way I knew I looked wearing my special dress and my hair all smooth. I saw myself in peoples eyes when they came towards me how they wanted to be near me talk to me have me smile at them. I saw men looking and I felt the stirring of that power Id almost forgotten. One time there were some people working on the stall opposite. They were selling soap and candles. They were hippies, a man and two women and they had a van all painted and the man watched me all morning. It was hot and one of the women cut up a watermelon, I saw the juice drip dark in to the dust and I could smell it. The other girl from the ashram who was helping on our stall went off to the toilets and Silver crawled out from under the bench like a hungry dog. The man smiled then he brought two slices of the melon over and held them out. Whats your name? he said to Silver but she didnt answer just stared like she always did and grabbed the melon and gulped it like he might change his mind and take it back. Well whats your name then? His eyes were blue against his tanned skin they moved over me and I could feel my old strength coming back. I cant remember what we talked about, him standing with one arm over the rack of clothes but his eyes never left me and there was opportunity there and the heat in my skin hummed with hope and life and by the time my workmate returned there was a plan and I wouldnt look back.

I still went to the creek sometimes, when Dan wasn't around. But more and more I didn't have to go that far to find Ian — often he'd already be there, waiting just behind the fallen tree, or even closer, lying hidden in the overgrown grass part-way down on our side.

I accepted this unthinkingly, as if it was natural that Ian would fall in with my own changed pattern, would wait, ready, for whenever I felt like being with him. It did not occur to me that he might be put out by my preoccupation with Dan. I was immune to doubt, bursting as I was with keen and undiscerning fascination. The tables had turned: now I was the talker, and Ian the listener.

'Dan says Bob Dylan is the greatest songwriter of all time.'

'His favourite is Champion Ruby, but if he can't get that then he doesn't mind Doctor Pat's.'

'When Dan gets to New York, he's going straight to CBGB, that's a club, where all the best bands play. He's going to go there every night until he finds a band to join.'

'Dan says it's a drag getting up early, but sometimes the sky makes it all worthwhile, the dawn can be so pretty. He says every time he lifts another crate of asparagus, he thinks, *another twenty cents towards my ticket, another inch closer to New York.*'

I blathered on, conveying every minute detail, and Ian listened with an interest that, had I not been so blinded by my own devotion, might have surprised me.

I did feel bad when I took the money creeping through the morning dark carefully opening the cupboard feeling for the box, I knew they kept in it all the takings from the market. Youve worked hard I told myself, for more than three years, they owe you some thing surely. I didnt take much any way, I could have taken more there was quite a lot there. I got Silver from the bedroom she was still sleeping her head on my shoulder all hot and heavy. I had my old case packed, I went down the hallway without a sound, one thing Id learned after all this time was how to be quiet. Out in the cool air I sat on the low brick wall with Silver in my arms and the case by my feet. I felt like a husk had been stripped away. I felt strong and so much love for the world for the new sun pink in the sky. I could even feel love for the ashram I could look back and through all the work the loneliness the disappointment and see that still The Path had given me the chance to become who I was now, Ishtar. The van came chugging up the street and I stood. I lifted my case and felt Silvers weight and the love rushed even stronger for her it didnt matter what had happened before, this love was here for her now she was at the centre of it. Everything Id done had been for her and because of her and she would never know, I promised myself. Id turn things around and she would be loved and happy and never feel like a burden never feel blame.

It took two days to drive to the commune along the coast. We stopped and swam at beaches along the way and slept in the dunes. Randal and the women were brown all over, at first I felt embarassed about my white body that had been kept in side for so long but Randal didnt mind, he swam up and touched me in the water. At night when Silver was asleep wrapped in a blanket and the other two women lying talking by the fire he led me to the van. There was a mattress in the back. My head was heavy from the joint we had smoked, my first one and I kept wanting to laugh and had to try not to because I didnt want to not be cool in front of him. We took off our clothes and kissed and touched each other and it was amazing after so long to do those things again it was actually much better than I remembered but every time we got close to doing what he wanted I stopped him, Id learned enough by then to know that was how you got a baby. Arent you on the pill? he said. What pill? I said. He laughed. Sister you need educating he said. He lay back and I stayed sitting up I could feel him watching me my outline in the faint light and I arched my back. After creeping round the ashrams for so long being nobody it was so good to be noticed. Come on he kept saying. No I said, I realy cant. Everything was slow from the pot but still some where I felt fear, he was strong he was older he could just make me. He reached up and put his hand to the back of my head but it was gentle, he guided me down. Okay then he said, I will show you some thing we can do.

One afternoon I went up the hill to the tree and Ian wasn't there. Not sure I could be bothered going any further in search of him, I stayed where I was, leaning over the top of the silvery-smooth trunk to look down on Hope. I'd thought Dan was out, because his truck hadn't been there when I got home from school, but as I watched I saw him appear on the kitchen steps, standing with one hand tucked into the opposite armpit, smoking a cigarette. I was about to go running to talk to him when I heard a sound off to one side of me. It was Ian. He was lying in the grass not far away, propped on his elbows with the camera pressed to his face.

As I watched he took a rapid round of shots, the clicks and whirs tumbling over each other, his thumb stabbing aggressively at the winder. I could see the jut of his shoulders, the tense, focused straining of his whole body as he aimed down the slope at Dan. Then he did a little forward wriggle, his pointy bottom lifting for a moment and showing level with the grass, and I got a sudden sense of being the accidental observer of a private moment. I turned away. The view in the opposite direction was of what everyone at Hope called the back paddocks — the land that ran from behind the mud-brick building alongside the hill to the section of the creek bank that was full of blackberry. There was blackberry in the further back paddock, too, a ragged dark island of it right in the middle, and beyond, near the fence line, a half-collapsed shed. I'd gone there only once. Near the shed was a pile of grey bones — the remains of a cow, or maybe a horse; the skull was big and long-nosed. They lay in a patch of bald dirt, in a trough-shaped depression that had made me imagine the animal dying, raking at the ground with its hooves, stretching its neck and rolling in terror.

Unease slid, cold, through my belly. What was Ian doing?

I didn't want to turn around. Just like at night when a coat hung on the back of a door becomes a figure about to slip down and spring towards the bed, I began to imagine that the person writhing in the grass behind me, all hungry angles, oblivious to everything but his target below, wasn't actually Ian but some monster, nightmare version of him.

I heard the kitchen door bang. Dan must have gone back inside. Maybe half a minute later there was a peripheral movement, a swishing of grass, and the settling of another body against the timber beside me.

'Hello,' said Ian, and when I turned it was the regular old him, of course, but there was a pink, wind-stung guiltiness to his face.

I looked away again. 'Hi.'

We leaned side-by-side, chins propped on our arms. Down below, smoke rose from the chimney and was rubbed out by the wind.

For some reason Jindi's voice came into my head: *Is Miller coming back? Will you leave, too?* A terrible ebbing sensation came over me — as if the lightness of the past couple of weeks had been deftly, conclusively, punctured.

What had I been thinking, following Dan around? That he would somehow take my hand and guide me into a different place, a different life, magically throw the world wide open for me? Tears prickled, and I cast a low, sideways look at Ian. He held the camera part-way under his jacket, attempting to conceal it, and it was this pathetic, furtive act that brought rage scalding and bitter to the back of my throat.

'What are you doing?' I burst out. 'Creeping round like that, taking photos of people without them knowing?'

Ian went still. I could feel the shame coming off him, and embarrassment of my own made my lips feel numb. But I gritted my teeth and waited.

When he spoke his voice was strained, trying for breeziness and failing. 'It's a *science*, my friend. Have you not heard of anthropology? The study of *peoples*? I am merely taking an interest in the rituals and traditions of a particular *type*. The hippie.' He threw out his hand, open-fingered, but kept his face averted, the smile on it stiff and awful.

I couldn't look at him, wretched ridiculous scarecrow. I hated him for making me feel pity when I wanted to be angry. 'Well whatever you're doing, just stop, okay. It's weird. And wrong.'

At the last word his smile came unstuck. His lips drew closed, trembling, and he seemed to shrink in on himself, his shoulders like folded wings through his jacket. He gave a long, shuddering sigh and adjusted the strap around his neck. 'I know,' he said, and his voice was so completely miserable that the pity won over the anger, and I found myself clapping him brusquely on the arm.

'It's all right,' I said. 'It's not that much of a big deal. It's just a bit weird.'

He stood with his head lowered, drooping.

I tried to touch his arm again, but he drew away as if wounded. Why was he so upset? I felt myself blinking into a great void of confusion, at the edges of which something — some dawning understanding — hovered.

'What's the matter?' I said, but he had turned and was marching away, up and over the crest of the hill.

Things weren't the same after that. Some kind of rupture had occurred, and the half-sensed reason for Ian's behaviour that day went on bumping with gentle persistence at the edge of my consciousness. I tried gamely to ignore it, to claw my way back into the thoughtlessness of the previous couple of weeks. Ian continued to appear at the fallen tree, but without his camera. We went to the creek together and did all our usual stuff, and I was glad to fall into the safety of this, full of an oddly powerful sense of gratitude to him for going along with me in pretending nothing had happened.

My crush on Dan felt different now too. I still had a fervent interest in him, but it was interspersed with far more moments of excruciating self-consciousness, when I saw myself as an annoying, desperate loser — or worse, creepy, like Ian squirming on his belly in the long grass. Through force of habit I'd seek Dan out in the places I knew I'd be likely to find him alone — chopping wood, or working on the engine of his truck — and plunge into my litany of questions. Where would he live in New York again? Did it hurt his back lifting crates of asparagus all the time? How long had he had his truck, and where did he get it from? Then the seesaw would tip, and I'd be caught in the beam of my own awareness and, stinging with shame, scurry away.

At school I wrote my answers to the activities Mr Dickerson set us, my pencilled letters round and even; the dots over my 'i's careful, miniature circles. My good marks continued, but the couple of times I didn't get a perfect score there was more than my usual feeling of irritation — I churned and fizzed with a restless sense of failure that took a long time to dissipate.

'Hey Hippie Shit!' a kid yelled as I got on the bus after school. 'I can smell yer from here!' I went on climbing the steps with my usual show of indifference, but once safely in my seat surprised myself with a spray of tears, which I hid by leaning against the window and pressing my face into the crook of my arm.

Softening winds sent the half-grown lambs in the paddocks lining the school bus route bucking and plunging, and there was a similar wildness to the mobs of uniformed kids that covered the oval at lunchtimes, hair aflutter. Everything seemed to be leaping with life, taking off. But I felt assaulted; I wanted to anchor myself with repetition, to take shelter in secure, static zones.

I did my best, retreating into books, into my tidy rows of correct answers at school, my test papers marked with tick after tick in Mr Dickerson's red pen, into the world of the creek that was so reassuringly constant and indifferent.

When we got to the commune one of the first things I did was ask one of the women to help me get the pill. Bet, the woman was called she took me to a doctor in a town nearby, it was a doctor she knew was cool. The girl in the chemist made me think of Evie Dyer folding over the paper bag and pushing it across the counter not looking at me. I smiled at her any way. At the commune I learned how to make soap and candles. There were other children, Silver played with them a bit but mostly she wanted to be near me. It was easier there than in the ashrams to have her around, there werent so many rules and more women to help with the cooking and things like that. I slept with Randal in his hut Silver slept there too. After dinner I would put her to bed and lie with her face to face how we used to and we would whisper together for a while and then once she was asleep I would go back out side and sit with the others round the fire. We smoked joints and some times there was LSD then it would be a real party, often it would go on all night and in to the next day, we wandered through the paddocks and scrub we lay naked under the stars or swam in the dam we made up songs and dances and did shows for each other and for the kids if they were awake and they did shows for us. Silver never joined in but I think she liked watching. There was never much money all mine was gone. Someone told me about a new pension for single mothers but I didnt know how to get it, I worried they might want information I didnt have like my birth certificate. Some of the others were on pensions some of the men worked jobs in the town or for farmers and there was the money from the markets and we grew vegetables and traded what we didnt eat ourselves. There were other groups of people like us in the area some had milking cows or beehives. Everyone just put in what they could to buy what we needed. At first it felt good being Randals woman. I loved when he sat with his arm around me like I belonged to him, even when we went some where and he left me waiting with the van I didnt care if people stared, when he came back I hoped someone would see who I was waiting for, my man. He was kind to Silver and it took a long time but she started to like him. In the mornings she would crawl up from her little mattress at the foot of our big one and get in with us. At first she would only lie on the out side edge beside me then eventually she started climbing in to the middle and we would all laugh and tickle or me and Randal would wrap our arms around each other and squash her, the Silver sandwich we called it. How about you stop taking the pill? Randal said. We could make a baby. It seemed crazy after all I had gone through but I got this little thrill of excitement when he said it at the thought of him wanting me that much. I kissed him and said nothing I tasted the thrill I enjoyed it I even imagined the baby that would make us properly in to a family, it would be a boy I thought with eyes like Randals. I didnt stop taking the pills though, I wasnt that stupid.

Then Miller came back, and he brought with him a woman. I watched her being taken from the car — Miller bending, one hand at her elbow, another at the small of her back. It was the exact opposite of how he handled Ishtar, grabbing, squeezing, lifting her bodily. This woman he treated as if she was very old, or somehow breakable.

Slowly she emerged from the passenger seat, blinking, her small, white hand laid over his in a way that made me think of old-fashioned pictures of people at dances, in ballgowns and suits, wearing gloves. She was little and wispy, with dandelion-silk hair. Her clothes were dark, black and grey, her legs twig-like in close-cut slacks. She fumbled in the pocket of her coat and took out a pair of sunglasses, which she raised with trembling hands to her face.

'Come in where it's warm,' said Miller, his voice smooth.

'So,' said Val later, in the kitchen. 'A wife.'

'In name only.' Ishtar scooped a cup into the big rice jar and then poured the grains into a saucepan.

'He's full of surprises, isn't he?'

'I knew.'

A snort from Val.

'He's never hidden anything from me.'

Val's eyebrows went up. 'Don't tell me you're still holding out for your money.'

Ishtar didn't answer. She measured more rice, her face as strong and unyieldingly beautiful as always.

Miller's wife was called Dawn, and she mostly stayed in the mud-brick building. He spent a lot of time there with her, and took out her meals. She was, he said, recovering, although he didn't say from what. Sometimes he cooked for her himself, scooping eggs from boiling water. He tucked a tea towel into the front of his pants, and sang songs in what sounded like Italian or French, the rounded, trilling notes cramming the air, sliding off the steamed-up window.

His apparent devotion to Dawn — or at least his commitment to feeding her — didn't stop him from continuing to grab Ishtar whenever he got the chance, or from burying his face in her neck with smacking kisses.

'Be patient,' I heard him whisper. 'Wait for me.'

She let him touch her, her body pliable in his grasp. But her face was set, and her arms didn't go round him in return. When he asked her to wait, she looked away and sighed.

A woman came she had a little boy who was about four, a bit older than Silver, she slept in the hut I thought of as the mothers hut. A few women slept there they were older and had a bunch of kids between them and they always had things to say at the group meetings, everything was a heavy trip for them and they were always asking others to lighten there load. I kept away from them as much as possible. They gave me a bad feeling. Then the new woman came she wasnt as old as them but she had a thin face and lines at the sides of her mouth and between her eyebrows, everything about her was lean and hard. Her kid had some thing wrong with him he couldnt talk he screamed a lot and still wore nappies he was only satisfied when he was sitting with a bucket scooping up water in a cup and pouring it out again over and over. Someone told me he was obsessed with water and his mother had to watch him every moment because hed just go for the dam or one of the water troughs and she was terrified hed drown. At night round the fire she sat with him held against her with her arms so tight around him she seemed to have to almost crush him to make him sleep. She sat with him like that she didnt join in the talk. Her face frightened me I tried to sit away from her on the other side so I couldnt see through the smoke and flames. Then one morning I saw her with Randal they were standing by his van the kid was a little way off under a tree with his bucket and cup pouring water. Randal had his hands in his pockets and his head down and she was realy having a go at him, I could almost see the words pelt out of her. She pointed her finger at the kid then she put her hand over her eyes. Randal took money from his pocket he counted it and gave her some. She waited with her hand out and he gave her more. She took it and walked away. Randal got in the van and drove off. I think I knew already, the kid had those bright blue eyes like the ones Id imagined for our baby the same colour exactly.

I didnt say any thing to Randal, I went to one of the mothers and she told me. I felt sick. The woman left the next day and took the kid with her but still I couldnt forget. I waited for Randal to say some thing but he didnt he acted completely the same like nothing had happened. I waited and a month went by and another month. Randal said again I should go off the pill. Then one day he asked why I was being so cold why I was bringing him down so much. I didnt answer. I thought if he doesnt know then some thing is realy wrong. His child his own flesh and blood and him doing nothing to help just handing over a bit of money like thats all he owed her. We went on a markets tour, him and me and Silver up the coast sleeping in the van. Every night he went out, some times he didnt come back until the next day. I always had to stay with the van because of Silver but then one time it was in a town with lots of hippies and there was a festival that went in to the night. Randal went off and left me with the stall and some thing changed in me. It got late and Silver fell asleep under the trestle table. I had to pack everything up by myself and put it in the van. I got the legs of the trestle in but I couldnt lift the top by myself, it was supposed to slide in under the mattress but it was too heavy for me and I had to leave it on the ground. I tucked Silver in and closed the doors then I went to the toilet. There were people everywhere there was a big stage set up and performances all hippie stuff, puppets and things people singing songs from Hair, the usual. I was so angry with Randal I felt like my anger carried me along like the crowd parted before it. I thought I saw him sitting with a group around a little fire but I didnt bother looking properly I didnt care what he was doing or who he was with. The festival had been set up in a big park there was a sports oval next to it. I found the toilets under the grandstand. Someone had drawn breasts and arms with hair under them onto the figure wearing a triangle dress on the toilet door then crossed out Ladys and put Women. The toilets were filthy one broken and overflowing, no paper in any. I washed my face in the sink and I looked at myself in the mirror. Youre so beautiful said the girl next to me. She leaned over, her shoulder bumped mine and I saw she was tripping, the pupils in her eyes huge. Youre so beautiful she said again. I looked in the mirror, I saw what the anger did to my face how my cheekbones stood out my lips looked swollen my eyes huge. I smoothed down my hair then I went out side and looked for people to sit with, a joint to share, for a man to notice me. It didnt take long. When I went to get Silver it was nearly morning, I could hear birds. Randal wasnt there. I took Silver wrapped in a blanket then I took the money it was only the takings from the last night, thats all that was there, Randal had the rest. I carried Silver over the grass all covered with rubbish and sleeping people to the tent of the new man.

Ishtar had put her things back with mine in the Joni Mitchell room. She came to bed late and got up early — sometimes I couldn't even tell that she'd been there at all.

One afternoon I returned from school to find the door to the room closed, the muted burr of Miller's voice behind it, and then the answering ripple of hers. I took this as my cue to drop my bag in the hallway and head straight to the creek, and was part-way across the mean little rectangle of dirt and weeds at the bottom of the back steps when Dawn stopped me.

She was standing in the dark entrance to the mud-brick building, almost invisible in her black clothes. She didn't speak, but raised one of her hands and it caught at the edge of my vision. I halted in surprise. For some reason I'd imagined her asleep, curled there in the musty burrow of Miller's room.

I glanced around, tapped my own chest. '*Me?*' I mouthed.

She moved forward, holding the doorframe, lowering herself from the threshold. The hand went up again, the fingers fluttering. Her voice was barely audible. 'Do you mind?'

I went over and she took my arm. She wasn't much taller than me.

'Do you mind?' she said again. 'I'm not used to outside loos. I'm afraid of spiders.' There was something old-fashioned about her speech; it had the same clearly defined syllables as Miller's radio newsreader voice. 'Will you check for me?'

'Okay.' Together we walked to the crooked lean-to. Her arm through mine felt weightless. I swung the door open and went in and scanned the cobwebbed walls, checked under the timber seat.

'No spiders.'

We swapped places and she closed the door behind her. I hovered, wondering if I was expected to hang around, and then the door opened again and she came, carefully, slowly, down the step and took my arm once more.

'Come on,' she said, in that same insubstantial voice, and I found myself moving with her through the weeds and into the tunnel-like hallway.

A chock of discomfort formed in my throat and I glanced over my shoulder at the receding rectangle of light. What if Miller came in? But Dawn's feather-light arm, surprisingly insistent, guided me on.

In the room she settled on the bed, propped against pillows, and pulled a blanket over her knees, hands clasped regally. She closed her eyes. Her lashes were sparse and long, an ashy colour, white at the tips.

I stood by, feeling big and clumsy. With relief I saw that Miller's grotesque drawing was gone from the wall. Otherwise, apart from the absence of Ishtar's few belongings, the room was the same. Worse, in fact: now there were plates lying round, crusted with food, and cups and glasses in a similar state. There were chocolate bar wrappers, too — and my keen eye noted four pristine-looking Cherry Ripes lined up on top of a pile of books. A tall glass bong stood on the floor at the foot of the bed, its shaft stained misty brown. On the far side, past Dawn, was a square upholstered case like a sewing box, green with a pattern of flowers in metallic gold. It had a hinged lid that was open, showing a slippery-looking lining of deeper green and a confusion of medicine bottles and packets. Some appeared to have overflowed onto the floor, and on the side of the bed where I stood there was a bottle on its side with the lid off, a scatter of bright red pills like jewels in the half-light. One had been stepped on, crushed into a little pat of brilliant crumbles. Over

Miller's rank billygoat smell there was now a layer of chemical, powdery sweetness.

Dawn's eyes opened and she reached out to a second case that lay beside the medicine one: a small suitcase with the same glittery, quilted exterior and moss-coloured lining. She took out what looked like a book, bound in cream leather, and settled it in her lap. The teeth of a zipper winked at the object's edge, and Dawn's white fingers caught the tiny, dangling tag and drew it round. The thing was an album of some kind, with plastic pockets that had photos slotted into them. She leafed slowly through the pages and then stopped. 'Look,' she breathed.

It was a young woman, posed formally in a studio, a head and shoulders shot. The background was a simple screen, but there was something in the lighting and the quality of the image — as well as in the glossy lushness of the girl herself, her skin, hair, and clothes — that conveyed an impression of luxury, of expense. I had never seen a photo like this up close. How far away this portrait was from Ian's windswept gypsy-girl one of me, or from the ones taken at school with their perfunctory lighting, their messiness, their rows of bodies at mismatched angles.

I was so distracted by the aesthetic of the photo that it took me a few moments to realise that the girl in it was actually Dawn. She really was almost unrecognisable, the roundness of her cheeks shocking, her hair shiny and thicker, her eyelashes painted black and assembled into upward-sweeping spines. Over one of her collarbones a small clump of flowers was attached to her dress, the stamen of the central bloom dark and spiky like the lashes.

'Is that …' I knew it might seem rude, but couldn't help myself. 'Is that you?'

171

She made a jerky, nasal sound that I realised was a laugh. 'It's hard to believe, isn't it?'

I bent closer, my fascination pushing aside any worry about Miller coming in. It was astonishing that this vision, so creamy, so vital, smiling boldly up from behind its plastic sleeve, could be the same person who was cradling the album in her sunken lap, fingering the corners of it with starved-looking hands, the shape of her skull ghoulishly visible under the dandelion hair.

'And look. Our wedding.' Dawn angled the album to show the facing page, which was sideways, a landscape shot. A group of people stood on some stone steps in front of a pair of tall ornate wooden doors. That same shining younger Dawn was at the centre, wearing a triangular white dress that showed her stick legs, a band of flowers across the top of her head. Beside her was an almost-as-unrecognisable Miller, beardless, his exposed face ruddy and smooth, his hair cut very short, revealing unexpectedly small ears.

'He wanted to wear a suit of a more interesting colour,' said Dawn. 'He wanted pink. There was a beautiful pink suit in Georges, just beautiful, and a lovely shirt and tie to match, but I said, "Oh darling, with your colouring you'd be like a great big boiled lolly. Too much pink — too much!"' Her voice had risen into a lisping silliness and she gave a sobbing sort of giggle. 'I was always telling him he was too much.'

In the photo Miller's eyebrows looked thinner, and his eyes more prominent. The beefiness was there though, the solid, compact body, and those oddly delicate hands — one through the crook of Dawn's arm, the other cupped at waist height as if part-way into one of his gestures. The suit he was wearing was plain and dark.

'We can be a bit formidable, the three of us, Mum and Dad and me.' Dawn gave a feathery sigh. 'But really, it wasn't about whether it suited him or not. Really we wouldn't let him because we were worried about what people might think.' Suddenly she looked directly at me, with grey eyes that seemed to strain slightly from their sockets, the whites yellowed and splotched with blood vessels. 'Do you see the joke there? What people might think — what people might *say*.'

I gaped blankly, trying to come up with an appropriate response, but before I could think of anything she shifted on her pillows and brought her face closer to mine.

'To think we were so concerned about a *suit*, when only two years later I — would go — completely — *mad*.'

Her whisper sliced the air; her breath smelled of pills and I tried not to recoil. This lurch into close, hissing confession was unnerving. And her manner — she was like some monstrous combination of an Enid Blyton character and Miss Havisham. My urge to leave had returned, the feeling of fear at being trapped in this cave at the far end of the passageway — but at the same time there was a sense of perverse enthrallment, like the desire to stare at an accident of some sort.

My own voice was soft: 'What happened?'

She didn't say anything right away, and when she did speak again it wasn't clear if she was responding to my question or musing to herself. 'Mum was so cross with Miller. She said he hadn't been taking care of me at all, letting me get in such a state. I was simply exhausted, she said. All I needed was a good rest. But of course that just wasn't true, and she knew it.' She lay back again and gave a low, slurred laugh. 'How am I supposed to know what's real and what isn't when I'm surrounded by people who don't tell the truth, who pretend things never happened?' She was staring sightlessly up at the ceiling. 'I missed half of my last year at school. They were always getting in different doctors, giving me pills. I can't remember what it was like now, not to be a bit woozy most of the time. Nobody knew what was wrong. I didn't either. I had been all right. As a child I was fine — fine.'

Somewhere outside, a chicken abruptly began to announce the laying of an egg with arduous cries. I jumped, but Dawn didn't seem to hear.

'So of course it wasn't the first time, the breakdown. It was just that nobody ever knew about what had happened before, nobody except Mum and Dad. Not even Miller. That's why they settled for him you know. He wasn't from the right kind of family, but they were just glad someone would take me.'

I began to straighten up, to indicate that it was time to go.

But Dawn ignored me, her fingers moving in absent circles over the plastic pages.

'His family weren't there at the wedding. He hasn't seen them since he left home at sixteen. He finished school early, you know, because he was so brilliant. So brilliant.' A wan smile lifted her cheekbones. 'Oh, he could talk me right up into the sky, that man, till I was flying through the clouds. He wrote me poems. That was when we first met. I wasn't at the university, I couldn't go because I hadn't got my matriculation. Mum had found me a job, and I was doing quite well. I did get invited along to some of the university things though, by girls I'd been to school with. They invited me out of pity, I imagine, but who cares — I met him, didn't I?'

I could see her thin chest heaving, and had to drop my eyes from the sight of the smile stretching her face. Outside, the chicken had paused for a few moments but now resumed its laboured broadcast.

'I'd better ...' I stepped away from the bed, nodding towards the hallway. Dawn didn't look at me or respond. 'Okay then,' I murmured. 'Bye.'

So Randal was the first and Bert was the second. Bert who had been camping at the same festival but was from a different commune closer to Brisbane. The time with Bert shouldnt have lasted as long as it did, he turned out to be no good always jealous he frightened me in the end and I had to sneak away in the night. I took Silver back to the city after that, she was old enough to go to school. There was a group house Id heard about, only women. It was a safe place and I got a job in a milk bar while Silver was at school. The women were in to being powerful taking there own lives in to there hands fighting the system all that stuff. I went along with it for a while went to some rallies with them and the groups they held, consciousness raising they called it where they all sat around talking. I understood there ideas I respected them but I didnt feel like they could help me. You should go to university they said, Its free now. I was too embarassed to tell them I hadnt finished high school and even if I had stayed I wouldnt have got the marks any way, nursing was what my parents had thought I might do but I dont even know if Id have got in to that youd need to be better at reading and writing, they were my real problems. It felt strange to think back on that. It seemed so long ago and how funny to think my only troubles then were bluffing my way through English classes fingers crossed under the desk Id never be called on to read out loud. There was some thing in these women I was afraid of they were so tough they were always saying women could do any thing there was no reason why not, I didnt think theyd understand if I tried to explain about my reading and writing theyd be like my mother and just say I wasnt trying. Then I met somebody else he was a teacher and he played the piano. But some thing went wrong like always, I was starting to expect it even when things were so new and beautiful I always knew nothing that good could last. Towards the end he started saying things like We can do this its worth saving, but the more he said those things the less I was able to even try. Well he said, It seems to me you want this to end, this thing between us. I never answered I just started to pack. He was a good man and I still feel sad I couldnt make it work between us. The house of women had gone the group broken up so I went back to The Path for a while to the first ashram. There was nowhere else to go and I knew theyd take me in, they had to they had to always be kind and generous it was there basic rule. Mira wasnt there any more, nobody was from the old days and even the teachers had changed. That made it easier. There were a lot of things that were easier this time. I wasnt as scared of everyone I didnt feel like there was some thing wrong with me because nothing happened when I did the special meditations. I realised that I didnt need to work as hard as I had in the past as long as I contributed enough nobody could realy say any thing against me and if I needed time off to do things for Silver I just said I had to go and they couldnt do any thing about it. They didnt like it but they couldnt stop me they needed me too much to stir up trouble over an afternoon of missed work. Still I never slacked off I only took the time if there was some thing I had to do. I got a job at night cleaning offices, I thought I could save up but I didnt even know what for, I just wanted money of my own but more than that I wanted to work. I worked and worked all day for the ashram and then at night for myself, it was like my own meditation it took me out of myself it emptied my mind.

When I left Randal and went with Bert it took Silver a while but she settled in she started to make friends with other kids I think she liked it that I was happy again I started putting her to bed the old way, lay with her and whispered. I was open to her again because I was open to everything I was set on a new course and full of hope. But then when things went bad the same old gap opened up the weight came down on me the slowness I had nothing left over to give her I stopped touching her and kissing her I just couldnt do it. Then when we left Bert, packed up and ran off in the night and hitchhiked to the city I swung back the other way the heaviness lifted and the love came easily again but this time it was her that turned away. In the womens group house, even with the piano playing man when I was the happiest Ive ever been, she wasnt there with me she was holding some thing back she reminded me of a dog I saw once on a jetty with its ears tipped to the water showing through the gaps body all flat not trusting. She had learned to look after herself pretty well, I saw that when I compared her with other children some of them couldnt do any thing for themselves. She knew not to ask for much from me. Shes a good kid people would say and she was but I didnt feel proud, I never felt proud again like I had when she was just born. I hadnt made her good she just was because she had to be. Now it seemed impossible that she had ever been in side me ever fed from my body ever slept in my arms.

I'm not sure what made me willingly submit to another visit with Dawn. Boredom, maybe, or the car-crash fascination that had gripped me the first time. After only that first encounter I couldn't know, I suppose, what another might hold; perhaps she might show me something else from one of those beautiful upholstered cases, things from the past life that, beyond the confronting reality of her present one — grey, withered, piteous — held such a calm, understated, and intriguingly foreign glow of wealth and privilege. I thought of pearls and gold, of evening dresses. It's possible I also thought of the Cherry Ripes.

Whatever the reason, only a couple of days afterwards — again, in the late afternoon, Miller having driven off somewhere in the brown station wagon and Ishtar still at work — I found myself lurking near the mud-brick building and watching for her. Eventually she did appear, tottering out with surprising speed to take my arm. We enacted the same routine as the first time, me checking the toilet for spiders and then waiting uncertainly before being guided by her insubstantial yet strangely compelling touch down the tunnel of the mud-brick hallway and into the foetid room. I stood at my post by the bedside while she settled against the pillows and took up the zippered album. The chocolate bars, I noted sadly, had disappeared. Dawn made no reference to our previous encounter but simply began talking, starting, to my astonishment, at exactly the same place — the photograph of herself. As if the first time hadn't happened at all, we went through the whole thing again: the studio portrait, the wedding shot, the madness and breakdowns. Even the way in which she told it was almost exactly the same — some phrases were repeated, I was sure, word-for-word — and I recognised this time the tone of a

179

storyteller settling into the worn grooves of repetition.

The rustling voice rose and fell, and again she went from the reclining, dreamy reminiscence to clutching at my hand and pulling me down so she could hiss right into my face. I endured this, tuning in and out while nervously keeping an ear open to the hallway, until she got up to where we'd left off last time.

She was lying back, her fingers curled round mine, and I was half kneeling. 'They didn't want me to go with him again,' she said, 'to come here. Well, we go through this every time. Mum asks why he never visits me when I'm unwell, and when I say it's because he just can't stand to see me in those places and to feel so helpless, she says, "Yes, well, I feel that way, too, but I keep coming, don't I, because I know it's the right thing to do." They're so concerned, Mum and Dad, with what's the right thing to do. They simply could never understand someone like Miller, who allows himself to be led by his instinct, rather than by rules.'

She glanced at me and I gave an obedient nod.

'Dad says he's just after money, that's the only reason he keeps coming back. Dad really has a very poor opinion of Miller now — he won't even speak to him. He says he's a degenerate who thinks the world owes him a living. But what upsets me most is when he says that Miller never really intended to be a lawyer, it was just a ruse to make them think he was respectable. He *had wanted* to be a lawyer. He was *passionate* about the law. Or at least what he thought the law was. He thought he was going to be able to *effect change*.' An echo of Miller's speech-making voice entered hers, and she gave a weak chop at the air with her free hand. 'But then he became very disillusioned with the legal system. He had thought it was all about justice, about truth — but, really, more often than not it's about trickery, about pulling the wool over people's eyes. And that, you know, I think that broke his heart. Made him lose his way.'

My mind grated at this impossible image of Miller as some kind of vulnerable being, deserving of tenderness.

'Do you know,' said Dawn, 'I'd rather see him destitute and full of happiness than trudging in the door of that flat — which was pretty dismal, I have to say, even if it was in South Yarra — trudging in after a day in court, looking so … so *beaten down*. That morning, when he sold the flat, I sat outside in the car and I'd been feeling very worried, thinking, oh god what is Dad going to say about all this, but then Miller came back — and he'd signed the papers and he was just *beaming*, he was so full of excitement about moving up north, buying the land.'

She lay in silence for a while, and I eased my hand out of hers, hoping perhaps she'd finished. But she sighed and went on.

'I wish Dad hadn't been so mean, about the loan. It's not as if he needed the money. He just can't stand someone not doing exactly as he says — someone having ideas of their own. Even if the macadamias had been a tremendous success and Miller had paid him back ten times over, Dad still would have disapproved.'

Abruptly, she turned on the mattress and began clinking through the medicine case. Selecting a bottle, she tipped some tablets out into her palm and picked up a glass of water. I took the opportunity to have another look round for the Cherry Ripes, but there was no sign of them.

'But they can't stop me from being here with him,' Dawn went on, sipping and throwing back her head as she swallowed. 'I'm his wife. Dad threatened to cut me off, but I know he won't, Mum won't let him.' She returned to the album, the pages making plasticky sounds as she leafed through them.

'See?' she said. 'See how happy we were?'

In the photo, they stand against a backdrop of small, round-topped trees. Gone are the suit and the dress — they both wear jeans and t-shirts, although with the same stagey, unsullied look that set Miller apart from the farmers at the supply shed now — a crispness in the denim, a richness to the colours. Miller's hair has already begun to rise like one of the blobs of dough Ishtar sometimes set in tins on top of the hot-water boiler to perform their gradual, yeasty expansions. Dawn is still sleek and alive-looking — her mouth opened in laughter, her teeth showing, the sunlight turning her hair a bright platinum. Miller reaches across to hold one hand over her stomach.

'Don't we look happy?' said Dawn, her voice quieter than ever, the words coming more slowly.

'Yes, you do.' I allowed my eyes to lose focus on the photo album, and the pages became blobs of green and pink. I no longer felt afraid of Miller coming in and finding me there in his room. Nor was I resistant to hearing these things spoken in Dawn's dried-up voice. I had entered a kind of dream state. None of this could be real. The Miller I knew, who was so full of hidden menace, who changed all the time for no reason, speaking in different voices and descending unexpectedly to lift people into the air — and who had drawn those pictures of Ishtar's body being invaded so brutally by his rainbow explosions — this could not be the same man Dawn was speaking of. A man who had lost his way. How could anyone so huge, so loud, so terrifying, be *lost*?

Dawn slipped lower on the mattress and her head lolled.

I blinked and tried to gather myself. I felt incredibly weary, as if her weakness had been somehow leaching into me, transferred, perhaps, by that bitter breath. 'I'd better go,' I whispered.

The wind bit as I ran up the hill, joined the whoosh of my breaths to fill my ears. I welcomed it, desperate to shake off the dreamy feeling, to wake up. Ian wasn't at the log. He wasn't at the creek either, but I didn't mind. I crouched with my hands in the water until they lost sensation, and gulped air that made my lungs hurt. I jumped up and down on the spot and ran recklessly, dodging branches, until the blood stung in my face and my thawed fingers throbbed. After that I sat tucked into the base of a tree until a wallaby came, the nap of its fur dark and solid-looking, its ears swinging as it lengthened its neck.

Back at Hope I took an apple and a book and read in the front room until it filled up with people and it was dinnertime. And later, when I went to bed, I was able to fall asleep without much trouble.

I kept well away from Dawn after that, sneaking carefully any time I went near the mud-brick building. When I did see her again, getting into the car with Miller, it was from a distance; she had her dark glasses on and seemed once again a mysterious figure, unknown to me.

One dinnertime, in the usual chaos of everyone moving in and out of the kitchen, loading up their plates and carrying them off to the front room, Miller reached past me and I saw his ear. It was deep and shadowed within the sandy frizz of his hair, but small and neat nonetheless, and that young, eager, exposed-looking face from the photo popped into my mind. I saw him standing on the church steps with one hand part-way raised, and I heard Dawn's words — *lost his way* — and a strange pang of pity ran through me with the suddenness of an electric shock.

But it only lasted a moment — he straightened and went round to the other side of the table and, before helping himself to the dahl, shoved closer to where Ishtar stood by the stove in order to run his fingers up the back of her thigh and between her legs, and it was a relief to feel the regular current of my hatred take up again.

I wanted to get my licence so I could drive legally. I knew how to drive, Randal taught me so I could help on the long trips in the van. In the back of my mind I had the idea that if I saved up enough money I could buy a car maybe I could start a business on my own selling things at markets like Randal had, I knew how to make the soap and candles. I went to the place where they did the tests but they said I needed proper identification like a birth certificate or a passport. I just went back to the ashram and kept working, I didnt think about it for a long time. Then one Saturday morning I said I had an appointment, I left Silver with the house mother and I caught the bus to Toowoomba then another bus to my parents house. I didnt even know if they lived there any more but then I saw the car in the drive, the same car still. I stood across the road for a long time. The vacant block wasnt vacant any more, there was a whole house there it looked newer than the other houses on the street but it didnt look that new. That was when I realised how long it had been, seven years. My father had taken care of the car, it looked almost the same just a bit faded. There was a kids bike lying in the drive way of number fourteen, I wondered if he still lived there if that bike belonged to his kid but it didnt make me feel any thing much. I had never thought about him even when I saw things in Silver that didnt come from me I never thought of them as having come from him, like the parts of her that were different belonged to her only. It was winter and I had a coat on, I tugged it straight and did up the belt I smoothed my hair and crossed the road I went up the path without stopping and rang the bell. My father opened the door. He looked so old. He stared at me for a while then I said Its me, and he said Bloody hell and then he said my old name, it was strange to hear it after so long. Well what do you know? he said. Come in, Lindas on her way actually. I stayed where I was. What about Mum? I said.

Oh he said and looked around like he thought she might be hiding some where. Well … But then I heard a car, the slam of its door and heels clicking up the path and it was Linda. Sorry Im late she called, I had to catch up on a Biology prac and my lab partner didnt … Then she saw me. She froze and stared like my father had. Then Oh my goodness she said, Oh my goodness and she came forward and grabbed me and squeezed me close. She was taller than me she was so tall she smelled like shampoo and perfume she was like a grown woman in her long boots and a miniskirt, I would not have known her if Id seen her in the street. Look at you! she said. Come in, you girls said my father, Get out of the cold Linda, you havent got enough clothes on. I looked past him down the hall, I wondered where my mother was. Its all right Linda whispered, Shes not here. She took my arm and made me go in.

The house smelled the way it always had except sort of stale, the carpets looked like they needed a clean and the furniture was much shabbier than I remembered. We went in to the kitchen. My father tried to say some thing but he couldnt he got his hanky out and kept blowing his nose then he left the room. Mums sick said Linda. Shes in a hospice now, its cancer, she doesnt have long to go. In the light I saw the dark circles under her eyes, she was thin and I could see her collar bones under her shirt. Still it didnt seem real to me, I kept expecting my mother to come in to take off her hat to look at the floor and say What a mess what a state this place is in, to go to the cupboard and get out the carpet sweeper. It didnt seem possible that this house could exist without her. I will make some tea said Linda, So did Dads message finally get through? I said What message? He went looking for you said Linda, He went to Brisbane and waited in the city for those, for your ... people and he asked if they knew you, he took a photo to show and everything. He asked them to get you to contact us. I didnt hear I said. Ive been away. Oh said Linda, Have you left the, the ... are you no longer a member? She smiled, she looked so happy. I knew it! she said, I read this book on cults and it said that even highly intelligent people could be brainwashed but still I always thought — Its not a cult I said, they didnt brainwash me. Oh. She looked confused she turned to the bench. Its just she said, You were always so smart I could never understand why you just suddenly decided to go off and ... My father came back in then just as I realised. At first I didnt even feel angry I just couldnt believe it. I stared at him. My voice came out very quiet. You never told Linda? I said. Told me what? said Linda. My father put his hands in his pockets and then took them out again. Well he said, Your mother — Dont blame it on her I said quickly and the anger was there then it sprang up and hissed in my voice and they both went quiet. The kettle gurgled and switched itself off. I breathed slowly trying to calm my voice. I said, I came to get my birth certificate, can I have it please. My father stood there for a while then he said Oh. Then he said Yes, yes of course. He went out again to his study. What didnt he tell me? said Linda. I looked at her with her nice clothes and her shampooed hair her university classes her car, I thought about the damp room in the ashram where there werent enough blankets on the bed and it was always a bit too cold where I would get up in the morning to dress Silver in her second hand clothes and rush her down to school before a day of pamphlets or workshop, rushing back to pick her up then help prepare dinner and sit through satsang then put her to bed before rushing off to the other job. Linda said my old name. I looked at her. I could feel how hard my face was. Ishtar I said. What? My name is Ishtar. I thought of the goddess with her bow and arrow her strength her cruel beauty. Linda just stared. Then my father came back with an envelope. What didnt you tell me? Linda said to him. I took the envelope, I went towards the hallway then I stopped. Answer me one thing I said. Is she sorry for what she did to me? Has she ever said that? He just stood there. I didnt think so, I said. He started to cry then, he got his hanky out again. Maybe if she saw you he said. I went to the door. Wait called Linda, Let me drive you. I will catch the bus I said. Wait she called again, she ran after me, she stopped at the door. Its called Hillcrest, she called as I went down the path. The hospice, its in Rockville.

Miller went off with Dawn in the car quite a few times, and I heard one of the women report to Val that she'd seen them at the bank in town, and both women made knowing faces at each other.

Then one Saturday afternoon there was a low, meaty engine sound from the direction of the dirt road and someone gave a yell, and then everyone rushed out onto the porch in time to see Miller come trundling down the driveway on a blue tractor that blazed with newness, every bit of chrome dazzling, the paintwork spotless, even the zig-zagged treads of its giant tyres twinkling, black and fresh in the sun. From high in the seat he waved, jouncing and grinning, then reached to honk the horn.

Jindi shrieked and squirmed with excitement, and had to be held back from running down the steps and into the path of the huge contraption, which Miller guided, elbows wide, round the side of the house. Once released, Jindi ran after him, followed by Val and a small group of others. Ishtar, who had been one of the last to come out onto the porch, went back inside.

I was left with two women — Rita, Jez's girlfriend, and Sue, who often helped Val in the kitchen and who I'd once heard say about Ishtar that, 'she thinks she's the bee's fucken knees.' It had been Rita who'd reported on Miller and Dawn's activities in town. Now the two exchanged glances, and Rita said, 'So that's what they were doing at the bank.'

Sue grinned. She had a tooth missing on one side. 'Yeah,' she said. 'And now we know what he sees in her, miserable little scrubber that she is.'

'Oh she's loaded,' said Rita. 'Rolling in it. You can tell just by the look of her. And did you see the suitcases? I saw when he was carrying them in. All matching, and they've got her initials on them in little gold letters.'

I never got my licence. I hadnt realised there was a written test for it. I didnt bother trying, it cost money and I knew I would fail. I went to the pension office to ask about the single mothers pension and they said I had to be living alone not with a man. I tried to explain there were men at the ashram but I wasnt with any of them but they said Who pays for things where you live? I tried to explain. They said Are you the sole provider in the household? No I said, But — You need to be the sole provider they said. At the big bus terminal while I was waiting for mine I saw the bus for Toowoomba again. I decided to walk, my own bus wasnt coming and I had to get back I needed to get Silver from school.

I met some people at the markets. They were heading north they said, they were going to set up a commune and run a farm to support themselves. I should have known it would come to nothing the way they talked all these ideas but no real plan. Still I gave them my money put it in the pool for farming equipment for supplies, I guess I just wanted to get away. They came to pick me up, it wasnt early morning this time and I didnt have to sneak out I just said I needed to go and thanks. They came around lunchtime they had two cars and a van travelling in convoy. There was a nice house mother at that time, Kharna she was called. I liked her she was the only one I was sad to leave. She waved from the doorway, it was just her, everyone else was at work. She was an Indian woman she was a teacher as well as house mother so she wore the robes they were bright against her dark skin her palm pink when she waved. Silver cried and that surprised me she hardly ever cried she must have realy liked Kharna too. Dont cry I whispered, We are going to a new place some where good youll be happy. She twisted away her face close to the window looking back. We drove through the streets we drove along the highway and Silver fell asleep. Someone passed a joint and flying down the road with the sun through the trees I felt like my body was disintegrating in to particles to join with the world. I was released from work from the ashram all damp and quiet from the city from buses to Toowoomba it was a new start a new beginning it was like every one before and all the ones that would come after. I ignored the crawling pit of doubts, I leapt across and went rushing in to the light.

I woke to footsteps outside my door.

'What's going on?' came a voice, and there was an indistinct reply. Then I registered properly the other sound, which was already there, writhing faintly in the black of my sleep, and had now increased in volume. Someone was screaming, a dreadful, thin sound, breaking off every now and then into speech, which was stabbing, accusatory. There was a second voice too, lower, lapping in long, deep, soothing strokes — Miller's.

The space beside me on the mattress was empty. I got up and went out into the hallway.

The screaming was coming from the front room — Val and Gav and Sue were clustered at the doorway, looking in, Val and Sue both in shapeless men's pyjamas, Gav's hairy white calves poking from the bottom of a robe. The purplish-blue blanket that hung in the doorway had been torn down and lay in a puddle between the feet of the onlookers, and Miller, Dawn, and Ishtar.

'Let go of me!' Dawn was shrieking. Her thin arms were raised, bare and shockingly pale, her tiny fists clenched. She had some kind of nightdress on, flimsy and short — her legs thrashing as she struggled against Miller's grip. 'Let go!'

'Dawn, Dawn.' Miller drew her to his chest, which I saw now was bare, furred with a shorter layer of the same coppery fuzz that grew from his head. I glimpsed also his muscled thighs — he was either naked or very close to it.

'Let go of me,' sobbed Dawn. Then she sagged in his arms. Her breaths were loud and rough.

'Dawn, darling, it's all right, you've had a bad dream.'

'What dream?' Dawn threw herself sideways. 'I wasn't dreaming! I saw!'

'Dawn, please, you mustn't get upset.'

Dawn made another effort to get out of his grasp, lunging towards Ishtar. When she spoke again the words crackled like water in a hot pan: 'You bitch, you slut, you get away from here and don't come back. Worming your way in while I was lying there ill.'

Ishtar had her back to me, the glimmering flesh of her shoulders visible each side of the veil of long hair. She had something wrapped round her — it looked like a man's shirt; I could see one of the sleeves dangling — and her legs were also bare below it.

'No, no, darling,' Miller was saying. 'Nothing happened, you imagined it, you were dreaming.'

Dawn's fingers raked in Ishtar's direction. 'Come here,' she said, 'just let me get my hands on you, let me have another go at that face. You think just because you're beautiful you can get anything you want? You think you can have my husband, right in front of me?' She fell back again, sobbing, and when Miller — who, I saw before I had a chance to look away, was completely naked — began to guide her towards the doorway, she let him. Gav, Sue, and Val made room for them to pass, and I crept quickly back to the dark safety of the Joni Mitchell room and into bed. I left the door open though, and watched — through slitted eyes, to protect myself from the full sight of Miller nude — as they passed.

'I couldn't find you,' Dawn was saying. 'I woke up, and —'

'Shh, shh.'

'Don't you shush me!' She resisted for a moment, pushing back against him. 'I know what I saw. Don't think I —'

'Come on now, let's get you back into bed. You shouldn't be out in this cold.'

He got her moving again and they passed out of sight and

hearing. Soon afterwards there were more footsteps, and Gav and Sue appeared. 'Wow,' said Gav. 'Heavy shit.'

Sue giggled, a rising, frothing sound.

'Oh shut up, you two,' came Val's voice. 'Come on, show's over. I'm going back to bed.'

There was a bit more shuffling back and forth, and then all went quiet.

I lay awake for a while, waiting, but Ishtar didn't come in. She must have gone to sleep in the front room, on the mattress there.

The next morning she was in the kitchen as usual, putting out plates and bowls while Val stirred the porridge. She had her hair pulled round to hang over one shoulder, and I saw that under it there were two long scratches down the side of her face, a dark crumb of dried blood near the top of one of them.

Sue and Gav, sleep-bleared, made no mention of what had happened. I saw glances sliding round though, and Val, leaning at her station against the sink, had the look of a teacher keeping order.

Eventually the room cleared, leaving me, watchful over my bowl of cold porridge, Ishtar, and Val. Ishtar ran the tap, pushing back the sleeves of her jumper.

Val seemed to be about to say something, but then the door opened and Miller stepped in. Val looked over at me, shrugged, tucked her chin under in a disapproving kind of way, and left the room. A moment later a protesting squawk came from the hallway — Jindi — and then Val's growl: 'No, you can't go in there.'

Ishtar glanced over her shoulder. 'You'll miss the bus, Silver.'

I stayed where I was, staring down at my porridge, half

expecting her to follow up, to order me to leave. It didn't happen though, and then I was stuck, wondering if I wanted to hear what they were going to say after all.

'I'm sorry about last night,' began Miller. 'Poor Dawn, she gets confused. Her moods are very fragile. And sometimes she misunderstands and then she gets herself in such a state —'

'You said she was all right with it.' Ishtar's voice was barely audible above the slosh of water — she hadn't stopped washing the dishes. 'With us.'

Miller moved closer, put a hand low on her back. 'She's like a child. One day she understands something, the next day she doesn't, she's forgotten, it's gone.' The hand moved up, the fingers in her hair. 'But it doesn't matter what she knows or thinks. What matters is us. We've got the tractor now, just think what we can get done with this place. There's still time to get crops in for this season.'

Ishtar scrubbed and rinsed, and put the dishes in the rack. Her reddened hands shone under frills of bubbles.

Miller's voice dropped. His fingers moved in her hair like baby rats in a nest. 'She won't always be here, you know. She'll manage a bit longer under my care, but then eventually she always needs to go back. Last year she was in hospital five months.'

Ishtar's elbows kept up their in-and-out gliding and the pile of dishes rose.

'Ishtar?'

I wished I had left the room when I had the chance. Now everything was so quiet I didn't dare move.

'Ishtar?' Miller's woolly head nuzzled at her. 'If it's about the money, I can get it for you.'

'When?' Her voice was like something dragging over gravel.

'In a month.'

'All of it?'

He pushed her hair aside, kissed her neck. 'Of course.'

She stopped doing the dishes and turned towards him, her wet hands held out from her sides. She kept them there as he crawled his kisses up along her jaw and to her mouth. Her body stayed stiff, but when he got to her mouth her eyes closed and her head went back, yielding.

I slipped out of my chair and crept away.

So there was that try at a commune and then a different one and another man and then some one else and then back to the ashram again for a while. On and on. Maybe you could say at first I was young and silly but by the time Miller came along I should have been old enough to know better. You would think I would have learnt some thing over all those years but now here I was at Hope and in a worse situation than ever before you could almost laugh it was so predictable. Some times I could just about hear my mothers voice saying I knew youd end up coming to nothing having no pride being taken advantage of there was always some thing wrong with you. Nothing to laugh about there. And nothing to do but keep going.

One morning I was hanging up washing and I felt someone standing behind me. It was her, Dawn. It had been a week but she remembered, maybe she wasnt as crazy as Miller said. Why are you still here? she said in a whispery voice, I told you to leave. I didnt turn around I kept doing the clothes but my heart started thumping. Youll leave if you know whats good for you she said, I dont know what hes promised but I can tell you absolutely right now you wont get it. Her voice was so soft I wondered if I was imagining it but I looked quickly while I was bending to the basket and she was there like a skinny stick swaying in the wind. Hes wilful she said. I expect it I expect him to be led by his passions. He has all these silly ideas and some times he gets other people involved. And I let him go. But only so far. She came closer she was right behind me. I turned around and stepped back. She had her hand up and I thought she was going to go for me again but she had it curled like she was holding a leash. He will always come back to me she said in that whispery voice. He is my husband, mine. I was watching that hand so I hadnt seen what was in the other one and it was only when Miller ran over and grabbed her and picked her up and carried her away that I saw it there fallen in to the long grass, one of the kitchen knives. He took her to there room and I got the knife and went and put it away. My hands were shaking and I had to walk to my room and sit down but it wasnt because of Dawn and the knife it was because I needed to think. It was hard to get my mind properly working because I felt so sick and all I wanted to do was lie down and sleep but that was nothing to do with what just happened either. I knew the real reason, the signs had been there for days now but I just couldnt believe it could be true. And for it to happen then when I was so stuck all that money gone and Miller promising and promising, and staying not because I believed him but because I just couldnt face starting again with nothing.

Later he came and found me. Im so sorry he said. Shes never been like this before. Shes asleep now. I dont think shes been taking the right pills. He sighed and sat down beside me. Poor Dawn he said, and his voice sounded all choked. There was hope for us once, long ago. There was going to be a baby. But then she lost it and ... He wiped his face and sat there for a minute blowing like a horse. Then he cleared his throat and rubbed his hands slowly together. Hed remembered what he came for now he was doing that thing where he acted like he was my father a wise old man who knows best. Ishtar he said, I think you need to be some where safe until the coast is clear again. He touched my cheek. I am going to have to hide you away my precious jewel. He was whispering even though there wasnt anybody else around. It was so funny now to see the tricks he used making me feel special, well it would have been funny if I didnt feel so stupid for falling for it all this time. He held up one finger. I have an idea. And remember its just till shes gone again. Can I show you? We went to his car he drove out the drive and then partway up the dirt road and turned off. Id seen that entrance before, it was just a gap in the bush no gate or any thing. I hadnt realised it was a little track. The car hardly fit, branches scratched down its sides. We bumped along around some bends and then he stopped again. There was a house there, a shack hardly standing up. We got out and went over to it. Everything was so quiet just birds and that sound trees make like breathing. Its an old miners cottage said Miller. There are a few of them round here mostly derelict. This ones not too bad, looks to have been inhabited until quite recently. He pushed open the door. It was a wreck, there was some furniture but it was all broken and covered in dust there was rubbish everywhere it stank like possums holes in the floor there was just one main room and another tiny one no kitchen no bathroom. I saw myself through my mothers eyes then how low Id fallen and taken poor Silver with me. Miller lifted up a chair that was on its side and tried to bang the dust off it. I will fix it up for you he said. He knelt down and took my hands. I will make it lovely for you my queen. I knew he wouldnt. It was strange to think how it used to be me always looking up to him how he was like the sun dazzling me filling everything how just the sound of his voice made me feel like all my joints had come undone. And now here I was the one looking down on him kneeling. He pushed his face against the backs of my hands he licked my knuckles. Please he said, It wont be for long. All right I said. Just until you pay me back. One month. He grinned up at me then he started undoing my jeans. Full of secret power thats how I should have felt but I didnt. Or angry that he thought I believed him that I was so dumb such a sucker. But I was so tired and even though under the fog there was an idea coming for a way out I felt scared I felt like I was seventeen again and suddenly just like a voice said it in my ear I heard my old name. Miller pushed me onto the filthy chair and my breasts hurt when he sucked at them, I looked up at the cobwebs strung like ropes I swallowed down on my sick fear and waited for him to finish.

'We're moving,' was all Ishtar said.

I was horrified when I first saw the place. Cold, stale air. Thin light from a small, dirty window. A low roof, close walls, all made of the same dark timber. Broken-off floorboards leaving long holes. Rubbish in drifts — newspapers, old beer cans with the colour gone. Rusted springs leering from the torn seat of a chair.

'We won't be here long,' she said, dropping her bags on the floor. 'A month.'

'And then will we go back to Hope?'

'Probably not.'

'Where, then?'

But she had moved away, gone into the other, tiny, room, where the rasping of a broom started up.

Miller, who had brought us there in the car, stayed — much to my relief — for only a minute or two. He strode around tapping on the walls. 'Beautiful timber,' he said. 'Local hardwood, last a thousand years. And see this craftsmanship?' He ran a hand along the place where the mantel, which had names and swear words gouged into it and was scattered with empty cans, joined the wall. 'Absolutely superb. You won't see skill like that these days.'

Ishtar moved round him with the broom, collecting mounds of rubbish and pushing them out the door. At one point he made a grab for her, but she sidestepped and went on sweeping.

'Won't take us long, will it?' said Miller. 'To get the place in order.'

Ishtar said nothing. She took a cushion off the rickety little couch and swept underneath it.

Miller rocked up onto his toes and back. Then he went out to where the ghost of the little house's long-ago garden glimmered in rose briars and thickened fruit trees and a patch of weedy grass, bright against the background of silty bush. Round he paced, hands clasped behind his back, as if doing some kind of official inspection. Soon he moved out of sight, back along the track to where the car was parked, and after a few moments there were the sounds of the engine starting and him driving away.

'Who's going to live here?' I said to Ishtar.

She raised the broom and began knocking the cans off the mantelpiece. 'Us.'

'You and me?'

'Yeah.'

'And Miller?'

She paused for a moment. Her skin looked strange, moist — I thought of damp clay with its muddy smell. 'No,' she said. 'Just us.'

'Why?'

She shrugged and swept the cans into a rattling pile.

'Is it because of Dawn?' My ears were getting hot.

'What do you mean?'

I had a teetering, dizzy feeling. I thought back to the kitchen the other morning, to the way she had told me to go or I'd miss the bus, but then hadn't made me leave. There was some kind of rule there, I knew, to do with listening but pretending not to understand — and now I was breaking it. I swallowed. 'Because she's his wife?'

Ishtar looked at me. 'Yeah,' she said, the word descending between us. Then she went back to sweeping.

It was Dan who came to help, that first day. He brought lengths of scrap timber that he sawed to fit into the holes in the floor. He went off again and found a camping stove and spirit lamp at the op shop, and a card table and a couple of chairs, and rigged up shelving with bricks and planks. He stuck a broom up the chimney and shook down a hail of black dust and cinders. He brought milk crates and more timber to make beds for us, topped with mattresses also from the op shop. I heard Ishtar offer him money, but he said no. He brought a bucket for getting water from the creek and a shallow tin tub for us to wash in, standing up, like they had at Hope that time.

At first I kept my distance, stepping round the edges of their busyness. This was much worse than Dan's adoring eyes at dinnertime. Here he was rushing round like some pathetic servant while Ishtar barely spoke to either of us, but went on grimly working, her expression remote and closed. And why were they doing all this anyway? The place was a ruin. Why didn't we just leave, Ishtar and me? Why did she always treat me like this, never protecting me from anything and then when I tried to enter her world, to ask about things like I just had, slamming down a shutter?

I went to the creek for a while, following a trail that sloped through the bush. It came out near a big wattle, which was the place I'd met Ian that first time. But Ian himself didn't appear, and eventually I got bored and went back.

Dan was outside, cutting a plank of wood that he held in place with one knee on a tall stump. The panting of the saw echoed round the clearing. He had lit a fire to burn the rubbish and there were the fresh smells of smoke and sawdust. When he paused in his work, using his forearm to push the hair out of his face, and smiled at me, my resentment and my lonely disdain faltered.

'Did you see your room?'

'My room?'

'Yeah. The little one. You should go and have a look. We've set up the bed.'

I went in, past Ishtar, who was working at one of the walls of the main room with a scrubbing brush. There was hardly space in the second room for anything more than a single bed, but like Dan said, someone — him, I was sure — had set one up, and even made it with sheets that, although worn and musty-smelling and with garish patterns that didn't match, were tucked neatly in. There was also an upended wooden crate for a little table, holding a candle in a saucer and a box of matches. There was still the smell of animal urine and, despite all the sweeping, a layer of dust and grit on the floor underfoot. But something turned over in my chest at the sight of that little room, at the care that had been taken. The rest of my ill will fell away, stiff and crumpled, and was replaced unexpectedly by tremulous, tentative excitement. I knelt on the bed and peered through the small window. Past the thorny branches of a runaway rose bush, the scrub made a dense wall. Hope — Dawn and Jindi, and Willow and Gav, and even Miller — seemed very far away.

I went back outside and Dan handed me a spade. He indicated the pile of rubbish that lay outside the door. 'Shove some of that load on the fire, will you?'

We got it all done in that one day. I carried water from the creek till my arms hurt and both palms felt raw from the bucket handle. I shovelled up the swathes of rubbish that Ishtar had sent pouring from the doorway like vomit from a gaping mouth and fed them to the fire, black tissues of ash rising to kiss the backs of my hands. Ishtar swept and scrubbed and Dan sawed and hammered, and came and went in his truck.

It was dark when we finished. Dan drove off one last time and returned with fish and chips, and we sat on the rickety chairs round the card table. The traces of possum were barely discernable under the smells of White Lily and the bunch of creamy ti-tree blossoms that Dan had stuck in a jar — and now the salty, hot smell of the food. The spirit lamp burred and threw out white glare; over near Ishtar's bed, with its Indian quilt, the firelight was softer, reflecting pink and orange in the timber. Dan had gotten a rug from somewhere — it was worn and had holes at one end, but it covered most of the patched floor. Someone had arranged a folded tablecloth over the crass carvings on the mantelpiece. The place had the quality of a cubby, or a campsite — a kind of makeshift homeliness that seems heartbreaking now, but at the time worked a kind of magic on me.

I was so tired and warm with the day's unexpected happiness that I didn't even notice Ishtar's wilted posture and the weary, mechanical way she stuffed the food into her mouth — not until Dan cleared his throat.

'You all right, Ishtar?'

'Just tired.' But she didn't look up.

My old irritation stirred at the sight of Dan's soft, concerned face, and I took a last handful of chips and got up and went into my new room. Closing the door behind me, I sat on the edge of the bed in the almost-dark and ate the chips one by one, licking my fingers and wiping them on my jeans. Then I kicked off my boots and got into the bed with all my clothes on and lay listening to the sigh and murmur of the bush outside. I didn't hear any further talk between Dan and Ishtar, and not long after there were the sounds of him leaving.

I turned over and stretched out my legs luxuriously. My own bed, in my own room, in my own house. Heavy with fatigue, I fell easily into sleep.

SUMMER

When I go back to that time in my mind — Hope, and Miller and Dawn, and Dan and Ishtar, and Ian, and the series of collisions we were all sliding towards — that little hut glows at the centre of my recollections as some kind of gift, a fluked idyll, all the more beautiful for how fragile, how short-lived, how untenable it was.

There was no logical reason for my feeling safe there. Miller was just down the road, and something bad was definitely going on with Ishtar, who became more and more withdrawn and uncommunicative. Yet during those first couple of weeks I experienced a sense of real happiness. I can only put it down to the actual place, which, after that incredible first day's transformation, represented what I had always fantasised about: a house that was just mine and Ishtar's, where we lived together, just the two of us. In a strange and completely unexpected way I had gotten what I'd always wanted — and even though I knew it wouldn't last, that was the comfort I held close as I fell asleep at night.

I loved being alone in the hut. After school, with Ishtar still at work, I lit a fire even if it wasn't cold, and swept the floor, straightened the meagre supply of crockery and the few jars and tins on the shelf. I put my school knapsack under the end of my bed and smoothed the blanket. Through the four small panes of wavery glass that made up the window in my room, the overgrown arm of the old rose bush presented fairy-tale orbs of rusty fruit. Even though I didn't like tea much, I boiled the kettle on the camp stove and made a cup, and sat with it at the card table, or outside on the sagging bench by the front door, holding it under my chin to feel the steam. I did everything slowly, thoughtfully, with a sense of spaciousness, almost of languor — even when heading out into the morning chill with the trowel and the roll of toilet paper, or lugging bucketfuls of water from the creek.

No more sneaking around, evading Jindi. No more overcrowded, noisy mealtimes, no more raucous late-night parties, no more tripping over other people's things, no more crying baby. Each morning, I woke and lay listening to the tick and whisper of the bush, and felt untouchable, sheltered in its cushioned heart.

Ishtar was sick. She didn't seem to have a cold or anything, and still went off to work each day, walking out to the dirt road in the mornings to flag down Gav or whoever else was driving past from Hope. But when she wasn't at work she mostly lay in bed. Sometimes she slept — often she was asleep even before it got dark — but other times she just lay there.

I was the one who kept the place clean, who washed the dishes in the tub and lit the fire and the lamp. She did buy some groceries, but she didn't cook — the two of us ate muesli and fried eggs, raw carrots and apples. Sometimes I would cook a pot of rice, which we ate just with salt and pepper. Ishtar chewed and swallowed in a joyless, methodical way, like someone taking medicine — even though, strangely, she seemed to be eating more than usual.

Our interactions were reduced, if that was possible, to the most basic of practical exchanges. 'We're out of rice,' she might say, not lifting her head from the pillow. 'Go round to Hope and get some. Take those oranges and do a swap.' Or at the sound of Dan's truck, 'I'm asleep,' huddled with her face to the wall — and I would open the door and shake my head at Dan, who nodded and went away again.

She didn't invite Dan in at all after that first day. Same with Miller, who turned up at odd hours, his knock resounding with entitlement. Ishtar dealt with him; I saw only a slice of his solid torso and glowing hair as, murmuring, she pushed the cracked-open door closed again.

'I'm sick.' Her voice was final. 'I need to rest.'

Dulled, uneasy realisations threatened at the back of my mind, but lying on my new bed in the honeyed afternoon light, or sitting on the outside bench with my cup of tea, or moving soft-footed and quiet as a wallaby through the bush, I could ignore them.

The hut, the bush, the creek; the soft eruptions of blossom that swayed, damp and fragrant, as I went out with the bucket in the pink mornings. The band of sweet, moist air that sat over the water's surface, coating my hands and forearms as I plunged the bucket in. The push of my thighs as I stood, made a scoop with my palm, and drank. The taste, mineral and ancient, sent me down into the brown water, into that sinewy, tail-flicking world, layers of silt and ooze, secret openings in the flanks of rocks.

The branches beckoned and up I went, cutting and banking, riding air. Or bracken passageways called, and my paws knew the powdery soil, my body telescoped and dived, my animal heart pattering.

If I could, I would have melted into that world, leaving my old self slumped on the bank, unwieldy, slow, and human.

I went to the doctor and made sure. Even though I knew any way it shook me up to be told it was true. All those years on the pill I always felt so safe but it can happen the doctor said, its just bad luck. You have a plan I kept saying to myself, this could be a disaster but realy its not its actually a way out. But I had that sickness and I couldnt think straight and the worst thing was it was just like last time. I tried to think about how to do it I had to get it right choose the right moment. I lay on my bed and tried but I just fell asleep straight after work, I fell asleep and didnt wake up till it was night and then when I did wake up, before I opened my eyes there was the sick feeling and my breasts all hard and sore and I kept hearing that old name Id almost forgotten and it was like I was back there again. I opened my eyes and there was the fire and the lamp hissing and Silver on the couch with her book all grown in to the stranger she was. I hadnt thought about any of it for so long it shouldve felt very far off but it didnt now it seemed very near just over my shoulder.

I had hardly seen Ian since I'd caught him taking the photos of Dan. We did run into each other by the creek one time and I told him about the move, but he showed little interest, which would have surprised me had I been more tuned in. Dean Price was giving him a hard time at school, I'd noticed that — seen the two of them at the centre of a scrum in the courtyard near the library. A teacher intervened, breaking up the knot of bodies and sending Ian, taut with rumpled dignity, off in one direction and Dean Price and his gang in the other. In the bush I had caught sight of him flitting through the trees, but something in his bearing kept me from calling out or running after him. Besides, I knew where he would be headed. I let him go, and managed to put him, along with Ishtar and her strange behaviour, out of my mind as I lay on my bed in the calm of the empty hut.

Then one morning I climbed the steps of the bus to find a new man in the driver's seat. He had rounded shoulders and a beaky nose, and a pang of worry went off in me at the sight of his hands, which were not draped casually like the old driver's but clamped stiffly either side of the wheel. When he pulled the lever to close the door it was with a desperate, grabbing motion, and even the way the vehicle accelerated under his control seemed nervy, irregular.

It was hard to say what exactly gave the usual bus driver his authority. The same went for Mr Dickerson. There were no readily identifiable signs, but it was clearly there, an air of confidence, of clout — and it was just as obvious that this man did not have those qualities, and in fact exuded weakness like an odour.

As we trundled uncertainly along the road it began: hoots

and yells from the back seats, kids getting up and moving around — something the regular driver would not have allowed for a moment. Then a school bag went sliding down the aisle. The driver didn't respond, but his posture seemed to grow more defensive.

By the time the bus pulled into the school car park the noise from the back had reached zoo-like levels and, in the chaos of everyone getting off, Ian's jumper was snatched and tossed overhead from thug to thug. The driver just sat, hands still on the wheel, gazing out the windscreen like someone who has unexpectedly survived the first round of an unwinnable fight.

As I crossed the asphalt I saw Ian walking evenly, as if nothing at all had happened, to retrieve his jumper from where it had been stuffed into a rubbish bin. His words echoed in my head — *When they find you, you just have to endure* — and I was almost thrown off my own casual-seeming course by the strength of the strange, pity-laced admiration that filled me.

The same driver was back again that afternoon, and Dean Price got on our bus instead of his own. Three stops before mine and Ian's, he and his mob made a mass exit. Down the aisle they rumbled in a mute, grey herd, from which a hammy hand appeared, pulling Ian off his seat and along with the jumble of bodies.

I saw his jumper pulled up close round his neck, the raw-looking fingers gripping it in a bundle, his grim face pressed sideways into the back of the boy in front, his feet groping at the floor, barely reaching. I glimpsed the waiting roadside, empty of adults, of protection, and Ian's words flashed up in my mind like red-pen headings in an exercise book — avoidance, resilience, *revenge* — and, from nowhere, the thought gaped, of the black mineshaft going down into deadly depths.

They were off, and the driver was lunging for the lever again. I called, 'Wait, please,' in a voice that came out so puny I was surprised he heard — and then I was scrambling down the steps and the bus, with a shudder and a burst of warm fumes, was gone, the sound of the engine fading into a sudden, terrible, wind-blown hush.

Four or five boys were standing in a bunch by the barbed-wire fence, their bags at their feet. Behind them a paddock bent its long grass to the wind. Dean Price, with Ian still in his grip, was nearer to the road. All of them — including Ian, a groove of disapproval between his eyebrows — were staring at me.

Dean Price's fat tongue lolled at his lips. 'What's she doin' here?'

I had never heard his speaking voice before. It was surprisingly high, and raspy. Some of the cronies shrugged.

'She a friend of yours, Munro?'

Ian didn't respond. His eyes dropped from my face.

Dean Price regarded me for a moment longer, then spat on the ground and turned back to Ian.

'Now.' He let go of Ian's collar at last. 'I hear you've got something interesting to show us, Munro, yer little ponce.'

Ian kept his head down.

'Newt reckons he caught you in the darkroom, saw what you've been up to, snapping away with your little camera. That right, Newt?'

A ruddy boy with white-blond hair blown into a crest grinned.

Dean Price raised his hand, palm up, and wiggled his fingers. 'Come on, then,' he said. 'Giss a look.'

Ian didn't move.

Dean Price gave an exaggerated sigh. 'For fuck's sake,' he said. Then Newt came over and seized Ian from behind, pinning his arms to his sides and lifting him off the ground. Dean Price ripped the bag from Ian's hands, opened it, and tipped out the contents. Some loose papers were snatched immediately by the wind and went whipping past me and off along the grassy roadside. A red plastic lunchbox and some books fell to the ground, as well as one of the white A4 envelopes photography students used to protect their prints, which Dean Price quickly put his foot on.

'Aha!' Casting a jubilant look round, he bent and picked up the envelope. 'This looks interesting, hey Munro?'

What happened after that happened very quickly, and almost all at once.

A vehicle pulled up, a small truck that I recognised with a throb of incredulous relief.

Ian suddenly twisted and kicked at Newt's shins, who released his grip for a moment. Ian then grabbed at the envelope in Dean Price's fist and the envelope tore, releasing a clutch of postcard-sized photographs that scattered and then tumbled over the grass in my direction, borne along by gusts of wind. As they went, they showed glimpses of their printed sides, which were more a washed-out grey than black-and-white: two shapes, indistinct but recognisably people — and clearly naked. Arms reaching, a head thrown back, a grainy but obvious bare breast, an unmistakable clump of dark pubic hair. Someone let out a whistle.

'Catch them!' yelled Dean Price, and every boy except Ian stumbled into action. But the photos somersaulted on, and before anyone had moved three paces they had all vanished — apart from the one I'd trapped under my foot and the two that had leapt like eager pets to press themselves against the skirt of my school dress.

I stood still as a post, feeling the plasticky shudder against my thighs, the threat of the wind.

The mob halted and looked to Dean Price for instruction.

But Dan had climbed out of the truck now and was walking over, calling, 'Hey,' and it was in the shadow of his approaching, adult, presence that all the boys stood, paralysed, and watched as I groped cautiously for the photos that had blown against my skirt and bent to retrieve the other one, then put all three into my bag.

'What's going on?' Dan stopped between Dean Price and Newt. He had his hands in his pockets, and was wearing a pair of sunglasses I'd never seen before, with mirrored lenses — and he looked unusually, and blessedly, grown up. Newt and Dean Price stared at the ground. Ian stood, silent, off to one side.

Dan's voice wasn't loud, but its authority was undeniable. He stood head and shoulders above Dean Price, who dangled his hands like a chastened toddler. I stole nearer. Dan took out a cigarette and lit it, cupping it close against the wind and taking his time. He drew on it a few times in silence, then moved closer to Dean Price, ducking to see into the boy's face.

'These two,' said Dan in that same low voice, 'are friends of mine.' He let out a stream of smoke.

Dean Price blinked.

'So you're going to leave them alone from now on.'

A nod from Dean Price.

'Am I right?'

Another nod.

'Am I right?' Dan's repeated the words in almost exactly the same tone, but this time he clipped the end of *right* with a metallic sound that somehow conveyed startling menace.

'Yeah. Yeah. You're right.'

'You okay?' said Dan to Ian, speaking across me sitting in the middle of the ute's bench seat.

'Yes.' The spots over Ian's cheekbones had gone pink, and he was staring down at his knees.

'You sure?'

'Yes. I'm fine.' He faced the window. 'I'm fine,' he said again, sounding almost irritated. His breaths were jerking in and out through his nose as if it hurt to draw them.

'Where do you live then?' said Dan. 'I'll drop you home.'

'Not the next left, but the one after.' Now he was mumbling, like someone who'd been hauled up in front of the class by a teacher. He lifted a hand to push back his hair and I saw that his fingers were shaking.

My own hands I kept firmly on my school bag.

We drove the short distance in silence.

'Here?' said Dan, and Ian didn't answer or even nod, only took hold of the handle and began to open the door before the truck had fully stopped. Away he stalked, onto the ridged dirt of the lane that led to his family's property, his ears pink, his collar gaping pitifully as always round his weedy neck, not turning to wave or call goodbye.

'He all right?' said Dan.

'Yeah.' My voice sounded thin. 'He's just embarrassed.'

But I knew he wasn't all right, and I knew what was the matter. Everything had changed in the moments in which Dan had walked towards Dean Price, in the moments in which I had rescued the photos trapped against my skirt and under my shoe, and they had flashed their messages to me. I knew something that I hadn't known before — but I couldn't acknowledge it yet, give it space, not while I was sitting there beside Dan.

'Next stop your place?'

I didn't answer. I stared out at the black and green stripes of tree trunks. When he pulled up at the hut I did the same as Ian, jumping out as fast as possible — although I did manage to blurt the word 'thanks' as I slammed the door, looking away.

I had seen who it was in the photos, recognised the figures as I slipped them into my bag. I needed to check again though, just to be sure, and as soon as Dan had driven off I went inside and into my room, closing both doors behind me. Ishtar was at work, and not due back for a while yet, but still I listened out as I took the prints from my bag and put them on the bed.

They were of Dan and Ishtar, in the outdoor bath at Hope. Ian must have taken them from his hiding spot up on the hill and then blown them up in the darkroom. He'd had to zoom so far into them that they barely qualified as photographs — they were almost impressionistic, the figures ghostly, swimming among spots of grain like flecks in an old mirror, their features blowzy and dreamlike. They were recognisable, though — instantly so — Dan's rangy build, the way his dark hair fell at the back of his neck; Ishtar's long throat, the calm smudges of her eyes.

I was glad for the smokiness of the images, for their vagueness, as I looked them over, skittering my gaze past the lower reaches of Dan's nakedness in the one where he was still climbing in, and the blotches of his lips as they met Ishtar's in the second print and bled into the creamy round of her breast in the third.

I twisted my fingers in the blanket. More than anything, I felt anger at myself for being so stupid, for never suspecting. Of course Ishtar would have done this — taken what Dan had to offer, if and when it suited her.

Picking up the photos, I slid them into a pile. Where had I been when they were taken? Washed-out as they were, the prints still gave an impression of brightness, of saturation of light, and I could guess at how they might look had they been printed as they should have been, showing distance — the two small, illuminated figures, the bath like a white boat in the long grass, the backdrop of Hope's sleeping buildings, the open sky above, everything brimming with the liquid radiance of early morning. I remembered finding Jindi in the lukewarm bath that time, after the party during Miller's absence. That must have been it — Dan and Ishtar, the last ones awake, lighting the fire as the sun rose, taking off their clothes. Ian creeping over the hill with his camera.

I shook the image away. It didn't matter. We would move soon and I could forget about Dan, forget what an idiot I'd been. The wind creaked and tapped and sent a bramble flailing at the window. My stomach ached. Maybe I was going to get my period again; it had only happened that one time, a while ago now. A memory came, of Dan smiling at me in the hallway one of those mornings after our mortifying first encounter, and I allowed myself a brief lapse into wishing I could go back and feel it again — the gradual recognition of his kindness, his respect for me, and the uncomplicated joy, the soaring delight of that thoughtless, babyish crush. Then the weary, adult feeling settled in once more.

Looking up at the window, pressing the corners of the photos with my thumbs, I turned my mind to the other thing. I didn't need to look again to see what else the pictures revealed. The understanding that had buzzed, unwanted, at the edge of my mind ever since that day I'd caught Ian squirming in the grass with the camera, ravenously whirring and clicking, had crystallised — and the question of what was *the matter* with him had been answered. Ishtar was in those photos, but only just, and only the parts of her that were near or touching Dan. In all three photos most of her back and even parts of her head were cut off, while Dan was right in the centre of the frame. Even exploded into spacey, unreal drifts of grey it was there: the essence, the purpose of these photographs — and my mind couldn't help sharpening the images, filling in the details, the droplets clinging to the scatter of dark hairs on Dan's chest, the gradation of stubble along his jaw, the swell and dip of muscle beneath that luminous skin. This was what Ian had sought to trap, to take for himself.

I thought about him in the truck, his agony. And all those earlier times, when I'd talked on and on about Dan and he'd listened with such avid interest. He was possessed, like Ishtar had been when Miller carried her up the stairs and her head fell back and her whole face softened. Ian's symptoms were different — where Ishtar's were joyous, lush, expansive, his were anguished and furtive, acutely self-conscious — but what was the same was the total transformation, the loss of control.

I knew about homosexuality. At every school I'd been to this was the greatest crime. *Poofter. Faggot. Lezzo.* And, despite all the lip service that was paid to the ideas of diversity and doing away with labels in the various group houses Ishtar and I had lived in — and despite being told that sex didn't have to be only between a man and a woman — I had never actually met anyone who was openly gay. I did, from those frank and excruciating kitchen-table discussions in the group houses and also from the probably less reliable things kids at school said, have some idea of what gay men did when they had sex, but this all belonged to some speculative, theoretical realm. And so, when I thought about Ian being in love with Dan, I didn't think about sex. Not consciously anyway; if it was there, it was in some screened-off area of my mind.

So Dan, with his own enslavement — watching Ishtar in the dinnertime firelight, running round doing chores for her — was responsible for Ian's suffering and didn't even know it. I closed my eyes. It was like a chain of dominoes toppling down, each person hurting the other. And however much I tried to place myself on the outside, an untouchable observer full of disdain or pity, the truth was that I was in there too, somewhere, falling.

Before Ishtar got back I wrapped the photos in paper and then a plastic bag, and grabbing the trowel, took them out into the bush. Halfway down to the creek I dug a hole under a crooked flowering gum and buried the package there, smoothing the dirt and covering the place with leaves.

A few days later I was walking back from the bus stop when Dan came past in his truck and stopped to offer me a lift. I could hardly say no, and so found myself sitting again in loaded silence beside him as we bumped along.

'You and your friend all right?' he said. 'After the other day?'

'Yeah.' I tried not to look at the dark hairs that showed at his wrists, to think about him and Ishtar, the blurred limbs, the saturated light.

'They been leaving you alone, those boys?'

'Yeah.' It was true; who knew how long it might last, but they hadn't bothered either of us since Dan's intervention. I sat forward in the seat. We had reached the turn-off for the hut. 'I can get out here.'

'Sure?'

'Yep.' I reached for the door handle, and was unexpectedly seized by a bout of meanness. How pathetic he was, hanging round Ishtar for so long when she wouldn't even see him. 'Unless you want to come in?'

He gave a tiny laugh. 'No.'

'Why not? Don't you want to see Ishtar?' It was the blade-like voice of one of the prissy girls at school, hand on hip, eyes narrowed.

Dan waited for a few moments, and then when he spoke it was so directly, so honestly, that my nastiness immediately collapsed. 'Of course I do,' he said. 'But I know she doesn't want to see me.'

I sat in mute shame. Suddenly, all I felt was a deep, deep tiredness, and the same secret desire I used to get with Ishtar, but that I hadn't felt for ages — to be younger, smaller, carried in his arms, wrapped in a blanket maybe, or held in his lap, looked after.

'Thanks for the lift.' I climbed down to stand in the lee of the open door.

'It's okay.' He smiled and tipped his head in the direction of the hut. 'I can't help it, you know. It's not something you get to choose.'

I looked at him, his lean figure behind the wheel, the length of his legs, the hands loose in his lap. Like the slightest warm breath it came sliding in, that sense I'd had when I first met him, of openness, of potential, of all the freedom and opportunity in the world sprawling beyond as if he was some kind of portal. I thought of Ishtar when she was low — in the place she was now — the endless, joyless, downcast tramping of her circular paths: work, chores, sleep, work. The shadows that reached from her, that sapped, that snaked and tightened like a smothering vine. It was too good, Dan's light, his freedom — too good to waste.

'How much have you saved?'

'What,' he said, 'money?'

'Yeah.'

He squinted, calculating. 'Well ...'

'Enough for the ticket?'

'Yeah. Easily.'

The urge to cry filled me like the quick, upward wicking of the tabs of litmus paper we dipped in liquid in Science class. 'You should go then,' I said, and shut the door and turned to the tunnel of leaves.

The morning after the incident with Dean Price, Ian had been back at the bus stop as if nothing had happened, but I didn't see him out in the bush for a few days. Then one afternoon we ran into each other on the creek path and there wasn't time for either of us to escape.

'Oh, hello,' he said, gazing into the high branches of a tree. 'Hi.'

We stood for a few moments, mired in awkwardness. Surely something had to be said. I knew what I could say, what I wanted to: that I didn't care about the photos, that I didn't mind how he felt about Dan, that none of it mattered really, everyone did silly things, I had too. But he didn't want to talk about it, that was obvious, and suddenly I could feel, like an invisible audience, all the jeering faces of the whole school, and hear the insults — *poofter, faggot* — and it occurred to me that if I did say anything about Dan then Ian would probably just deny it. In the end all I could manage was to mumble, 'I got rid of those photos.'

It was as if I hadn't spoken. He went on studying the tree. Then he took a greaseproof-paper package from his pocket. 'Cake?' He held it out. 'It's lemon.'

With a mixture of relief and guilt — because I knew that by quailing before that imaginary crowd of onlookers, I'd failed him as a friend somehow, even if it was what he wanted — I unwrapped it and bit into the crumbly, yellow slab.

He took the paper and screwed it up, tossed it in the air, tried to catch it, missed, and bent to retrieve it. 'So,' he said, 'shall we *repair* to the bridge?'

I swallowed the lumpy mouthful. 'Okay.'

We were at the bridge — maybe it was that day, or another around the same time — when Jindi appeared, stumping along the edge of the dirt road. She was wearing a mustard-coloured velour dress with stains down the front, and running shoes that were too big.

'Jindi.' I checked the road behind her. 'What are you doing here all by yourself?'

Ignoring this question, she came right up to us and stood, gripping the railing. 'Miller's lady's kicked him out,' she announced.

'Jindi ...' I didn't like her being out here; she belonged at Hope, safely confined. She was only five — wasn't someone supposed to be looking after her?

'What lady?' said Ian.

Jindi leaned against the rail. 'You know. His lady who whispers and who he used to keep in his room.'

Ian widened his eyes at me.

'But she comes out now,' Jindi went on. 'Val makes her soup and they play cards in the kitchen. Sometimes I play too, but her hands make me feel sick. They're all yellow, the nails, and she drops her cards they shake so much.'

'It's his wife,' I said to Ian. 'There's something wrong with her.' With relief, I spotted someone — an adult — coming up the road.

'Wife?' Ian threw up his hands. 'A wife? This sounds *dramatic.*'

'It's not really,' I said. 'They're married, but they're not — together, you know. It's just because she's rich, I think. He gets money from her.' I turned to Jindi. 'What do you mean, kicked him out? Where's he gone?'

'He's living in the bad paddock. You know, where the bones are.'

I looked down the road again. It was Gav; I could see the flash of his bare legs under his sarong, and the glint of his glasses.

'The *back* paddock, you mean?'

'Yeah. In the shed. He's got a bed in there, and a fire. I'm too scared to go close, but I hear him, he sings and calls out. Even at night. I heard him when I was going to the dunny.' A cobweb hung from the side of her head; there was a leaf caught in it that quivered as she spoke. 'When we were having dinner he came in and he was crying.'

'He was crying?'

'Yeah. It was scary. So loud.'

'Did he say anything?'

'Yeah.'

'Well, what?'

'He said, "Dawn, it was nothing, take me back, don't you need me."' Jindi's eyes bulged with the effort of her performance, and the leaf danced up and down.

'This is better than *Days of Our Lives*,' said Ian. 'And what did Dawn say?'

Jindi grinned. 'She said, "No, I don't, you can buy your own damn tractor next time, and your own damn shirts."'

'Jindi!' called Gav, who had stopped a small distance away. 'Come on! Don't run off like that — we didn't know where you were!'

'Then what happened?' said Ian.

'Well.' Jindi drew herself up, making the most of the time she had left. 'He went away again, and Dawn asked Val for a glass of wine.'

I went to have a look myself, creeping down the side of the hill to hide behind the island of blackberry. It was more a shelter than a shed; it only had three walls. Peering through the looping, barbed branches, I saw the mattress, pillow, and blanket, and the place where he'd had a fire — but Miller himself wasn't there. Scanning in every direction and seeing no one, I went closer, to where an outcrop of brambles provided a last hiding spot. There were whisky bottles and cardboard wine casks and their emptied silver innards scattered round, and beside the mattress the big bong from his room, and a couple of Dawn's pill bottles.

I heard him before I saw him, coming back from the direction of the outdoor toilet. He was singing, one of his trumpeting, foreign songs, although the vowels were slurred and he broke off now and then. As I scurried round the far side of the blackberry mound, his head appeared above the seed tassels that whistled and sighed at the tips of the long grass, and there was something short-sighted and bleary in the way he was listing along that I recognised: he was drunk or stoned, or both. I took off up the hill, bent low. When I got to the tree I looked back down; he was on the mattress, just a horizontal streak of colour from this distance, browny-gold and pink.

We had been at the hut maybe two weeks when I walked in from the dirt road one afternoon to find his car parked on the track and Miller seated on the bench outside the door. I froze, still under the cover of overhanging branches. He sat with one leg cocked, the ankle propped on the other knee; his head was tipped back against the wall. I waited. It was hard to tell — I wasn't quite close enough — but I thought his eyes were closed. I stood still for a long time. He didn't stir, but then when I tiptoed past, heading towards the creek, I was sure I caught a movement — an open slit under one lid, the tracking glide of an eyeball. I tried not to but couldn't help breaking into a run.

I hid and read until the sun got low. When I returned I was sure he must be gone, but as I got closer I heard the rumble of his voice, and I stopped and stayed by the side wall, peeking carefully round the corner. He was up off the bench and standing, blocking the doorway. Ishtar was on the other side of him, in her work clothes, arms folded.

'No,' she said quietly.

Miller opened his arms as if appealing to the whole world. There were dark patches at his armpits. I noticed also that there was a tidemark of grime where his skin met the fuzz of his beard and hair, and the collarless pink shirt he was wearing was covered in stains and black at the neckline and cuffs.

'You have to,' he said. 'You must.'

Ishtar didn't answer.

'This morning,' said Miller. 'Early. I saw two cockatoos. In the pink sky.' He raised an arm, skimmed his hand. 'They made a big circle, right over Hope, and then over here. And then they took off.' He fluttered his fingers. 'They went north.' He smiled. 'See?'

Nothing from Ishtar.

'I needed a sign,' said Miller. 'I asked for one and it came.' He stepped nearer to her and my stomach clenched. He reached and took her hand, which lay limp and unwilling in his. 'Don't you see?' It sounded as if he was making an enormous effort not to shout. 'We need to get away. Just the two of us. We need to make our own life, away from here. Away from other people. I'm ready. The car is full of petrol.'

Ishtar didn't move or speak.

'What is it?' He lifted her hand, as if trying to tug out a

response. 'Is it Dawn? You think I'm a bad husband, abandoning her?' He peered into Ishtar's face, his eyebrows lifted. 'That's what you're thinking, isn't it? But! Aha!' He stepped back again and dropped her hand, raised a forefinger and smiled, a slow, droop-eyed smile that broadened until his whole head seemed to nod with the weight of it. 'This is what has come to me, Ishtar. This is what I now see. I will be freeing her. I will be releasing her. Because our marriage cannot be saved, and do you know why?'

Ishtar stood, silent.

He went on. 'It was hard for me to see this, because it meant seeing weakness in myself.' The smile dropped away. 'I was weak, Ishtar. For a long time I have been. I used her. Her money.'

I tried to see Ishtar's face, to gauge her reaction, but her head was lowered.

Miller began to pace. 'I told myself it was only fair, since I looked after her, that it belonged to me too, since she was my wife. But that wasn't true. I was just being weak. A coward. I was shackled just like everyone else, to comfort, to the easy way.'

I fixed my eyes on Ishtar, the screen of her hair, making the magic shape with my fingers. *Don't listen to him.*

Miller paced and turned. 'But did it bring us happiness, either of us? No. Does she have respect for me? No.' He paused and looked down at himself, then made scrubbing motions at his torso and thighs. 'Can't you see how tainted I am? Anger. Frustration. Resentment.' With each word he scrabbled his fingers as if brushing away insects. Then suddenly he dropped to his knees. He put his palms to his face and began to make deep, groaning sobs. 'There was love, when we met, Dawn and I. But I should have seen that there was corruption too, already. I should have got her away from them — her parents, the doctors.'

Ishtar pulled her jacket closer round herself. Miller's hair was brushing at her legs and she took a step back. 'I need to go inside now,' she said.

He grabbed her round the knees, and I dug my nails into the hut wall. He rose, keeping hold of her, the hem of her jacket, then her shoulder. When he was standing again, he put one hand in under her hair at her neck. His thumb was at her throat, the black-rimmed fingernail pushing into the groove alongside her windpipe.

The trees swayed, the air sang, the pulse of insects sounded urgent and coded. My body was rigid against the timber, arms locked, legs tensed but unmoving. I could hear Miller's sobbing breaths and see the tears going down into his beard, but Ishtar made no sound at all. Her eyes were closed, her body still.

'I could just take you,' he said, quietly, almost whispering. Another sob, and his voice went thin and high. 'I could do it that way. I could.' His wet face glittered in the sunlight, his teeth shone. Without releasing his hold he let his head droop, his cheek lie against her shoulder. 'I could do it that way … but I won't, my love. I won't. Because it will be better when you come of your own accord. Can't you see what has happened? I'm free. I'm a free man. And you need to come with me as a free woman.'

He stayed like that for a few moments, and his breathing quietened. Then he let her go and she turned and went straight into the hut and closed the door behind her.

He didn't try to follow — he just stood there for a while. Then he humped his shoulders and gave a short, barking laugh. He tipped back his head and turned in a slow circle, staggering slightly, reaching into the air as if trying to grab at something invisible. He was muttering, but I couldn't catch the words. He circled twice, then lowered his arms and stood looking into his hands. I could see his lips moving, and hear a droning buzz, like a swarm of bees. Eventually he let the imaginary thing drop and trudged off to his car, which drove away with spasmodic revs of the engine.

The next day Ishtar brought home a bolt, which she fitted to the inside of the door using a screwdriver of Dan's that had been left behind. Now, when we were both inside at night, she slid it closed. She did it the way she did everything — neatly, quietly, like it was nobody else's business.

That Saturday she stayed in bed all morning, and I went down to the creek to escape the sight of her under the quilt and the dank air of the hut, which seemed to carry a sweetish, bodily smell that made the nervous feeling in my gut worse. Ian didn't show up, and I found myself scanning the implacable rise on the far side of the water, unable to block a vision of him kneeling, pinch-faced, at the lip of that black opening, dropping things in: a handful of leaves, spit from his mouth, all his rage and fear and the long tangles of lonely shame that even I, his one friend, was banned from sharing and could only guess at. He needed that hole — I understood that more than ever now — but that didn't make it any less terrifying.

When I went back to get something to eat, Ishtar was still in the bed. I mixed up some milk and made a bowl of muesli, moving quietly, but she must have been awake anyway. When she spoke, her voice was lucid, collected.

'I need you to go over to Hope,' she said. 'Get Val for me. Tell her I need her help.' She had her back to me, but it was as if she saw my hesitation, the way I sat swirling my spoon through the milk, which had globs of yellowy, undissolved powder in it, floating with the oats and sultanas. 'Go now,' she said.

I went, ducking through the bush, the muesli sitting in a lump under my ribs. At the top of the hill I squatted in the grass and peered round, but there was no sign of anyone. When I got to the tree, I recognised Miller's shape lying on the mattress in the back-paddock shed. He had a fire going; smoke laddered the sky above the buckled roof.

Heart racing, I half ran, half slid down the rest of the hill. Jindi was outside playing with a bunch of half-grown chicks. When she saw me approaching she scooped one up and stood, toes turned out, holding the chick at waist height like an award she was waiting to present. Her round face was grave and patient; her too-small pants strained at her thighs.

I ignored her and went straight to the kitchen door. In passing I glanced at the entry to the mud-brick building, and wondered if what she had said at the bridge was true, that it was Dawn who had banished Miller to the shed. It didn't seem possible that tiny, wispy Dawn with her feathery hair and sticks of arms could have so much power. But it wasn't always about who was bigger. I thought of her arrival, the way he'd guided her from the car, his large form so reverent, and the careless, entitled way her frail hand lay over his.

The kitchen was empty and I went through to the hall, calling Val's name in a low, self-conscious way. The room she and Jindi slept in was empty too, the wide-open door showing the bedcovers thrown back and four pairs of Val's shoes — all elastic-sided boots in varying states of wear — set out under the window, alongside a bit of cardboard with the words *Shoo shop* smearily printed on it in crayon. Rita was lying in her bed and I passed quickly without seeing if she was awake or asleep. The other bedrooms were either closed or uninhabited. There were voices coming from the front room though, and just as I reached the curtain, Val came through it; I caught sight of Dawn in there, her drooping figure in one of the armchairs, chin in hand.

'Silver,' said Val, but didn't stop. She went on bustling back towards the kitchen, and I found myself drawn along behind, mumbling my message.

'What's that?' She went into the little laundry room and lifted the lid of the washing machine. 'What's she need help with?'

'I don't know.' I waited for her to sigh in a long-suffering way, or say she couldn't come, she was too busy. But she turned and gave me a hard look, then abruptly reached out and prodded with her forefinger into my ribs.

'You need a good meal.' Pushing past me, she began rustling round on the dresser shelf for her car keys.

She drove, in her rusted yellow station wagon, with me and Jindi in the back seat. When she had parked outside the hut she sat for a moment regarding the blind-looking building with its shuttered door and black window and I felt keenly aware of how run down it still looked, how small and shabby.

'You girls wait here.' Val got out of the car, marched over to

233

the door and rapped on it. It opened and she went in.

'Is this where you live now?' Jindi moved closer and her thigh lolled against mine. 'It looks like a shed.'

'It's actually a miner's cottage.'

'It's okay, you know, to live in sheds. Miller does now.'

I tried to ignore her. The sun had come out and the air in the car was heating up. There was a cloying smell, like damp woollen jumpers and sleep.

She sighed luxuriously, leaning into me. 'The shed people,' she said in a grand voice. 'Now I know two shed people. You, and Miller. No, three — you, and Miller, and Ishtar.'

'It's not a shed. It's a miner's cottage.' I got out and went to the door of the hut, which was ajar.

'So you don't know how many weeks?' came Val's voice from inside. 'You sick? You look sick.'

Ishtar's answer was inaudible.

'Yeah, probably not too far gone then,' said Val. 'Well, I'll ask around. Don't worry, it'll be all right. Even if it's a bit late they can deal with it.'

Something more from Ishtar, a murmur.

'You just take it easy.' Val's voice was unusually tender, but when she came out of the door she was brisk as ever, hustling Jindi back into the car.

'Come down any time,' she called to me from the open window. 'If you're hungry.'

She returned the next evening with some bean stew and rice in an enamel dish, and a piece of paper she handed to Ishtar.

'Good luck.'

'Thanks.' Ishtar went back to the bed and sat on its edge.

'No worries.' Val stopped in the doorway. She spoke in her usual rough, joking way, but her eyes were careful. 'Miller's gone off his rocker a bit. He hasn't been bothering you, has he?'

Images bobbed up: Miller kneeling, the explosions of his sobs; his red face with smears of black; his great hands reaching as Ishtar walked away.

Ishtar didn't even look up. 'No.'

Val folded her arms and rested her hip against the doorframe. 'Too much acid, I reckon. Seen it before. Fries yer brain. Silly bugger.' She let air out between her teeth with a pensive, comfortable sound. 'Ah, well. They'll be gone soon. Dawn's turned out to be all right. Funny how these things happen — you get these pathetic, victim women who wouldn't say boo to a goose, and then their bloke falls in a heap and suddenly out they come with all this hidden strength.'

Now Ishtar's head lifted. 'They're going?'

'Pretty soon, I reckon. She's kicked him out, but she'll take him back. She's just punishing him a bit.' A brief smile, but still those eyes on Ishtar's face, assessing. 'She says she wants to get a place of her own, she's had enough of him. But she'll take him with her, I reckon. Wouldn't be surprised if this kind of thing's happened before. I dunno, maybe they like the drama.'

Ishtar straightened. 'She's kicked him out?'

'Well, out of their room, anyway. He's camping down in the back paddock, poor bastard.'

When Val had gone, Ishtar stared at nothing for a long time. She still had the piece of paper in her hand. After a while she put it away in her bag without even looking at it. Then she got into the bed.

'I have to go to Melbourne tomorrow,' she said. 'For a few days. You can stay at Hope.'

Later, when she was asleep, I took the bit of paper out. All it had written on it was *Doctor Parker*, and a phone number. I refolded it and put it back.

I got up early. It was still dark and I crept out without waking Silver
and went through the cold along the creek path. The sky was just
getting light all the leaves were ghostly pale I felt like a hurt animal
dragging myself along, my legs so heavy and that swollen feeling in my
breasts and the sickness always there I couldnt wait to be rid of it.
Val had been right he was in the shed in the back paddock. From the
top of the hill I could see a burned down fire a red dot in the silvery
blue. I went to the mud brick and opened the door quietly then felt
my way in the dark to her room. I hadnt thought about the dark,
all I could see when I got there was the blue square of the window
I couldnt even make out the bed. But I felt around and there was a
candle and matches in the same place as before. She looked like she
was dead lying there her face all still and bony. Dawn I whispered,
Wake up. I had to squat down and shake her skinny shoulder. She
opened her eyes. Its me I whispered, Ishtar. She just stared at me.
Are you awake? Get out she said, but I held up my hand. You want
to hear this. I am making you an offer. She sat up. I told her slowly,
the way Id been practicing. Im pregnant. Its Millers. Eight hundred
dollars and youll never see me again either of you. Her eyes went
up and down my body. Suddenly her hand shot out and down my
top her cold fingers on my tight hot breast. I couldnt help making
a noise, it hurt. She poked around, she had a kind of empty look
on her face. Its not enough just feeling someones breast I should
have thought better about it and got proof got the doctor to write
it down and sign it or some thing but she believed me any way I
could tell. Maybe she could just see it the way Val could the way my
mother could all those years ago, some thing in my face my skin.
Maybe she remembered what it was like. He would leave you I said,
If he found out. If I told him. He wouldnt care about your money any
more he would leave you for this baby. She made a face like she was

237

in pain. I had her now she couldnt stand the thought of him getting someone else pregnant I knew that would be her weakness. But I wont tell him I said. And I wont keep it. Eight hundred dollars and I go to Melbourne I get an abortion and I get on a plane. Youll never see me again and he will never know. Straight away she said But how can I be sure youll do it? I will do it I said. I would do it any way but I dont have any money he took it all. I have nowhere to go. If you want to see me gone youll have to pay for it. I dont have that much she said. Not on you I said. But you can get it. I will need to make a telephone call she said, It might take a day or two. You write out the check now I said, And date it for Friday I wont cash it till then. That gives you four days. She squinted her eyes. I had her I was pretty sure but just in case I said If you dont give me the money I will get rid of it any way but I will tell Miller and just think what that would do to him. She made that face again. I sat back and waited. I thought about a hippie wedding I went to once where a guru wrapped the couples hands up together in a long cloth round and round. My fingers twitched. I was holding it up the dead dream that kept her and Miller together that they had worried and worn at till the spaces showed in the weave, I was holding it up with both hands and I was ready to rip. All right she said. Let me get my check book.

When I woke, Ishtar was up already, packing.

I went down to the creek for water, and when I got back Dan was there. He was standing right in the doorway, and when I came up behind him he threw me a funny look, a kind of forced, wan grin, and then crossed the room in two long steps and sat down at the table like a dog that knew it was doing something punishable.

Ishtar went on folding clothes and putting them in her duffel bag.

'Thought you might like a ride.' Dan's voice was hoarse. 'To the station.'

She didn't look up. 'I'm all right.'

His long fingers tapped at his knees. 'Too cold still to be hitching, this early in the morning.'

The quiet swam round us, broken by the rustle of Ishtar's movements. I saw Dan's eyes on her, the lost look of them, and the old anger stirred. I went into my room and closed the door. *Just give up*, I thought, sinking down on the bed. I wished I could grow into a giant and reach down and scrub him out, him and his stupid, gentle, enduring hope. *Just go to America.*

Through the door I could hear him perfectly. 'Val told me what's happening,' he said.

No reply.

'You don't have to do this,' he went on. 'You could always keep it — I can help you. It doesn't matter who the father is. I don't care.'

I got up, skin prickling, went closer to the door, straining for Ishtar's response. What was he talking about?

Dan continued. 'I've got money saved, and I can get a better job. We could move to Melbourne, with Silver, all of us. I could —'

'Dan.'

'I want to help you.' His voice was urgent. 'Please let me.'

'The decision's made.'

There was a pause. I stood, trying to arrange my thoughts, to properly understand. Did Dan want to be my *father*, was that what he was saying? A house in Melbourne, all of us — I tried to clamp down on the warm shiver that ran through me. Surely that wasn't what he meant, and anyway, what decision had Ishtar made? We must be leaving, after she'd gotten back. Maybe she was organising somewhere for us to go. But the phone number had been for a doctor — I'd thought that was what the trip was for, because she was sick.

Dan spoke again. 'But either way, come to Melbourne with me, let's —'

'How old are you?' Ishtar's voice rose, cutting him off.

'Twenty-two.'

'I'm almost ten years older than you.'

'But that doesn't matter!'

'Wait. I had Silver when I was seventeen.'

My breathing felt strange. I had never heard Ishtar say anything like this, talk at all about herself, her own life, or me and my birth.

She went on, quietly. 'I've never even been overseas.'

'But you could still do that,' said Dan. 'We could go together.'

I was only half-listening now. It hadn't taken much. It wasn't as if Ishtar had actually said, *Silver is a burden to me, she has ruined my life*, but in what she did say — *I've never even been overseas* — and in the tone of her voice, in which thirteen years of helpless longing and dissatisfaction seemed to be held, that's what I heard. I squeezed my hands into fists, digging my nails in.

You knew, anyway, I told myself. *You already knew.* But it was like something had solidified, taken on a definite shape. *A burden.* The word made me feel squashed and drooping, like something heavy-centred that had collapsed, that would have to be scraped up in order to lift.

'Why not?' Dan was saying. 'It would be easier. I could help, you know, with Silver. It would be great for her, she'd love it. We could go anywhere. Europe, America, India — wherever you want.'

At the sound of my name, I tuned back in. *With Silver. All together.* What did this mean? Did Dan really like me, want us to be together, the three of us? The warm shiver again. My throat hurt, like there was a sound there wanting to come out. I gazed at the closed door. *Please, please.* In my mind I saw myself open it, walk out there — their two questioning faces turning to me. *What do you want?* My voice, clear and strong: *Please, let's go, the three of us.*

But Ishtar was talking again. 'No,' she was saying, 'you don't understand. I need to do things by myself. Without a man. That's what I'm still waiting for.'

The image shrank and vanished.

There was a long silence, and I heard Dan's breathing, loud and compressed, as if he had his hands over his face. When he spoke again his voice was weak. 'All right,' he said. 'But at least let me drive you to the station.'

There were footsteps and my door opened. It was Ishtar. Her eyes, unhelpful, met mine. 'Come on,' she said, 'we can drop you at the bus stop.'

It was in the truck, sitting between them, staring at the narrow rush of road ahead, that I realised what they had been talking about, what I had misunderstood. Like something from nature — a flower, a leaf unfolding — it moved into the centre of my mind and eased itself open. It wasn't me Dan had meant when he'd talked about being the father, about *keeping it*.

There was a picture I'd seen in a book once, of a human embryo: the tiny curled shape, pink on black; the oversized head with dark, obscured rounds of undeveloped eyes; the beginnings of limbs sticking out, flipper-like. I stole a look at Ishtar, at her body, bundled in secretive layers, arms folded over the top. Her shuttered face. I didn't even know what an abortion actually was, how it was done, just that it meant getting rid of a baby before it really grew into a baby.

Dan pulled over at the school bus stop and Ishtar made room for me to get out. 'I'll be back by Thursday,' she said. 'Friday at the latest. Stay at Hope. Val'll feed you and give you a bed.'

I got down. I tried not to but couldn't help glancing up at Dan, catching his sad face. I couldn't imagine growing into a giant now — I felt tiny, helpless, an embryo myself, floating in my own dark space, stumpy limbs twitching uselessly.

The truck moved off along the road. It got smaller and smaller and then disappeared.

I didn't go to Hope. After school I just went to the creek and hung around with Ian as if nothing was different. When it got dark and he went home I went up to the hut and made a fire and heated a can of beans, which I was eating on the couch when Dan tapped on the door.

In the faint light, there were shadows under his eyes. 'Just wanted to check you're okay,' he said. 'Val was going to come, but I thought you'd probably prefer me.'

We exchanged thin smiles.

'Yeah,' I said. 'I'm okay.'

Cold air was rushing past him, and the night outside looked very dark. I opened the door further, stepped back. 'Do you want to come in?'

'If that's all right with you.'

I had that feeling again, like when we'd talked in his truck and I'd told him to forget about Ishtar and go to America — the fast descent of a deep and sapping exhaustion. I saw, as if from a distance, the little hut with its dimly lit windows, a speck in the sea of bush. I saw myself, an even tinier speck of a figure, tending its flicker of a fire — the smallness of my actions, the frailty of my hold against the vast black all around.

'It's okay. I'm tired though. I might go to bed soon.'

'That's fine. I'll just sit by the fire for a while. Keep you company. I can let myself out.'

We stood in the cave of shadows. Ishtar's bed glowed orangey-pink in the firelight. Her absence gaped.

'Cold night,' said Dan.

'Yeah.'

The kettle on the camp stove began to hiss.

I leaned against the table. I felt so tired I could barely stand. 'I was just going to make myself a hot water bottle.'

'I'll do it.'

I watched as his big hands unscrewed the stopper, held up the rubbery neck, tipped the kettle.

'Here.'

I took it and held the sloshing, hot weight against myself.

'Goodnight.' He went to the couch and sat down, slipped a paperback from his jacket pocket and opened it. Then he looked over at me. 'You sure you don't mind if I hang round for a while?'

'No. It's fine.'

I went into my room and shut the door. Changed quickly and got under the covers, huddling round the hot water bottle. It was easy to fall asleep, listening to the shift of the fire, the turning of pages. The hut felt bigger with him in it, warmer, fuller.

He was gone in the morning. But I thought I heard the truck as I woke, and when I went out into the other room the fire was high, banked with fresh wood, and I could smell him still, his tobacco.

The same thing happened the next two nights.

We didn't talk. He arrived late, and I went to bed more or less straight away, to bed and into black sleep. And I didn't feel anything much. Not my old, grown-up sad irritation, and not the helpless, embryo feeling either — I just felt tired, and grateful, and relieved that he didn't seem to want to talk about anything. Both times he was gone again when I woke up but the fire was left freshly tended, and heading out to the bus stop I felt boosted somehow.

Ishtar didn't come back on Thursday, or Friday.

'She must have got held up,' said Dan, and then, when I didn't answer, 'I'm sure she'll be back tomorrow.'

On Saturday morning I stayed in bed, trying to read and not able to stop myself from listening out. She would be on foot,

I assumed, if she'd hitched from the station. Unless someone drove her all the way in. But no sound came — neither car nor footsteps — and the time crawled.

I stared at the page. What if Miller and Dawn left, like Val had said? What if Ishtar came back — recovered, awakened, her switch flicked — and saw that she didn't have to worry about Miller, about hiding from him, about being trapped, and saw everything that was so good about this place, where we had our own house and she had a job?

A series of images took off in my mind, reeling through with the same bright, licking light as the films we sometimes watched at school, projected on the wall of the classroom, never quite in focus: Ishtar stooping to step under the branches of the big wattle down by the creek, then looking up to smile; the two of us sitting at the table eating dinner; her sewing while I did my homework, side by side in the clear circle of the spirit lamp. And Dan, his grinning face alongside hers under the wattle branch, or him turning from the camping stove with a frying pan, scooting fried eggs onto plates, his lanky body folded into one of the chairs, his elbow on the table. But here the vision broke down, and I came to with a flare of annoyance. What was the point of thinking about this stuff? It wasn't what Ishtar wanted, and she was in charge. She didn't want Dan — or me, for that matter. What she wanted was to be alone, to go overseas, to do things by herself.

Eventually I got up and opened her case, which held our papers. I ignored the passports, not wanting to remember that trip to the chemist, the jellybeans, the wood smoke, Ishtar's arm around me. I went through the other things. There was my birth certificate, with *Unknown* typed in the space for the father's name and *Karen Mary Landes* in the space for the mother's. Karen Mary Landes was Ishtar's other name — I had always known this, although I couldn't remember ever actually being told so. I had just heard it occasionally, drifting over my head, spoken by adults, but it had never seemed to have any fixed reference; it certainly never seemed to belong to her. It had an official sound, and lived in the same realm of vague meaning as words like *proprietary limited* and *stat dec.*

There was also Ishtar's — Karen's — own birth certificate, which was more faded than mine and soft at the creases. *BIRTH,* it said at the top, like mine, but where on mine the word was unadorned, on hers it had an ornate frame of lines and scrolls. Karen Mary Landes had been born in August 1955, and had both a mother and a father, Mary Evelyn Landes nee Thomas and Robert Donald Landes, whose address was 8 Walkers Drive, Toowoomba West. I had seen Toowoomba on a map — it wasn't far from Brisbane, but I'd never been there. Walkers Drive, along with Mary Evelyn and Robert Donald, had never felt real anyway — they all had the same distant ring to them. My mother, the woman I lived with and followed everywhere, the only constant in my life, clear and alive and blotting out all background names and places, was not Karen Mary Landes — she was Ishtar.

I glanced over the certificates, then moved on to the two photos: the one of me at about Jindi's age, sitting with some other kids on a bench, squint-smiling into the sun, and the one of Ishtar holding me as a toddler, my hand gripping her hair, the two of us looking round as if taken by surprise.

My usual irritation rose. I'd seen these things too many times — when I looked at them my eyes moved as if on a track, touching on certain features in a particular order. There was always the feeling that, if only I could break out of the habit and see properly, look at them as if for the first time, some truth might be revealed to me.

It was as I was putting the photos back that I noticed the lump under the lining of the case. The lining was tartan, a red and green pattern, frayed and thin, the ribs of the case palpable through it; as I ran my hand over it again, it became obvious that there was something in there, between the fabric and the shell, something with corners and a wadded, dense feel — papers.

I felt around the edges until I found the slit. It was held closed with a pin, tucked in right along the lip of the case. The room seemed to fall into a deeper hush and I found myself glancing round, my heartbeat quickening. I got up and went to the door, looked out, and listened. Nothing. I shut it and slid the bolt across.

Paying close attention to the way it had been put in, I took the pin out and laid it on the table. The opening was not much wider than my hand, and I had to work the papers out with care, feeling for the shorter end of the rectangular bundle.

They were letters, held together with a rubber band. I undid them, taking note of their order. There were three, in their envelopes, and they were all addressed, in the same handwriting, to Ishtar — but with her name misspelled — and to a post-office box. On the top and middle letters, the PO box address had been crossed out, and new addresses written on, in two different handwritings. The first letter — the one on the bottom of the pile — had not been redirected. All three had been opened; the folded paper inside showed at the torn tops. The return address on the flap was different for each, but the name the same: *L. Landes.* One of the addresses was for 8 Walkers Drive, Toowoomba West. My stomach contracted.

I read them in chronological order, slowly, finding the writing difficult — a spiny, sloping script, close on the page.

5th August 1979

Dear Ishtah,
I hope this reaches you.
 The funeral was yesterday. I don't know if you saw in the paper. We did try to find you again, and they said they'd pass on a message, but maybe you didn't get it. Or maybe you didn't want to come.
 Mum's death was peaceful, and Dad and I were both with her.
 I think Dad was very upset you didn't come to the funeral.
 I am sorry that you and Mum weren't able to resolve your differences. I know Dad is sorry too.
 Please write back to me. I would love to see you again.
Love,
Linda

20th May 1981

Dear Ishtah,
I hope this reaches you. Sometimes I think none of these letters do.
 Dad's condition has taken a downhill turn.

The doctors have finally listened to me and done some further tests and they have changed their diagnosis from Alzheimer's to something called fronto-temporal dementia, which is what I suspected all along. It's been much too quick for Alzheimer's.

I took some time off so I could be home with him, but even though I have a good understanding of the illness and know what to expect I am finding it too much, and even though it's not what I wanted I am afraid he will have to go into care.

It's been very sad seeing him deteriorate like this. In some ways it was worse early on, when he was still mostly 'all there', because he understood what was happening to him and he would become so frustrated and very angry at himself.

I thought he might have another year or so but the way it's looking it actually may not be too much longer.

I can't help but feel that I have missed an opportunity with Dad. Remember when you visited that night, and you said there was something he hadn't told me? After you left I asked him what it was, and what it was Mum should be sorry for. He said the reason you left was that you and Mum had a falling out, but that was all he would say, that it was 'a difference of values'.

It was very difficult to get him to say even that, and I got the sense that there was more to the story. But when I pressed him he became agitated, and said I must not bother Mum about it because she needed peace at this time.

He had already started to withdraw while Mum was

sick, and then after she died he got much worse. Later
though, once the dementia had taken hold and he lost
his words, he went through a phase of obviously trying
to communicate something to me. He would get terribly
upset, and I would go through the list of possible causes
and obviously one of them was you, and he did seem to
have a strong response to that.

I thought I should let you know what is happening
in case you would like to see him. He still does have the
very rare moment of apparent clarity, but I have to be
honest and say he is not likely to recognise you. You might
want to see him for your own reasons, though.

I am home with him now, so you can write to this
address, and the phone number's still the same.
Love,
Linda

15th December 1983

Dear Ishtah,
I hope you are well, and, as always, that you get this letter.

I don't have any news, really. I just wanted to give you
my new address and phone number, as I've moved again.
I'm in Sydney now, doing research in immunology. I find
it interesting work.

I am still on my own. It's been over three years now.
I heard that Jamie is married and has a baby. It's actually
been quite difficult for me to recover from that break-up,
even though I knew it was for the best. I don't find it easy
to trust and commit to a relationship. I know I'm not old

yet but I can't help but feel there won't be anyone else for
me. Actually, I think I've given up. I don't mind really. I
have my work. I suppose I've become one of those strange
women who's lived alone for too long.

Christmas is a bit of a hard time, though. I do tend
to feel the loneliness then.

I wonder where you are, and what you're doing.
Love, and many fond thoughts,
Your sister, Linda

I read the letters over three times each. Then I sat for long minutes with them in front of me. I had a groggy, dazzled feeling, as if I'd come out of a dark cinema into daylight, and in my mind swam illuminated figures, human — with human movements and features — but elusive, their faces indistinct. Of course these people had existed; Ishtar didn't spring from nowhere, and there had always been those flimsy, empty-sounding names on her birth certificate. But now an extra dimension had been added, and for the first time it properly hit me: somewhere — in Toowoomba West, that dot on the map — they had been in the world, living and breathing, at the same time as me. And now were gone, dead.

The figures moved across the screen of my mind, unreachable, their smudged faces averted. I looked at the letters again, the name at the bottom of the uppermost one: *Linda*. Linda. She was still there, in Sydney — or had been, two years ago. Ishtar had a sister. But the sister didn't know anything about us, or even where we were. She didn't even know how to spell Ishtar's name.

I put the letters back in their envelopes and replaced the

rubber band. I eased them in under the lining. Then I stuck the pin carefully in and closed the case and put it away.

Ishtar was there when I returned from school the next day. She was in bed, facing the wall. If my coming in woke her she showed no sign of it. I crept out again, and down to the creek.

When I returned at dusk there was food on the table — rice and some raw vegetable sticks — and she got up and served a plate for me.

'Did they look after you all right over at Hope?'

I didn't answer.

She wasn't listening anyway. She went out, for the toilet, and then got into bed again.

I finished my food and went into my room.

At first I just assumed she was recovering physically. I could only guess how long this might take. But a week passed and, while she went straight back to work, in most other ways she was no different from how she'd been before her trip to Melbourne. In fact, she was worse. She hardly ate anything. Sometimes she would prepare food for me, but not often. The moist look had gone from her skin — now it had a puffy, dry appearance, and for the first time I noticed lines at the corners of her eyes and around her mouth.

She kept the door bolted, and if anyone knocked she didn't respond, unless it was me — I had to call out to her. Dan came, twice, tapped and waited awhile, then left. Miller didn't come.

'When are we leaving?' I asked one morning, when she was up, sitting dully at the table.

'Soon.'

'Where will we go?'

But she didn't answer, and when I came back from school she was in the bed again.

Every night I thought tomorrow I will do it get packed and go. I had the money, Id cashed the check and it came through like Dawn promised so it was all there in my bag. Whenever I wanted I could just take Silver to Melbourne, get the tickets and go. But then when I woke up I had no energy. I hadnt expected that. I thought Id just get it over with and it would be a big relief and Id feel good again ready to get on with things. I kept thinking about one time when I was a kid we went to Brisbane for the day and drove past this group of people demonstrating out side a church. There werent that many of them and they werent chanting or any thing just standing there, a woman turned and shook her sign at us, it had a picture of a baby on it Abortion is Murder, it said. I kept seeing that sign I kept hearing my mothers voice saying What have you done? One night I dreamt I was following my father as he pushed the lawnmower. Help me help me I dont know what to do I shouted but the mower was so loud and he wouldnt turn around.

Everywhere there was a feeling of change, of approaching endings. Suddenly the days were warm, and sometimes even hot. From the bus window I saw Christmas decorations in the streets of Tarrina, and signs for end-of-year events: a visit from the Lion's Club Santa Claus, a family bush dance, a carol service. The school year was almost over. Final tests were taken, projects were handed back, pleas came over the loudspeakers for lost property to be claimed. Teachers, even Mr Dickerson, became distracted and more lenient. Classrooms buzzed with whispers. Windows were opened and breezes ruffled papers. At lunchtime the noise was extra frantic — it rang in the brick courtyards and swooped and eddied in the air above the oval.

The evening of the last day of term I recognised the sound of Val's car, and there was a rap at the door of the hut.

I opened it. Ishtar was in bed as usual, apparently asleep.

Right on the doorstep was Jindi, standing very straight, her hands clasped. Val stood a few steps behind her.

'Good evening!' said Jindi in a rehearsed kind of way.

'Shh.' I stepped out, shooing her away from the door and closing it behind me.

'Sorry.' Jindi began to speak in a very loud whisper, almost louder than her regular talking voice. 'Good evening,' she repeated. 'I have come to invite you to a party. To celebrate the summer ...' She faltered for a moment, frowning, then brightened again, drew herself up, arranged her lips, and enunciated with care: 'solt-a-sis.'

'Oh,' I said. 'Thanks.'

Jindi frowned again, and then steadied herself. 'It's going to be on … on … um. Not tonight …'

'Tomorrow night,' said Val. 'And it's the summer solstice.'

Jindi dropped her ceremonial stance and began to wriggle on the spot. 'Can you come, Silver?' she burst out in her normal voice. 'We're going to make decorations, and dress up in costumes, and Val says there'll be a *chocolate cake.*'

Val began to walk towards her car, but called as she went: 'Silver?'

'Yeah?'

'Tell your mum she's invited, okay?'

'Okay.'

Jindi was advancing on me, writhing. 'Will you come? Silver? Will you dress up? What will you wear? I'm going to be a summer flower fairy. Val says she'll make me a crown of flowers, and I'm going to wear my flower dress, and —'

'Come on, Jindi,' called Val. 'Time to go.'

I didn't tell Ishtar. Something was building in me, slowly expanding, and it was to do with the letters, with Linda. I felt it when I crouched by the creek with the bucket the next morning, and when I lay on my bed trying to read. It was the first day of the holidays, but there was no feeling of calm, of space. Outside, the bush swirled with bright, uneasy winds, and I lay staring at the knots in the timber wall and feeling the thing swell, like a bloat in my belly.

I went out again, along the creek and across the road, to climb the hill and look down on Hope. Miller was there, a distant figure, horizontal on his pallet in the open-sided shed; I saw an arm lift and move through the air, a slow stirring action, before lowering again to curve over the tawny blur that was his head. I thought of the film I'd seen at school about lions in Africa that showed a group of them lying in the grass, the casual drape of their bodies, the lazy shifting of their great paws.

Over at the house, someone came out of the mud-brick building and paused in the clearing near the kitchen steps. Dawn. I recognised her brittle frame, the pin legs braced as she adjusted something in her hands — a plate it looked like, with a cup balanced on top — before moving on, into the main house.

So they were still there. I made the magic shape and squinted my eyes. *Go away.*

Dan's green bike was propped against a tree near the hut when I got back. As I approached I saw him jiggling the handle and pushing with his shoulder at the door.

'Has she put a lock on this?' he said when he noticed me.

'Yeah.'

He stepped back. 'How is she?'

'She's okay.'

'Is she sick?' He spoke in a hushed voice, and beckoned me away from the hut. We went across the clearing and he sat down on a stump. 'I'm worried that —'

'It's not to do with the abortion.'

His face changed. 'I didn't know if you —'

'I'm not stupid.'

His lips twisted in a smile, but his eyes were sad. 'I know you're not.'

I glanced at the closed door. 'She just goes like this sometimes.'

'Silver.' He looked down at his hands. 'I'm leaving tomorrow.'

'What?' A shaken, seasick feeling came over me.

'My time here's over.'

'But ...' Tears rushed into my eyes; the ground seemed to tilt. None of it mattered — Dan and Ishtar in the bath, his pathetic devotion to her, my embarrassment at following him around like a fool all that time — all I could think about was those nights while she was away, his quiet presence in the hut, falling asleep in my bed knowing he was out there by the fire. I looked over at the bike and tried to steady myself. I would never see him again, never catch his white smile, never perch on the crossbar in the tearing wind and feel his arms either side of me and his solid warmth at my back, the vibration of his laugh between my shoulder blades.

I wiped the tears quickly away. 'But what about Ishtar, and what you said, about moving to Melbourne — or all of us going overseas?'

He smiled another sad smile. 'Did you like the sound of that?'

I nodded, sniffling furtively.

'Yeah, me too. But Ishtar's not ...' He sighed. 'She's not ready for —'

'She's so mean.' To my horror, I began to sob like a little kid. 'All she ever thinks of is herself. I *hate* her.'

Dan reached for me, but I twisted away and stood with my back to him. I was appalled at how childish I was being, but I couldn't seem to stop. 'And now you're leaving me here with her, and she won't get out of bed; she's never been this bad before and I don't know what's going to happen.'

He got up and tried to put his arms around me, but I pulled away again.

'Silver,' he said. 'I think Ishtar just needs a break. She's had a rough time. She kind of got scammed by Miller, you know, and —'

'Yeah right, of course you take her side, everyone always cares about *her*, wants *her* to be happy.'

'I didn't mean —'

'Leave me alone! Go away!'

I couldn't hold the crying back now it had gotten going, and I still wouldn't let him comfort me, so we stood there like two strangers waiting under the same shelter for a storm to pass. When at last I had managed to pull myself together, he spoke again.

'I didn't mean that I don't care about you, Silver. I do. I really care about you. I think you're a great kid.' He reached out again, this time to hold my hand, and I let him.

'Take me with you, then.' It just came out, like the crying, and even as I said it I knew how stupid it was. Of course I couldn't go with him; for a start it wasn't legal — he wasn't my parent, or guardian. But for a moment a ridiculous, babyish hope fluttered in my stomach.

He sighed, and the hope dissolved, and even before he spoke I was slipping my hand out of his.

'I wish I could,' he said. 'But you know I can't.'

'Don't worry about it.' My voice was stiff. I felt my face flush, and put my head down to hide it. What an idiot I was. He didn't want me for myself — it was Ishtar he really wanted; I was just an extra he wouldn't mind having along.

'Silver.' He drew an envelope from his pocket and held it out.

I took it. It was small, but packed solid. 'What's this?'

'It's the money I've been saving. It's for both of you. There's enough for two tickets, plus a bit extra.'

'Tickets?'

He nodded. 'Plane tickets. To Europe. Or India. Or wherever.'

This shook me part-way out of my miserable embarrassment. I stared. 'But it's yours. It's your money you've been saving. To go to America. To play in bands.'

He took out his tobacco pouch. 'It's all right. I can still go.'

'But how?'

Slowly, he lit a cigarette. Then he said. 'You might not understand this … and it's a bit embarrassing.'

I waited.

'I didn't need to save any money.' He blew smoke upwards. 'I have a bank account with enough in it for a round-the-world ticket. I've had it for a year — it was a present from my parents for my twenty-first. But I didn't want to use it. I wanted to pay my own way.' He glanced at me and grinned. 'Yeah. Stupid, right? But, you see, I'd never had to work for anything. My life had always been so easy.' His eyes drifted. He sat in silence for a moment, then shook his head. 'I wanted to take a stand, I s'pose — the kind of stand only a spoilt private-school boy is privileged enough to take.'

I gripped the envelope with both hands; the paper was growing damp. None of this seemed real — it was too much. There was the taste of metal in my mouth and a faint whirring in my ears.

'Silver?' Dan was leaning towards me. 'You okay?'

I nodded.

'So you take that money, all right? And you tell Ishtar what I just told you.'

I nodded again.

'I'll see you tomorrow. I'll come and say goodbye before I

go. And …' His voice softened, and I didn't have to look at him to know he had what I'd come to think of as his Ishtar face on. 'There's a party tonight, at Hope. Will you tell Ishtar? Maybe she'd like to come down, if she's feeling better.'

'Okay.' I started dazedly towards the hut, gripping the envelope, but stopped and turned back to him. 'Dan?'

'Yeah?'

'Why are you doing this?' I indicated the envelope. 'When she's so mean to you? When she doesn't love you back?'

He took a while to answer. 'There's love there,' he said at last, hesitating. 'There's love between us. Maybe it's not equal, maybe there's more on one side than the other, but that's not the point. The point is, if you love somebody and you can help them, then you do it, don't you?'

I watched him bump away down the track, the white rims of the tyres flashing as he entered the gloom of the overhanging trees.

Before going inside I sat for a while on the bench outside the hut. The day was hot already. My upper half was shaded, but the sun on my legs was strong and sweat began to pop at my armpits and under my nose. I still had the dizzy feeling, and there were black, quivery spots at the edges of my vision.

I looked down at the envelope in my lap. We would go now, surely — there was no reason for Ishtar to stay. This money would be the boost she needed, the trigger, swinging her into action. We would go overseas: I saw myself, pulled along in her wake through crowded markets, waiting while she laughed with some new man, putting myself to bed in dingy hostel rooms, trying not to wonder what I would do if she wasn't there when I woke in the morning. No school, no friends, always moving on.

I blinked into the bright clearing. The shadows between the tree trunks opposite trembled.

Ishtar took the envelope and opened it while I delivered Dan's message. She didn't look up or say anything, even when the money fell out on the sheet in a little gust of fragrant air. Despite my numbness, a thrill went through my gut; it was more money than I'd ever seen.

'He said it's enough for tickets for both of us.'

She didn't answer. She didn't count the notes, just gathered them with shaking fingers, stuffed them back into the envelope, and put it under her pillow. Then she lay down again and turned away from me.

'Ishtar?'

She lay still.

'What's going to happen?'

No answer.

'Where will we go? Which country?'

I waited but she didn't respond. I felt like a balloon, my head expanded and echoing, my feet barely touching the floor. I took an apple from the bag Dan had left for us on the bench out the front last week. From the entrance to my bedroom I looked back at the motionless length of her body under the sheet. The shut-in air seemed to hang over her, stained like the walls.

I closed the door behind me and lay on my own bed. I bit into the apple and the sharp juice ran down my throat.

The day went on forever. It got hotter and hotter. I took off my jeans and lay under the sheet in my t-shirt and undies. The sun moved until it came in my little window, and fell relentlessly across the mattress. At some point I went to sleep, my mouth sticky with apple juice.

I woke up to her standing over me.

'Silver.' She had the envelope, and she held it out. 'Take this to Hope. Give it back to Dan. Don't give it to anyone else. If he's not there, hold onto it, bring it back here.'

The sun was low, but it wasn't dark outside yet. The room was full of orange light. I sat up and tried to focus, to understand what was happening.

'But …'

She cut me off with a quick, firm shake of the envelope. Then she let it drop onto the bed and went out of the room.

I sat staring down at it. The overinflated, spacey feeling came back and I gripped the sheet in bunches. I hated her new starts, I didn't trust them, but even with their fleeting flimsiness they were at least familiar, recognisable. This — this flatness without end, this lack of response to an opportunity — I did not understand. I was lost, spinning in black, grabbing at nothing. We couldn't stay here with her like this, with her not moving or eating, with no money, and no one to care — no Dan. A vision descended: Val taking charge, installing Ishtar in one of the rooms at Hope to lie with staring eyes and yellow fingers, another Dawn, another half-person. Ishtar and Dawn, and Miller out in his shed, wallowing and raving on his mattress — three mad patients in the Hope Farm asylum. And me stuck forever, or at least until I finished school and could get a job.

We had to get away. I would go to Dan and explain, ask for

help. He wouldn't leave me with her like this. I put on some shorts and my sandshoes and went out, the envelope in my pocket. She was drinking a glass of water, one hand on the back of a chair. She didn't look up. For a few moments I stood there. I hadn't, in my balloon state, planned on saying anything, but like they had earlier with Dan, words just seemed to come out of nowhere.

'Why didn't you get an abortion when you were pregnant with me?'

Her eyes looked huge in the dim light. 'What?'

Quickly, the floating feeling went and my body seemed to tighten from the outside, gather in and consolidate round the sharp, central core that was this question. I didn't know where it had come from, but it was there, stabbing, insistent, undeniable — like a stick poking through rubber.

'Why didn't you get an abortion?' I repeated. 'When you were pregnant with me?'

Silence. Slowly, she moved round the chair and sat in it, put her elbows on the table and her head in her hands. When she spoke, her voice was blurred. 'I couldn't,' she said. 'You couldn't get them in those days, not in Brisbane. Or maybe you could … but I didn't know how.'

There was a sound in my head, a crack, and then a roar. She was still speaking, but I couldn't hear. My fingers were on the bolt, the door was open, my shoulder glancing off the frame, my bare legs flicking through the weeds as I ran.

The creek reeled in front of me and I went facedown onto the bank, my breath jarring with my fall and the shock of water on my arms. I waited for my fingers to lose sensation but they didn't — the top layer was almost warm — so I splashed my face instead. It felt cold then, prickling against my sweat, but the jangling, deafening howl that beat through me didn't stop. I lay in its grip, panting.

It was the droplets beading on the skin of my own forearms that gave me the idea, set it sawing in my mind. A crow barked like a warning, but I ignored it, jumped up, and ran again.

Under the crippled gum I dug with my fingers, dirt packing under my nails, filaments of blossom whirling, riding my ragged breaths.

He was asleep when I got to him. I kicked him, felt my toes glance off the barrel of his ribs. Through the black-edged pinpoint of my vision he looked small, far away, the mattress a little white oblong like the cakes of motel soap Ishtar used to bring back from her cleaning jobs, and him a miniature doll on top. With one foot I could flip it, send him flying — if I could just get my legs to move properly. But I could only manage these weak, mistimed kicks, and anyway I didn't want to send him flying now, I wanted him to wake up and hear what I was yelling, my voice stretched over the roaring in my ears.

I wasn't afraid of him any more. I wasn't afraid of anything. I was a blunt-limbed pink nothing, twitching in blackness; I mattered to no one and no one mattered to me — and she had done this, she had made me into this.

I hate her, I hate her, I hate her.

'What? What?' He sat up.

His face wavered. Was I on my feet still, or had I fallen to my knees? There was dirt under my hands, then air; I had dropped the photos. Something crackled and bit at the backs of my legs. My breaths kept seizing, my voice dumping its message too hard, again and again, like waves on a rock, smashing it up. I stared at his smeared face until the ground levelled and the mattress got a bit bigger, and I stepped forward because it was his fire behind me, I realised, burning my legs, and I caught his stench and like ink in water a hint of what I was doing came and dispersed and was gone. I let it go. I wanted the anger — and it had its own force anyway, after all this time. There were the photos, still sealed in their layers of paper and plastic; I kicked them forward and sent my voice out through the squalling static.

'Ishtar was fucking Dan while you were away. And she was pregnant, but she went to Melbourne and got an abortion. Ask Val, she knows. Ask Dan.'

Then I was up on the hill again, lying on my face behind the fallen tree, dirt in my mouth. I pressed my knuckles to my eyes and the roaring went on for what felt like a long time, before gradually breaking into chunks that at first seemed random but eventually settled into a rhythm. Then I felt that my hands were wet, and realised that the rhythm was my breathing, and that my breaths were sobs, and that I was crying. I lifted my head and opened my eyes and the air stung, bright and clear. A bird — one of Miller's white cockatoos — went ripping across the sky, and as if unzipped by its call the howling stopped and everything was quiet again, my sobbing small rounded waves that didn't break. I sat like that for a while, on my knees.

I had my eyes open, but I wasn't seeing what was in front of me — the side of the hill, trembling tassels of bleached grass against darkening blue; the last streaks of light turning pink — what I saw was a clear space, colourless, glaring almost too brightly to bear. It quivered, taut, shimmering and ready, and I knew what was coming, because I closed my eyes again and covered them, but that didn't work. I made a noise, an animal squawk, and then in it dropped, the understanding; the full acknowledgement of what I had just done. Black and viscous, a roiling glob, it hung for just a moment before exploding to fill everything.

Miller pacing in the room at the ashram that first day, stirring a whirlpool of light-soaked air. Miller snatching up Jindi and thrusting her towards the night sky. Miller's brute arms around Ishtar in the kitchen, the yielding of her neck to his kisses, her closed eyes. His drawings, the vicious penetrations of her body, the fierce sprays of conquering sperm. The wagging of his head in the clearing outside the hut, the groping of his hands. The power that hummed in him as he lay by his fire, that boiled under the addled, cracked exterior, covered but not dampened by the bong and the wine and the whisky and the pills, blindly seething, waiting for an opening, a clear path, a calling-out. And I had called it out. I had set it on Ishtar.

I got up. It was properly dark now, and a fat yellow moon sat right at the bottom of the sky. A song came drifting, something I half recognised — chiming guitars and a warbling, female vocal. I looked down and saw that Hope was lit up, every window golden, the flutter of candles on the kitchen windowsill and even the back steps. For once the place looked beautiful, and for a dizzy moment I wondered if I was in a dream — but then I remembered the party. Miller's fire was still there, off on its own to the side, just a dot. But where was he? I tried to remember what had happened once I'd spoken, once I'd said those words, what he'd said or done, but I couldn't — there was just a jump, a gap, to me lying in the dirt behind the log.

My heart knocking, I began to half-run back down the slope. There was the thought — very faint, hopeless really — that he hadn't noticed the photos, hadn't unwrapped and looked at them; that I could sneak in and steal them back again. But beyond that I had no plan. All my dull, blunt rage was gone. There was no roaring, no pinpointed vision, no sense of hugeness and power. Now I felt everything: the thump of my heart, the jag of my breaths, the whip of grass against my shins — and, wedged solid and straining at my chest as I ran, the raw fact of what I had done.

He was still there, I saw as I got down onto the flat and closer — and he had seen the photos. Their torn packaging lay to one side, and I could see a small rectangular object in Miller's fist where he squatted over the flames. He had taken off his shirt. Three or four wine cask bladders shone in the murk at the edge of the fire's circle, and there were papers and bottles spread further around than before — he had been throwing things. The mattress now lay slumped against one of the shed's side walls. There was a wet patch on the back wall, with trickles running down, and broken glass caught the firelight on the dark earth below. Miller's head nodded, and wordless noises rose from him, snaking to meet the tinny party sounds that drifted from Hope.

I waited a moment, watching that great head-shadow loom and bounce, then change shape as he turned to one side, letting the photos drop. The shaft of the glass bong glinted in the red light, and the voice broke off — and although I wasn't close enough to hear, I imagined the long burbling sound of him drawing up the smoke — and then the voice resumed, louder, and I caught a word this time: *Ishtar*. The shadow expanded, contracted; I saw him stand and stagger, then return to squatting, snatching up the photos and tossing them onto the fire. Another word detached itself from the flow: *witch*, or maybe *bitch*.

Something was going to happen. He was gathering himself, working up to — what? I thought of the press of his black thumbnail into Ishtar's skin. *I could just take you*. Whatever it was, it would be bad. I tried to think, to force myself beyond just feeling, beyond the slap and scrape of the world against me, and the swelling of guilt. Dan. I needed to find Dan. To ask for help and — I now realised, with an extra pang of shame — to warn him.

As I turned, Miller's voice broke into some kind of crescendo, a summoning yell, and when I snatched a look over my shoulder I glimpsed him on his feet, gesturing. Had he seen me? I ran faster. The dark shape of the mud-brick drew closer, bumping up and down against the starred sky, and I was almost at the gap between it and the outside toilet when the sight of figures there in the clearing — one of them unmistakably frail and twiggy, the yellow light in her ghostly cap of hair — sent me swerving around the back of the toilet and past the unused tractor gleaming in the moonlight. I didn't want to be stopped by anyone. I'd go round the other side of the house and see if Dan was out the front, which was where the music and voices were coming from.

Behind the shed that housed Miller's tools and boxes of seeds I collided with Ian. He was crouched at the far end of the back wall, and must have been peering round the corner — at Dawn, or at Sue, who was dancing by herself at the bottom of the kitchen steps — but he was so low and in such a pool of shadows I didn't see him, and fell right over him. We lay for a few moments of silent recognition and recovery, and before he could move I gripped his arm.

'Shh,' I whispered.

He sat up.

I knelt beside him, my mouth close to his ear, struggling to keep my voice under control. 'Miller's gone … I don't know — he's gone crazy. He's, he's, I think he's going to do something to Ishtar.'

'*Yikes.*'

'Can — can you help me?' The whispers sputtered out as if from a tiny, broken machine gun. 'You have to hel-help. Help me find Dan.'

He nodded.

I pointed. 'Out the front, out the front.'

Ian stuck his head out and then ducked back again. '*He's coming,*' he mouthed, nodding towards the mud-brick building.

We cowered, listening.

Dawn's voice sounded, abrupt but thin. 'What are you doing?'

I peered out, enough to see Sue, who wasn't dancing any more, but just standing at the foot of the kitchen steps staring at where Miller and Dawn must have been.

'Miller?' came Dawn's voice again. 'Where're you —' She broke off into a weak, protesting cry.

Sue started forward, and I put my head further out in time to see Miller go lumbering away, along the rutted driveway where he'd ridden in on the tractor that day, honking and waving, high and jubilant behind the big wheel. Now he moved with the crooked, menacing advance of a scorpion, his great arms out for balance, his legs widened as if for better purchase. Dawn was on the ground, Sue beside her, beginning to help her up.

'Quick.' Ian took off and I followed. We ran to the other side of the house, which was crowded by bushes and junk — rusted rolls of chicken-wire, piles of rot-soft planks, an old washing machine, car parts shot through with weeds — and scrambled through as fast and as quietly as possible to emerge under the cover of a largish, shaggy shrub at the end of the porch.

There seemed to be a lot of people on and in front of the porch, but it was probably only twenty or so — all the Hope residents, plus whatever guests they had managed to muster. There were candles stuck here and there, on the railings and the sill of the open windows. Two big metal drums with fires burning in them illuminated the parked cars. Some chairs had been brought out, and I caught sight of Willow on one, and Val, wilted flowers in her hair. No sign of Jindi; she must have exhausted herself with excitement and been put to bed. Dan was there, I saw with relief, sitting on the edge of the porch with his legs dangling.

All of this I took in very quickly, in the moments before Miller appeared from around the far side of the building. Into the shadowy crowd he moved, his bare torso wet with grease or sweat, and as he came he broke open a path of commotion. People stood up, backed away; Willow was knocked and went sliding from her chair to her knees, clutching her glass; another chair, empty, flew to one side like spray from a biting axe.

'Shit,' I heard Ian murmur beside me, and I started towards Dan. But then I stopped. What was I going to say? My shame gave a wrench, and I stayed where I was.

Past the first fire drum Miller strode. He tripped as he reached the porch, and almost fell in Dan's lap — and I saw the bemused almost-smile that crossed Dan's face in the moment before Miller took hold of him, the friendly way his hand went up to Miller's shoulder. Then they were on the ground, a conjoined mess of limbs, thrashing furiously back and forth. The small crowd made way.

'Whoa, easy,' someone called.

Another thrash, a swift slipping-through, and Dan was up, scrambling to his feet. He was hurt, though — he hobbled a few steps then stood crookedly, one knee bent, wiping at the blood that was coming from his nose, shining on his lips.

Miller, behind him, took longer to get up, but showed no sign of injury. He steadied himself, blowing, before advancing again on Dan.

'Look out,' somebody yelled, and Dan turned — but then Miller had him, one hand at the side of his head, the other at his throat. Dan's fingers clamped over his, their arms interlocked and taut. Back went Dan and forward went Miller, their steps slow and trembling.

'Miller,' said Dan in a gasping voice. 'Miller, calm down.'

Miller didn't speak. His mouth was open and with each breath came a moaning sound, breaking into grunts as he pressed forward, bull-like, his head lowered. Back and back stepped Dan, until he reached one of the cars and stopped. Miller kept pushing; Dan's knees bent and he sat on the car's bonnet. Miller pushed further and Dan's upper half gave and gave until he was lying flat and Miller had him pinned against the bonnet. Dan's arms were up, hands braced against Miller's chest, but still the downward force continued, still Miller bent over him, slowly, slowly, Dan's shaking arms giving way.

'Miller,' Dan wheezed again. 'What are you doing?'

From where I stood, paralysed, I could see the gap closing between them, Miller's face inching closer to Dan's. I caught the wet shine of Miller's lips, his open mouth. *He's going to bite him*, I thought. *He's going to bite his face off.*

'Help,' I heard myself croak, and I scanned the shadowy group of frozen onlookers. 'Someone.'

'Miller!' came Val's voice from the back of the crowd. 'Get off him!'

Gav made a tentative step forward, hands raised like someone being arrested in a TV show. 'Hey, hey,' he said weakly. 'Everyone just calm down, shall we?'

Heedlessly, Miller's face went on moving towards Dan's.

'Help him, someone!' This time my voice was loud and shrill, and Gav took another reluctant step closer.

'Come on, now,' he said. 'Let's just all settle down —'

He didn't get to finish his appeal though, because at my yell Ian had shot out from beside me and across the dark ground. Silent and fast he went — and before I could wonder what he was doing, heading not for Miller but for the house, and before Gav could work his way any nearer to the two figures bent over the car, Ian was up the steps, gripping the rail. Through went his body, swinging into space, skinny legs punching, feet connecting with the rim of one of the fire drums — the one further from where I was, but nearer to Miller and Dan — and the rusted cylinder was tipping, swinging over and down in a great whoosh of sparks. Like living things the burning wood leapt out, propelled by a landslide of livid coals, spilling right to Miller's heels — one long, char-striped piece landing, propped like a dog begging, against the back of his knee.

Miller roared and spun, swiping at his legs. He staggered

away from the fire, which lay like a rug patterned hot white and orange, its edge curling at the timber coffee table.

'Move the table!' someone called.

'Get some water!'

The crowd milled and jabbered. Somebody stumbled, fell to the ground. They were like bees drowning, uselessly buzzing at the foot of the porch, caught in the twin pools of darkness either side of the spilled fire.

'Tip beer on it!' called a voice, followed by a slow, rattling laugh.

Somewhere among the stoned dithering I caught sight of Dan, still at the car, grimacing as he tried to walk.

Miller hunched and moaned, batting at his leg. Then he straightened. He heaved a great sigh, and tipped his head back as if appealing to the stars. His fists went up and I saw them shake as he squeezed them. 'That,' he growled, 'was *my* baby, *mine*!' He rammed at his own temples. His burned leg twitched as if of its own accord. Like an enormous toddler distracted from a tantrum, he appeared to have completely forgotten about Dan. Heavily, he rotated his vast body and began to shamble in the opposite direction, along the row of cars. 'Ishtar,' he grunted. He stopped and put a hand on the bonnet of his brown station wagon, like a rider greeting his horse.

A fresh jolt of fear hit me. He was going to the hut. I couldn't stop him, and how could I warn her — how could I possibly get there first? I looked again for Dan, but there was something else catching at my attention, a sound, rustling below the voices — a busy, papery sound — and from the direction of the house there came a flaring of bright light. I saw it gild Miller, dancing in the raw-looking skin at the back of his leg where his pants had been burned away. I turned.

The little carpet of burning wood and coals that Ian had spilled was still there, licking at the table, which no one had moved. But the light, and the heat I was beginning to feel now, building, rolling outwards, were coming from the house, from one of the front windows and the front door. The house was on fire.

My mind dashed back to Miller and Dan on the ground, the panicked retreat of onlookers, some jumping up onto the porch. The open windows and candle-lined sills. I pictured the candle knocked, tipping, falling inside the room, lying there unnoticed, the crawl of its flame at the base of the curtain, its steady climb and creeping growth, feeding on the perished fabric, the aged, porous timber floor and walls.

But this fire was not creeping now. This fire was big already, shockingly, frighteningly big, and growing as I watched — bank after bank of orange blooms unfurling. At first I could see the open window, with the flames coming up from inside, and the beginnings of flames only at one side of the front door; then within moments the flames were filling both spaces, tearing upwards in vigorous sheets, the window's curtain showing only as a strip to one side, exploding into liquid white and then gone. Then the frames of both window and door were not visible any more either — there were just two holes, one vaguely square and one vaguely rectangular, with the flames rushing from them, pouring out, and up.

There was a sudden, frenzied stirring in the middle of the small crowd, and then first Val's shout — '*Jindi!*' — followed by gibbering from Willow.

'The kids!' someone yelled.

'Quick!' came another voice. 'Round the back!' There was a rush down the side of the house, leaving a few people stomping at the small fire and milling round in the glare of the big one, calling to each other.

'Where's the phone? Someone call triple-oh!'

'Get the hose.'

'Buckets!'

Dan was still near the other car. He didn't seem able to walk, but I could hear him shouting directions, pointing to the tap.

I knew I should help; I knew where buckets were, in the laundry and the shed. I knew there was a hose round the back. But Miller — and Ishtar. Teetering on my toes, I hung in an agonised moment that felt like forever. The sound of the fire stretched and warped in my ears. Miller's steps thudded in slow motion; his hand reached for the door of the station wagon.

And then I saw the movement behind the windscreen, the wisp of a figure sitting there. Dawn. I saw her lean across, her pallid face staring out at Miller as he tugged uselessly at the door handle. I saw the bunch of keys dangling from her finger, then swallowed by her closing fist.

Miller pulled at the handle. Again, hard. Then he tried the back door. Slowly, disbelievingly, he circled the car, going from door to door, rattling uselessly at each.

The engine started and, with Miller howling and slapping uselessly at its exterior, the car backed — wobblingly, almost stalling — out from between those parked either side and then around in a semicircle. There was a scraping of gears and it leapt forward, almost hitting Miller, and with a triumphant blast of the horn started up the driveway, gathering speed. Just before it reached the gate, the headlights went on, and the bright beam lapped at the opening in the band of trees, the sandy surface of the road. Then, its one working tail-light bobbing, the car exited the gateway, turned, and disappeared in the direction of the main road.

Miller, out on the packed dirt, had dropped to a crouch, hands to his temples.

Dawn. I couldn't believe it. Even as I turned and began to run towards the back of the house, calling, 'I'll get the hose,' I had a fleeting urge to laugh, to whoop out loud. *Dawn!*

Hot air rippled the stars overhead, and one of the side windows already showed flickering, the weatherboards pocking with pink, black-edged splotches. It was amazing how quickly the fire had taken hold. The kitchen was full of yelling, and people running in and out; as I tried to marshal the hose into loops neat enough to carry I caught sight of Sue trying to hold onto Willow, who was swaying like a spooked animal, bleating wordlessly.

I was almost back to the porch, half dragging the hose, when Ian appeared by my side.

'He's walking,' he said, low and terse.

'What?'

Someone — Gav; the light slashed across his glasses and I caught a whiff of patchouli — took the hose from me and hurried off with it.

Ian nodded towards the track that led up to the main gate. 'Miller. He's gone off on foot. If we're quick we can go the back way and beat him there.'

Once we were at the bottom of the hill and out of earshot it was as if the fire didn't exist. But when we crossed the road and entered the bush, the moonlight turned everything to shades of ash, and it was so still it felt as if all the air had been taken, dragged away.

We plunged along the path, the creek beside us silvered and silent. Scratches stung on my bare legs, and my chest ached from the smoke.

Ian led, made the turn-off at the big wattle — but when we got to the cleared area and the hut revealed itself, a dark rectangle, no light showing anywhere, he slowed and waited for me to draw level. We paused. There were no noises other than insect ones.

'Come on,' whispered Ian, but he didn't move.

I went first, my breath hitched up short, edging across the clearing and then around the side of the building.

The front door was open, showing dark space. I froze, motioned to Ian. Waited. No sound. I inched closer, reached the bench, which stretched — a pointing arrow — to the open door. I could feel Ian right behind me, his breath on the back of my neck.

At the doorway I put my ear to the opening. Nothing. I poked my head in, stared into the darkness until shapes began to form: the fireplace, the couch, Ishtar's bed — empty.

Slowly we stepped in.

'Ishtar?'

No answer. It was hard to see properly — things looked different in the dark; puddles of shadow like black liquid; shapes squatting, still and sinister. I went to the bench and found the torch, clicked it on.

The bed with the sheet thrown back. Dirty plates in a pile on the table. The bag of apples, dull red in the torch's beam. Cobwebs, dust. Everything shabbier, uglier in the weak cone of light, but no more than the usual mess — and no blood, no signs of struggle or force.

Ian's whisper was barely audible. 'Are we too late?'

I shrugged. Went to my room, shone the torch all round it. Nothing. My bed, my own dank, kicked-off sheet. The apple core on the mattress.

'Ishtar?'

The room sang its emptiness but still I knelt and reached with the wand of light under the bed, glaring on balls of dust and more cobwebs.

'We're too late,' whispered Ian behind me.

I looked up at him. 'Or maybe she's already gone? Maybe she —'

He raised a hand. Someone was coming.

I got up.

It was him — the heavy tread outside, the low, sonorous voice coming into earshot, spooling out.

I switched off the torch.

Even though the main door was open already he rammed into it, sending it back against the wall with a clap. He moved so quickly into the room he hit the couch, and it went scraping over the floor. He reeled back and collected himself, standing with that loose-armed, ready posture, head swivelling.

All this I saw in silhouette, against the moon-bright rectangle of doorway.

'Ishtar?' said Miller thickly, and then resumed his humming, his breath-sucking. His black form bent over her bed, great paws fumbling. 'Ishtar?'

Ian took my arm, pulled. Together, as if one merged body, we lowered ourselves to the floor, began to climb into the space under my bed. Ian was halfway under, his arm unhooking from mine, when I dropped the torch. It banged to the floor and rolled noisily. I froze.

Miller's humming stopped and I saw him straighten and swing round.

'Ian.' I mouthed the word; it hardly sounded. My pulse hammered in my ears. We were small, we were quick — we could slip past, dash by him. I reached for Ian, pulled at his shirt. I began to get to my feet.

But Miller was there, he was charging towards us, he was filling the tiny doorway, his big arms were out — he had me, his fingers a vice above my elbow. He tugged, and pain rang through my shoulder. My feet left the ground; I bent my knees and landed on the mattress.

He held me like that, kneeling on the bed, my head level with his so I couldn't avoid the hot, rotten breath that spurted from his beard as he ran his hands over my hair and face.

'It's the kid,' he muttered. He paused for a moment but didn't let go. The light from the window behind me caught the surfaces of his eyes, the wetness of his open mouth. Then, so close I felt his beard touch my chin, he shouted, 'Where is she?'

I pulled back as far as I could, angling my head away.

'Where's Ishtar?'

Spit landed on my cheek. He shook me and my teeth clattered. He pushed me down on the bed and then wrenched me up again. I heard a frail mew, then realised I was the one who had made it.

'I know where she is.'

It was Ian. He had crept past Miller to the doorway and was just visible, a slight dark figure against the lesser shadows.

Miller looked round. I felt his fingers slacken slightly. He reeked. That rank, creature smell that had been in his room, but ten times riper.

'I know where she is. She's hiding.' Ian's voice was level. 'I can take you to her. But you have to let go of Silver.'

Miller's huge head shook, slowly, from side to side. His fingers stayed clenched around my arm. His breaths were loud and wet, like a baby's.

'Well, she can come too, then,' said Ian pleasantly, as if suggesting a picnic or some other benign activity. 'We can all go together.'

Miller's arm swept back to his side and I was pulled from the bed, scrambling to land on my feet. One of my shoes caught on the edge of the mattress and went flying. Miller stepped towards Ian and I was dragged along. Then, gradually, his fingers unlocked, and I felt the air on my damp skin. He took a fistful of my t-shirt at the back.

'No running,' he said.

I could just see Ian's eyes — they were fixed on mine. I gave him a tiny nod.

He turned for the door. 'This way.'

We went slowly this time, along the grey path, through the shadow-dappled bush. The moon wasn't yellow any more — it was high and white, its light cold. Ian led again, followed by me, lopsided in my one shoe, and then Miller, his heavy grip at my back, the heat of his knuckles through my top, his bare toes every now and then colliding with one of my heels. Along to the bridge and over, and then up the avenue of sparser growth that marked the old miners' trail.

Miller resumed his broken humming, and panted loudly. Once, he stumbled, pulling me down with him, my elbow sliding against the wet mat of his chest-hair, revulsion jamming my throat. We got to the two trees, and Ian went between their luminous trunks. I hesitated; Miller barged into me and we came to a clumsy halt.

Ian turned. The pinkish branches between us hung like human limbs bent at impossible angles. 'Come on,' he said. 'Almost there.'

I tried to see past him into the clearing but everything was shadows. I blinked and the shadow shapes seemed to wobble and drift, resetting in a slightly different formation. Where was it, exactly? Was it even visible — maybe Ian had left it covered, set up as a trap. 'Ian ...' My voice sounded very small. My pulse was loud in my ears.

'Come on.' Ian turned back, and took a step.

I strained again to see into the darkness. *Watch him*, I told myself. *He knows where it is.* But I couldn't see him any more.

Miller's fist gave a shove between my shoulder blades and I propped like a panicked horse, head thrown back. 'Ian!'

'Come on,' came the call.

Miller gave one of his breathy, sighing moans, and began shunting me along before him as if I weighed nothing. Then something caught at my ankle and I fell forward with him on top of me.

It was the fence. The collapsed fence — I felt its slack lines, the grit of rust on my fingers as I untangled my foot. My heel slipped out of the second sandshoe and I let it go, kicked it away. Miller had climbed off me, to one side, and was on his knees.

'What ...?' he said.

Then Ian was beside me, pulling me up, and I grabbed his arm and squeezed it, one sharp squeeze to send a message. 'You go first,' I hissed, pushing him, and we were running, and behind was Miller's roar, the heavy sounds of him getting to his feet.

Ian's back, Ian's legs, the soles of his shoes, *one-two, one-two*. I knew it was only a short distance, only a few steps, and I watched for him to swerve or jump, staring so hard my eyes felt like they would pop out of my head, every muscle in my own legs electric. *One-two, one-two*, and there it was — uncovered, a bigger, darker patch of shadow among the other shadows — and Ian jumped. I saw him hurdle, the arc of him through the air, and Miller was coming with his crashing feet, right behind me, Miller's fingers bumping at my back, just missing, and I only had two more steps to go, one more step, and I was on it, I was leaping, the burning split of my legs opening, the pull of every tendon, the desperate reaching, reaching for length.

Landing, the shock of real, hard ground, jarring my ankles, slamming my knees. But not stopping, shoving up and forward, half crawling, scrabbling across the dirt, away from the feeling of falling, the cold, stale-breathed drop. And behind me, Miller went down.

We heard him, the yelp he gave. We heard the two bumps he made as he hit the sides, one almost straight away, and then another, not as loud, after a long, slow, couple of moments. And then we heard, floating up from very far away, very deep, a final, heavy, wet thud.

I reached for Ian at the same time as he reached for me, and we grabbed onto each other. I bent my head and pressed one ear to his chest, and jammed my shoulder up to block the other one, so all I could hear was the rabbit race of our two hearts running in double time.

We went up, higher, further into the bush. We just walked together, without talking, following mining trails feathered with saplings and bracken, which offered easier passage between the trees.

We passed other shafts with fences hanging, half collapsed, signs blank-faced in the dim light.

I got cold. My feet hurt, and my ankle where I'd scraped it on the fence wire.

Slower and slower we walked, and then we stopped and sat down at the base of a big tree. Side by side we stared into the sifting shadows. The moon was no longer visible, although its white light still filtered through the branches. The stars in the patch of sky above were bright and hard-looking. I couldn't stop shivering.

After a while we lay down, back to back, pressed close for warmth. I curled up my knees and tucked in my arms.

I don't know if I slept but when I opened my eyes the sky had a wash of pink in it. I thought I'd heard noises. I lay still, feeling Ian breathing behind me. Light was creeping into the scrub around us. A bird hopped through the leaf litter, then disappeared under an archway of fern fronds. Other birds called, and when I looked again the pink in the sky had turned to gold.

Then I did hear it. Voices, calling. Not close — down on the other side of the creek. They were calling us.

'Ian?'

'Yeah?'

'Listen.'

He sat up, and I did the same.

Everything hurt — every muscle in my over-stretched legs, my scraped, cut feet, my shoulder where Miller had yanked it. I ached with thirst and my tongue felt thick and strange. I eased my legs straight. 'We should go.'

'Yeah.'

We looked at each other. I licked my lips. 'So what do we …?'

He shook his head, just slightly. 'We say we went to tell your mum about the fire, and she wasn't there. So then we went to look for her, and we got lost, we got confused, and we slept up here in the bush.'

'But what about …?'

'We don't say anything about him. The last time we saw him was at Hope, when he was fighting with Dan.' He stood and brushed down his shorts. 'Just don't say anything and it'll be okay. Come on.'

We were both whispering, standing close, but we didn't make eye contact.

'My shoe. It's there. It fell off.'

'Okay. I'll get it.'

I swallowed. 'Thanks.'

The voices sounded again.

'Come on,' said Ian. 'We'd better go.'

We went downhill, vaguely following the trails, and came out on the main one, just above the turn-off signposted by the twin trees. In silence Ian went in; in silence he came out with the shoe. He handed it to me and we continued walking.

On and on the voices went, bouncing off the water. They had shifted along the creek's bank, closer to Hope. They were men's voices — I didn't recognise them.

'Should we call back?'

Ian shook his head. 'Let's get a bit closer first.'

It was strange, hearing my name shouted over and over by an unknown man. As we neared the bridge we both slowed down. A new heaviness descended. I glanced at Ian; he was barely moving, feet dragging, head down. He felt it too, I could tell — the need to wait, to spin it out a while longer, this time, this lull, before we showed ourselves, brought the reality of our secret into lasting, hardened being.

When the bridge came into sight we stopped. Something bumped my hand. It was Ian — his fingers groped at mine, caught and held them.

Then there were feet on the bridge, the flicker of blue uniforms, and they were there, the two policemen — they saw us and came striding over, still calling our names — and Ian let go of my hand.

The ruin of Hope sat like a pair of jaws pulled back to the morning sky, jag-edged, heaped with ash, exhaling breaths of smoke. The ugly mud-brick building, apparently untouched, squatted in attendance. At one end of the row of parked cars was a fire truck; at the other a police car. People stood in clusters, arms folded.

The policemen had been carrying blankets — they'd

wrapped me and Ian in one each, and we wore them like cloaks as we walked. At first, as we'd crossed the road and climbed through the fence, they had tried to talk to us, saying rehearsed-sounding things about taking us to our families. They'd stayed close, guiding arms on our shoulders, helping us through the fence wires. But as we moved up the hill, they quietened and fell back, allowing us to walk together, to lead the way.

Going downhill we fell into a rhythm, footfalls aligning, blankets swishing, and a kind of emptied feeling moved into me, a strange, clear, helplessness. Things were going to happen now and I had no control over what they might be. I could only submit.

I suppose if I had been able to think of anything, to predict anything, I might have expected Ishtar not to be there. I might have imagined her vanished, gone at last, having left the night before while it was all happening — the fight, the fire — silently exiting the violent whirl of drama that, at its centre, in its conception, held her image.

What I didn't expect was for her to break from one of the groups of figures, to run up the slope towards me, to grab me in her arms and pull me so close my breath caught and my feet left the ground. I didn't expect her to cry.

Her ribs jumped with her sobbing. Her tears wet my scalp. I was still holding the sandshoe; wedged between us, it smelled of rubber and canvas, of school changing rooms. She hung onto me until I started to resist, and then she let me down and put her palms either side of my face and kissed me again and again and her kisses caught the morning air and slapped it against my skin.

Behind her the smoke, as if lost, as if having forgotten its reason for being, drifted in the gaping space above the remains, the piles of black stuff, the sullen rectangle of the outer foundations, which must have been brick or some tougher, harder timber. The kitchen steps still stood, a lone grey tooth in a rotten, gummy grin; it took me a while to recognise a paler lump among the debris as the fridge, half melted, and shrouded in ash.

'What happened with Jindi, and the baby?'

'They're okay.' Her voice broke, and she wiped her face with her sleeve.

I couldn't stop looking at the ruin, the impossible, shocking blankness of that emptied space, the missing roof and walls. Two firemen in uniform stood at its edge, talking with a policeman. One of them pointed into the wreckage and shook his head.

Ishtar pressed her lips to my cheek again. I barely caught her whisper: 'I thought you were in there.'

I looked across and saw Ian and his parents, standing in their own close huddle. I could only see the back of Ian's head, his thin, shaking shoulders, the ridge of his spine through his clothes. But I saw his mother's face with its undeniable, narrow likeness, and I saw the clutch of her hands at his shirt. The father was taller, his posture sagging. Ian's leanness was there, his stork-like limbs, and also something of his removed, reined-in manner, his fastidiousness. But as I watched, the father moved closer. He put his arms around both of the others. His long face rested on the top of Ian's head, and his eyes squeezed shut.

A woman and a man wearing some other kind of uniform made me sit on the grass and drink sugary tea from a paper cup, and eat a sandwich. My fingers made black marks on the bread. The cheese was cut too thick, and the slices of tomato made me think of flesh.

The helmeted, heavy-suited firemen were packing up the truck now, winding the flaccid hose back in. The second bite of sandwich wouldn't go down; I spat it into the paper bag while no one was looking.

'Ishtar.' The word hardly came out, but she heard me. 'Can we go?'

She helped me up.

'Oh, are you off are you? I'm not sure ...' began the sandwich and tea woman, but Ishtar ignored her.

We went over to the cars, where Val stood. Jindi lay asleep across the back seat of the yellow station wagon.

Val's embrace was as unexpected as Ishtar's, hot and close and long. 'Thank god,' she said in her grainy voice, letting me go and then pulling me back again. 'Thank god.'

Ishtar helped me in and Jindi's dirty feet twitched and then resettled against my thigh.

'We'll go and you can get changed,' said Ishtar. 'Then Val's going to drive us to see Dan.'

'Dan?'

'Yeah. He hurt his ankle. He's at the hospital, in Tarrina.'

The front door of the hut was wide open, the couch still up against the fireplace as if trying to hide. There were the torch and the single sandshoe, lying in the doorway to my room. I hurried over, put the shoe I was holding down with its mate and grabbed the torch, which I set on the table. I could feel Ishtar watching.

My hands shook as I changed, and when I took off my shorts, their legs creased and stiff with dirt, the envelope fell out onto the floor. I put it carefully on the bed, and watched it as I finished dressing. Then I took it to Ishtar.

It seemed to me the smell of Miller was there still, in the rooms.

I held out the envelope. 'I didn't get a chance.'

She took it, her fingers closing over mine, and when I tried to pull my hand away she caught it and held on.

'I'm sorry,' she said.

'It's okay.' The words jumped out automatically. I tried again to draw my hand back, but she wouldn't let go.

'I shouldn't have sent you,' she said, 'without explaining. I actually changed my mind, last night — I went down, to Hope. I thought I might catch you. But I was too late. Nobody knew where you were. Nobody could say for sure you weren't inside when the fire …' She put her palm to her chest and breathed deeply for a few seconds. Then her eyes left my face and moved round the room, over the shoved-into couch and her own empty bed with its sullied sheet to the reunited sandshoes in the doorway. They came back, met mine. 'Nobody knew where you were.'

I dropped my gaze to the table, to the torch. We must have passed each other somewhere. I saw it as if on an aerial map, our trails visible, coming near but not touching, hers running down the hill and to one side of the shed, or the fallen log, or the compost heap, ours heading upwards on the other side. And, forming the other half of a crooked circle, Miller's path, by the road.

I heard myself rush the words, realising even as I said them how guilty they made me sound — answering a question that had not been asked. 'We came to find you, to tell you about the fire. But you weren't here, and then we went looking for you, and we got lost …'

She looked again at the shoes, then turned to the kitchen bench. When she spoke again her voice was brisk. 'You hungry?'

'No.' My stomach clenched. I didn't understand why I felt so angry. This was what was supposed to happen. She had believed the story. She came closer to me again and reached for my hand, but I pulled it back.

'Don't touch me,' I said.

She poured water into a dish and put it and a flannel on the table in front of me.

'We need to leave.' I gestured at the empty duffel bags folded in the bottom of her shelves, the case on its side under the end of her bed. 'Now. Move out, I mean. Straight away.'

She didn't ask why. She had her head down. 'Okay.'

I stared at what I could see of her lowered face, her foreshortened features, the hair falling either side. *This is all your fault.* The words were inside me, pressing outwards, wanting to stab at her. But I didn't let them.

Val drove us to Tarrina. Jindi was still asleep in the car and I slept too, waking as Val pulled on the handbrake, my neck stiff, sweat beading at the backs of my knees.

The hospital buildings were modern and tidy, their car park bordered by roses in small, circular beds. Behind the reception desk a woman frowned, eyes darting at my face, which I probably hadn't cleaned very well.

'We're here to see Dan Cohen,' said Ishtar. 'Daniel.'

The woman looked at something on her desk. 'Cohen,' she said, and then her face changed. 'Oh yes,' she said, 'the fire. Gosh, that must have been quite a shock.' She leaned forward.

'You look like you've been through the wringer, love,' she said. 'What happened? You weren't inside —'

'Can we see Dan, please?' said Ishtar.

'Oh yes, sorry.' The woman pinched her lips together and pointed along a corridor. 'Ward Five.'

Dan was down the end of the row of beds. He was lying on his back, a blanket drawn up to his hips. His legs looked very long under the thin fabric, which was white, and perforated with tiny square holes; one foot stuck out the end, with a big cast on it. He had no top on.

When he saw us approaching he put one hand across his eyes, then slid it down and looked over it like someone removing a blindfold. He shook his head, grinning. 'Jesus, kid,' he said. 'We were worried about you.' Then his expression changed. 'And your friend?'

'He's okay.'

His soft face, unguarded, turned up to me, the smoothness of his brown skin, flushed slightly at the throat, the sparse, dark hairs at the hollow of his breastbone and around his nipples — I shuffled my gaze from one part of him to the next, an embarrassed tenderness curling in me.

Ishtar pulled the curtain round and she and I sat down on two plastic chairs. 'We sure were,' she said. She put her hand to Dan's face, tucked it in between his cheek and the pillow. 'And how are you?'

'I'm okay. Broken ankle. Hurts.' A quick grimace of a smile. 'And so what about the fire? They were just getting it under control when I ...'

'The house burnt right down,' said Ishtar. 'There's nothing left.'

Dan raised his eyebrows and whistled between his teeth.

There was silence for a while, then he turned to me. 'Silver, that fight was pretty scary. I'm sorry you had to see it. Miller just — he just lost it for a moment. Adults do stupid stuff, you know that.'

At the sound of Miller's name my heart began to hammer so hard I was sure they must be able to hear it.

Ishtar leaned forward. 'I'm sorry Miller hurt you.'

'It doesn't matter.' He put his hand over hers. 'Everyone's okay, that's what matters.'

She pulled their joined hands closer and kissed them.

I stared down at my lap.

'He's missing,' said Ishtar. 'Miller.'

My heart went into overdrive.

'Shit,' said Dan. 'But he wasn't inside —'

'No. Somebody saw him walk up to the road. That was the last anyone saw of him.'

'Yeah, that's what I thought. I was worried he was going after you, that he was ...'

I tried to make the magic shape but my fingers were shaking too much. I tucked my hands between my thighs.

'Anyway,' said Dan, 'I was so relieved when you turned up. You only just missed him. Lucky.'

'Yeah.'

'He was pretty well out of it. He probably just fell asleep somewhere. He'll turn up.'

Miller slamming into the hut, colliding with the couch. His grip on my arm in the darkness, his shouting face in mine. Limping up the hill in my one shoe. The black shaft. The sounds he made, as he fell.

Ishtar was quiet, but I imagined I could feel her attention on me, like some invisible beam — radar, or sonar. When I raised my head though, it was Dan who was looking my way.

'Silver?' he said. 'You okay?'

I nodded and fixed my gaze on the end of the bed, the big white cast. My breathing felt strange, as if I couldn't get enough air in.

Ishtar took out the envelope and they argued about the money for a while, but I couldn't pay attention. Ishtar said something about already having enough, which did trigger a blip of surprise on the far side of my panic, but I was in too much of a state to understand what she meant. In the end Dan made her keep it anyway.

I still regret that the rest of that goodbye was so heavily obscured by my terror at the thought of being found out, by my throbbing heart and strangled breaths, by the weight that had entered the air with the mention of Miller's name. I don't think I was at all able to grasp the fact that this was the last time I would see Dan. He kissed me, there is a memory of that, but it's a distant, unfeeling one. I wish now that I could go back and have that goodbye again, untainted, to be able to thank him for his kindness, his friendship, to be able to feel straight, childish sadness at such a loss.

Val took us to the train station.

'Now you take care,' she said, as we got our things out of the boot. When Ishtar tried to give her some money for petrol she flapped her hand. 'You just take care,' she said again.

'See you soon!' called Jindi through her open window as they drove away.

I didn't think about the fact that we wouldn't see them soon, or later — or ever again. And that the same went for Willow, Gav, and Sue. And Ian. I was still jangling so hard with paranoid guilt that I could barely think at all.

I'd reached some kind of limit though, and when I sat on a bench to wait while Ishtar bought the tickets, my heart finally slowed, my limbs grew heavy and my mind emptied. The train came and we got on it, into a completely empty carriage, and I lay across a seat and slept and slept and slept.

In Melbourne we went to a pub that was walking distance from the station. The room, two flights up, was tiny, almost completely filled by the twin single beds, only a slim aisle of space between.

We went straight back downstairs for dinner. Chips and some kind of meat. A wan bit of lettuce and a slice of tomato. Ishtar drank a glass of beer and I had lemonade. My hunger was there at last, and I ate until my stomach hurt. There was light still in the street outside, late and golden, but the city seemed empty, the view of the building opposite unbroken by pedestrians, only one or two passengerless trams trundling past during our meal.

'Sunday night,' said the man behind the bar.

After dinner I went to the shared bathroom two doors down from our room. The shower tiles were dark with mould, and clots of other people's hair sat at the edge of the shower drain like miniature, thirsty animals. The bath was clean though, and I filled it up. There was a key in the door, but I couldn't turn it. I tried and tried until my fingers hurt and tears popped into my eyes. I gave up and sat on the wonky chair. Footsteps passed, and men's voices sounded. I crossed my arms over my still-clothed chest.

I went back to the room.

'What happened?' said Ishtar.

There was a feeling now, which had been there since the morning — since the shock of her embrace and the hand-holding — of something taking up the space between us, something dense and deadening, rising from me; a mute, numb blockage.

'I thought you were going to have a bath,' said Ishtar.

I mumbled something and flopped onto the bed.

'What?'

I spoke to the wall. 'I can't lock the door.'

There was the sound of her standing up. 'Come on.'

Under the bathroom's bare globe she jiggled the key. Took it out and put it back in again. Tried it with the door open. Tried from the outside, then the inside again. Eventually she shrugged and left it, took the wobbly chair and put it against the door and sat on it. 'I'll stand guard,' she said.

I looked at her.

'What?' She gave a forced laugh. 'I'm not going to sit out in the corridor.'

The laugh, as it echoed off the tiles, took on a strange, wretched quality. The cloud of tension intensified.

'Don't be ridiculous,' she said, after a few moments, and then she sighed and turned sideways, angling her head in a show of not-looking.

I took off my clothes and got in, facing away from her. I lathered the soap and washed myself, and the surface of the water clouded with grey scum.

The room had a window, but the glass was frosted. Through

it a brick wall was discernable, very close. Pigeons were calling somewhere, and a tram rattled down on the street.

'This is where I stayed,' she said. 'When I came last time.'

I knew what she meant, but I didn't answer. I wasn't going to help her.

She said it so quietly I almost could have imagined it. 'For the abortion.'

My knees stuck up out of the soapy water, two pink islands, slicked with milky tide lines. I took the flannel and wiped my face with it. My eyes stung and I kept them closed — and there it was, the tiny foetus, floating against its wet black background, its eyeball showing under the film of skin.

'You wanted to know,' she said, the words stronger now, the effort in them audible, 'why I didn't get an abortion when I was pregnant with you.'

I kept my eyes closed. The creature twitched a flipper, bobbed in its glistening darkness.

'Like I said,' her voice went on, 'I couldn't, in Brisbane, back then. You couldn't get one. Or if you could, I didn't know where. Or how. I was only seventeen years old. I didn't even know how you got pregnant, if you could believe that.' She gave a faint, weary snort.

The small room held its damp breath. The bath was the same temperature as the air, and with my eyes shut I couldn't tell which parts of me were under and which were not. When I spoke, the words seemed to dissolve almost as soon as they came out. 'But what if you could have got one?'

'You mean if I could go back and have that choice now?'

'Yeah.'

Then there was a sudden movement and she was kneeling

beside me, both arms around me, sleeves in the water.

'No. Of course not. I've got you now. I couldn't go back and undo you.'

That was our chance, I suppose. To reconnect. To take the stiffened hinge that joined us and wrench it into mobility. When I go over it all in my mind, that's the part I imagine changing, doing differently. I imagine turning to her, sitting up in the water to return her embrace, pressing my face into her neck. That, I tell myself, was probably all it would have taken.

But that's not what happened. I wasn't strong enough, or brave enough; the accumulated resentment was too firmly rusted on. She stayed like that for a while as I lay limp and unresponsive, and then she let go again, and I got out and dried myself and put on the only nightclothes I owned — a cotton slip that was far too small and reached just halfway down my thighs — and went back to the room and got into bed, leaving her still sitting on the chair.

The next morning we had breakfast in a coffee shop. The city was trussed up in tinsel, pointy gold and silver stars hanging from the tramlines. I'd missed that somehow, in our exhaustion-fogged arrival. Also, overnight it seemed to have filled with people — crowds of them now flowed up and down the footpaths. It was like a completely different place.

Ishtar ate in silence. I wasn't hungry. My egg was overcooked, the yolk splitting to show its hardened inner. I left it and drank my glass of orange juice, but it went down too fast and sloshed around in my stomach. I'd slept like a stone on the hotel mattress, which dipped in the middle, keeping me immobile on my back like an overturned beetle. Ishtar had had to wake me. But still I felt soaked with a deep tiredness, pulled low in my seat.

She leaned across, put her hand by mine on the tabletop. 'You okay?'

'Yeah.' I ignored her attempt at eye contact and squinted through the window at the tramping figures criss-crossing in the glitter and glare of the hot morning.

After a few moments she appeared to give up. She sat back and looked around the room, and I turned from the window — and at the same moment both of our eyes fell on a folded newspaper that lay on the counter. Imaginary headlines flew through my mind: *Dead man found. Murder victim in mineshaft. Girl suspect sought.* I pictured the plump man behind the counter opening the paper and reading, then lowering it and frowning at me. I tried to summon Ian in my head: *Don't be ridiculous. Nobody knows.* The juice began to feel like it was crawling back up my throat.

Ishtar got up and went to pay for the food, and I sat, replaying Ian's words: *Just don't say anything and it'll be okay.* 'It'll be okay,' I murmured to myself, but I didn't feel any better.

When she had finished Ishtar walked to the door, and I started to get to my feet, clattering the cutlery. My chair got stuck and I struggled to get out from behind the table. I caught sight of the newspaper again and with a snap the anger was back, the urge to attack her with words, to force something on her, or out of her.

You know Miller went to the hut. You know something happened. You saw the mess. You didn't even ask me where I was.

She had stopped in the doorway. I got free of the furniture and stepped towards her, staring into her face, my eyes so wide they started to water.

Ask me what happened. Ask me.

The door opened and she went out.

I followed, bumping into a man, then a woman with shopping bags that banged at my legs. 'Sorry.' I dodged round her and darted after Ishtar, who seemed to glide with rapid ease through the crowd. Lunging, I caught the back of her shirt.

We stood, facing one another, joggled by the streams of passing people.

'Ishtar.'

'Yeah?'

The straining, desperate rage wobbled. I swallowed. I thought of Ian shaking his head, his voice, gentle but firm: *We don't say anything about him.*

'Silver. What is it?'

I looked down at the pavement. 'I need to make a phone call.'

She didn't ask any questions, just led me to a phone box and gave me some coins, then stood outside with her back turned.

I pushed the door closed and fumbled my way through the phone book until I realised it was only for the city and surrounding suburbs. Then I found a number for directory assistance and called, and got the listing for Munro in Kooralang.

Ian answered, and at the sound of his voice I started to cry, the same mortifying crying that had happened with Dan — loud, wet, and obvious.

'Silver? Is that you?'

'Yes,' I managed to blub.

'Are you okay?'

'Yes.' I took the receiver away from my ear for a few moments and put my face in the crook of my arm, wiping it and trying to breathe evenly. The tears didn't stop completely, but I did manage to regain some control over my voice. I lifted the receiver again. 'I'm scared.'

'Right.' There was a warning in his tone.

I glanced at Ishtar, who still had her back turned, and lowered my voice. 'I'm not saying anything. I haven't said anything, don't worry. But I'm scared.'

This time his voice was reassuring. 'It will be okay. I promise.'

The tears kept running down my face. The phone box smelled of newspapers and urine. I pressed the earpiece close. 'How are you?'

'Oh, I'm fine. You know, school holidays.' He spoke as if from the depths of normalcy, from a place so mundane and settled as to be boring, as if nothing bad had ever happened, and I strained to catch every word, every nuance of his rusty voice. 'I'm *slaving* for the parents, painting the verandah. I am *heartily sick* of the colour brown, let me tell you.'

A brief laugh erupted through my tears; I felt the pop of a snot bubble and scrubbed at my face with my sleeve again.

'So where are you?'

'In a hotel. In Melbourne.'

'A *hotel*. Sounds exciting.'

'It's not. It's pretty crap, actually.'

'Where will you go from there?'

'I don't know.' The red light on the phone was flashing. 'I think we're about to get cut off.'

301

'Silver, tell me your address when you have one.'

'Okay.'

'I mean it. We can write to each other.'

'Okay.'

'Do it.'

'All right!' But we had been disconnected. I hung up and let out a long, quavering sigh. My ear was hot. He still felt so close. My snot eruption had made me think of Jindi too, and I pictured her in her stained velour dress and ill-fitting runners, standing with her toes turned out, grubby hands clasped. I wiped my face again and realised I was smiling.

'Ready?'

I nodded, and Ishtar turned and rejoined the tide of pedestrians, leaving me to follow once more. We rounded a corner, then another, and then she entered a shop.

Travel Agent, said the sign on the door, which I caught on its backswing. A smaller sign below had come unstuck at one corner: *Budget Deals!* Inside, Ishtar was already taking a seat at one of the three desks. The man behind it motioned me over, indicating a second chair. I went in and sat down slowly. The room was hot; an overhead fan ticked round in a fatigued kind of way, but there was no detectable movement of air.

'… cheapest tickets,' Ishtar was saying. 'For me and my daughter. She's thirteen.'

The man nodded and pulled out a folder. He flipped through the pages and then turned it round. 'What I would recommend …' he began.

His voice seemed to warp in my ears, then recede. I felt dizzy.

I held onto the seat with one hand and made the magic shape with the other, fixing my gaze on a poster that showed a guard on a horse outside Buckingham Palace, wearing a red coat and one of those tall furry black hats.

Ishtar's voice droned and wove itself through a space left by the man's, and then the two voices joined to form a fat rope of sound that circled me slowly and began to close its coils like a boa constrictor. I fixed my eyes on the pillar of the guard's hat. My stomach felt strange and my mouth kept filling up with saliva. I swallowed and tightened my fingers into the shape, but it didn't help. The guard's hat wavered; his horse appeared to nod its head.

'Silver?'

Ishtar's voice lifted in a separate, more clearly defined coil.

'Silver?'

I tried to focus.

She had turned towards me. 'Are you all right?'

I heard myself make a thick, negative sound.

Her face filled my vision, shimmering. Her mouth didn't seem to be moving in synch with her words. 'Do you need a drink of —'

I jumped up, knees banging the desk, and made for the door, feeling impossibly slow, my hands outstretched, groping for the handle.

Ishtar's voice behind me: 'Silver —'

My fingers under the handle, heaving at the door, my arms trembling, then out, and barging through the foot traffic to the pavement's edge to bend at the waist, the blast of watery orange vomit scouring my throat and nostrils, splashing into the grey cobbled gutter. My legs giving, dropping to my knees, the feel of hot concrete on the palm of one hand as I wiped my face with the other.

Ishtar beside me, crouching, her arm around my shoulders, tentative. 'You all right?'

The raw feeling in my mouth, my teeth furred, acid at the back of my nose. The sun behind her so she was just a shape, huge, dark, taking up all the sky. With a click my hearing returned to normal. A tram bell rang, pigeons rolled out fat calls, footsteps clipped and trudged, each sound moving clearly, spaciously, without limit.

My voice joined them. 'I don't want to go,' I said, to Ishtar's sun-blotting shape. 'I don't want to go overseas, or anywhere. I don't want to keep moving all the time. I just want to stay in the one place.'

'But we don't have anywhere. I mean, we can't stay in that hotel. And this money, it's an opportunity.'

Her hand lay on my back, light as a leaf. I shook myself like a dog and it was gone. I stared down into the gutter, at my wet splash drying already at the edges. 'It's what you want,' I said. 'It's not what I want.'

There was a pause and then she touched me again, took my arm, helped me up, and took me to a bench a few shops further along. We sat down. I could see her face now, and she bent and looked directly at me. 'Okay,' she said. 'What do you want?'

After

I suppose it was a test. I suppose I wanted her to stay, to choose me, to somehow push through my defences and make me accept her love. To know that that was what I really wanted, even if I'd been unable say it.

I did feel abandoned as I watched her walk towards those tall doors, the vinyl airline bag that had come free with her ticket hooked over one arm, a rude, fresh red against her worn jeans and jacket. The habit of watchfulness and the fear of being left behind must have been so ingrained in me that when she stopped and waved, the urge to run after her — to throw myself at her, to somehow grab on before she could vanish — was overwhelming and I had to get away. While she was still facing me, still looking, her hand still raised, I turned and pushed back through the loose crowd and the tall stranger who was my aunt was forced to drop her own hand and turn also, and follow.

But Ishtar had asked me what I wanted, and I gave my answer, and it's not worth wasting time considering why I wasn't able to be properly honest. In any case, I suspect I had some sort of pre-emptive instinct to get it out of the way, to avoid future pain and further confusion by forcing — sooner rather than later — a separation that was inevitable.

It was certainly an immediate, definitive commitment. I had

met Linda for the first time the evening before, in the so-called dining room of the hotel, where the three of us ate dinner, mostly in silence. The other patrons were all boozy-looking old men, and the waitress — who was also the barmaid — was especially friendly to us. When she came to clear our table she leaned over me. 'Excited, love?' she said, and I gaped, flushing with embarrassment, wondering how she could possibly know about my decision.

Ishtar looked equally as lost, and it was Linda who came to my rescue. 'About Christmas,' she said, in a low voice.

I continued to stare helplessly at the barmaid, who grinned and reached for my plate. 'Only two more sleeps!' she trilled.

When she'd finished, Ishtar got up and without explanation also walked away, through the door marked *Ladies*.

Linda folded her long fingers together. 'Ishtar,' she said, the word slightly off kilter on her tongue, 'told me what you want to do.'

I nodded.

'Are you,' she leaned forward, 'completely sure?'

I nodded again.

She stayed like that for a few moments, gazing intently into my face while I made an effort not to look away. Then she gave a single nod. 'All right, then.'

The next morning — Christmas Eve — after Ishtar had gone, Linda and I returned to the city in her small, clean car and she took me to Myer, where I chose a fountain pen and a package of ink cartridges as my Christmas gift from her. The fifty-dollar note Ishtar had given me stayed in its blank envelope — no card, no words spoken as she handed it over at the departure gate — in my pocket. I still have it.

Over tea and sandwiches in the department store's cafeteria — it was only midmorning; we'd had to get up early to be at the airport on time — Linda clasped her hands again. 'When would you like to leave?' she said. 'It's a long drive, but it's still early in the day.'

I looked into her grave, waiting face. 'I'm ready now,' I said.

We were in Sydney, and I was putting my things down on the floor of her spare room, by midnight.

I can't recall much about the early days at Linda's. I slept a lot. I remember her bringing trays of food to me in bed, as if I was sick, and feeling too exhausted to resist, and the slightly removed sense of relief and comfort that came with giving in to her care. It was like those nights in the hut with Dan — some part of my mind switched off and I became an animal, hungry, tired, burrowing into blankets.

My memory clears at the point when she returned to work, and time became more structured. There were still another couple of weeks to go before the beginning of term, when I would be starting at yet another new school, and I spent the weekdays alone. Linda's flat was on the second floor, with large windows; it was a quiet place, filled with light, smelling of laundry powder and books. There were only the two bedrooms, a bathroom, and one living space that was open to the kitchen, but the rooms were a decent size, and there was a sense of space and order.

Once Linda had left for work I sank into the stillness, moving round slowly like an invalid, setting up little nests on the couch or the balcony with my book, cushions, blankets, a cup of tea. Often I went back to bed and slept or just lay, dozing. I watched soap operas on television. I didn't follow the storylines or even keep track of which character was which, but swam into their soft rhythms, the endless interiors, the shifting, bright faces, the gentle sparkle of jewellery, teeth, and hair.

Sometimes, lying on the couch, I would feel as if I had fallen victim to some rupture in time and space, like in a book — *Tom's Midnight Garden* or *Playing Beattie Bow* — and that I should really be with Ishtar, wherever she was, but instead had been transported somehow to the flat of an unknown woman. I would have to get up and look at something of Linda's, and the image of her hands would come to me, using that thing. *Linda*. She was real. I was supposed to be here. There, on the kitchen table, was the sandwich she had left for my lunch, wrapped in greaseproof paper like Ian's mother had used.

It didn't help that the room I slept in still felt like a spare room, with anonymous bedding and a framed Van Gogh print on the wall.

'It's your room now,' she had said. 'You can change it around if you like. Put up some posters.' But I was unable to change anything, to make my mark. With my clothes in the chest of drawers and my new pyjamas under the pillow, there was no evidence of my existence. My empty duffel bag lay at the bottom of the freshly cleared wardrobe — every now and then I knelt and reached in to check for it, the familiar thick folds of its worn canvas.

I spent a lot of time looking in the bathroom mirror. I'd never had such free and uninterrupted access to a mirror before — it seemed I'd only caught my reflection in hurried moments, and in mirrors that were small and dark, spotted or cracked. The mirror in Linda's bathroom was a clean wide rectangle, well lit by three small, frosted windows above. In it I could see myself from the hips up. After my shower in the mornings I dried myself without looking, mindful of Linda's nearby presence. But later, fully dressed and with her gone, I indulged in long sessions of gazing. I couldn't get used to the sight of my own face, and examined it from every angle, peering out of the corners of my eyes. I lifted my hair into a snaky pile that left my neck looking naked and skinny, or plaited it into a rope that fell over one shoulder.

Sometimes I lifted my top and looked at my puffed-out nipples and the small pads of flesh that were appearing around them. I did this nervously, listening out even though Linda wasn't due back for hours. I dropped my top again and stood with my shoulders brought forward, hiding the breasts, then back, pushing them out. I smiled, nodded, shrugged. I mouthed words. *Hi, I'm Silver. I'm new. I live with my aunt.*

In the afternoons I would often go down onto the street, and around the corner to a long strip of parkland where I would walk along the paths, dazed in the muggy heat. The spectre of Hope — always ready, just at the edge of consciousness — seemed distant but clear, as if etched with lines that were very fine, glittering and chill. Here trees stirred dully, through thicker air.

Other people passed me, joggers, bike riders, dog walkers, parents with children, their yells and footfalls and whizzing tyres rushing in streaks that stretched and faded. I kept my hand in my pocket, my fingers around the keys Linda had given me, one for the door to the flat and one for the main door downstairs. I felt light on the path, insubstantial. I scuffed my shoes to make a sound of my own. Often I would find myself returning to the flat at a panicky trot, the top of my head burning from the sun, shying at the dark branches of the monkey-puzzle trees. When the key turned and I burst in to find everything just as I'd left it, the feeling of relief was cool and flooding.

Each day, as the time for Linda's return from work approached, a different kind of anxiety began to accumulate. I was no longer afraid of not existing or of being in the wrong place. I was here and she knew it; now the problem was that she was on her way, and we were both going to be here together. What were we going to talk about? What were we going to do? By a quarter past five I would be driven to distraction, unable to read or watch television. I paced, feeling enormous, as though I took up too much space. I sat on the end of my bed, not wanting to be in the living room, the first thing she saw when she walked in.

When she did come though, the feelings of suspension and anxiety — amazingly — lifted. The key in the lock. The door opening. Her level voice: 'Hello? Silver?'

As I got up and went out to meet her, the drumming of my heart would already be easing, my breaths loosening. After putting down her briefcase she would take off her shoes and flex her long toes on the carpet, then perch on the arm of the couch and look up at me. 'How was your day?'

'Fine.'

'Did you get outside?'

'Yes.'

The exchange was almost always exactly the same every time. What happened during the rest of the evening was also predictable. If we needed groceries we would walk together to the supermarket; if not she sat at her desk for a while, opening her mail and sometimes looking over work papers, and I went into my room and read. Then I would help her with dinner, and we would eat together at the small round table. After that we played Scrabble or watched television — Linda liked cosy British murder mysteries, but also *Countdown*; any television was compelling to me — until bedtime.

I can see now that this regularity was probably intentional. She is someone who likes order, certainly, but I think she made things even more structured for my sake. The impression she gave at the time was that it was easy for her to accommodate me — but of course it couldn't have been like that. She hadn't even known I existed until two days before I moved in.

The phone rang one evening while she had her hands full in the kitchen, dicing chicken I think it was. 'You get it,' she said, and I picked it up, feeling clumsy.

'Hello?'

A woman's voice, jolly and brisk. 'Hello? That's not Linda, is it?'

'No.' My answer came out slowly, and sounded very childlike. 'It's Silver. I'm her — her niece.'

'Oh yes, of course, well, hello Silver, it's Margaret here from the film club, just wondering when Linda will be joining us again.'

I stood with the phone to my ear, still rattled by the foreign sound of my own words — *her niece* — and the woman's unquestioning response, the recognition in her voice. I don't know what I'd expected. For her to say *Who?* perhaps, or for Linda to wipe her hands and take the phone, explaining in hushed tones. I hadn't expected this casual acceptance, this obvious prior knowledge. I felt my face redden.

'Silver? Are you there?'

'Oh. Yes. Sorry, hold on a minute.'

I explained to Linda. 'Not for a while,' she said. 'Tell her maybe next month.'

It wasn't until later, lying in bed, that the slightly inflated, pleased feeling abated enough for me to consider what the call had actually been about. *I* was the reason Linda wasn't going to her film club. She was staying home to be with me. Now, of course, I can see the significance in this, how it was emblematic of any number of hidden sacrifices, but at the time, while it made me feel slightly uncomfortable as well as grateful, I was happy to let it go, to retreat into sleep, knowing that the next day would be the same as the others, and that they all were gradually linking into a solid mass.

I rang Ian one afternoon, from a pay phone. He complained at length about the boring jobs his parents had him doing around the farm, and I listened greedily. Then, as my pile of coins began to diminish, with a sick feeling and a querulous, loaded voice, I asked: 'Any news?'

'Oh gosh no, nothing's happening around *here*.'

Thinking he'd missed my meaning, I tried to come up with a better way of hinting at what I didn't want to speak out loud, but before I could he spoke again: 'Well there is *one* thing everyone's been talking about. Did you know about Miller?' His tone was so convincing — serious but slightly salacious — that for a moment I floundered.

'No?' I managed, weakly, my cheeks burning.

Like one actor covering for another who kept forgetting her lines, Ian forged on. 'Wow, I can't believe you haven't heard.

Well, he went missing. Was seen wandering off into the bush the night of the fire, very drunk, and never came back. Left all his things — there was another building that didn't burn down, apparently, and they were in there. Anyway, they did a big search, police stomping around all through the bush, but they didn't find anything.'

I leaned against the glass. My heart was knocking so hard I could barely hear.

'Silver?' came Ian's voice. 'You still there?'

'Yes.'

'Oh, I thought you'd gone. There are all these mineshafts, you see, up in the hills, and they're really old and *really* deep, and there's just no way to get down into them, the technology simply does not exist. So everyone's saying he probably fell into one of them, but there's no way of finding him.'

I swallowed. 'They can't get down the mineshafts?'

'Some of them they can, but lots of them they can't. Too dangerous, and too deep.'

'So they didn't find him, his …?'

'No, they didn't. There was a thing in the paper — they gave up.'

'So that's it then?'

'Yep. That's it. Case closed.'

The rest of the phone call he filled with inane chatter while I stood in a daze, only half hearing. His skill in conveying the information about Miller, and in maintaining such a credibly natural tone throughout the whole conversation was such that I might have believed him to be genuinely uncaring, were it not for one tiny revelation, right at the end of the call.

'I don't know how I'm going to *cope*,' he said, 'with going back to school. I'll *never* be able to get up in the mornings — I've started sleeping in so late. I've been having trouble …' There was a long pause, into which he allowed a deep, weary exhalation. 'I've been having trouble falling asleep at night.'

After that, we wrote to each other, letters that were so superficial as to appear to be in some kind of code.

> *Yesterday I ate almost a whole watermelon and nearly vomited. Linda makes really good cheesecake.*

> *Both verandahs are now glorious mission brown but Dad couldn't bear to let any paint go to waste so out with the roller again and I have been getting acquainted with the shed.*

> *There are two dogs in one of the downstairs flats. They are called Fluffy and Max. Max is cute but Fluffy has this skin thing that is so disgusting, her whole back is nearly bald.*

> *For my birthday this year Mum's taking me to Melbourne to see* The Mikado *at the State Theatre. It's an opera, by the way. I have to pay for some of the ticket but that's all right, I've got plenty saved up.*

> *I am SO BORED!!!!*

It was a code, of sorts. When I wrote to Ian I used what I thought to be the voice of an ordinary teenager, bored during school holidays, and he wrote back to me in the same voice. *We are normal*, we told each other. *We are getting on with our normal lives.*

The days seemed to hinge on dinnertime. I came to look forward to helping Linda prepare the meals, which seemed exotic at first, with their firm textures and fresh colours, their discrete elements that sat so cleanly on our plates. Slices of smoked trout served with tiny, whole potatoes and neat mounds of chopped salad; lamb cutlets, steamed baby carrots and green beans. I pored over the glossy pictures in Linda's recipe books, the detailed, sensible instructions. *Chop carrots into matchstick-sized pieces and add to broccoli florets. Toss with dressing and set aside.* I took pleasure in getting to know the kitchen, which implements to use for which purpose, where everything was kept. Cooking fumes and steam vanished into the range hood above the stove. The plates, bowls, and cups all matched. There were placemats and napkins; the table would be cleared completely, even though we only needed the two places. Afterwards, I washed the dishes, which barely filled the rack, and wiped the benches clean.

I don't recall what we spoke about over dinner. I don't think we spoke much, but it didn't matter. I do remember the times she tried to press me on things, coming to stand in the doorway to my room. Her soft, apologetic voice: 'Silver?'

'Yes?' My insides already contracting with discomfort.

'Is there anything you'd like to talk about?'

'No.'

317

'Well, if there ever is anything, I'm here to listen.'

'There isn't anything.'

Unlike Ian, I had no trouble falling asleep. This was when I felt safest, curled in the dark, Linda's bedtime sounds — the creak of her desk chair, soft footsteps, the running of a tap — at the far edges of my drifting consciousness. It was in the early mornings that the terror came, wrenching me awake, my heart galloping. The gaping blackness. His hands, his breath, the awful cry.

I got a Walkman, which helped. I listened to the quizzes on AM radio, soothed myself with the comfortable wash of voices, the mild to-and-fro.

On the weekends we went to see films, or drove to the beach. There was a picnic with Linda's friends. They were all women, none of them married, and this was something they apparently spoke about quite often, in a blithe way. One of them, Suzie — who was glamorous, with bleached hair and pink lipstick — had just broken up with a boyfriend. 'I'm just devastated,' she said brightly, tearing a drumstick from a cold chicken. She had sunglasses in a 1950s style.

'Well I've given up,' said Margaret, who was short with spiky hair and tanned skin that crinkled at the corners of her eyes. 'It's been a relief, I can tell you.'

They drank white wine, and the talk and laughter was constant. Linda was the quietest in the group, but she smiled, following the conversation, and when Suzie leaned into her, laughing, lipstick on her teeth, Linda laughed too and patted Suzie's hand.

I sat on the periphery with a book. Across the grass I saw some teenagers, lying around under another tree. I watched them covertly, burning with embarrassment at Linda and her loud friends, their womanliness, their lack of shame. The dash of pink on Suzie's teeth suddenly bothered me, and Linda's thighs, soft and pale at the cuffs of her shorts. I made shields either side of my face with my hands and bent to the book in my lap.

Driving back, Linda asked if I was okay. I made a noncommittal sound.

'I suppose it's a bit boring for you,' she said. 'A grown-up event like that.'

It was evening, the sun low. We were passing through a beachside suburb and a group of kids around my age, girls and boys, ran across the road in front of us. Linda slowed down. They were in swimmers, towels wrapped around their waists, and they were so close I could see the colours of a woven bracelet on a girl's wrist, the sand clinging to their tanned calves.

'Mandy, wait!' yelled one of the boys, his voice cracking against the tarmac, the deepening sky. They reached the kerb with a flick of heels; Linda accelerated and they were gone.

We went to Grace Brothers to buy me new clothes. I selected the plainest things I could find.

'What about this?' Linda held up a dress, white cotton with small navy polka-dots and a ruffled skirt. 'For if you go out.' The question of where I might go, and with whom, remained unspoken.

I shook my head miserably.

She put it back. 'No,' she said. 'You're right. It's a bit frilly.'

We went to the underwear section, and I chose navy socks and two six-packs of regular underpants. It was Linda who picked up the bras. Two of them. They were a plain, sports kind, no lace. 'I think these would be your size,' she murmured, standing close beside me and holding them discreetly folded over themselves.

I didn't thank her for her delicacy. Wordlessly I took them and shoved them under my arm.

Now that I live in a flat of my own, dependent on my own routines, I wonder what it must have been like for Linda to have her home and her life so suddenly invaded by this stranger. And a child at that — or worse, a teenager, with a teenager's inwardness. A responsibility she had been given no time to prepare for and which came with no instructions — Linda with her lists, her weekly meal plans, Linda who kept the manuals for every domestic appliance in a folder, in alphabetical order. What irritations did she hide, and what fears?

She did her homework — I saw books on parenting and adolescence beside her bed — and I like to think I felt some vague gratitude, or at least moments of recognition, like the one that night after Margaret's phone call, but I suspect that I mostly just took what she offered and forged ahead without much thought for her, her feelings or the sacrifices she might be making.

I have apologised, since, for this. With typical gravity she accepted the apology, but said that at the time she was relieved to recognise anything at all like the behaviour of a normal teenager.

'You were supposed to be selfish,' she said. 'Whenever you were, I knew I must be doing something right.'

I started school. I didn't make friends. I didn't wear frilly dresses and go out, or run across roads in my swimmers with boys. I worked. I sat quietly in each class, and listened and made notes, and I did all my homework and all the extension work the teachers began giving me. By the middle of the year Linda and I had decided that I would apply for a selective-entry school and change again in Year Nine.

Eventually I did rearrange the spare room — my room. She bought me a desk, which just squeezed in beside the chest of drawers, and I stuck study notes above it, my certificates, my academic awards, and a poster of Albert Einstein.

The letters to and from Ian petered out. Keeping up the exchange of trivial information had become exhausting, and neither of us seemed willing or able to break out of our pretend voices and say anything real. I thought about him less and less often.

I hardly thought about Ishtar at all. Consciously, that is. There was a feeling though, like the cold, etched one that belonged to Hope — always there, ready to overtake me. The Ishtar feeling was warm and sweet and smoky, and came with snapshot images: the swing of her hair, a long-legged step in jeans and boots, the length of her throat and the slip of its creamy-gold skin into the rough wool of a jumper. It was primitive and desperate, and I hated it and the way it arrived with apparent randomness, and no warning. I deflected it as best I could.

Perhaps on some basic level I simply saw Linda as a better bet, and having made that investment, I went on to protect it. It did not occur to me at any stage that I could have them both in my life. Even when Ishtar returned to Australia and the two of them began to take steps — so shuffling, so tentative as to barely qualify as action — in the direction of reconciliation, my old mistrust and my newly inflamed resentment were, combined, so powerful that I could only see risk in that scenario. And the ease with which I was able to thwart them — the hardness of my resolve in comparison to the uncertainty of theirs, which on Ishtar's part I read as simple lack of interest — seemed to me proof of the veracity of my instinct. And she had stayed away so long.

Linda did what she could. She stuck Ishtar's postcards on the fridge; she spoke about their childhood, their parents; she showed me photos. I could see the effort this took — her voice quavered, and she would occasionally blot at her eyes with a tissue. There was always a sense of relief at the conclusion of these conversations — or sessions, as I came to think of them — and I suspected it was on her part as well as mine. A kind of resentful gloom would come over me when I saw her getting down the photo album with its cover of bumpy, porridge-coloured fabric, and I found myself retreating into abstraction, overcome by fits of yawning.

It was during one of these sessions, the two of us kneeling on the living-room floor, that Linda said, seemingly out of the blue: 'Do you know why Karen — Ishtar — left home?'

I came part-way out of my torpor. Did this mean she knew something, had found something out? 'No,' I said. 'Why? Do you?'

'No, no.' She shifted the album that lay across her lap. 'I just wondered. What did she tell you?'

'Nothing.'

'Well.' Linda was using her extra-careful voice. 'You have a right to more information, you know.'

I shrugged.

'You wouldn't have to speak with … Ishtar … if you didn't want to.' The name never sounded quite right when she said it. 'If it felt too difficult to ask directly. You could write a letter.'

Anger ground in me, like gears clashing. I got up. 'What would be the point of that?' I said. 'She wouldn't be able to read it.'

Later she came and sat on the end of my bed and began to speak, quietly. 'I was fifteen,' she said. 'Karen and I went to the same school, but we didn't have much to do with each other. I was what they called a conch — all I cared about was studying. I wasn't into sports or the social scene. She was very different. She was popular because of her looks, but I think she lacked confidence. Anyway, she did have a bit of a reputation at school. There were whispers. Not that I ever knew what she actually did to earn it, I was so socially unaware. But I do remember some boys at the bus stop one day, saying something about her, something … unpleasant.'

I lay staring at the wall.

'One day I came home and she just wasn't there. Our mother said she'd gone away for a while, to a special school, to help with her literacy. I just didn't question it. Then later on the truth came out — about The Path, that she'd left to join them. Now that I do the sums, I think she must have become pregnant with you almost straightaway. Or even …' She was silent for a while, and when she spoke again it was in a more direct, decisive tone. 'She came back to visit once, when our mother was very sick — about to die — and she and Dad argued about something. She said there was something Mum and Dad hadn't told me about, something that had to do with her leaving.'

'I know,' I said. 'I saw the letter you sent.'

'Really?' She shifted on the bed. 'So she got the letters? I never knew that.'

'She got some of them. I found them. She kept them hidden.'

Linda lapsed back into silence. Eventually she stirred again. 'Now, the thing is,' she said, 'I wonder if she might have already been pregnant with you — if that might have been what caused the falling-out. Our mother was very religious. She wouldn't have stood for a child born out of wedlock. Maybe she said they had to get married, and Karen didn't want to. Or maybe the fellow wasn't interested — or maybe he was, but our mother found him unsuitable.'

There was another long pause. The sluggish, resistant feeling had overtaken me again.

'Silver, I wonder if it might help you, help the way you're feeling about your mum, to speak with her about these things?'

I didn't respond.

Linda put a hand on my leg, through the duvet. 'Only if you want to.'

'No thanks,' I said.

I think there was a good six months after her return in which Ishtar made an obvious effort. A visit was arranged but I cancelled it, claiming it would interfere with my studies. I was in my final year of school by then, heading for a perfect score, barricaded in my fortress of overachievement.

She wrote letters: clunky, bare-bones accounts of the rainforest retreat she was working at, or the yoga course she was doing. Reading them, the litany of logged activities, devoid of reflection or analysis, you would think she was the child, reporting dutifully to some distant relative. Our phone calls — which were as frequent as weekly in those first months — were not much better, but to be fair she was working against my already-entrenched unhelpfulness; they were essentially one-way, and she had never been much of a talker.

I had cut her off, and the skin had grown over the severed connection, and we all — Linda included — knew this. And none of us, not even those who wanted to, had the necessary resources to make any kind of difference.

There was also the false security of time. Linda clearly believed the day would come when I'd want to reconnect with Ishtar and, while it's difficult to say in hindsight, I think the idea was there in the back of my mind also — some unexamined assumption that with age and experience I might come to feel, if not actual forgiveness then at least a desire for a better understanding.

We did see each other once, when she came to my high-school graduation ceremony, during which I was presented with a prize for academic excellence. She arrived late and I didn't even know if she was in the audience, and out of pride did not allow myself to scan the rows of faces for hers. Afterwards, as the other girls flung off their blazers and whooped and shrieked, I stood at the base of the stage and watched the two of them approach from different directions — both holding back, each deferring to the other. I had an urge to escape, to disappear through some back door, leaving them to their infuriating cautiousness. At last they joined me, Ishtar first by a slight margin, and there was an awkward round of brief, bony embraces. I was as tall as Ishtar, which felt wrong.

'Congratulations,' she said.

'Thanks,' I mumbled.

Linda began to explain the scholarships offered by various universities, and then stopped abruptly, even though Ishtar was listening and nodding politely.

A teacher saved us, wanting to take a photo for the school's magazine.

'Would you all …?' He gestured with his camera for us to line up in front of the stage, and Linda and Ishtar both lowered their heads.

'Go on,' said Linda. 'I think you should.'

'No, no,' said Ishtar. 'You.'

I stepped into the space alone, my certificate scrolled moistly in my hand. The teacher waited a few moments, his smile wilting, then gave a defeated sort of shrug, pointed, clicked, and moved on.

I don't recall any more about the rest of that reunion. There is just one other, very small, memory. When the teacher lowered the camera and walked away, and the silver-blue burst of the flash cleared from my eyes, I found I was looking right at Ishtar, and for a moment we stared into each other's faces with the intense, bold interest of very young children.

In that picture in the magazine, which I still have, I am

scraggle-haired as ever, the collar of my uniform crooked under my blazer. But my chin is tilted and a power crackles in the fierce planes of my face; the empty space on either side of me blazes, unbreachable. I look like my mother.

A better understanding of Ishtar did come, but not in the way I might have anticipated. In 1995, when I was twenty-three and she was forty, she was killed in a car accident in Queensland, where she was living at the time.

Linda called me with the news. It was evening; I was in my room, reading, in the house I shared with two other young women who were both nurses and rarely home. Linda spoke in tightly cropped sentences; between them I could hear her crying.

Ishtar had been a passenger — it was a hired car, apparently, being used by a group of backpackers. She did not know them; they were giving her a ride somewhere. The car was full, and Ishtar had crammed in and was therefore not wearing a seatbelt.

The next morning Linda collected me in her little hatchback and together we drove up to the town where Ishtar had been renting a unit. It took two days — we stayed in a motel overnight, and I slept badly. Linda kept crying, and the more she cried the further I seemed to withdraw — I felt guilty, as if her crying was some form of accusation, even though I knew it wasn't.

The town was small and, I thought, uninspiring. It was September, a weekday, midafternoon by the time we arrived, and very warm. The sky was low and grey, with darker clouds hunkering over the domed mountains that stuck up out of the horizon.

We checked in to a motel on the main street. The police

station was visible, just a bit further down the road.

'I think you should stay here,' said Linda, when we had carried our overnight bags in. 'While I do the identification.'

'Okay.' I sat on the edge of one of the beds.

'I think that's best, don't you?'

'Okay.'

When she had gone I lay down and tried to picture what Linda would be doing. Going into some small room, somewhere, at the police station perhaps, or in a funeral home — I didn't know how these things worked. Chill air, stainless steel, a sheet being lifted. Ishtar's body. Well, her remains anyway — she was badly smashed up in the accident, Linda had told me in that initial phone call. *Damaged*, was the word she'd used.

I stared up at the ceiling. What happened, then, to people without families? Who remained unclaimed? What became of their bodies?

I fell asleep, and woke when she came back in, eyes small from crying. She sat on the end of the other bed. Eventually, she said: 'She would not have experienced any pain. It would have been absolutely instant.' She turned to me. 'I can *guarantee* you that.'

I looked at her, her long, unused-looking legs jutting from the mattress's edge, her soft hands folded between her thighs. I thought of those years I had lived with her, her constant, gentle company, the meals she prepared, the cups of tea brought to my desk while I studied. She hadn't known I existed until the day before we met. And despite her general hesitance, her unworldliness — traits that she wore, unquestioningly, like a uniform — she had not for one moment showed any sign of reluctance or resentment.

The removed, put-upon feeling dropped away, and was replaced by a wave of gratitude. She had done her best for me — she really had. I moved down to the end of my own bed and reached across and took her hand.

We went to the unit the following morning, to pack up Ishtar's things.

The landlord was waiting out the front, an elderly Italian man, pants cinched high over his belly.

'I am very sorry,' he said, when we had got out of the car and unpacked our flattened boxes and Linda's industrial sticky-tape dispenser. He stepped to the side, holding the screen door open for us. 'The furniture belong here,' he said. 'Is just her things, her clothes.'

'Thank you,' said Linda.

'Please.' He bowed his head. 'When you are finish, you just pull the door, all right? I will come later and check is all okay.'

It was dark inside, and I walked into Linda, who had gone first.

'Sorry,' she whispered, and I heard her grope along the wall, then the click of the switch, and the light came on overhead.

We were in the living room, which was very small, with the kitchen adjoining, off to one side. On the bench was a bowl with fruit in it still, and tiny insects circling above. There was a smell of damp, and of stale pot and overripe bananas.

No pictures were on any of the walls. Nothing was stuck to the fridge. On the bench beside the fruit bowl were a couple of letters — bills, in their impersonal envelopes — and a copy of a local newspaper.

'She hadn't been here very long,' said Linda, as if this might serve as a reasonable explanation for how dismal the place was.

I went into the bedroom. It was also bare, but the old Indian quilt was on the bed, and the smell was different — it smelled like Ishtar in there, the way I remembered her. I suppose it hit me then, that I had lost her.

On the top of the chest of drawers, there were two framed photographs. One was my formal university graduation photo, from my first degree. Linda must have sent her a copy. The other was one of the old ones that had always been in the suitcase — Ishtar holding the toddler me, our twin gazes, unprepared and wary.

I found it very difficult to lift that quilt, to fold it and push it into a box. My hands shook.

Linda suggested we sorted as we went, so we could take the things we didn't want to an op shop rather than lug them all the way back to Sydney. But I found I wasn't able to let anything go. There wasn't much anyway — her clothes, including shoes, only filled three boxes. Then there was one box of books, mostly photographic ones about nature; another two of bedding and towels; some balls of wool, knitting and crochet needles, though no sign of any work in progress; and the old case, which at the time I couldn't bring myself to open. In the tiny bathroom, there was soap and shampoo, nothing else.

I stood in the middle of the living room and saw myself, a lick of shadow, reflected in the blank square of the small television screen. I tried to imagine what it was Ishtar had done every night in this place, after returning from some menial cash-paying job.

Did she watch television? Sitting on this scrappy, uncomfortable-looking couch? She didn't read, I knew that much. An old instinct, surprisingly strong, had caused me to check each room for evidence of a man, a lover, either live-in or visiting — but there were absolutely no signs.

I found myself thinking about our hut near Hope, trying to remember it. Had it been as grim as this, as soulless, as empty? How strong my desire for a home must have been, to lend that place softness, comfort — to see the honey in the timber and the warm glow radiate from that bedspread.

On the coffee table was a lighter, some cigarette papers, and an ashtray with a couple of ground-out roaches in it. I went to the cardboardy-looking cabinet that stood against one wall and slid out a drawer. A small stash of leaf marijuana; I took it and dropped it into the garbage bag we'd filled with the food from the fridge.

Linda went out the back door first, into the little courtyard. I saw her stop short, and the slight drawing-in of her chin that I knew signified fright or discomfort. I went over.

There was the black plastic council recycling tub, full to the brim, and lined up behind it, against the wall, were five or six old milk crates loaded with empty beer and whisky bottles. Alongside them were two piles of flattened beer cartons.

'Maybe she had a party,' I said, and the unlikelihood of this immediately seemed to resonate in the bare, walled space, the lonely rooms behind us.

'Silver.' Linda made a face at me, a sort of brave grimace. 'The police told me she was known to them, that they'd picked her up a few times, drunk. They said she used to drink at the local pub with the backpackers. I suppose that's why she was in the car with those people.' She squeezed her hands together. 'I just can't help thinking we should have done more for her. Supported her more.'

It wasn't an accusation, but still I put my head down, folded my arms — and up rose my anger, hot and prickling and as strong as if it had been yesterday that Ishtar had ignored the mess in the hut and my shoes in the doorway and instead asked if I was hungry — putting the cover over my secret, leaving me alone with it.

Linda lifted one of the crates. 'We'd better take these to the tip,' she said in a forced, businesslike tone. 'They'll probably have a recycling service.' She clinked past me without meeting my eye, and went back inside. I stepped into the middle of the paved square, breathing the yeasty smell of old beer. There was one palm tree; its leaves rattled in the clammy breeze.

The carload of boxes went into storage in Linda's spare room — my old bedroom. The suitcase I took to my house and put under my bed.

Linda had made arrangements for Ishtar's remains to be cremated, and the ashes arrived by mail the next week. Over dinner we discussed what to do with them — at least, Linda kept saying it was up to me, and I kept saying I didn't know what to do. In the end we put the decision off and the plastic urn with its heavy, gravelly-sounding contents went into the spare room as well.

I sank gratefully back into work on my master's degree, resumed my every-second-day swims at the local pool, met with Linda once a fortnight for lunch or dinner.

It wasn't until the study year was over and I found myself adrift as usual in those vacant couple of months, swimming every day for want of something to do, reading gluttonously, and looking forward a bit too much to the newspaper's cryptic crosswords, that I took the suitcase out from under the bed and opened it and found the notebook.

It was on top, a slim exercise book, like the ones used in schools. On the cover, in the box with spaces for *Name* and *Subject*, a single word had been printed: *Ishtar*. My skin tightened.

I set it aside. Underneath, as well as what I'd expected to find — Ishtar's expired passport, her birth certificate, the remaining photo of me and the other hippie kids — there was a large sheet of a slippery kind of paper, folded in half. I pulled this out first and unfolded it.

It was a copy of a page from a newspaper dated 6th January 1986. It wasn't a photocopy — the paper was different; it had the same slick surface on the inside as well, and the quality wasn't quite as good. I ran my fingers over it with recognition. At school, we'd visited the state library and been shown the microfilm machines — how you could flick through collections of newspapers, select a page, and have it printed out. That was what this was. She must have found it herself, after her return from overseas. Pity twanged in me at the thought of her poring over dates and headlines, inching her finger along the words the way she used to do if nobody was looking. I smoothed the page where it lay on the carpet. *Search Ends for Missing Man*, read the headline.

The search for a man who went missing in central Gippsland over a week ago has ended with no success.

*Walter Ronald Miller, aged 36, has not been seen
since the night of 20th December when he left a party at a
property near Kooralang, in central Gippsland.*

*Miller was seen leaving the party in a confused state
and thought to be under the influence of alcohol and drugs.
Police believe it is possible Miller fell into one of many
abandoned mineshafts located in bushland adjacent to the
property, some of which are too deep and unstable to be
searched.*

So it had stayed with her as well. She had gone to the
library and looked up this article — it probably took her a
whole day — and copied it, and then kept it, here with her
skimpy collection of meaningful things. She had cared enough
to do all that.

Pushing myself away from the case and its contents, I leaned
against the wall. I had learned to stop asking myself this question
— it made me angry, and there was nowhere for that feeling to go.
But here it came again, scuttling in uninvited, trailing its strands
of rage. What did Ishtar suspect that morning when we returned
to the messed-up hut? What conclusion did she draw from the
obvious signs of upheaval? And from my actions: my hasty, guilty
retrieval of the torch; my pathetic, pre-emptive explanation? She
had known Miller had headed for the hut — Dan had told her.
The anger slapped up against me, caught and clung. How could
she have left it at that? She knew I was involved in whatever had
happened. Why didn't she shake it out of me, the truth, relieve
me of it? She was my *mother*.

Her face came into my mind, during that moment at my
school graduation night, when she'd looked at me as if I was a

stranger, someone she was interested in. Who was I, to her? A burden first, and then a stranger.

I refolded the slippery bit of paper. Now a different kind of anger was moving in, big and blockish. What was I supposed to do with my secret, now that she was gone?

I no longer woke with the fear of discovery snatching my breath: police at the door — the kind of fears you have in the middle of the night when you're a kid. I had dealt with those fears, chipped away at them with logic. Even if it all came out — if Ian for some crazy reason confessed after all this time — we had acted in self-defence. We were running away from him, we were terrified. But I think that, tied up with that half-buried, postponed idea of eventually coming to some understanding of Ishtar, there had been the assumption that, one day, I would tell her. I would unload, make her take it — her share of the burden, the guilt.

I put the article away and took out the notebook, and a loose piece of paper fell from between its pages. Ishtar's laboured boxy writing, scored with crossings-out, only a few lines:

To my daughter Silver Lakshmi Liberty Landes,
I have to tell you some things. I have kept all this a secret
because I never wanted you to feel like any of it was your
fault.
  Some times I think you should never be told. But some
times I think it will help

It broke off there. I turned the paper over but there wasn't any more.

My throat was hurting. I went back to the notebook and flipped through it.

It was filled — every page. I'd never seen so much of her handwriting in the one place; I'd only ever seen it in isolated lines, printed on forms mostly. Here the words were densely packed, covering the pages so completely they seemed to pulse, wave-like. There were no paragraphs, just infrequent line breaks that stood out like beacons.

I turned to the first page and read the opening line: *I saw him watching.*

I am older now than she was when we said goodbye at the airport. I'm older than she was when she died. I see women in their early thirties and they look so young to me, still plumped with youth, full of strength and forward momentum. If they do harbour secrets — like my mother did, like I do — then perhaps they have not yet slowed down enough for them to catch up, to really take hold.

Ishtar stepped through those gates, tall and strong and unknowable as ever, defined by her stunting, unshared past, fashioned from it. I was her daughter and I never knew her story. I am older than she ever got to be and even now I don't think I could come close to imagining what it would be like to have such a choice — if you could call it that — forced on you at that age, to have to make it with your soft, unfinished mind. And then to have to go on with the outcome — to bind your young self to it, to merge with it and its attendant doubts until they became a part of you. To do that alone. I suppose you would have to live something like that to understand.

I kept expecting the past to fade, but as time has gone on I've found myself thinking about it more instead of less. Of course, it's so much easier now to make contact with the past — or at least with things that connect you to it. Perhaps that's it, the lure: the irresistible availability of information. Whatever the reason, just recently I have begun looking people up. Not to make contact — just to see what is out there, in the public domain, about them. What *profile* they have.

When I took the first step — typing *Ian Munro* into Google — I was incredibly nervous. I suppose I'm showing my age, my lack of affinity with this type of technology. It's ridiculous, but I felt furtive. Despite — or perhaps because of — my reasonably good understanding of how it works, I don't entirely trust the internet.

Ian is an actor. Stage, not screen. He lives in the UK, in Brighton. He seems to be quite successful; I have read reviews of his performances that use words like *luminous* and *captivating* — words I couldn't help hearing in his rusty fourteen-year-old voice, loaded with wry emphasis. There are a few images. One or two formal, publicity-type headshots in which he stares down the camera, chin resting on the knuckles of one folded hand. His cheekbones are extraordinary; he has that sort of clever, fine-featured look that makes me think of racehorses and greyhounds. *Noble* — that's the word. These photos are posed though; their effect is intentional. It's another image of him I keep going back to, that brings tears to my eyes every time I see it. It's of him on stage, performing. He is wearing a suit coat and slim-cut pants, his shirt unbuttoned at the collar, and he is stepping forward, arms raised. The angle is from below, so the impression is of length and height — he grew into a tall man — but I see the child in him, the gangliness, the skittishness. I see him by the creek, darting through the trees, frenetic and elusive, his private misery a crackling aura, white-hot against the shadows. I hope that now there is no part of himself that he feels he needs to hold back.

I googled the word 'Jindi', but could only find sites about a cheese-making company of the same name, and about businesses associated with a town called Jindivick, in eastern Victoria. Maybe she changed her name. Val I have no chance of finding; I never knew her as anything other than Val.

Dan Cohen is a common name; Dan and Daniel Cohens are a dime a dozen on the internet. There is one I have found though who lives in Austin, Texas, and is a very well-regarded sound engineer and producer. The available information about him is almost all about his work, but one article describes him as 'Australian born', and mentions a background in New York's post-punk scene of the mid to late 1980s. There are no images of him online. Sometimes I think about digging deeper, but then I imagine discovering I've got the wrong Dan, and that my Dan is some ordinary bloke, with a Facebook account showing him on holiday with his family, or renovating his house in an outer suburb of Melbourne. Of course, there is no shame in being an ordinary bloke — and Dan would have made a very good and probably quite happy husband and father and renovator of houses — but I suspect I would be disappointed by this outcome.

I can still see him opening his packages of records, the eagerness of his fingers; I can still feel him behind me on the bike as we blaze down the road, carving apart the grey evening, the lowering sky, sending tremors through the paddocks. I am still quite attached to that vision of his lanky figure walking calmly out into the world, climbing on board a plane, setting off without fanfare to do what he'd always meant to do.

There are labels that could be applied to Miller, explanations for his behaviour. Drug-induced psychosis. Bipolar disorder. Borderline or narcissistic personality disorder. But if those terms existed back then, they weren't commonly used the way they are now, and what would they have meant to a thirteen-year-old, anyway? To me he was monstrous — endlessly powerful, endlessly threatening. He was the only person I ever saw challenge Ishtar's power, meet it, send shock waves through its implacable force field. He was the chisel's blade, smashing down on all of us, sending everything flying apart.

Very occasionally I am able to think of him as vulnerable, damaged in his own fashion. I remember Dawn's rustling whisper — *lost his way* — and the image of that ear hiding among the hair, small and pink, and unexpectedly pitiful. Of course he had lost his way, at some point. Maybe Dawn's story of genuine young love being gradually eroded was valid — or maybe he had manipulated her from the beginning. There's no way of telling. The important thing is, whether it happened in his twenties or earlier, he had turned. And when you think about it, what made him monstrous to me was not actually him — it was Ishtar's failure to come between the two of us, to shield her child as a mother should. In any case, it's been easier to stick with the fictional Miller, the monster. It's been easier, in my mind, to lay a monster to rest.

Linda and I still meet for dinner once a fortnight. Afterwards we go to see a film together. I have never shown her the notebook or told her about it. I don't believe in honesty for its own sake. If her parents were still alive it might be different. But they're not, and what good could it do her to alter her memories of them now, to sully them? As for her memories of or regard for Ishtar — as far as I am concerned there is nothing to correct there. Linda never judged; she has always been too guileless, too decent.

Ishtar's ashes remain in storage, in the cupboard in the spare room of my own flat now, along with her other possessions — and the fifty-dollar note she gave me for Christmas that morning. I am still unable to decide what to do with them. When someone dies, people talk about *what they would have wanted*, about respecting this and making decisions accordingly. So what do you do when you have no idea what the person might have wanted? When their desires, their ambitions — what it was, if anything, that might have brought them true, lasting joy — are more or less unknown to you?

Linda has suggested that I make the decision based on what *I* want, on what would help me put Ishtar to rest — the Ishtar in my mind. This seems a valid option, but I have not yet been able to commit to it. I have thought about scattering them at Hope, in the bush surrounding the hut, or in the creek. To honour what it was I felt there with her — almost-happiness, or potential happiness. But that would mean going back and I'm not ready to do that, to find the hut a ruin once more or perhaps gone altogether. To face the ghosts, or go anywhere near Miller's secret grave for fear of disturbing the seal I've put on him in my mind. And because, underneath all my rationalisations about what happened, about it not being actual murder, I do still fear inviting suspicion — the slim but real possibility that some local stickybeak, collector of stories, clipper of newspaper columns, might spot me stumbling around up on that hill in my city clothes and remember the missing man, might take down my number plate and get on the phone to the police.

A few years ago I went to see a therapist. I only went for a few sessions. She kept accusing me of *managing* things, of intellectualising instead of feeling.

I look at my life and I see what she means. My small, tidy flat. My safe job, my research, my office where I have things the way I want them and enjoy just the right level of friendly distance from my colleagues. One evening a week I work as a volunteer, tutoring young students from disadvantaged backgrounds. I probably have my own versions of Linda's cloistered speech idiosyncrasies. I have a group of friends like hers, single women who have 'given up'. I haven't had much luck with long-term relationships. I don't like change. I still swim.

All this, yes, is managing.

I think of Ishtar raking out that chicken coop. Chopping wood, sweeping, sewing. The swing and twist of her patterns: opening, closing, beginning, ending, arriving, leaving. Moving on, moving on, moving on. And I think that sometimes, perhaps, managing is all that can be done.

She was not right, though — the therapist — about the feelings. Not completely right, anyway. They can't be avoided altogether. They are there. They seem to exist on some plane of their own, and I have simply learned to live, as unobtrusively as possible, alongside.

Some mornings as I wake up, before coming fully to consciousness, I am visited by a memory so profound it is a bodily experience. I am a child, lying with her in bed. A mattress on the floor somewhere, in some half-furnished room — it doesn't matter which one.

She has her back to me as always, but it is her — her body against mine, its living, warm weight. I don't know if she's asleep or awake, but she hasn't moved yet, hasn't risen and dressed and gone.

She breathes.

I can smell her. Her hair, her skin.

I feel it, then.